*Portrait of the Artist
as a Young Dog*
and Other Fiction

Portrait of the Artist as a Young Dog
and Other Fiction

Dylan Thomas

ALMA CLASSICS

ALMA CLASSICS
an imprint of

ALMA BOOKS LTD
Thornton House
Thornton Road
Wimbledon Village
London SW19 4NG
United Kingdom
www.almaclassics.com

For the publication details of the individual stories in this collection see the relevant note to each title

This edition of Dylan Thomas's collected stories first published by Alma Classics in 2024

Cover © David Wardle

Printed in Great Britain by CPI Group (UK) Ltd, Croydon CR0 4YY

ISBN: 978-1-84749-915-8

All rights reserved. No part of this publication may be reproduced, stored in or introduced into a retrieval system, or transmitted, in any form or by any means (electronic, mechanical, photocopying, recording or otherwise), without the prior written permission of the publisher. This book is sold subject to the condition that it shall not be resold, lent, hired out or otherwise circulated without the express prior consent of the publisher.

Contents

Portrait of the Artist as a Young Dog and Other Fiction ... 1

PORTRAIT OF THE ARTIST AS A YOUNG DOG ... 3
- The Peaches ... 5
- A Visit to Grandpa's ... 20
- Patricia, Edith and Arnold ... 25
- The Fight ... 34
- Extraordinary Little Cough ... 45
- Just Like Little Dogs ... 53
- Where Tawe Flows ... 59
- Who Do You Wish Was with Us? ... 73
- Old Garbo ... 82
- One Warm Saturday ... 94

EARLY STORIES ... 113
- Brember ... 115
- Jarley's ... 117
- After the Fair ... 120
- The Enemies ... 124
- In the Garden ... 129
- Gaspar, Melchior, Balthasar ... 132
- The End of the River ... 134
- The Tree ... 139
- The Visitor ... 146
- The Dress ... 153
- The Lemon ... 156
- The Burning Baby ... 161
- The Horse's Ha ... 167
- The Orchards ... 172

The School for Witches	180
The Mouse and the Woman	186
A Prospect of the Sea	199
The Holy Six	206
Prologue to an Adventure	214
The Map of Love	219
In the Direction of the Beginning	224
An Adventure from a Work in Progress	226
The True Story	230
The Vest	233
ADVENTURES IN THE SKIN TRADE	237
A Fine Beginning	239
Plenty of Furniture	257
Four Lost Souls	272
LATE STORIES	289
Memories of Christmas	291
Quite Early One Morning	296
Holiday Memory	301
The Crumbs of One Man's Year	307
The Followers	312
A Story	320
Abbreviations	328
Note on the Texts	329
Notes	329

Portrait of the Artist as a Young Dog
and Other Fiction

PORTRAIT OF THE ARTIST
AS A YOUNG DOG*

The Peaches*

The grass-green cart, with "J. Jones, Gorsehill"* painted shakily on it, stopped in the cobblestone passage between the Hare's Foot and the Pure Drop. It was late on an April evening. Uncle Jim, in his black-market suit with a stiff white shirt and no collar, loud new boots and a plaid cap, creaked and climbed down. He dragged out a thick wicker basket from a heap of straw in the corner of the cart and swung it over his shoulder. I heard a squeal from the basket and saw the tip of a pink tail curling out as Uncle Jim opened the public door of the Pure Drop.

"I won't be two minutes," he said to me. The bar was full; two fat women in bright dresses sat near the door, one with a small dark child on her knee; they saw Uncle Jim and nudged up on the bench.

"I'll be out straight away," he said fiercely, as though I had contradicted him, "you stay there quiet."

The woman without the child raised up her hands. "Oh, Mr Jones," she said in a high laughing voice. She shook like a jelly.

Then the door closed and the voices were muffled.

I sat alone on the shaft of the cart in the narrow passage, staring through a side window of the Hare's Foot. A stained blind was drawn half over it. I could see into half of a smoky, secret room, where four men were playing cards. One man was huge and swarthy, with a handlebar moustache and a love curl on his forehead; seated by his side was a thin, bald, pale old man with his cheeks in his mouth; the faces of the other two were in shadow. They all drank out of brown pint tankards and never spoke, laying the cards down with a smack, scraping at their matchboxes, puffing at their pipes, swallowing unhappily, ringing the brass bell, ordering more, by a sign of the fingers, from a sour woman with a flowered blouse and a man's cap.

The passage grew dark too suddenly, the walls crowded in, and the roofs crouched down. To me, staring timidly there in the dark passage in a strange town, the swarthy man appeared like a giant in a cage surrounded by clouds, and the bald old man withered into a black hump with a white top; two white hands darted out of the corner with invisible cards. A man with spring-heeled boots and a two-edged knife might be bouncing towards me from Union Street.

I called "Uncle Jim, Uncle Jim" softly, so that he should not hear.

I began to whistle between my teeth, but when I stopped I thought the sound went hissing on behind me. I climbed down from the shaft and stepped close to the half-blind window; a hand clawed up the pane to the tassel of the blind; in the little, packed space between me on the cobbles and the card players at the table, I could not tell which side of the glass was the hand that dragged the blind down slowly. I was cut from the night by a stained square. A story I had made in the warm, safe island of my bed, with sleepy midnight Swansea flowing and rolling round outside the house, came blowing down to me then with a noise on the cobbles. I remembered the demon in the story, with his wings and hooks, who clung like a bat to my hair as I battled up and down Wales after a tall, wise, golden, royal girl from Swansea convent. I tried to remember her true name, her proper, long, black-stockinged legs, her giggle and paper curls, but the hooked wings tore at me, and the colour of her hair and eyes faded and vanished like the grass-green of the cart that was a dark, grey mountain now standing between the passage walls.

And all this time the old, broad, patient, nameless mare stood without stirring, not stamping once on the cobbles or shaking her reins. I called her a good girl and stood on tiptoe to try to stroke her ears as the door of the Pure Drop swung open and the warm lamplight from the bar dazzled me and burned my story up. I felt frightened no longer, only angry and hungry. The two fat women near the door giggled "Goodnight, Mr Jones" out of the rich noise and the comfortable smells. The child lay curled asleep under the bench. Uncle Jim kissed the two women on the lips.

"Goodnight."

"Goodnight."

"Goodnight."

Then the passage was dark again,

He backed the mare into Union Street, lurching against her side, cursing her patience and patting her nose, and we both climbed into the cart.

"There are too many drunken Gypsies," he said as we rolled and rattled through the flickering lamplit town.

He sang hymns all the way to Gorsehill in an affectionate bass voice, and conducted the wind with his whip. He did not need to touch the reins. Once on the rough road, between hedges twisting out to twig the mare by the bridle and poke our caps, we stopped at a whispered "Whoa" for Uncle to light his pipe and set the darkness on fire and show his long, red, drunken fox's face to me, with its bristling side bushes and wet, sensitive nose. A white house with a light in one bedroom window shone in a field on a short hill beyond the road.

Uncle whispered "Easy, easy, girl" to the mare, though she was standing calmly, and said to me over his shoulder in a suddenly loud voice: "A hangman lived there."

He stamped on the shaft, and we rattled on through a cutting wind. Uncle shivered, pulling down his cap to hide his ears, but the mare was like a clumsy statue trotting, and all the demons of my stories, if they trotted by her side or crowded together and grinned into her eyes, would not make her shake her head or hurry.

"I wish he'd have hung Mrs Jesus,"* Uncle said.

Between hymns he cursed the mare in Welsh. The white house was left behind, the light and the hill were swallowed up.

"Nobody lives there now," he said.

We drove into the farmyard of Gorsehill, where the cobbles rang and the black, empty stables took up the ringing and hollowed it so that we drew up in a hollow circle of darkness and the mare was a hollow animal and nothing lived in the hollow house at the end of the yard but two sticks with faces scooped out of turnips.

"You run and see Annie," said Uncle. "There'll be hot broth and potatoes."

He led the hollow, shaggy* statue towards the stable – clop, clop to the mice house. I heard locks rattle as I ran to the farmhouse door.

The front of the house was the single side of a black shell, and the arched door was the listening ear. I pushed the door open and walked into the passage out of the wind. I might have been walking into the hollow night and the wind, passing through a tall vertical shell on an inland seashore. Then a door at the end of the passage opened; I saw the plates on the shelves, the lighted lamp on the long, oilclothed table, "Prepare to Meet Thy God" knitted over the fireplace, the smiling china dogs, the brown-stained settle, the grandmother clock, and I ran into the kitchen and into Annie's arms.

There was a welcome, then. The clock struck twelve as she kissed me, and I stood among the shining and striking like a prince taking off his disguise. One minute I was small and cold, skulking dead-scared down a black passage in my stiff best suit, with my hollow belly thumping and my heart like a time bomb, clutching my grammar-school cap, unfamiliar to myself, a snub-nosed storyteller lost in his own adventures and longing to be home; the next I was a royal nephew in smart town clothes, embraced and welcomed, standing in the snug centre of my stories and listening to the clock announcing me. She hurried me to the seat in the side of the cavernous fireplace and took off my shoes. The bright lamps and the ceremonial gongs blazed and rang for me.

She made a mustard bath and strong tea, told me to put on a pair of my cousin Gwilym's* socks and an old coat of Uncle's that smelt of rabbit and tobacco. She fussed and clucked and nodded and told me, as she cut bread and butter, how Gwilym was still studying to be a minister, and how Aunt Rach Morgan, who was ninety years old, had fallen on her belly on a scythe.

Then Uncle Jim came in like the Devil with a red face and a wet nose and trembling, hairy hands. His walk was thick. He stumbled against the dresser and shook the coronation plates, and a lean cat shot booted out from the settle corner. Uncle looked nearly twice as tall as Annie. He could have carried her about under his coat and brought her out suddenly, a little, brown-skinned, toothless, hunchbacked woman with a cracked sing-song voice.

"You shouldn't have kept him out so long," she said, angry and timid.

He sat down in his special chair, which was the broken throne of a bankrupt bard, and lit his pipe and stretched his legs and puffed clouds at the ceiling.

"He might catch his death of cold," she said.

She talked at the back of his head while he wrapped himself in clouds. The cat slunk back. I sat at the table with my supper finished, and found a little empty bottle and a white balloon in the pockets of my coat.

"Run off to bed, there's a dear," Annie whispered.

"Can I go and look at the pigs?"

"In the morning, dear," she said.

So I said goodnight to Uncle Jim, who turned and smiled at me and winked through the smoke, and I kissed Annie and lit my candle.

"Goodnight."

"Goodnight."

"Goodnight."

I climbed the stairs; each had a different voice. The house smelt of rotten wood and damp and animals. I thought that I had been walking long, damp passages all my life, and climbing stairs in the dark, alone. I stopped outside Gwilym's door on the draughty landing.

"Goodnight."

The candle flame jumped in my bedroom, where a lamp was burning very low, and the curtains waved; the water in a glass on a round table by the bed stirred, I thought, as the door closed, and lapped against the sides. There was a stream below the window; I thought it lapped against the house all night until I slept.

"Can I go and see the pigs?" I asked Gwilym next morning. The hollow fear of the house was gone, and, running downstairs to my breakfast, I smelt the sweetness of wood and the fresh spring grass and the quiet untidy farmyard, with its tumbledown dirty-white cow-house and empty stables open.

Gwilym was a tall young man aged nearly twenty, with a thin stick of a body and spade-shaped face. You could dig the garden with him. He had a deep voice that cracked in half when he was excited, and he sang songs to himself, treble and bass, with the same sad hymn tune, and wrote hymns in the barn. He told me stories about girls who died for love. "And she put a rope round the tree, but it was too short," he said. "She stuck a penknife in her bosoms, but it was too blunt." We were sitting together on the straw heaps that day in the half-dark of the shuttered stable. He twisted and leant near to me, raising his big finger, and the straw creaked.

"She jumped in the cold river, she jumped," he said, his mouth against my ear, "arse over tip and Diu,* she was dead." He squeaked like a bat.

The pigsties were at the far end of the yard. We walked towards them, Gwilym dressed in minister's black, though it was a weekday morning, and me in a serge suit with a darned bottom, past three hens scrabbling the muddy cobbles and a collie with one eye, sleeping with it open. The ramshackle outhouses had tumbling, rotten roofs, jagged holes in their sides, broken shutters and peeling whitewash; rusty screws ripped out from the dangling, crooked boards; the lean cat of the night before sat snugly between the splintered jaws of bottles, cleaning its face, on the tip of the rubbish pile that rose triangular and smelling sweet and strong to the level of the riddled cart-house roof. There was nowhere like that farmyard in all the slapdash county, nowhere so poor and grand and dirty as that square of mud and rubbish and bad wood and falling stone, where a bucketful of old and bedraggled hens scratched and laid small eggs. A duck quacked out of the trough in one deserted sty. Now a young man and a curly boy stood staring and sniffing over a wall at a sow, with its tits on the mud, giving suck.

"How many pigs are there?"

"Five. The bitch ate one," said Gwilym.

We counted them as they squirmed and wriggled, rolled on their backs and bellies, edged and pinched and pushed and squealed about their mother. There were four. We counted again. Four pigs, four naked pink tails curling up as their mouths guzzled down and the sow grunted with pain and joy.

"She must have ate another," I said, and picked up a scratching stick and prodded the grunting sow and rubbed her crusted bristles backwards. "Or a fox jumped over the wall," I said.

"It wasn't the sow or the fox," said Gwilym. "It was Father."

I could see Uncle, tall and sly and red, holding the writhing pig in his two hairy hands, sinking his teeth in its thigh, crunching its trotters up: I could see him leaning over the wall of the sty with the pig's legs sticking out of his mouth. "Did Uncle Jim eat the pig?"

Now, at this minute, behind the rotting sheds, he was standing, knee-deep in feathers, chewing off the live heads of the poultry.

"He sold it to go on the drink," said Gwilym in his deepest rebuking whisper, his eyes fixed on the sky.

"Last Christmas he took a sheep over his shoulder, and he was pissed for ten days."

The sow rolled nearer the scratching stick, and the small pigs sucking at her, lost and squealing in the sudden darkness, struggling under her folds and pouches.

"Come and see my chapel," said Gwilym. He forgot the lost pig at once and began to talk about the towns he had visited on a religious tour, Neath and Bridgend and Bristol and Newport, with their lakes and luxury gardens, their bright, coloured streets roaring with temptation. We walked away from the sty and the disappointed sow.

"I met actress after actress," he said.

Gwilym's chapel was the last old barn before the field that led down to the river; it stood well above the farmyard, on a mucky hill. There was one whole door with a heavy padlock, but you could get in easily through the holes on either side of it. He took out a ring of keys and shook them gently and tried each one in the lock. "Very posh," he said. "I bought them from the junk shop in Carmarthen." We climbed into the chapel through a hole.

A dusty wagon with the name painted out and a whitewash cross on its side stood in the middle. "My pulpit cart," he said, and walked solemnly into it up the broken shaft. "You sit on the hay – mind the mice," he said. Then he brought out his deepest voice again, and cried to the heavens and the bat-lined rafters and the hanging webs: "Bless us this holy day, O Lord, bless me and Dylan and this Thy little chapel for ever and ever, amen. I've done a lot of improvements to this place."

I sat on the hay and stared at Gwilym preaching, and heard his voice rise and crack and sink to a whisper and break into singing and Welsh and ring triumphantly and be wild and meek. The sun through a hole shone on his praying shoulders, and he said: "O God, Thou art everywhere all the time, in the dew of the morning, in the frost of the evening, in the field and the town, in the preacher and the sinner, in the sparrow and the big buzzard. Thou canst see everything, right down deep in our hearts; Thou canst see us when the sun is gone; Thou canst see us when there aren't any stars, in the gravy blackness, in the deep, deep, deep, deep pit; Thou canst see and spy and watch us all the time, in the little black corners, in the big cowboys' prairies, under the blankets when we're snoring fast, in the terrible shadows – pitch black, pitch black; Thou canst see everything we do, in the night and day, in the day and the night, everything, everything; Thou canst see all the time. O God, mun,* you're like a bloody cat."

He let his clasped hands fall. The chapel in the barn was still, and shafted with sunlight. There was nobody to cry "Hallelujah" or "God bless" – I was too small and enamoured in the silence. The one duck quacked outside.

"Now I take a collection," Gwilym said.

He stepped down from the cart and groped about in the hay beneath it and held out a battered tin to me.

"I haven't got a proper box," he said.

I put two pennies in the tin.

"It's time for dinner," he said, and we went back to the house without a word.

Annie said, when we had finished dinner: "Put on your nice suit for this afternoon. The one with stripes."

It was to be a special afternoon, for my best friend, Jack Williams, from Swansea, was coming down with his rich mother in a motor car, and Jack was to spend a fortnight's holiday with me.

"Where's Uncle Jim?"

"He's gone to market," said Annie.

Gwilym made a small pig's noise. We knew where Uncle was: he was sitting in a public house with a heifer over his shoulder and two pigs nosing out of his pockets, and his lips wet with bull's blood.

"Is Mrs Williams very rich?" asked Gwilym.

I told him she had three motor cars and two houses, which was a lie. "She's the richest woman in Wales, and once she was a mayoress," I said. "Are we going to have tea in the best room?"

Annie nodded. "And a large tin of peaches," she said.

"That old tin's been in the cupboard since Christmas," said Gwilym. "Mother's been keeping it for a day like this."

"They're lovely peaches," Annie said. She went upstairs to dress like Sunday.

The best room smelt of mothballs and fur and damp and dead plants and stale, sour air. Two glass cases on wooden coffin boxes lined the window wall. You looked at the weed-grown vegetable garden through a stuffed fox's legs, over a partridge's head, along the red-paint-stained breast of a stiff wild duck. A case of china and pewter, trinkets, teeth, family brooches, stood beyond the bandy table; there was a large oil lamp on the patchwork tablecloth, a Bible with a clasp, a tall vase with a draped woman about to bathe on it, and a framed photograph of Annie, Uncle Jim and Gwilym smiling in front of a fern pot. On the mantelpiece were two clocks, some dogs, brass candlesticks, a shepherdess, a man in a kilt and a tinted photograph of Annie, with high hair and her breasts coming out. There were chairs around the table and in each corner, straight, curved, stained, padded, all with lace cloths hanging over their backs. A patched white sheet shrouded the harmonium. The fireplace was full of brass tongs, shovels and pokers. The best room was rarely used. Annie dusted and brushed and polished there once a week, but the carpet still sent up a grey cloud when you trod on it, and dust lay evenly on the seats of the chairs, and balls of cotton and dirt and black stuffing and long black horse hairs were wedged in the cracks of the sofa. I blew on the glass to see the pictures. Gwilym and castles and cattle.

"Change your suit now," said Gwilym.

I wanted to wear my old suit, to look like a proper farm boy and have manure in my shoes and hear it squelch as I walked, to see a cow have calves and a bull on top of a cow, to run down in the dingle and wet my stockings, to go out and shout "Come on, you b——" and pelt the hens and talk in a proper voice. But I went upstairs to put my striped suit on.

From my bedroom I heard the noise of a motor car drawing up the yard. It was Jack Williams and his mother.

Gwilym shouted "They're here, in a Daimler!" from the foot of the stairs, and I ran down to meet them with my tie undone and my hair uncombed.

Annie was saying at the door: "Good afternoon, Mrs Williams, good afternoon. Come right in, it's a lovely day, Mrs Williams. Did you have a nice journey, then? This way, Mrs Williams, mind the step."

Annie wore a black, shining dress that smelt of mothballs, like the chair covers in the best room; she had forgotten to change her gym shoes, which were caked with mud and all holes. She fussed on before Mrs Williams down the stone passage, darting her head round, clucking, fidgeting, excusing the small house, anxiously tidying her hair with one rough, stubby hand.

Mrs Williams was tall and stout, with a jutting bosom and thick legs, her ankles swollen over her pointed shoes; she was fitted out like a mayoress or a ship, and she swayed after Annie into the best room.

She said: "Please don't put yourself out for me, Mrs Jones, there's a dear." She dusted the seat of a chair with a lace handkerchief from her bag before sitting down.

"I can't stop, you know," she said.

"Oh, you must stay for a cup of tea," said Annie, shifting and scraping the chairs away from the table so that nobody could move and Mrs Williams was hemmed in fast with her bosom and her rings and her bag, opening the china cupboard, upsetting the Bible on the floor, picking it up, dusting it hurriedly with her sleeve.

"And peaches," Gwilym said. He was standing in the passage with his hat on.

Annie said, "Take your hat off, Gwilym, make Mrs Williams comfortable," and she put the lamp on the shrouded harmonium and spread out a white tablecloth that had a tea stain in the centre, and brought out the china and laid knives and cups for five.

"Don't bother about me, there's a dear," said Mrs Williams.

"There's a lovely fox!" She flashed a finger of rings at the glass case.

"It's real blood," I told Jack, and we climbed over the sofa to the table.

"No it isn't," he said, "it's red ink."

"Oh, your shoes!" said Annie.

"Don't tread on the sofa, Jack, there's a dear."

"If it isn't ink, it's paint then."

Gwilym said: "Shall I get you a bit of cake, Mrs Williams?"

Annie rattled the teacups. "There isn't a single bit of cake in the house," she said. "We forgot to order it from the shop – not a single bit. Oh, Mrs Williams!"

Mrs Williams said: "Just a cup of tea, thanks." She was still sweating, because she had walked all the way from the car. It spoilt her powder. She sparkled her rings and dabbed at her face.

"Three lumps," she said. "And I'm sure Jack will be very happy here."

"Happy as sandboys." Gwilym sat down.

"Now you must have some peaches, Mrs Williams, they're lovely."
"They should be, they've been here long enough," said Gwilym.
Annie rattled the teacups at him again.
"No peaches, thanks," Mrs Williams said.
"Oh, you must, Mrs Williams, just one. With cream."
"No, no, Mrs Jones, thanks the same," she said. "I don't mind pears or chunks, but I can't bear peaches."

Jack and I had stopped talking. Annie stared down at her gym shoes. One of the clocks on the mantelpiece coughed and struck. Mrs Williams struggled from her chair.

"There, time flies!" she said.

She pushed her way past the furniture, jostled against the sideboard, rattled the trinkets and brooches and kissed Jack on the forehead.

"You've got scent on," he said.

She patted my head.

"Now behave yourselves."

To Annie, she said in a whisper: "And remember, Mrs Jones, just good plain food. No spoiling his appetite."

Annie followed her out of the room. She moved slowly now.

"I'll do my very best, Mrs Williams."

We heard her say "Goodbye then, Mrs Williams" and go down the steps of the kitchen and close the door. The motor car roared in the yard, then the noise grew softer and died.

Down the thick dingle Jack and I ran shouting, scalping the brambles with our thin stick-hatchets, dancing, hallooing. We skidded to a stop and prowled on the bushy banks of the stream. Up above sat one-eyed, dead-eyed, sinister, slim, ten-notched Gwilym,* loading his guns in Gallows Farm. We crawled and rattatted through the bushes, hid, at a whistled signal, in the deep grass, and crouched there, waiting for the crack of a twig or the secret breaking of boughs.

On my haunches, eager and alone, casting an ebony shadow, with the Gorsehill jungle swarming, the violent, impossible birds and fishes leaping, hidden under four-stemmed flowers the height of horses, in the early evening in a dingle near Carmarthen, my friend Jack Williams invisibly near me, I felt all my young body like an excited animal surrounding me, the torn knees bent, the bumping heart, the long heat and depth between the legs, the sweat prickling in the hands, the tunnels down to the eardrums, the little balls of dirt between the toes, the eyes in the sockets, the tucked-up voice, the blood racing, the memory around and within flying, jumping, swimming and waiting to pounce. There, playing Indians in the evening, I was aware of me myself in the exact middle of a living story, and my body was my adventure and my name. I sprang with excitement and scrambled up through the scratching brambles again.

Jack cried: "I see you! I see you!" He scampered after me. "Bang! Bang! You're dead!"

But I was young and loud and alive, though I lay down obediently.

"Now you try and kill me," said Jack. "Count a hundred."

I closed one eye, saw him rush and stamp towards the upper field, then tiptoe back and begin to climb a tree, and I counted fifty and ran to the foot of the tree and killed him as he climbed. "You fall down," I said.

He refused to fall, so I climbed too, and we clung to the top branches and stared down at the lavatory in the corner of the field. Gwilym was sitting on the seat with his trousers down. He looked small and black. He was reading a book and moving his hands.

"We can see you!" we shouted.

He snatched his trousers up and put the book in his pocket.

"We can see you, Gwilym!"

He came out into the field. "Where are you, then?"

We waved our caps at him.

"In the sky!" Jack shouted.

"Flying!" I shouted.

We stretched our arms out like wings.

"Fly down here."

We swung and laughed on the branches.

"There's birds!" cried Gwilym.

Our jackets were torn and our stockings were wet and our shoes were sticky; we had green moss and brown bark on our hands and faces when we went in for supper and a scolding. Annie was quiet that night, though she called me a ragamuffin and said she didn't know what Mrs Williams would think and told Gwilym he should know better. We made faces at Gwilym and put salt in his tea, but after supper he said: "You can come to the chapel if you like. Just before bed."

He lit a candle on the top of the pulpit cart. It was a small light in the big barn. The bats were gone. Shadows still clung upside down along the roof. Gwilym was no longer my cousin in a Sunday suit, but a tall stranger shaped like a spade in a cloak, and his voice grew too deep. The straw heaps were lively. I thought of the sermon on the cart: we were watched,

Jack's heart was watched, Gwilym's tongue was marked down, my whisper, "Look at the little eyes", was remembered always.

"Now I take confessions," said Gwilym from the cart.

Jack and I stood bareheaded in the circle of the candle, and I could feel the trembling of Jack's body.

"You first." Gwilym's finger, as bright as though he had held it in the candle flame until it burned, pointed me out, and I took a step towards the pulpit cart, raising my head.

"Now you confess," said Gwilym.

"What have I got to confess?"

"The worst thing you've done."

I let Edgar Reynolds be whipped because I had taken his homework; I stole from my mother's bag; I stole from Gwyneth's bag; I stole twelve books in three visits from the library, and threw them away in the park; I drank a cup of my water to see what it tasted like; I beat a dog with a stick so that it would roll over and lick my hand afterwards; I looked with Dan Jones through the keyhole while his maid had a bath; I cut my knee with a penknife, and put the blood on my handkerchief and said it had come out of my ears so that I could pretend I was ill and frighten my mother; I pulled my trousers down and showed Jack Williams; I saw Billy Jones beat a pigeon to death with a fire shovel, and laughed and got sick; Cedric Williams and I broke into Mrs Samuels's house and poured ink over the bedclothes.

I said: "I haven't done anything bad."

"Go on, confess," said Gwilym. He was frowning down at me.

"I can't! I can't!" I said. "I haven't done anything bad."

"Go on, confess!"

"I won't! I won't!"

Jack began to cry. "I want to go home," he said.

Gwilym opened the chapel door, and we followed him into the yard, down past the black, humped sheds, towards the house, and Jack sobbed all the way.

In bed together, Jack and I confessed our sins.

"I steal from my mother's bag too – there are pounds and pounds."

"How much do you steal?"

"Threepence."

"I killed a man once."

"No you didn't then."

"Honest to Christ, I shot him through the heart."

"What was his name?"

"Williams."

"Did he bleed?"

I thought the stream was lapping against the house.

"Like a bloody pig," I said.

Jack's tears had dried. "I don't like Gwilym, he's barmy."

"No he isn't. I found a lot of poems in his bedroom once. They were all written to girls. And he showed them to me afterwards, and he'd changed all the girls' names to God."

"He's religious."

"No he isn't, he goes with actresses. He knows Corinne Griffith."*

Our door was open. I liked the door locked at night, because I would rather have a ghost in the bedroom than think of one coming in, but Jack liked it open, and we tossed and he won. We heard the front door rattle and footsteps in the kitchen passage.

"That's Uncle Jim."

"What's he like?"

"He's like a fox, he eats pigs and chickens."

The ceiling was thin, and we heard every sound, the creaking of the bard's chair, the clatter of plates, Annie's voice saying: "Midnight!"

"He's drunk," I said. We lay quite still, hoping to hear a quarrel.

"Perhaps he'll throw plates," I said.

But Annie scolded him softly. "There's a fine state, Jim."

He murmured to her.

"There's one pig gone," she said. "Oh, why do you have to do it, Jim? There's nothing left now. We'll never be able to carry on."

"Money! Money! Money!" he said. I knew he would be lighting his pipe.

Then Annie's voice grew so soft we could not hear the words, and Uncle said: "Did she pay you the thirty shillings?"

"They're talking about your mother," I told Jack.

For a long time Annie spoke in a low voice, and we waited for words. "Mrs Williams", she said, and "motor car", and "Jack", and "peaches". I thought she was crying, for her voice broke on the last word.

Uncle Jim's chair creaked again; he might have struck his fist on the table, and we heard him shout: "I'll give her peaches! Peaches, peaches! Who does she think she is? Aren't peaches good enough for her? To hell with her bloody motor car and her bloody son! Making us small."

"Don't, don't Jim!" Annie said. "You'll wake the boys."

"I'll wake them and whip the hell out of them, too!"

"Please, please, Jim!"

"You send the boy away," he said, "or I'll do it myself. Back to his three bloody houses."

Jack pulled the bedclothes over his head and sobbed into the pillow: "I don't want to hear, I don't want to hear. I'll write to my mother. She'll take me away."

I climbed out to close the door. Jack would not talk to me again, and I fell asleep to the noise of the voices below, which soon grew gentle.

Uncle Jim was not at breakfast. When we came down, Jack's shoes were cleaned for him, and his jacket was darned and pressed. Annie gave two boiled eggs to Jack and one to me. She forgave me when I drank tea from the saucer.

After breakfast, Jack walked to the post office. I took the one-eyed collie to chase rabbits in the upper fields, but it barked at ducks and brought me a tramp's shoe from a hedge, and lay down with its tail wagging in a rabbit hole. I threw stones at the deserted duck pond, and the collie ambled back with sticks.

Jack went skulking into the damp dingle, his hands in his pockets, his cap over one eye. I left the collie sniffing at a molehill, and climbed to the treetop in the corner of the lavatory field. Below me, Jack was playing Indians all alone, scalping through the bushes, surprising himself round a tree, hiding from himself in the grass. I called to him once, but he pretended not to hear. He played alone, silently and savagely. I saw him standing with his hands in his pockets, swaying like a Kelly,* on the mudbank by the stream at the foot of the dingle. My bough lurched; the heads of the dingle bushes spun up towards me like green tops; "I'm falling!" I cried; my trousers saved me; I swung and grasped – this was one minute of wild adventure, but Jack did not look up, and the minute was lost. I climbed, without dignity, to the ground.

Early in the afternoon, after a silent meal, when Gwilym was reading the Scriptures or writing hymns to girls or sleeping in his chapel, Annie was baking bread and I was cutting a wooden whistle in the loft over the stable, the motor car drove up in the yard again.

Out of the house Jack, in his best suit, ran to meet his mother, and I heard him say, as she stepped, raising her short skirts, onto the cobbles: "And he called you a bloody cow, and he said he'd whip the hell out of me, and Gwilym took me to the barn in the dark and let the mice run over me, and Dylan's a thief, and that old woman's spoilt my jacket."

Mrs Williams sent the chauffeur for Jack's luggage. Annie came to the door, trying to smile and curtsy, tidying her hair, wiping her hands on her pinafore.

Mrs Williams said "Good afternoon" and sat with Jack in the back of the car and stared at the ruin of Gorsehill.

The chauffeur came back. The car drove off, scattering the hens. I ran out of the stable to wave to Jack. He sat still and stiff by his mother's side. I waved my handkerchief.

A Visit to Grandpa's*

In the middle of the night I woke from a dream full of whips and lariats* as long as serpents, and runaway coaches on mountain passes, and wide, windy gallops over cactus fields, and I heard the man in the next room crying "Gee-up!" and "Whoa!" and trotting his tongue on the roof of his mouth.

It was the first time I had stayed in Grandpa's house. The floorboards had squeaked like mice as I climbed into bed, and the mice between the walls had creaked like wood as though another visitor was walking on them. It was a mild summer night, but curtains had flapped and branches beaten against the window. I had pulled the sheets over my head, and soon was roaring and riding in a book.

"Whoa there, my beauties!" cried Grandpa. His voice sounded very young and loud, and his tongue had powerful hooves, and he made his bedroom into a great meadow. I thought I would see if he was ill, or had set his bedclothes on fire, for my mother had said that he lit his pipe under the blankets, and had warned me to run to his help if I smelt smoke in the night. I went on tiptoe through the darkness to his bedroom door, brushing against the furniture and upsetting a candlestick with a thump. When I saw there was a light in the room, I felt frightened, and as I opened the door I heard Grandpa shout "Gee-up!" as loudly as a bull with a megaphone.

He was sitting straight up in bed and rocking from side to side as though the bed were on a rough road; the knotted edges of the counterpane were his reins; his invisible horse stood in a shadow beyond the bedside candle. Over a white flannel nightshirt he was wearing a red waistcoat with walnut-sized brass buttons. The overfilled bowl of his pipe smouldered among his whiskers like a little burning hayrick on a stick. At the sight of me, his hands dropped from the reins and lay blue and quiet, the bed stopped still on a level road, he muffled his tongue into silence, and the horses drew softly up.

"Is there anything the matter, Grandpa?" I asked, though the clothes were not on fire. His face in the candlelight looked like a ragged quilt pinned upright on the black air and patched all over with goat's-beard.

He stared at me mildly. Then he blew down his pipe, scattering the sparks and making a high, wet dog whistle of the stem, and shouted: "Ask no questions."

After a pause, he said slyly: "Do you ever have nightmares, boy?"

I said: "No."

"Oh yes, you do," he said.

I said I was woken by a voice that was shouting to horses.

"What did I tell you?" he said. "You eat too much. Who ever heard of horses in a bedroom?"

He fumbled under his pillow, brought out a small tinkling bag and carefully untied its strings. He put a sovereign in my hand and said: "Buy a cake." I thanked him and wished him goodnight.

As I closed my bedroom door, I heard his voice crying loudly and gaily, "Gee-up! Gee-up!" and the rocking of the travelling bed.

In the morning I woke from a dream of fiery horses on a plain that was littered with furniture, and of large, cloudy men who rode six horses at a time and whipped them with burning bedclothes. Grandpa was at breakfast, dressed in deep black. After breakfast he said "There was a terrible loud wind last night", and sat in his armchair by the hearth to make clay balls for the fire. Later in the morning he took me for a walk, through Johnstown village and into the fields on the Llansteffan road.

A man with a whippet said "There's a nice morning, Mr Thomas" – and when he had gone, leanly as his dog, into the short-treed green wood he should not have entered because of the notices, Grandpa said: "There, do you hear what he called you? Mister!"

We passed by small cottages, and all the men who leant on the gates congratulated Grandpa on the fine morning. We passed through the wood full of pigeons, and their wings broke the branches as they rushed to the tops of the trees. Among the soft, contented voices and the loud, timid flying, Grandpa said, like a man calling across a field: "If you heard those old birds in the night, you'd wake me up and say there were horses in the trees."

We walked back slowly, for he was tired, and the lean man stalked out of the forbidden wood with a rabbit held as gently over his arm as a girl's arm in a warm sleeve.

On the last day but one of my visit I was taken to Llansteffan in a governess cart* pulled by a short, weak pony. Grandpa might have been driving a bison, so tightly he held the reins, so ferociously cracked the long whip, so blasphemously shouted warning to boys who played in the road, so stoutly stood with his gaitered legs apart and cursed the demon strength and wilfulness of his tottering pony.

"Look out, boy!" he cried when we came to each corner, and pulled and tugged and jerked and sweated and waved his whip like a rubber sword. And when the pony had crept miserably round each corner, Grandpa turned to me with a sighing smile: "We weathered that one, boy."

When we came to Llansteffan village at the top of the hill, he left the cart by the Edwinsford Arms and patted the pony's muzzle and gave it sugar, saying: "You're a weak little pony, Jim, to pull big men like us."

He had strong beer and I had lemonade, and he paid Mrs Edwinsford with a sovereign out of the tinkling bag; she enquired after his health, and he said that Llangadog was better for the tubes. We went to look at the churchyard and the sea, and sat in the wood called the Sticks, and stood on the concert platform in the middle of the wood where visitors sang on midsummer nights and, year by year, the innocent of the village was elected mayor. Grandpa paused at the churchyard and pointed over the iron gate at the angelic headstones and the poor wooden crosses. "There's no sense in lying there," he said.

We journeyed back furiously: Jim was a bison again.

I woke late on my last morning, out of dreams where the Llansteffan sea carried bright sailing boats as long as liners, and heavenly choirs in the Sticks, dressed in bards' robes and brass-buttoned waistcoats, sang in a strange Welsh to the departing sailors. Grandpa was not at breakfast – he rose early. I walked in the fields with a new sling, and shot at the Towy gulls* and the rooks in the parsonage trees. A warm wind blew from the summer points of the weather; a morning mist climbed from the ground and floated among the trees and hid the noisy birds; in the mist and the wind my pebbles flew lightly up like hailstones in a world on its head. The morning passed without a bird falling.

I broke my sling and returned for the midday meal through the parson's orchard. Once, Grandpa told me, the parson had bought three ducks at Carmarthen Fair and made a pond for them in the centre of the garden, but they waddled to the gutter under the crumbling doorsteps of the house, and swam and quacked there. When I reached the end of the orchard path, I looked through a hole in the hedge and saw that the parson had made a tunnel through the rockery that was between the gutter and the pond and had set up a notice in plain writing: "This way to the pond."

The ducks were still swimming under the steps.

Grandpa was not in the cottage. I went into the garden, but Grandpa was not staring at the fruit trees. I called across to a man who leant on a spade in the field beyond the garden hedge: "Have you seen my grandpa this morning?"

He did not stop digging, and answered over his shoulder: "I seen him in his fancy waistcoat."

Griff, the barber, lived in the next cottage. I called to him through the open door: "Mr Griff, have you seen my grandpa?" The barber came out in his shirtsleeves.

I said: "He's wearing his best waistcoat." I did not know if it was important, but Grandpa wore his waistcoat only in the night.

"Has Grandpa been to Llansteffan?" asked Mr Griff anxiously.

"He went there yesterday in a little trap," I said.

He hurried indoors, and I heard him talking in Welsh, and he came out again with his white coat on, and he carried a striped and coloured walking stick. He strode down the village street, and I ran by his side.

When we stopped at the tailor's shop, he cried out "Dan!" – and Dan Tailor stepped from his window, where he sat like an Indian priest but wearing a derby hat. "Dai Thomas has got his waistcoat on," said Mr Griff, "and he's been to Llansteffan."

As Dan Tailor searched for his overcoat, Mr Griff was striding on. "Will Evans," he called outside the carpenter's shop, "Dai Thomas has been to Llansteffan, and he's got his waistcoat on."

"I'll tell Morgan now," said the carpenter's wife out of the hammering, sawing darkness of the shop.

We called at the butcher's shop and Mr Price's house, and Mr Griff repeated his message like a town crier.

We gathered together in Johnstown square. Dan Tailor had his bicycle, Mr Price his pony trap. Mr Griff, the butcher, Morgan carpenter and I climbed into the shaking trap, and we trotted off towards Carmarthen town. The tailor led the way, ringing his bell as though there were a fire or a robbery, and an old woman by the gate of a cottage at the end of the street ran inside like a pelted hen. Another woman waved a bright handkerchief.

"Where are we going?" I asked.

Grandpa's neighbours were as solemn as old men with black hats and jackets on the outskirts of a fair. Mr Griff shook his head and mourned: "I didn't expect this again from Dai Thomas."

"Not after last time," said Mr Price sadly.

We trotted on, we crept up Constitution Hill, we rattled down into Lammas Street, and the tailor still rang his bell and a dog ran, squealing, in front of his wheels. As we clip-clopped over the cobbles that led down to the Towy bridge, I remembered Grandpa's nightly noisy journeys that rocked the bed and shook the walls, and I saw his gay waistcoat in a vision and his patchwork head tufted and smiling in the candlelight. The tailor before us turned round on his saddle; his bicycle wobbled and skidded. "I see Dai Thomas!" he cried.

The trap rattled onto the bridge, and I saw Grandpa there: the buttons of his waistcoat shone in the sun; he wore his tight, black Sunday trousers and a tall, dusty hat I had seen in a cupboard in the attic, and he carried an ancient bag. He bowed to us. "Good morning, Mr Price," he said, "and Mr Griff and Mr Morgan and Mr Evans." To me he said: "Good morning, boy."

Mr Griff pointed his coloured stick at him.

"And what do you think you are doing on Carmarthen bridge in the middle of the afternoon," he said sternly, "with your best waistcoat and your old hat?"

Grandpa did not answer, but inclined his face to the river wind, so that his beard was set dancing and wagging as though he talked, and watched the coracle* men move, like turtles, on the shore.

Mr Griff raised his stunted barber's pole. "And where do you think you are going," he said, "with your old black bag?"

Grandpa said: "I am going to Llangadog to be buried." And he watched the coracle shells slip into the water lightly, and the gulls complain over the fish-filled water as bitterly as Mr Price complained:

"But you aren't dead yet, Dai Thomas."

For a moment Grandpa reflected, then: "There's no sense in lying dead in Llansteffan," he said. "The ground is comfy in Llangadog – you can twitch your legs without putting them in the sea."

His neighbours moved close to him. They said: "You aren't dead, Mr Thomas."

"How can you be buried, then?"

"Nobody's going to bury you in Llansteffan."

"Come on home, Mr Thomas."

"There's strong beer for tea."

"And cake."

But Grandpa stood firmly on the bridge, and clutched his bag to his side, and stared at the flowing river and the sky, like a prophet who has no doubt.

Patricia, Edith and Arnold*

The small boy in his invisible engine, the Cwmdonkin Special,* its wheels, polished to dazzle, crunching on the small back garden scattered with breadcrumbs for the birds and white with yesterday's snow, its smoke rising thin and pale as breath in the cold afternoon, hooted under the wash line, kicked the dog's plate at the wash-house stop and puffed and pistoned slower and slower while the servant girl lowered the pole, unpegged the swinging vests, showed the brown stains under her arms and called over the wall: "Edith, Edith, come here, I want you."

Edith climbed on two tubs on the other side of the wall and called back: "I'm here, Patricia." Her head bobbed up above the broken glass.

He backed the *Flying Welshman** from the wash house to the open door of the coal hole and pulled hard on the brake that was a hammer in his pocket: assistants in uniform ran out with fuel; he spoke to a saluting fireman, and the engine shuffled off, round the barbed walls of China that kept the cats away, by the frozen rivers in the sink, in and out of the coal-hole tunnel. But he was listening carefully all the time, through the squeals and whistles, to Patricia and the next-door servant, who belonged to Mrs Lewis, talking when they should have been working, calling his mother Mrs T., being rude about Mrs L.

He heard Patricia say: "Mrs T. won't be back till six."

And Edith next door replied: "Old Mrs L. has gone to Neath to look for Mr Robert."

"He's on the randy* again," Patricia whispered.

"Randy, sandy, bandy!" cried the boy out of the coal hole.

"You get your face dirty, I'll kill you," Patricia said absent-mindedly.

She did not try to stop him when he climbed up the coal heap. He stood quietly on the top, King of the Coal Castle, his head touching the roof, and listened to the worried voices of the girls. Patricia was almost in tears; Edith was sobbing and rocking on the unsteady tubs. "I'm standing on top of the coal," he said, and waited for Patricia's anger.

She said: "I don't want to see him, you go alone."

"We must, we must go together," said Edith. "I've got to know."

"I don't want to know."

"I can't stand it, Patricia, you must go with me."

"You go alone, he's waiting for you."

"Please, Patricia!"

"I'm lying on my face in the coal," said the boy.

"No, it's your day with him. I don't want to know. I just want to think he loves me."

"Oh, talk sense, Patricia, please! Will you come or no? I've got to hear what he says."

"All right then, in half an hour. I'll shout over the wall."

"You'd better come soon," the boy said. "I'm dirty as Christ knows what."

Patricia ran to the coal hole. "The language! Come out of there at once!" she said.

The tubs began to slide, and Edith vanished.

"Don't you dare use language like that again. Oh! Your suit!" Patricia took him indoors.

She made him change his suit in front of her. "Otherwise there's no telling." He took off his trousers and danced around her, crying: "Look at me, Patricia!"

"You be decent," she said, "or I won't take you to the park."

"Am I going to the park, then?"

"Yes, we're all going to the park – you and me and Edith next door."

He dressed himself neatly, not to annoy her, and spat on his hands before parting his hair. She appeared not to notice his silence and neatness. Her large hands were clasped together; she stared down at the white brooch on her chest. She was a tall, thick girl with awkward hands; her fingers were like toes, her shoulders were wide as a man's.

"Am I satisfactory?" he asked.

"There's a long word," she said, and looked at him lovingly. She lifted him up and seated him on the top of the chest of drawers. "Now you're as tall as I am."

"But I'm not so old," he said.

He knew that this was an afternoon on which anything might happen; it might snow enough for sliding on a tray; uncles from America, where he had no uncles, might arrive with revolvers and St Bernards; Ferguson's shop might catch on fire and all the piece packets fall on the pavements; and he was not surprised when she put her black, straight-haired heavy head on his shoulder and whispered into his collar: "Arnold, Arnold Matthews."

"There, there," he said, and rubbed her parting with his finger and winked at himself in the mirror behind her and looked down her dress at the back.

"Are you crying?"

"No."

"Yes you are, I can feel the wet."

She dried her eyes on her sleeve. "Don't you let on that I was crying."

"I'll tell everybody – I'll tell Mrs T. and Mrs L., I'll tell the policeman and Edith and my dad and Mr Chapman: Patricia was crying on my shoulder like a nanny goat; she cried for two hours, she cried enough to fill a kettle. I won't really," he said.

As soon as he and Patricia and Edith set off for the park, it began to snow. Big flakes unexpectedly fell on the rocky hill, and the sky grew dark as dusk, though it was only three in the afternoon. Another boy, somewhere in the allotments behind the houses, shouted as the first flakes fell. Mrs Ocky Evans opened the top bay windows of Springmead and thrust her head and hands out, as though to catch the snow. He waited, without revolt, for Patricia to say "Quick! Hurry back, it's snowing!" and to pack him in out of the day before his feet were wet. Patricia can't have seen the snow, he thought at the top of the hill, though it was falling heavily, sweeping against her face, covering her black hat. He dared not speak for fear of waking her, as they turned the corner into the road that led down to the park. He lagged behind to take his cap off and catch the snow in his mouth.

"Put on your cap," said Patricia, turning. "Do you want to catch your death of cold?"

She tucked his muffler inside his coat, and said to Edith: "Will he be there in the snow, do you think? He's bound to be there, isn't he? He was always there on my Wednesdays, wet or fine." The tip of her nose was red; her cheeks glowed like coals; she looked handsomer in the snow than in the summer, when her hair would lie limp on her wet forehead and a warm patch spread on her back.

"He'll be there," Edith said. "One Friday it was pelting down and he was there. He hasn't got anywhere else to go, he's always there. Poor Arnold!" She looked white and tidy in a coat with a fur piece, and twice as small as Patricia; she stepped through the thick snow as though she were going shopping.

"Wonders will never cease," he said aloud to himself. This was Patricia letting him walk in the snow, this was striding along in a storm with two big girls. He sat down in the road. "I'm on a sledge," he said. "Pull me, Patricia, pull me like an Eskimo."

"Up you get, you moochin,* or I'll take you home."

He saw that she did not mean it. "Lovely Patricia, beautiful Patricia," he said, "pull me along on my bottom."

"Any more dirty words, and you know who I'll tell."

"Arnold Matthews," he said.

Patricia and Edith drew closer together.

"He notices everything," Patricia whispered.

Edith said: "I'm glad I haven't got your job."

"Oh," said Patricia, catching him by the hand and pressing it on her arm, "I wouldn't change him for the world!"

He ran down the gravel path onto the upper walk of the park.

"I'm spoilt!" he shouted. "I'm spoilt! Patricia spoils me!"

Soon the park would be white all over; already the trees were blurred round the reservoir and fountain, and the training college on the gorse hill was hidden in a cloud. Patricia and Edith took the steep path down to the shelter. Following on the forbidden grass, he slid past them straight into a bare bush, but the bump and the pricks left him shouting and unhurt. The girls gossiped sadly now. They shook their coats in the deserted shelter, scattering snow on the seats, and sat down, close together still, outside the bowling-club window.

"We're only just on time," said Edith. "It's hard to be punctual in the snow."

"Can I play by here?"

Patricia nodded. "Play quietly then – don't be rough with the snow."

"Snow! Snow! Snow!" he said, and scooped it out of the gutter and made a small ball.

"Perhaps he's found a job," Patricia said.

"Not Arnold."

"What if he doesn't come at all?"

"He's bound to come, Patricia – don't say things like that."

"Have you brought your letters?"

"They're in my bag. How many have you got?"

"No, how many have you got, Edith?"

"I haven't counted."

"Show me one of yours," Patricia said.

He was used to their talk by this time; they were old and cuckoo, sitting in the empty shelter sobbing over nothing. Patricia was reading a letter and moving her lips.

"He told me that too," she said, "that I was his star."

"Did he begin: 'Dear Heart'?"

"Always 'Dear Heart'."

Edith broke into real loud tears. With a snowball in his hand, he watched her sway on the seat and hide her face in Patricia's snowy coat.

Patricia said, patting and calming Edith, rocking her head: "I'll give him a piece of my mind when he comes!"

When who comes? He threw the snowball high into the silently driving fall. Edith's crying in the deadened park was clear and thin as a whistle, and, disowning the soft girls and standing away from them in case a stranger passed, a man with boots to his thighs, or a sneering, bigger boy from the Uplands,* he piled the snow against the wire of the tennis court and thrust his hands into the snow like a baker making bread. As he delved and moulded the snow into loaves, saying under his breath "This is the way it is done, ladies and gentlemen", Edith raised her head and said: "Patricia, promise me, don't be cross with him. Let's all be quiet and friendly."

"Writing 'Dear Heart' to us both," said Patricia angrily. "Did he ever take off your shoes and pull your toes and—"

"No, no, you mustn't, don't go on, you mustn't speak like that!"

Edith put her fingers to her cheeks. "Yes, he did," she said.

"Somebody has been pulling Edith's toes," he said to himself, and ran round the other side of the shelter, chuckling. "Edith went to market," he laughed aloud, and stopped at the sight of a young man without an overcoat sitting in the corner seat and cupping his hands and blowing into them. The young man wore a white muffler and a check cap. When he saw the boy, he pulled his cap down over his eyes. His hands were pale blue, and the ends of his fingers yellow.

The boy ran back to Patricia. "Patricia, there's a man!" he cried.

"Where's a man?"

"On the other side of the shelter – he hasn't got an overcoat, and he's blowing in his hands like this."

Edith jumped up. "It's Arnold!"

"Arnold Matthews, Arnold Matthews, we know you're there!" Patricia called round the shelter, and, after a long minute, the young man, raising his cap and smiling, appeared at the corner and leant against a wooden pillar.

The trousers of his sleek blue suit were wide at the bottoms; the shoulders were high and hard, and sharp at the ends; his pointed patent shoes were shining; a red handkerchief stuck from his breast pocket; he had not been out in the snow.

"Fancy you two knowing each other!" he said loudly, facing the red-eyed girls and the motionless, open-mouthed boy who stood at Patricia's side with his pockets full of snowballs.

Patricia tossed her head, and her hat fell over one eye. As she straightened her hat, "You come and sit down here, Arnold Matthews, you've got some questions to answer!" she said in her washing-day voice.

Edith clutched at her arm: "Oh! Patricia, you promised." She picked at the edge of her handkerchief. A tear rolled down her cheek.

Arnold said softly then: "Tell the little boy to run away and play."

The boy ran round the shelter once and returned to hear Edith saying "There's a hole in your elbow, Arnold", and to see the young man kicking the snow at his feet and staring at the names and hearts cut on the wall behind the girls' heads.

"Who did you walk out with on Wednesdays?" Patricia asked.

Her clumsy hands held Edith's letter close to the sprinkled folds of her chest.

"You, Patricia."

"Who did you walk out with on Fridays?"

"With Edith, Patricia."

He said to the boy: "Here, son, can you roll a snowball as big as a football?"

"Yes, as big as two footballs."

Arnold turned back to Edith and said: "How did you come to know Patricia Davies? You work in Brynmill."*

"I just started work in Cwmdonkin," she said. "I haven't seen you since, to tell you. I was going to tell you today, but I found out. How could you, Arnold? Me on my afternoon off, and Patricia on Wednesdays."

The snowball had turned into a short snow man with a lopsided, dirty head and a face full of twigs, wearing a boy's cap and smoking a pencil.

"I didn't mean any harm," said Arnold. "I love you both."

Edith screamed. The boy jumped forward, and the snowman with a broken back collapsed.

"Don't tell your lies, how can you love two of us?" Edith cried, shaking her handbag at Arnold. The bag snapped open, and a bundle of letters fell on the snow.

"Don't you dare pick up those letters," Patricia said.

Arnold had not moved. The boy was searching for his pencil in the snowman's ruins.

"You make your choice, Arnold Matthews, here and now."

"Her or me," said Edith.

Patricia turned her back to him. Edith, with her bag in her hand hanging open, stood still. The sweeping snow turned up the top page of a letter.

"You two," he said, "you go off the handle. Sit down and talk. Don't cry like that, Edith. Hundreds of men love more than one woman: you're always reading about it. Give us a chance, Edith, there's a girl."

Patricia looked at the hearts and arrows and old names. Edith saw the letters curl.

"It's you, Patricia," said Arnold.

Still Patricia stood turned away from him. Edith opened her mouth to cry, and he put a finger to his lips. He made the shape of a whisper, too soft for Patricia to hear. The boy watched him soothing and promising Edith, but she screamed again and ran out of the shelter and down the path, her handbag beating against her side.

"Patricia," he said, "turn round to me. I had to say it. It's you, Patricia."

The boy bent down over the snowman and found his pencil driven through its head. When he stood up, he saw Patricia and Arnold arm in arm.

Snow dripped through his pockets, snow melted in his shoes, snow trickled down his collar into his vest. "Look at you now," said Patricia, rushing to him and holding him by the hands, "you're wringing wet."

"Only a bit of snow," said Arnold, suddenly alone in the shelter.

"A bit of snow indeed – he's as cold as ice, and his feet are like sponges. Come on home at once!"

The three of them climbed the path to the upper walk, and Patricia's footprints were large as a horse's in the thickening snow.

"Look, you can see our house, it's got a white roof!"

"We'll be there, ducky, soon."

"I'd rather stay out and make a snowman like Arnold Matthews."

"Hush! Hush! Your mother'll be waiting. You must come home."

"No she won't. She gone on a randy with Mr Robert. Randy, sandy, bandy!"

"You know very well she's shopping with Mrs Partridge, you mustn't tell wicked lies."

"Well, Arnold Matthews told lies. He said he loved you better than Edith, and he whispered behind your back to her."

"I swear I didn't, Patricia, I don't love Edith at all!"

Patricia stopped walking. "You don't love Edith?"

"No, I've told you, it's you. I don't love her at all," he said. "Oh! My God, what a day! Don't you believe me? It's you, Patricia. Edith isn't anything. I just used to meet her – I'm always in the park."

"But you told her you loved her."

The boy stood bewildered between them. Why was Patricia so angry and serious? Her face was flushed, and her eyes shone. Her chest moved up and down. He saw the long black hairs on her leg through a tear in her stockings. Her leg is as big as my middle, he thought. I'm cold; I want tea; I've got snow in my fly.

Arnold backed slowly down the path. "I had to tell her that, or she wouldn't have gone away. I had to, Patricia. You saw what she was like. I hate her. Cross my heart!"

"Bang! Bang!" cried the boy.

Patricia was smacking Arnold, tugging at his muffler, knocking him with her elbows. She pummelled him down the path, and shouted at the top of her voice: "I'll teach you to lie to Edith! You pig! You black! I'll teach you to break her heart!"

He shielded his face from her blows as he staggered back. "Patricia, Patricia, don't hit me! There's people!"

As Arnold fell, two women with umbrellas up peered through the whirling snow from behind a bush.

Patricia stood over him. "You lied to her and you'd lie to me," she said. "Get up, Arnold Matthews!"

He rose and set his muffler straight and wiped his eyes with the red handkerchief, and raised his cap and walked towards the shelter.

"And as for you," Patricia said, turning to the watching women, "you should be ashamed of yourselves! Two old women playing about in the snow."

They dodged behind the bush.

Patricia and the boy climbed, hand in hand, back to the upper walk.

"I've left my cap by the snowman," he remembered. "It's my cap with the Tottenham colours."

"Run back quickly," she said, "you can't get any wetter than you are."

He found his cap half hidden under snow. In a corner of the shelter, Arnold sat reading the letters that Edith had dropped, turning the wet pages slowly. He did not see the boy, and the boy, behind a pillar, did not interrupt him. Arnold read every letter carefully.

"You've been a long time finding your cap," Patricia said. "Did you see the young man?"

"No," he said, "he was gone."

At home, in the warm living room, Patricia made him change his clothes again. He held his hands in front of the fire, and soon they began to hurt.

"My hands are on fire," he told her, "and my toes, and my face." After she had comforted him, she said: "There, that's better. The hurting's gone. You won't call the king your uncle in a minute."* She was bustling about the room. "Now, we've all had a good cry today."

The Fight*

I was standing at the end of the lower playground and annoying Mr Samuels, who lived in the house just below the high railings. Mr Samuels complained once a week that boys from the school threw apples and stones and balls through his bedroom window. He sat in a deckchair in a small square of trim garden and tried to read the newspaper. I was only a few yards from him. I was staring him out. He pretended not to notice me, but I knew he knew I was standing there rudely and quietly. Every now and then he peeped at me from behind his newspaper, saw me still and serious and alone, with my eyes on his. As soon as he lost his temper, I was going to go home. Already I was late for dinner. I had almost beaten him, the newspaper was trembling, he was breathing heavily, when a strange boy,* whom I had not heard approach, pushed me down the bank.

I threw a stone at his face. He took off his spectacles, put them in his coat pocket, took off his coat, hung it neatly on the railings and attacked. Turning round as we wrestled on the top of the bank, I saw that Mr Samuels had folded his newspaper on the deckchair and was standing up to watch us. It was a mistake to turn round. The strange boy rabbit-punched me twice. Mr Samuels hopped with excitement as I fell against the railings. I was down in the dust, hot and scratched and biting, then up and dancing, and I butted the boy in the belly and we tumbled in a heap. I saw through a closing eye that his nose was bleeding. I hit his nose. He tore at my collar and spun me round by the hair.

"Come on! Come on!" I heard Mr Samuels cry.

We both turned towards him. He was shaking his fists and dodging about in the garden. He stopped then, and coughed, and set his panama straight, and avoided our eyes, and turned his back and walked slowly to the deckchair.

We both threw gravel at him.

"I'll give him 'Come on'!" the boy said, as we ran along the playground away from the shouts of Mr Samuels and down the steps onto the hill.

We walked home together. I admired his bloody nose. He said that my eye was like a poached egg, only black.

"I've never seen such a lot of blood," I said.

He said I had the best black eye in Wales, perhaps it was the best black eye in Europe; he bet Tunney* never had a black eye like that.

"And there's blood all over your shirt."

"Sometimes I bleed in dollops," he said.

On Walter's Road we passed a group of high-school girls, and I cocked my cap and hoped my eye was as big as a blue bag,* and he walked with his coat flung open to show the bloodstains.

I was a hooligan all during dinner, and a bully, and as bad as a boy from the Sandbanks,* and I should have more respect, and I sat silently, like Tunney, over the sago pudding. That afternoon I went to school with an eyeshade on. If I had had a black silk sling I would have been as gay and desperate as the wounded captain in the book that my sister used to read, and that I read under the bedclothes at night, secretly with a flash lamp.

On the road, a boy from an inferior school, where the parents did not have to pay anything, called me "One eye!" in a harsh, adult voice. I took no notice, but walked along whistling, my good eye on the summer clouds sailing, beyond insult, above Terrace Road.

The Mathematics master said: "I see that Mr Thomas at the back of the class has been straining his eyesight. But it isn't over his homework, is it, gentlemen?"

Gilbert Rees, next to me, laughed loudest.

"I'll break your leg after school!" I said.

He'd hobble, howling, up to the headmaster's study. A deep hush in the school. A message on a plate brought by the porter.

"The headmaster's compliments, sir, and will you come at once?"

"How did you happen to break this boy's leg?" "Oh! Damn and bottom, the agony!" cried Gilbert Rees. "Just a little twist," I would say. "I don't know my own strength. I apologize. But there's nothing to worry about. Let me set the leg, sir." A rapid manipulation, the click of a bone. "Doctor Thomas, sir, at your service." Mrs Rees was on her knees. "How can I thank you?"

"It's nothing at all, dear lady. Wash his ears every morning. Throw away his rulers. Pour his red and green inks down the sink."

In Mr Trotter's drawing class we drew naked girls inaccurately on sheets of paper under our drawings of a vase and passed them along under the desks. Some of the drawings were detailed strangely, others were tailed off like mermaids. Gilbert Rees drew the vase only.

"Sleep with your wife, sir?"

"What did you say?"

"Lend me a knife, sir?"

"What would you do if you had a million pounds?"

"I'd buy a Bugatti and a Rolls and a Bentley and I'd go two hundred miles an hour on Pendine Sands."*

"I'd buy a harem and keep the girls in the gym."

"I'd buy a house like Mrs Cotmore-Richard's, twice as big as hers, and a cricket field and a football field and a proper garage with mechanics and a lift."

"And a lavatory as big as… as big as the Melba Pavilion,* with plush seats and golden chains and—"

"And I'd smoke cigarettes with real gold tips, better than Morris's Blue Book."

"I'd buy all the railway trains, and only 4A could travel in them."

"And not Gilbert Rees either."

"What's the longest you've been?"

"I went to Edinburgh."

"My father went to Salonika in the war."*

"Where's that, Cyril?"

"Cyril, tell us about Mrs Pussie Edwards in Hanover Street."

"Well, my brother says he can do anything."

I drew a wild guess below the waist, and wrote Pussie Edwards in small letters at the foot of the page.

"Cave!"

"Hide your drawings."

"I bet you a greyhound can go faster than a horse."

Everybody liked the drawing class, except Mr Trotter.

In the evening, before calling on my new friend, I sat in my bedroom by the boiler and read through my exercise books full of poems. There were Danger Don'ts on the backs. On my bedroom walls were pictures of Shakespeare, Walter de la Mare torn from my father's Christmas *Bookman*, Robert Browning, Stacy Aumonier, Rupert Brooke, a bearded man who I had discovered was Whittier, Watts's *Hope** and a Sunday-school certificate I was ashamed to want to pull down. A poem I had had printed in the "Wales Day by Day" column of the *Western Mail* was pasted on the mirror to make me blush, but the shame of the poem had died.* Across the poem I had written, with a stolen quill and in flourishes: "Homer nods." I was always waiting for the opportunity to bring someone into my bedroom – "Come into my den; excuse the untidiness; take a chair. No! Not that one, it's broken!" – and force him to see the poem accidentally. "I put it there to make me blush." But nobody ever came in except my mother.

Walking to his house in the early dusk through solid, deserted professional avenues lined with trees, I recited pieces of my poems and heard my voice, like a stranger's voice in Park Drive accompanied by the tap-tapping of nailed boots, rise very thinly up through the respectable autumn evening.

> "My mind is fashioned
> In the ways of intertissue;
> Veiled and passioned
> Are the thoughts that issue
> From its well of furtive lust
> Raptured by the Devil's dust."

If I looked through a window onto the road, I would see a scarlet-capped boy with big boots striding down the middle, and would wonder who it could be. If I were a young girl watching, my face like Mona Lisa's, my coal-black hair coiled in earphones, I'd see beneath the "Boys' Department" suit a manly body with hair and sun tan, and call him and ask, "Will you have tea or cocktails?" and hear his voice reciting the 'Grass Blade's Psalm'* in the half-dark of the heavily curtained and coloured drawing room hung about with famous reproductions and glowing with books and wine bottles:

> "The frost has lain,
> Frost that is dark with flowered slain,
> Fragilely strewn
> With patches of illuminated moon,
> About my lonely head in flagged unlovely red.
>
> "The frost has spake,
> Frost secretive and thrilled in silent flake,
> With unseen lips of blue
> Glass in the glaze stars threw,
> Only to my ears, has spake in visionary tears.
>
> "The frost has known,
> From scattered conclave by the few winds blown,
> That the lone genius in my roots,
> Bare down there in a jungle of fruits,
> Has planted a green year, for praise in the heart of my upgrowing days.

"The frost has filled
My heart with longing that the night's sleeve spilled,
Frost of celestial vapour fraught,
Frost that the columns of unfallen snow have sought,
With desire for the fields of space hovering about my single place."

"Look! There's a strange boy, walking alone like a prince."

"No, no, like a wolf! Look at his long stride!" Sketty* church was shaking its bells for me.

"When I am strewn low
And all my ashes are
Dust in a dumb provoking show
Of minatory star..."

I recited. A young man and woman, arm in arm, suddenly appeared from a black lane between houses. I changed my recitation into a tune and hummed past them. They would be tittering together now, with their horrid bodies close. Cissy, moony, long hair. I whistled hard and loud, kicked a tradesmen's entrance and glanced back over my shoulder. The couple were gone. Here's a kick at "The Elms". "Where are the bleedy elms, mister?" Here's a handful of gravel, Mrs. "The Croft", right at your window. One night I would paint "Bum" all over the front gate of "Kia-ora".

A woman stood on "Lyndhurst" steps with a hissing Pom,* and, stuffing my cap in my pocket, I was off down the road; and there was Dan's house, "Warmley", with music coming loudly out of it.

He was a composer and a poet too; he had written seven historical novels before he was twelve, and he played the piano and the violin; his mother made wool pictures, his brother was a clerk at the docks and syncopated, his aunt kept a preparatory school on the first floor, and his father wrote music for the organ. All this he had told me as we walked home bleeding, strutting by the gym frocks waving to boys in the trams.

My new friend's mother answered the door with a ball of wool in her hand. Dan, in the upstairs drawing room, heard my arrival and played the piano faster.

"I didn't hear you come in," he said when I found him. He finished on a grand chord, stretching all his fingers.

The room was splendidly untidy, full of wool and paper and open cupboards stacked with things you could never find; all the expensive furniture had been kicked; a waistcoat hung on the chandelier. I thought I could live for ever in that room, writing and fighting and spilling ink, having my friends for picnics there after midnight with Waller's Rum-and-Butter and charlottes russes from Eynon's, and Cydrax and Vino.*

He showed me his books and his seven novels. All the novels were about battles, sieges and kings. "Just early stuff," he said.

He let me take out his violin and make a cat noise.

We sat on a sofa in the window and talked as though we had always known each other. Would the "Swans" beat the "Spurs"?* When could girls have babies? Was Arnott's average last year better than Clay's?*

That's my father outside there on the road," he said, "the tall one waving his arms."

Two men were talking on the tramlines. Mr Jenkyn looked as if he were trying to swim down Eversley Road, he breaststroked the air and beat on the ground with his feet, and then he limped and raised one shoulder higher than the other.

"Perhaps he's describing a fight," I said.

"Or telling Mr Morris a story about cripples," said Dan. "Can you play the piano?"

"I can do chords, but not tunes," I said.

We played a duet with crossed hands.

"Now, who's that sonata by?"

We made a Dr Percy, who was the greatest composer for four hands in the world, and I was Paul America, the pianist, and Dan was Winter Vaux.

I read him an exercise book full of poems. He listened wisely, like a boy aged a hundred, his head on one side and his spectacles shaking on his swollen nose. "This is called 'Warp',* I said:

"Like suns red from running tears,
Five suns in the glass,
Together, separate yet, yet separately round,
Red perhaps, but the glass is as pale as grass,
Glide, without sound.
In unity, five tears lid-awake, suns yet, but salt,
Five inscrutable spears in the head,
Each sun but an agony,
Twist perhaps, pain bled of hate,
Five into one, the one made of five into one, early
Suns distorted to late.

All of them now, madly and desolate,
Spun with the cloth of the five, run
Widely and foaming, wildly and desolate,
Shoot through and dive. One of the five is the sun."

The noise of the trams past the house clattered away as far as the sea or farther, into the dredgered bay. Nobody had ever listened like that before. The school had vanished, leaving on Mount Pleasant hill* a deep hole that smelt of cloakrooms and locker mice, and "Warmley"* shone in the dark of a town I did not know. In the still room, that had never been strange to me, sitting in heaps of coloured wool, swollen-nosed and one-eyed, we acknowledged our gifts. The future spread out beyond the window, over Singleton Park crowded with lovers messing about, and into smoky London paved with poems.

Mrs Jenkyn peered round the door and switched the light on.

"There, that's more homely," she said. "You aren't cats."

The future went out with the light, and we played a thumping piece by Dr Percy – "Have you ever heard anything so beautiful? Louder, louder, America!" said Dan. "Leave a bit of bass for me," I said – until the next-door wall was rapped.

"That's the Careys. Mr Carey's a Cape Horner,"* Dan said.

We played him one harsh, whaling piece before Mrs Jenkyn, with wool and needles, ran upstairs.

When she had gone, Dan said: "Why is a man always ashamed of his mother?"

"Perhaps he isn't when he is older," I said, but I doubted it. The week before I was walking down High Street with three boys after school, and I saw my mother with a Mrs Partridge outside the Kardomah.* I knew she would stop me in front of the others and say "Now you be home early for tea", and I wanted High Street to open and suck me down. I loved her and disowned her. "Let's cross over," I said, "there's some sailors' boots in Griffith's window." But there was only a dummy with a golf suit on, and a roll of tweed.

"Supper isn't for half an hour yet. What shall we do?"

"Let's see who can hold up that chair the longest," I said.

"No, let's edit a paper: you do the literature, I'll do the music."

"What shall we call it, then?"

He wrote "*The* ——, edited by D. Jenkyn and D. Thomas" on the back of a hatbox from under the sofa. The rhythm was better with D. Thomas and D. Jenkyn, but it was his house.

"What about *The Meistersingers*?"*

"No, that's too musical," I said.

"*The Warmley Magazine*?"

"No," I said, "I live in 'Glanrhyd'."*

After the hatbox was covered, we wrote.

"*The Thunderer*, edited by D. Jenkyn Thomas" in chalk on a piece of cardboard and pinned it on the wall.

"Would you like to see our maid's bedroom?" asked Dan. We whispered up to the attic.

"What's her name?"

"Hilda."

"Is she young?"

"No, she's twenty or thirty."

Her bed was untidy. "My mother says you can always smell a maid." We smelt the sheets. "I can't smell anything."

In her brass-bound box was a framed photograph of a young man wearing plus fours.

"That's her boy."

"Let's give him a moustache."

Somebody moved downstairs, a voice called "Supper now!" and we hurried out, leaving the box open. "One night we'll hide under her bed," Dan said as we opened the dining-room door.

Mr Jenkyn, Mrs Jenkyn, Dan's aunt and a Reverend Bevan and Mrs Bevan were seated at the table.

Mr Bevan said grace. When he stood up, it was just as though he were still sitting down, he was so short. "Bless our repast this evening," he said, as though he didn't like the food at all. But once "Amen" was over, he went at the cold meat like a dog.

Mrs Bevan didn't look all there. She stared at the tablecloth and made hesitant movements with her knife and fork. She appeared to be wondering which to cut up first, the meat or the cloth.

Dan and I stared at her with delight; he kicked me under the table, and I spilt the salt. In the commotion I managed to put some vinegar on his bread.

Mrs Jenkyn said, while everyone except Mr Bevan was watching Mrs Bevan moving her knife slowly along the edge of her plate: "I do hope you like cold lamb."

Mrs Bevan smiled at her, assured, and began to eat. She was grey-haired and grey-faced. Perhaps she was grey all over. I tried to undress her, but my mind grew frightened when it came to her short flannel petticoat and navy bloomers to the knees. I couldn't even dare unbutton her tall boots to see how grey her legs were. She looked up from her plate and gave me a wicked smile.

Blushing, I turned to answer Mr Jenkyn, who was asking me how old I was. I told him, but added one year. Why did I lie then? I wondered. If I lost my cap and found it in my bedroom, and my mother asked me where I had found it, I would say "In the attic", or "Under the hallstand". It was exciting to have to keep wary all the time in case I contradicted myself, to make up the story of a film I pretended to have seen and put Jack Holt in Richard Dix's place.*

"Fifteen and three-quarters," said Mr Jenkyn, "that's a very exact age. I see we have a mathematician with us. Now see if he can do this little sum."

He finished his supper and laid out matches on the plate.

"That's an old one, Dad," Dan said.

"Oh, I'd like to see it very much," I said in my best voice. I wanted to come to the house again. This was better than home, and there was a woman off her head, too.

When I failed to place the matches rightly, Mr Jenkyn showed me how it was done, and, still not understanding, I thanked him and asked him for another one. It was almost as good being a hypocrite as being a liar – it made you warm and shameful.

"What were you talking to Mr Morris about in the street, Dad?" asked Dan. "We saw you from upstairs."

"I was telling him how the Swansea and District Male Voice did the *Messiah*,* that's all. Why do you ask?"

Mr Bevan couldn't eat any more, he was full. For the first time since supper began, he looked round the table. He didn't seem to like what he saw. "How are studies progressing, Daniel?"

"Listen to Mr Bevan, Dan, he's asking you a question."

"Oh, so-so."

"So-so?"

"I mean they're going very well, thank you, Mr Bevan."

"Young people should attempt to say what they mean."

Mrs Bevan giggled, and asked for more meat. "More meat," she said.

"And you, young man, have you a mathematical bent?"

"No, sir," I said, "I like English."

"He's a poet," said Dan, and looked uncomfortable.

"A brother poet," Mr Bevan corrected, showing his teeth.

"Mr Bevan has published books," said Mr Jenkyn. "*Proserpine, Psyche*—"

"*Orpheus*," said Mr Bevan sharply.

"And *Orpheus*. You must show Mr Bevan some of your verses."

"I haven't got anything with me, Mr Jenkyn."

"A poet," said Mr Bevan, "should carry his verses in his head."

"I remember them all right," I said.

"Recite me your latest one – I'm always very interested."

"What a gathering," Mrs Jenkyn said. "Poets, musicians, preachers. We only want a painter now, don't we?"

"I don't think you'll like the very latest one," I said.

"Perhaps," said Mr Bevan, smiling. "I am the best judge of that."

"Frivolous is my hate,"* I said, wanting to die, watching Mr Bevan's teeth.

"Singed with bestial remorse
Of unfulfilment of desired force,
And lust of tearing late;

"Now could I raise
Her dead, dark body to my own
And hear the joyous rustle of her bone
And in her eyes see deathly blaze;

"Now could I wake
To passion after death, and taste
The rapture of her hating, tear the waste
Of body. Break, her dead, dark body, break."

Dan kicked my shins in the silence before Mr Bevan said: "The influence is obvious, of course. 'Break, break, break, on thy cold, grey stones, O sea.'"*

"Hubert knows Tennyson backwards," said Mrs Bevan. "Backwards."

"Can we go upstairs now?" Dan asked.

"No annoying Mr Carey then."

And we shut the door softly behind us and ran upstairs with our hands over our mouths.

"Damn! Damn! Damn!" said Dan. "Did you see the reverend's face?"

We imitated him up and down the room, and had a short fight on the carpet. Dan's nose began to bleed again. "That's nothing, it'll stop in a minute. I can bleed when I like."

"Tell me about Mrs Bevan. Is she mad?"

"She's terribly mad, she doesn't know who she is. She tried to throw herself out of the window, but he didn't take any notice, so she came up to our house and told Mother all about it."

Mrs Bevan knocked and walked in. "I hope I'm not interrupting you."
"No, of course not, Mrs Bevan."
"I wanted a little change of air," she said. She sat down in the wool on the sofa by the window.
"Isn't it a close night?" said Dan. "Would you like the window open?"
She looked at the window.
"I can easily open it for you," Dan said, and winked at me.
"Let me open it for you, Mrs Bevan," I said.
"It's good to have the window open."
"And this is a nice high window too."
"Plenty of air from the sea."
"Let it be, dear," she said. "I'll just sit here and wait for my husband."
She played with the balls of wool, picked up a needle and tapped it gently on the palm of her hand.
"Is Mr Bevan going to be long?"
"I'll just sit and wait for my husband," she said.
We talked to her some more about windows, but she only smiled and undid the wool, and once she put the blunt end of the long needle in her ear. Soon we grew tired of watching her, and Dan played the piano – "My twentieth sonata," he said, "this one is *Homage to Beethoven*" – and at half-past nine I had to go home.

I said goodnight to Mrs Bevan, who waved the needle and bowed sitting down, and Mr Bevan downstairs gave me his cold hand to shake, and Mr and Mrs Jenkyn told me to come again, and the quiet aunt gave me a Mars bar.

"I'll send you a bit of the way," said Dan.

Outside, on the pavement, in the warm night, we looked up at the lighted drawing-room window. It was the only light in the road.

"Look! There she is!"

Mrs Bevan's face was pressed against the glass, her hook nose flattened, her lips pressed tight, and we ran all the way down Eversley Road in case she jumped.

At the corner, Dan said: "I must leave you now, I've got to finish a string trio tonight."

"I'm working on a long poem," I said, "about the princes of Wales and the wizards and everybody."

We both went home to bed.

Extraordinary Little Cough*

One afternoon, in a particularly bright and glowing August, some years before I knew I was happy, George Hooping, whom we called Little Cough, Sidney Evans, Dan Davies and I sat on the roof of a lorry travelling to the end of the Peninsula.* It was a tall, six-wheeled lorry, from which we could spit on the roofs of the passing cars and throw our apple stumps at women on the pavement. One stump caught a man on a bicycle in the middle of the back; he swerved across the road; for a moment we sat quiet, and George Hooping's face grew pale. And if the lorry runs over him, I thought calmly as the man on the bicycle swayed towards the hedge, he'll get killed, and I'll be sick on my trousers and perhaps on Sidney's too, and we'll be arrested and hanged, except George Hooping, who didn't have an apple.

But the lorry swept past; behind us, the bicycle drove into the hedge; the man stood up and waved his fist, and I waved my cap back at him.

"You shouldn't have waved your cap," said Sidney Evans. "He'll know what school we're in." He was clever, dark and careful, and had a purse and a wallet.

"We're not in school now."

"Nobody can expel me," said Dan Davies. He was leaving next term to serve in his father's fruit shop for a salary.

We all wore haversacks, except George Hooping, whose mother had given him a brown-paper parcel that kept coming undone, and carried a suitcase each. I had placed a coat over my suitcase, because the initials on it were "N.T." and everybody would know that it belonged to my sister.* Inside the lorry were two tents, a box of food, a packing case of kettles and saucepans and knives and forks, an oil lamp, a Primus stove,* ground sheets and blankets, a gramophone with three records and a tablecloth from George Hooping's mother.

We were going to camp for a fortnight in Rhossili,* in a field above the sweeping five-mile beach. Sidney and Dan had stayed there last year, coming back brown and swearing, full of stories of campers' dances round the fires at midnight, and elderly girls from the training college who sunbathed naked on ledges of rocks surrounded by laughing boys, and singing in bed that lasted until dawn. But George had never left home for more than a night – and then, he told me one half-holiday when it was raining and there was nothing to do but stay in the wash house racing his guinea pigs giddily along the benches, it was only to stay in St Thomas, three miles from his house, with an aunt who could see through the walls and who knew what a Mrs Hoskin was doing in the kitchen.

"How much further?" asked George Hooping, clinging to his split parcel, trying in secret to push back socks and suspenders, enviously watching the solid green fields skim by as though the roof were a raft on an ocean with a motor in it. Anything upset his stomach, even liquorice and sherbet, but I alone knew that he wore long combinations* in the summer with his name stitched in red on them.

"Miles and miles," Dan said.

"Thousands of miles," I said. "It's Rhossili, USA. We're going to camp on a bit of rock that wobbles in the wind."

"And we have to tie the rock onto a tree."

"Cough can use his suspenders," Sidney said.

The lorry roared round a corner – "Upsy-daisy! Did you feel it then, Cough? It was on one wheel" – and below us, beyond fields and farms, the sea, with a steamer puffing on its far edge, shimmered.

"Do you see the sea down there? It's shimmering, Dan," I said.

George Hooping pretended to forget the lurch of the slippery roof and, from that height, the frightening smallness of the sea. Gripping the rail of the roof, he said: "My father saw a killer whale." The conviction in his voice died quickly as he began. He beat against the wind with his cracked treble voice, trying to make us believe. I knew he wanted to find a boast so big it would make our hair stand up and stop the wild lorry.

"Your father's a herbalist." But the smoke on the horizon was the white, curling fountain the whale blew through his nose, and its black nose was the bow of the poking ship.

"Where did he keep it, Cough, in the wash house?"

"He saw it in Madagascar. It had tusks as long as from here to… from here to…"

"From here to Madagascar."

All at once the threat of a steep hill disturbed him. No longer bothered about the adventures of his father, a small, dusty, skullcapped and alpaca-coated man standing and mumbling all day in a shop full of herbs and curtained holes in the wall, where old men with backache and young girls in trouble waited for consultations in the half-dark, he stared at the hill swooping up and clung to Dan and me.

EXTRAORDINARY LITTLE COUGH

"She's doing fifty!"

"The brakes have gone, Cough!"

He twisted away from us, caught hard with both hands on the rail, pulled and trembled, pressed on a case behind him with his foot, and steered the lorry to safety round a stone-walled corner and up a gentler hill to a gate of a battered farmhouse.

Leading down from the gate, there was a lane to the first beach. It was high tide, and we heard the sea dashing. Four boys on a roof – one tall, dark, regular-featured, precise of speech, in a good suit, a boy of the world; one squat, ungainly, red-haired, his red wrists fighting out of short, frayed sleeves; one heavily spectacled, small-paunched, with indoor shoulders and feet in always-unlaced boots wanting to go different ways; one small, thin, indecisively active, quick to get dirty, curly – saw their field in front of them, a fortnight's new home that had thick, pricking hedges for walls, the sea for a front garden, a green gutter for a lavatory and a windstruck tree in the very middle.

I helped Dan unload the lorry while Sidney tipped the driver and George struggled with the farmyard gate and looked at the ducks inside. The lorry drove away.

"Let's build our tents by the tree in the middle," said George.

"Pitch!" Sidney said, unlatching the gate for him.

We pitched our tents in a corner, out of the wind.

"One of us must light the Primus," Sidney said, and, after George had burnt his hand, we sat in a circle outside the sleeping tent talking about motor cars, content to be in the country, lazily easy in each other's company, thinking to ourselves as we talked, knowing always that the sea dashed on the rocks not far below us and rolled out into the world, and that tomorrow we would bathe and throw a ball on the sands and stone a bottle on a rock and perhaps meet three girls. The oldest would be for Sidney, the plainest for Dan and the youngest for me. George broke his spectacles when he spoke to girls; he had to walk off, blind as a bat, and the next morning he would say: "I'm sorry I had to leave you, but I remembered a message."

It was past five o'clock. My father and mother would have finished tea; the plates with famous castles on them were cleared from the table; Father with a newspaper, Mother with socks, were far away in the blue haze to the left, up a hill, in a villa, hearing from the park the faint cries of children drift over the public tennis court, and wondering where I was and what I was doing. I was alone with my friends in a field, with a blade of grass in my mouth, saying "Dempsey* would hit him cold" and thinking of the great whale that George's father never saw thrashing on the top of the sea, or plunging underneath, like a mountain.

"Bet you I can beat you to the end of the field."

Dan and I raced among the cow pads,* George thumping at our heels.

"Let's go down to the beach."

Sidney led the way, running straight as a soldier in his khaki shorts, over a stile, down fields to another, into a wooded valley, up through heather onto a clearing near the edge of the cliff, where two broad boys were wrestling outside a tent. I saw one bite the other in the leg; they both struck expertly and savagely at the face; one struggled clear, and, with a leap, the other had him face to the ground. They were Brazell and Skully.

"Hallo, Brazell and Skully!" said Dan.

Skully had Brazell's arm in a policeman's grip; he gave it two quick twists and stood up, smiling.

"Hallo, boys! Hallo, Little Cough! How's your father?"

"He's very well, thank you."

Brazell, on the grass, felt for broken bones. "Hallo, boys! How are your fathers?"

They were the worst and biggest boys in school. Every day for a term they caught me before class began and wedged me in the waste-paper basket and then put the basket on the master's desk. Sometimes I could get out and sometimes not. Brazell was lean, Skully was fat.

"We're camping in Button's field," said Sidney.

"We're taking a rest cure here," said Brazell. "And how is Little Cough these days? Father given him a pill?"

We wanted to run down to the beach, Dan and Sidney and George and I, to be alone together, to walk and shout by the sea in the country, throw stones at the waves, remember adventures and make more to remember.

"We'll come down to the beach with you," said Skully.

He linked arms with Brazell, and they strolled behind us, imitating George's wayward walk and slashing the grass with switches.

Dan said hopefully: "Are you camping here for long, Brazell and Skully?"

"For a whole nice fortnight, Davies and Thomas and Evans and Hooping."

When we reached Mewslade beach and flung ourselves down, as I scooped up sand and it trickled, grain by grain through my fingers, as George peered at the sea through his double lenses and Sidney and Dan heaped sand over his legs, Brazell and Skully sat behind us like two warders.

"We thought of going to Nice for a fortnight," said Brazell – he rhymed it with ice, dug Skully in the ribs – "but the air's nicer here for the complexion."

"It's as good as a herb," said Skully.

They shared an enormous joke, cuffing and biting and wrestling again, scattering sand in the eyes, until they fell back with laughter, and Brazell wiped the blood from his nose with a piece of picnic paper. George lay covered to the waist in sand. I watched the sea slipping out, with birds quarrelling over it, and the sun beginning to go down patiently.

"Look at Little Cough," said Brazell. "Isn't he extraordinary? He's growing out of the sand. Little Cough hasn't got any legs."

"Poor Little Cough," said Skully, "he's the most extraordinary boy in the world."

"Extraordinary Little Cough," they said together, "extraordinary, extraordinary, extraordinary." They made a song out of it, and both conducted with their switches.

"He can't swim."

"He can't run."

"He can't learn."

"He can't bowl."

"He can't bat."

"And I bet he can't make water."

George kicked the sand from his legs. "Yes, I can!"

"Can you swim?"

"Can you run?"

"Can you bowl?"

"Leave him alone," Dan said.

They shuffled nearer to us. The sea was racing out now. Brazell said in a serious voice, wagging his finger: "Now, quite truthfully, Cough, aren't you extraordinary? Very extraordinary? Say yes or no."

"Categorically, yes or no," said Skully.

"No," George said. "I can swim and I can run and I can play cricket. I'm not frightened of anybody."

I said: "He was second in the form last term."

"Now, isn't that extraordinary? If he can be second, he can be first. But no, that's too ordinary. Little Cough must be second."

"The question is answered," said Skully. "Little Cough is extraordinary." They began to sing again.

"He's a very good runner," Dan said.

"Well, let him prove it. Skully and I ran the whole length of Rhossili sands this morning, didn't we, Skull?"

"Every inch."

"Can Little Cough do it?"

"Yes," said George.

"Do it, then."

"I don't want to."

"Extraordinary Little Cough can't run," they sang, "can't run, can't run."

Three girls, all fair, came down the cliff side arm in arm, dressed in short white trousers. Their arms and legs and throats were brown as berries; I could see when they laughed that their teeth were very white; they stepped onto the beach, and Brazell and Skully stopped singing. Sidney smoothed his hair back, rose casually, put his hands in his pockets and walked towards the girls, who now stood close together, gold and brown, admiring the sunset with little attention, patting their scarves, turning smiles on each other. He stood in front of them, grinned and saluted: "Hallo, Gwyneth! Do you remember me?"

"La-di-da!" whispered Dan at my side, and made a mock salute to George still peering at the retreating sea.

"Well, if this isn't a surprise!" said the tallest girl. With little studied movements of her hands, as though she were distributing flowers, she introduced Peggy and Jean.

Fat Peggy, I thought, too jolly for me, with hockey legs and tomboy crop, was the girl for Dan; Sidney's Gwyneth was a distinguished piece and quite sixteen, as immaculate and unapproachable as a girl in Ben Evans's stores;* but Jean, shy and curly, with butter-coloured hair, was mine. Dan and I walked slowly to the girls.

I made up two remarks: "Fair's fair, Sidney, no bigamy abroad" and "Sorry we couldn't arrange to have the sea in when you came."

Jean smiled, wriggling her heel in the sand, and I raised my cap.

"Hallo!"

The cap dropped at her feet.

As I bent down, three lumps of sugar fell from my blazer pocket. "I've been feeding a horse," I said, and began to blush guiltily when all the girls laughed.

I could have swept the ground with my cap, kissed my hand gaily, called them señoritas and made them smile without tolerance. Or I could have stayed at a distance, and this would have been better still, my hair blown in the wind, though there was no wind at all that evening, wrapped in mystery and staring at the sun, too aloof to speak to girls; but I knew that all the time my ears would have been burning, my stomach would have been as hollow and as full of voices as a shell. "Speak to them quickly, before they go away!" a voice would have said insistently over the dramatic silence, as I stood like Valentino* on the edge of the bright, invisible bullring of the sands. "Isn't it lovely here?" I said.

I spoke to Jean alone – and this is love, I thought, as she nodded her head and swung her curls and said: "It's nicer than Porthcawl."*

Brazell and Skully were two big bullies in a nightmare; I forgot them when Jean and I walked up the cliff, and, looking back to see if they were baiting George again or wrestling together, I saw that George had disappeared around the corner of the rocks and that they were talking at the foot of the cliff with Sidney and the two girls.

"What's your name?"

I told her.

"That's Welsh," she said.

"You've got a beautiful name."

"Oh, it's just ordinary."

"Shall I see you again?"

"If you want to."

"I want to all right! We can go and bathe in the morning. And we can try to get an eagle's egg. Did you know that there were eagles here?"

"No," she said. "Who was that handsome boy on the beach, the tall one with dirty trousers?"

"He's not handsome, that's Brazell. He never washes or combs his hair or anything. He's a bully and he cheats."

"I think he's handsome."

We walked into Button's field, and I showed her inside the tents and gave her one of George's apples. "I'd like a cigarette," she said.

It was nearly dark when the others came. Brazell and Skully were with Gwyneth, one each side of her holding her arms, Sidney was with Peggy, and Dan walked, whistling, behind with his hands in his pockets.

"There's a pair," said Brazell. "They've been here all alone and they aren't even holding hands. You want a pill," he said to me.

"Build Britain's babies," said Skully.

"Go on!" Gwyneth said. She pushed him away from her, but she was laughing, and she said nothing when he put his arm around her waist.

"What about a bit of fire?" said Brazell.

Jean clapped her hands like an actress. Although I knew I loved her, I didn't like anything she said or did.

"Who's going to make it?"

"He's the best, I'm sure," she said, pointing at me.

Dan and I collected sticks, and by the time it was quite dark there was a fire crackling. Inside the sleeping tent, Brazell and Jean sat close together; her golden head was on his shoulder; Skully, near them, whispered to Gwyneth; Sidney unhappily held Peggy's hand.

"Did you ever see such a sloppy lot?" I said, watching Jean smile in the fiery dark.

"Kiss me, Charley!" said Dan.

We sat by the fire in the corner of the field. The sea, far out, was still making a noise. We heard a few night birds. "'Tu-whit! Tu-whoo!' Listen! I don't like owls," Dan said, "they scratch your eyes out!" – and tried not to listen to the soft voices in the tent. Gwyneth's laughter floated out over the suddenly moonlit field, but Jean, with the beast, was smiling and silent in the covered warmth; I knew her little hand was in Brazell's hand.

"Women!" I said.

Dan spat in the fire.

We were old and alone, sitting beyond desire in the middle of the night, when George appeared, like a ghost, in the firelight and stood there trembling until I said: "Where've you been? You've been gone hours. Why are you trembling like that?"

Brazell and Skully poked their heads out.

"Hallo, Cough my boy! How's your father? What have you been up to tonight?"

George Hooping could hardly stand. I put my hand on his shoulder to steady him, but he pushed it away.

"I've been running on Rhossili sands! I ran every bit of it! You said I couldn't, and I did! I've been running and running!"

Someone inside the tent had put a record on the gramophone. It was a selection from *No, No, Nanette*.*

"You've been running all the time in the dark, Little Cough?"

"And I bet I ran it quicker than you did, too!" George said.

"I bet you did," said Brazell.

"Do you think we'd run five miles?" said Skully.

Now the tune was 'Tea for Two'.

"Did you ever hear anything so extraordinary? I told you Cough was extraordinary. Little Cough's been running all night."

"Extraordinary, extraordinary, extraordinary Little Cough," they said.

Laughing from the shelter of the tent into the darkness, they looked like a boy with two heads. And when I stared round at George again, he was lying on his back fast asleep in the deep grass and his hair was touching the flames.

Just Like Little Dogs*

Standing alone under a railway arch out of the wind, I was looking at the miles of sands, long and dirty in the early dark, with only a few boys on the edge of the sea and one or two hurrying couples with their mackintoshes blown around them like balloons, when two young men joined me, it seemed out of nowhere, and struck matches for their cigarettes and illuminated their faces under bright-checked caps.

One had a pleasant face; his eyebrows slanted comically towards his temples, his eyes were warm, brown, deep and guileless, and his mouth was full and weak. The other man had a boxer's nose and a weighted chin ginger with bristles.

We watched the boys returning from the oily sea; they shouted under the echoing arch, then their voices faded. Soon there was not a single couple in sight; the lovers had disappeared among the sandhills and were lying down there with broken tins and bottles of the summer passed, old paper blowing by them, and nobody with any sense was about. The strangers, huddled against the wall, their hands deep in their pockets, their cigarettes sparkling, stared, I thought, at the thickening of the dark over the empty sands, but their eyes may have been closed. A train raced over us, and the arch shook. Over the shore, behind the vanishing train, smoke clouds flew together, rags of wings and hollow bodies of great birds black as tunnels, and broke up lazily; cinders fell through a sieve in the air, and the sparks were put out by the wet dark before they reached the sand. The night before, little quick scarecrows had bent and picked at the track line, and a solitary dignified scavenger wandered three miles by the edge with a crumpled coal sack and a park-keeper's steel-tipped stick. Now they were tucked up in sacks, asleep in a siding, their heads in bins, their beards in straw, in coal trucks thinking of fires, or lying beyond pickings on Jack Stiff's slab near the pub in the Fishguard Alley, where the methylated-spirit drinkers danced into the policemen's arms and women like lumps of clothes in a pool waited, in doorways and holes in the soaking wall, for vampires or firemen. Night was properly down on us now. The wind changed. Thin rain began. The sands themselves went out. We stood in the scooped, windy room of the arch, listening to the noises from the muffled town, a goods train shunting, a siren in the docks, the hoarse trams in the streets far behind, one bark of a dog, unplaceable sounds, iron being beaten, the distant creaking of wood, doors slamming where there were no houses, an engine coughing like a sheep on a hill.

The two young men were statues smoking, tough-capped and collarless watchers and witnesses carved out of the stone of the blowing room where they stood at my side with nowhere to go, nothing to do, and all the raining, almost winter, night before them. I cupped a match to let them see my face in a dramatic shadow, my eyes mysteriously sunk, perhaps, in a startling white face, my young looks savage in the sudden flicker of light, to make them wonder who I was as I puffed my last butt and puzzled about them. Why was the soft-faced young man, with his tame devil's eyebrows, standing like a stone figure with a glow-worm in it? He should have a nice girl to bully him gently and take him to cry in the pictures, or kids to bounce in a kitchen in Rodney Street. There was no sense in standing silent for hours under a railway arch on a hell of a night at the end of a bad summer when girls were waiting, ready to be hot and friendly, in chip shops and shop doorways and Rabaiotti's all-night café,* when the public bar of the Bay View at the corner had a fire and skittles and a swarthy, sensuous girl with different-coloured eyes, when the billiard saloons were open, except the one in High Street you couldn't go into without a collar and tie, when the closed parks had empty, covered bandstands and the railings were easy to climb.

A church clock somewhere struck a lot, faintly from the night on the right, but I didn't count.

The other young man, less than two feet from me, should be shouting with the boys, boasting in lanes, propping counters, prancing and clouting in the Mannesmann Hall,* or whispering around a bucket in a ring corner. Why was he humped here with a moody man and myself, listening to our breathing, to the sea, the wind scattering sand through the archway, a chained dog and a foghorn and the rumble of trams a dozen streets away, watching a match strike, a boy's fresh face spying in a shadow, the lighthouse beams, the movement of a hand to a fag, when the sprawling town in a drizzle, the pubs and the clubs and the coffee shops, the prowlers' streets, the arches near the promenade, were full of friends and enemies? He could be playing nap by a candle in a shed in a woodyard.

Families sat down to supper in rows of short houses, the wireless sets were on, the daughters' young men sat in the front rooms. In neighbouring houses they read the news off the tablecloth, and the potatoes from dinner were fried up. Cards were played in the front rooms of houses on the hills. In the houses on tops of the hills families were entertaining friends, and the blinds of the front rooms were not quite drawn. I heard the sea in a cold bit of the cheery night.

One of the strangers said suddenly, in a high, clear voice: "What are we all doing, then?"

"Standing under a bloody arch," said the other one.

"And it's cold," I said.

"It isn't very cosy," said the high voice of the young man with the pleasant face, now invisible. "I've been in better hotels than this."

"What about that night in the Majestic?" said the other voice.

There was a long silence.

"Do you often stand here?" said the pleasant man. His voice might never have broken.

"No, this is the first time here," I said. "Sometimes I stand in the Brynmill arch."

"Ever tried the old pier?"

"It's no good in the rain, is it?"

"Underneath the pier, I mean, in the girders."

"No, I haven't been there."

"Tom spends every Sunday under the pier," the pug-faced young man said bitterly. "I got to take him his dinner in a piece of paper."

"There's another train coming," I said. It tore over us, the arch bellowed, the wheels screamed through our heads, we were deafened and spark-blinded and crushed under the fiery weight and we rose again, like battered black men, in the grave of the arch. No noise at all from the swallowed town. The trams had rattled themselves dumb. A pressure of the hidden sea rubbed away the smudge of the docks. Only three young men were alive.

One said: "It's a sad life, without a home."

"Haven't you got a home, then?" I said.

"Oh yes, I've got a home all right."

"I got one, too."

"And I live near Cwmdonkin Park," I said.

"That's another place Tom sits in in the dark. He says he listens to the owls."

"I knew a chap once who lived in the country, near Bridgend," said Tom, "and they had a munition works there in the war, and it spoilt all the birds. The chap I know says you can always tell a cuckoo from Bridgend – it goes: 'Cuckbloodyoo! Cuckbloodyoo!'"

"Cuckbloodyoo!" echoed the arch.

"Why are you standing under the arch, then?" asked Tom. "It's warm at home. You can draw the curtains and sit by the fire, snug as a bug. Gracie's* on the wireless tonight. No shananacking* in the old moonlight."

"I don't want to go home, I don't want to sit by the fire. I've got nothing to do when I'm in, and I don't want to go to bed. I like standing about like this with nothing to do, in the dark all by myself," I said.

And I did, too. I was a lonely nightwalker and a steady stander-at-corners. I liked to walk through the wet town after midnight when the streets were deserted and the window lights out, alone and alive on the glistening tramlines in dead and empty High Street under the moon, gigantically sad in the damp streets by ghostly Ebenezer Chapel. And I never felt more a part of the remote and overpressing world, or more full of love and arrogance and pity and humility, not for myself alone, but for the living earth I suffered on and for the unfeeling systems in the upper air, Mars and Venus and Brazell and Skully, men in China and St Thomas,* scorning girls and ready girls, soldiers and bullies and policemen and sharp, suspicious buyers of second-hand books, bad, ragged women who'd pretend against the museum wall for a cup of tea, and perfect, unapproachable women out of the fashion magazines, seven feet high, sailing slowly in their flat, glazed creations through steel and glass and velvet. I leant against the wall of a derelict house in the residential areas or wandered in the empty rooms, stood terrified on the stairs or gazing through the smashed windows at the sea or at nothing, and the lights going out one by one in the avenues. Or I mooched in a half-built house, with the sky stuck in the roof and cats on the ladders and a wind shaking through the bare bones of the bedrooms.

"And you can talk," I said. "Why aren't you at home?"

"I don't want to be home," said Tom.

"I'm not particular," said his friend.

When a match flared, their heads rocked and spread on the wall, and shapes of winged bulls and buckets grew bigger and smaller. Tom began to tell a story. I thought of a new stranger walking on the sands past the arch and hearing all of a sudden that high voice out of a hole.

I missed the beginning of the story as I thought of the man on the sands listening in a panic or dodging, like a footballer, in and out among the jumping dark towards the lights behind the railway line, and remembered Tom's voice in the middle of a sentence.

"...went up to them and said it was a lovely night. It wasn't a lovely night at all. The sands were empty. We asked them what their names were, and they asked us what ours were. We were walking along by this time. Walter here was telling them about the glee party in the Melba and what went on in the ladies' cloakroom. You had to drag the tenors away like ferrets."

"What were their names?" I asked.

"Doris and Norma," Walter said.

"So we walked along the sands towards the dunes," Tom said, "and Walter was with Doris and I was with Norma. Norma worked in the steam laundry. We hadn't been walking and talking for more than a few minutes when, by God, I knew I was head over heels in love with the girl, and she wasn't the pretty one, either."

He described her. I saw her clearly. Her plump, kind face, jolly brown eyes, warm wide mouth, thick bobbed hair, rough body, bottle legs, broad bum, grew from a few words right out of Tom's story, and I saw her ambling solidly along the sands in a spotted frock in a showering autumn evening with fancy gloves on her hard hands, a gold bangle, with a voile handkerchief tucked in it, round her wrist, and a navy-blue handbag with letters and outing snaps, a compact, a bus ticket and a shilling.

"Doris was the pretty one," said Tom, "smart and touched up and sharp as a knife. I was twenty-six years old and I'd never been in love, and there I was, gawking at Norma in the middle of Tawe sands, too frightened to put my finger on her gloves. Walter had his arm round Doris then."

They sheltered behind a dune. The night dropped down on them quickly. Walter was a caution* with Doris, hugging and larking, and Tom sat close to Norma, brave enough to hold her hand in its cold glove and tell her all his secrets. He told her his age and his job. He liked staying in in the evenings with a good book. Norma liked dances. He liked dances, too. Norma and Doris were sisters. "I'd never have thought that," Tom said. "You're beautiful, I love you."

Now the storytelling night* in the arch gave place to the loving night in the dunes. The arch was as high as the sky. The faint town noises died. I lay like a pimp in a bush by Tom's side and squinted through to see him round his hands on Norma's breast. "Don't you dare!" Walter and Doris lay quietly near them. You could have heard a safety pin fall.

"And the curious thing was," said Tom, "that after a time we all sat up on the sand and smiled at each other, And then we all moved softly about on the sand in the dark, without saying a word. And Doris was lying with me, and Norma was with Walter."

"But why did you change over, if you loved her?" I asked.

"I never understood why," said Tom. "I think about it every night."

"That was in October," Walter said.

And Tom continued: "We didn't see much of the girls until July. I couldn't face Norma. Then they brought two paternity orders against us, and Mr Lewis, the magistrate, was eighty years old, and stone-deaf, too. He put a little trumpet by his ear, and Norma and Doris gave evidence. Then we gave evidence, and he couldn't decide whose was which. And at the end he shook his head back and fore and pointed his trumpet and said: 'Just like little dogs!'"

All at once I remembered how cold it was. I rubbed my numb hands together. Fancy standing all night in the cold. Fancy listening, I thought, to a long, unsatisfactory story in the frostbite night in a polar arch. "What happened then?" I asked.

Walter answered. "I married Norma," he said, "and Tom married Doris. We had to do the right thing by them, didn't we? That's why Tom won't go home. He never goes home till the early morning. I've got to keep him company. He's my brother."

It would take me ten minutes to run home. I put up my coat collar and pulled my cap down.

"And the curious thing is," said Tom, "that I love Norma and Walter doesn't love Norma or Doris. We've two nice little boys. I call mine Norman."

We all shook hands.

"See you again," said Walter.

"I'm always hanging about," said Tom.

"Abyssinia!"

I walked out of the arch, crossed Trafalgar Terrace and pelted up the steep streets.

Where Tawe Flows*

Mr Humphries, Mr Roberts and young Mr Thomas knocked on the front door of Mr Emlyn Evans's small villa, "Lavengro", punctually at nine o'clock in the evening. They waited, hidden behind a veronica bush, while Mr Evans shuffled in carpet slippers up the passage from the back room and had trouble with the bolts.

Mr Humphries was a schoolteacher – a tall, fair man with a stammer who had written an unsuccessful novel.

Mr Roberts, a cheerful, disreputable man of middle age, was a collector for an insurance company; they called him in the trade a "bodysnatcher", and he was known among his friends as Burke and Hare,* the Welsh Nationalist. He had once held a high position in a brewery office.

Young Mr Thomas was at the moment without employment, but it was understood that he would soon be leaving for London to make a career in Chelsea as a freelance journalist; he was penniless, and hoped, in a vague way, to live on women.

When Mr Evans opened the door and shone his torch down the narrow drive, lighting up the garage and hen run but missing altogether the whispering bush, the three friends bounded out and cried in threatening voices: "We're Ogpu* men, let us in!"

"We're looking for seditious literature," said Mr Humphries with difficulty, raising his hand in a salute.

"*Heil*, Saunders Lewis!* And we know where to find it," said Mr Roberts.

Mr Evans turned off his torch. "Come in out of the night air, boys, and have a drop of something. It's only parsnip wine," he added.

They removed their hats and coats, piled them on the end of the banister, spoke softly for fear of waking up the twins, George and Celia, and followed Mr Evans into his den.

"Where's the trouble and strife, Mr Evans?" said Mr Roberts in a cockney accent. He warmed his hands in front of the fire and regarded with a smile of surprise, though he visited the house every Friday, the neat rows of books, the ornate roll-top desk that made the parlour into a study, the shining grandfather clock, the photographs of children staring stiffly at a dicky bird, the still, delicious home-made wine, that had such an effect, in an old beer bottle, the sleeping tom on the frayed rug. "At home with the bourgeoisie."

He was himself a homeless bachelor with a past, much in debt, and nothing gave him more pleasure than to envy his friends their wives and comforts and to speak of them intimately and disparagingly.

"In the kitchen," said Mr Evans, handing out glasses.

"A woman's only place," said Mr Roberts heartily, "with one exception."

Mr Humphries and Mr Thomas arranged the chairs around the fire, and all four sat down, close and confidential and with full glasses in their hands. None of them spoke for a time. They gave one another sly looks, sipped and sighed, lit the cigarettes that Mr Evans produced from a draughts box, and once Mr Humphries glanced at the grandfather clock and winked and put his finger to his lips. Then, as the visitors grew warm and the wine worked and they forgot the bitter night outside, Mr Evans said, with a little shudder of forbidden delight: "The wife will be going to bed in half an hour. Then we can start the good work. Have you all got yours with you?"

"And the tools," said Mr Roberts, smacking his side pocket.

"What's the word until then?" said young Mr Thomas.

Mr Humphries winked again. "Mum!"

"I've been waiting for tonight to come round like I used to wait for Saturdays when I was a boy," said Mr Evans, "I got a penny then. And it all went on gob-stoppers and jelly babies, too."

He was a traveller in rubber, rubber toys and syringes and bath mats. Sometimes Mr Roberts called him "the poor man's friend" to make him blush. "No! No! No!" he would say. "You can look at my samples, there's nothing like that there." He was a socialist.

"I used to buy a packet of Cindrellas with my penny," said Mr Roberts, "and smoke them in the slaughterhouse. The sweetest little smoke in the world. You don't see them now."

"Do you remember old Jim, the caretaker, in the slaughterhouse?" asked Mr Evans.

"He was after my time – I'm no chicken, like you boys."

"You're not old, Mr Roberts, think of G.B.S."*

"No clean Shavianism for me, I'm an unrepentant eater of birds and beasts,"* said Mr Roberts.

"Do you eat flowers, too?"

"Oh! Oh! You literary men, don't you talk above my head now. I'm only a poor resurrectionist on the knocker."*

"He'd put his hand down in the guts box and bring you out a rat with its neck broken clean as a match for the price of a glass of beer."

"And it was beer then."

"Shop! Shop!" Mr Humphries beat on the table with his glass. "You mustn't waste stories, we'll need them all," he said. "Have you got the abattoir anecdote down in your memory book, Mr Thomas?"

"I'll remember it."

"Don't forget, you can only talk at random now," said Mr Humphries.

"OK, Roderick!" Mr Thomas said quickly.

Mr Roberts put his hands over his ears. "The conversation is getting esoteric," he said. "Excuse my French! Mr Evans, have you such a thing as a rook rifle? I want to scare the highbrows off. Did I ever tell you the time I lectured to the John O'London's Society* on 'The Utility of Uselessness'? That was a poser. I talked about Jack London* all the time, and when they said at the end that it wasn't a lecture about what I said it was going to be, I said, 'Well, it was useless lecturing about that, wasn't it?' – and they hadn't a word to say. Mrs Dr Davies was in the front row, you remember her? She gave that first lecture on W.J. Locke and got spoonered in the middle. Remember her talking about the '*Bevagged Loveabond*',* Mr Humphries?"

"Shop! Shop!" said Mr Humphries, groaning. "Keep it until after."

"More parsnip?"

"It goes down the throat like silk, Mr Evans."

"Like baby's milk."

"Say when, Mr Roberts."

"A word of four syllables denoting a period of time. Thank you! I read that on a matchbox."

"Why don't they have serials on matchboxes? You'd buy the shop up to see what Daphne did next," Mr Humphries said.

He stopped and looked round in embarrassment at the faces of his friends. Daphne was the name of the grass widow in Manselton* for whom Mr Roberts had lost both his reputation and his position in the brewery. He had been in the habit of delivering bottles to her house, free of charge, and he had bought her a cocktail cabinet and given her a hundred pounds and his mother's rings. In return she held large parties and never invited him. Only Mr Thomas had noticed the name, and he was saying: "No, Mr Humphries, on toilet rolls would be best."

"When I was in London," Mr Roberts said, "I stayed with a couple called Armitage in Palmers Green. He made curtains and blinds. They used to leave each other messages on the toilet paper every single day."

"If you want to make a venetian blind," said Mr Evans, "stick him in the eye with a hatpin." He felt, always, a little left out of his evenings at home, and he was waiting for Mrs Evans to come in, disapprovingly, from the kitchen.

"I've often had to use 'Dear Tom, don't forget the Watkinses are coming to tea', or 'To Peggy, from Tom, in remembrance'. Mr Armitage was a Mosleyite."*

"Thugs," said Mr Humphries.

"Seriously, what are we going to do about this uniformication of the individual?" Mr Evans asked. Maud was in the kitchen still; he heard her beating the plates.

"Answering your question with another," said Mr Roberts, putting one hand on Mr Evans's knee, "what individuality is there left? The mass age produces the mass man. The machine produces the robot."

"As its slave," Mr Humphries articulated clearly, "not, mark you, as its master."

"There you have it. There it is. Tyrannic dominance by a sparking plug, Mr Humphries, and it's flesh and blood that always pays."

"Any empty glasses?"

Mr Roberts turned his glass upside down. "That used to mean 'I'll take on the best man in the room in a bout of fisticuffs' in Llanelly. But seriously, as Mr Evans says, the old-fashioned individualist is a square peg now in a round hole."

"What a hole!" said Mr Thomas.

"Take our national – what did Onlooker say last week? – our national misleaders."

"You take them, Mr Roberts, we've got rats already," Mr Evans said with a nervous laugh. The kitchen was silent. Maud was ready.

"Onlooker is a nom de plume for Basil Gorse Williams," said Mr Humphries. "Did anyone know that?"

"*Nom de guerre*. Did you see his article on Ramsay Mac?* 'A sheep in wolf's clothing'."

"Know him!" Mr Roberts said scornfully. "I've been sick on him."

Mrs Evans heard the last remark as she came into the room. She was a thin woman with bitter lines, tired hands, the ruins of fine brown eyes and a superior nose. An unshockable woman, she had once listened to Mr Roberts's description of his haemorrhoids for over an hour on a New Year's Eve and had allowed him, without protest, to call them the "grapes of wrath".* When sober, Mr Roberts addressed her as "ma'am" and kept the talk to weather and colds. He sprang to his feet and offered her his chair.

"No, thank you, Mr Roberts," she said in a clear, hard voice, "I'm going to bed at once. The cold disagrees with me."

Go to bed, plain Maud,* thought young Mr Thomas. "Will you have a little warm, Mrs Evans, before you retire?" he said.

She shook her head, gave the friends a thin smile and said to Mr Evans: "Put the world right before you come to bed."

"Goodnight, Mrs Evans."

"It won't be after midnight this time, Maud, I promise. I'll put Sambo out in the back."

"Goodnight, ma'am."

Sleep tight, hoity.

"I won't disturb you gentlemen any more," she said. "What's left of the parsnip wine for Christmas is in the boot cupboard, Emlyn. Don't let it waste. Goodnight."

Mr Evans raised his eyebrows and whistled. "Whew, boys!" He pretended to fan his face with his tie. Then his hand stopped still in the air. "She was used to a big house," he said, "with servants."

Mr Roberts brought out pencils and fountain pens from his side pocket. "Where's the priceless MS? Tempus is fugiting."*

Mr Humphries and Mr Thomas put notebooks on their knees, took a pencil each and watched Mr Evans open the door of the grandfather clock. Beneath the swinging weights was a heap of papers tied in a blue bow. These Mr Evans placed on the desk.

"I call order," said Mr Roberts. "Let's see where we were. Have you got the minutes, Mr Thomas?"

"*Where Tawe Flows*," said Mr Thomas, "*a Novel of Provincial Life*. 'Chapter One: A Cross-Section Description of the Town, Dockland, Slums, Suburbia, etc.' We finished that. The title decided upon was: 'Chapter One: The Public Town'. Chapter Two is to be called 'The Private Lives', and Mr Humphries has proposed the following: 'Each of the collaborators take one character from each social sphere or stratum of the town and introduce him to the readers with a brief history of his life up to the point at which we commence the story, i.e. the winter of this very year. These introductions of the characters, hereafter to be regarded as the principal protagonists, and their biographical chronicles shall constitute the second chapter.' Any questions, gentlemen?"

Mr Humphries agreed with all he had said. His character was a sensitive schoolmaster of advanced opinions, who was misjudged and badly treated.

"No questions," said Mr Evans. He was in charge of suburbia. He rustled his notes and waited to begin.

"I haven't written anything yet," Mr Roberts said. "It's all in my head." He had chosen the slums.

"Personally," said Mr Thomas, "I haven't made up my mind whether to have a barmaid or a harlot."

"What about a barmaid who's a harlot too?" Mr Roberts suggested. "Or perhaps we could have a couple of characters each? I'd like to do an alderman. And a gold-digger."

"Who had a word for them, Mr Humphries?" said Mr Thomas.

"The Greeks."

Mr Roberts nudged Mr Evans and whispered: "I just thought of an opening sentence for my bit. Listen Emlyn. 'On the rickety table in the corner of the crowded, dilapidated room, a stranger might have seen, by the light of the flickering candle in the gin bottle, a broken cup, full of sick or custard.'"

"Be serious, Ted," said Mr Evans, laughing. "You wrote that sentence down."

"No, I swear, it came to me just like that!" He flicked his fingers. "And who's been reading my notes?"

"Have you put anything on paper yourself, Mr Thomas?"

"Not yet, Mr Evans." He had been writing, that week, the story of a cat who jumped over a woman the moment she died and turned her into a vampire. He had reached the part of the story where the woman was an undead children's governess, but he could not think how to fit it into the novel.

"There's no need, is there," he asked, "for us to avoid the fantastic altogether?"

"Wait a bit! Wait a bit!" said Mr Humphries. "Let's get our realism straight. Mr Thomas will be making all the characters Blue Birds before we know where we are. One thing at a time. Has anyone got the history of his character ready?" He had his biography in his hand, written in red ink. The writing was scholarly and neat and small.

"I think my character is ready to take the stage," said Mr Evans. "But I haven't written it out. I'll have to refer to the notes and make the rest up out of my head. It's a very silly story."

"Well, you must begin, of course," said Mr Humphries with disappointment.

"Everybody's biography is silly," Mr Roberts said. "My own would make a cat laugh."

Mr Humphries said: "I must disagree there. The life of that mythical common denominator, the man in the street, is dull as ditchwater, Mr Roberts. Capitalist society has made him a mere bundle of repressions and useless habits under that symbol of middle-class divinity, the bowler." He looked quickly away from the notes in the palm of his hand. "The ceaseless toil for bread and butter, the ogres of unemployment, the pettifogging gods of gentility, the hollow lies of the marriage bed. Marriage," he said, dropping his ash on the carpet, "legal monogamous prostitution."

"Whoa! Whoa! There he goes!"

"Mr Humphries is on his hobby horse again."

"I'm afraid," said Mr Evans, "that I lack our friend's extensive vocabulary. Have pity on a poor amateur. You're shaming my little story before I begin."

"I still think the life of the ordinary man is most extraordinary," Mr Roberts said, "take my own—"

"As the secretary," said Mr Thomas, "I vote we take Mr Evans's story. We must try to get *Tawe* finished for the spring list."

"My *Tomorrow and Tomorrow** was published in the summer in a heatwave," Mr Humphries said.

Mr Evans coughed, looked into the fire and began.

"Her name is Mary," he said, "but that's not her name really. I'm calling her that because she is a real woman and we don't want any libel. She lives in a house called 'Bellevue', but that's not the proper name, of course. A villa by any other name, Mr Humphries. I chose her for my character because her life is a little tragedy, but it's not without its touches of humour either. It's almost Russian. Mary – Mary Morgan now, but she was Mary Phillips before she was married, and that comes later, that's the anticlimax – wasn't a suburbanite from birth: she didn't live under the shadow of the bowler, like you and me. Or like me, anyway. I was born in 'The Poplars' and now I'm in 'Lavengro'. From bowler to bowler, though I must say, apropos of Mr Humphries's diatribe, and I'm the first to admire his point of view, that the everyday man's just as interesting a character as the neurotic poets of Bloomsbury."

"Remind me to shake your hand," said Mr Roberts.

"You've been reading the Sunday papers," said Mr Humphries accusingly.

"You two argue the toss later on," Mr Thomas said. "'Is the Ordinary Man a Mouse?' Now, what about Mary?"

"Mary Phillips," continued Mr Evans, "(and any more interruptions from the intelligentsia and I'll get Mr Roberts to tell you the story of his operations, no pardons granted) lived on a big farm in Carmarthenshire, I'm not going to tell you exactly where, and her father was a widower. He had any amount of what counts and he drank like a fish, but he was always a gentleman with it. Now, now! Forget the class war, I could see it smouldering. He came of a very good, solid family, but he raised his elbow, that's all there is to it."

Mr Roberts said: "Huntin', fishin' and boozin'."

"No, he wasn't quite county and he wasn't a nouveau riche either. No Philippstein about him, though I'm not anti-Semite. You've only got to think of Einstein and Freud. There are bad Christians, too. He was just what I'm telling you, if you'd only let me, a man of good farming stock who'd made his pile, and now he was spending it."

"Liquidating it."

"He'd only got one child, and that was Mary, and she was so prim and proper she couldn't bear to see him the worse for drink. Every night he came home, and he was always the worse; she'd shut herself in her bedroom and hear him rolling about the house and calling for her and breaking the china sometimes. But only sometimes, and he wouldn't have hurt a hair of her head. She was about eighteen and a fine-looking girl, not a film star, mind, not Mr Roberts's type at all, and perhaps she had an Oedipus complex, but she hated her father, and she was ashamed of him."

"What's my type, Mr Evans?"

"Don't pretend not to know, Mr Roberts. Mr Evans means the sort you can take home and show her your stamp collection."

"I will have hush," said Mr Thomas.

"'Ave 'ush, is the phrase," Mr Roberts said. "Mr Thomas, you're afraid we'll think you're patronizing the lower classes if you drop your aspirates."

"No nasturtiums,* Mr Roberts," said Mr Humphries.

"Mary Phillips fell in love with a young man whom I shall call Marcus David," Mr Evans went on, still staring at the fire, avoiding his friends' eyes and speaking to the burning pictures, "and she told her father: 'Father, Marcus and I want to be engaged. I'm bringing him home one night for supper, and you must promise me that you'll be sober.'

"He said: 'I'm always sober!' But he wasn't sober when he said it, and after a time he promised.

"'If you break your word, I'll never forgive you,' Mary said to him.

"Marcus was a wealthy farmer's son from another district, a bit of a Valentino in a bucolic way, if you can imagine that. She invited him to supper, and he came, very handsome, with larded hair. The servants were out. Mr Phillips had gone to a mart that morning and hadn't returned. She answered the door herself. It was a winter's evening.

"Picture the scene. A prim, well-bred country girl, full of fixations and phobias, proud as a duchess and blushing like a dairymaid, opening the door to her beloved and seeing him standing there on the pitch-black threshold, shy and handsome. This is from my notes.

"Her future hung on that evening as on a thread. 'Come in,' she insisted. They didn't kiss, but she wanted him to bow and print his lips on her hand. She took him over the house, which had been specially cleaned and polished, and showed him the case with Swansea china in it. There wasn't a portrait gallery, so she showed him the snaps of her mother in the hall and the photograph of her father, tall and young and sober, in the suit he hunted otters in. And all the time she was proudly parading their possessions, attempting to prove to Marcus, whose father was a JP, that her background was prosperous enough for her to be his bride, she was waiting fearfully the entrance of her father.

"'O God,' she was praying when they sat down to a cold supper, 'that my father will arrive presentable.' Call her a snob, if you will, but remember that the life of country gentry, or near gentry, was bound and dedicated by the antiquated totems and fetishes of possession. Over supper she told him her family tree and hoped the supper was to his taste. It should have been a hot supper, but she didn't want him to see the servants, who were old and dirty. Her father wouldn't change them, because they'd always been with him, and there you see the Toryism of this particular society rampant. To cut a long story (this is only the gist, Mr Thomas), they were halfway through supper, and their conversation was becoming more intimate, and she had almost forgotten her father, when the front door burst open and Mr Phillips staggered into the passage, drunk as a judge. The dining-room door was ajar, and they could see him plainly. I will not try to describe Mary's kaleidoscopic emotions as her father rocked and mumbled in a thick voice in the passage. He was a big man – I forgot to tell you – six foot and eighteen stone.

"'Quick! Quick! Under the table!' she whispered urgently, and she pulled Marcus by the hand and they crouched under the table. What bewilderment Marcus experienced we shall never know.

"Mr Phillips came in and saw nobody and sat down at the table and finished all the supper. He licked both plates clean, and under the table they heard him swearing and guzzling. Every time Marcus fidgeted, Mary said: 'Shhh!'

"When there was nothing left to eat, Mr Phillips wandered out of the room. They saw his legs. Then, somehow, he climbed upstairs, saying words that made Mary shudder under the table, words of three syllables."

"Give us three guesses," said Mr Roberts.

"And she heard him go into his bedroom. She and Marcus crept out of hiding and sat down in front of their empty plates.

"'I don't know how to apologize, Mr David,' she said, and she was nearly crying.

"'There's nothing the matter,' he said (he was an amenable young man by all accounts), 'he's only been to the mart at Carmarthen. I don't like TTs* myself.'

"'Drink makes men sodden beasts,' she said.

"He said she had nothing to worry about, and that he didn't mind, and she offered him fruit.

"'What will you think of us, Mr David? I've never seen him like that before.'

"The little adventure brought them closer together, and soon they were smiling at one another, and her wounded pride was almost healed again, but suddenly Mr Phillips opened his bedroom door and charged downstairs, eighteen stone of him, shaking the house.

"'Go away!' she cried softly to Marcus. 'Please go away before he comes in!'

"There wasn't time. Mr Phillips stood in the passage in the nude.

"She dragged Marcus under the table again, and she covered her eyes not to see her father. She could hear him fumbling in the hallstand for an umbrella, and she knew what he was going to do. He was going outside to obey a call of nature. 'O God,' she prayed, 'let him find an umbrella and go out. Not in the passage! Not in the passage!' They heard him shout for his umbrella. She uncovered her eyes and saw him pulling the front door down. He tore it off its hinges and held it flat above him and tottered out into the dark.

"'Hurry! Please hurry!' she said. 'Leave me now, Mr David.' She drove him out from under the table.

"'Please, please go now,' she said, 'we'll never meet again. Leave me to my shame.' She began to cry, and he ran out of the house. And she stayed under the table all night."

"Is that all?" said Mr Roberts. "A very moving incident, Emlyn. How did you come by it?"

"How can it be all?" said Mr Humphries. "It doesn't explain how Mary Phillips reached Bellevue. We've left her under a table in Carmarthenshire."

"I think Marcus is a fellow to be despised," Mr Thomas said. "I'd never leave a girl like that – would you, Mr Humphries?"

"Under a table, too. That's the bit I like. That's a position. Perspectives were different," said Mr Roberts, "in those days. That narrow puritanism is a spent force. Imagine Mrs Evans under the table. And what happened afterwards? Did the girl die of cramp?"

Mr Evans turned from the fire to reprove him. "Be as flippant as you will, but the fact remains that an incident like that has a lasting effect on a proud, sensitive girl like Mary. I'm not defending her sensitivity, the whole basis of her pride is outmoded. The social system, Mr Roberts, is not in the box. I'm telling you an incident that occurred. Its social implications are outside our concern."

"I'm put in my place, Mr Evans."

"What happened to Mary then?"

"Don't vex him, Mr Thomas: he'll bite your head off."

Mr Evans went out for more parsnip wine, and, returning, said:

"What happened next? Oh! Mary left her father, of course. She said she'd never forgive him, and she didn't, so she went to live with her uncle in Cardiganshire, a Dr Emyr Lloyd. He was a JP too, and rolling in it, about seventy-five – now, remember the age – with a big practice and influential friends. One of his oldest friends was John William Hughes – that's not his name – the London draper, who had a country house near his. Remember what the great Caradoc Evans* says? The Cardies always go back to Wales to die when they've rooked the cockneys and made a packet.

"And the only son, Henry William Hughes, who was a nicely educated young man, fell in love with Mary as soon as he saw her, and she forgot Marcus and her shame under the table and she fell in love with him. Now, don't look disappointed before I begin: this isn't a love story. But they decided to get married, and John William Hughes gave his consent, because Mary's uncle was one of the most respected men in the country and her father had money and it would come to her when he died, and he was doing his best.

"They were to be married quietly in London. Everything was arranged. Mr Phillips wasn't invited. Mary had her trousseau. Dr Lloyd was to give her away. Beatrice and Betti William Hughes were bridesmaids. Mary went up to London with Beatrice and Betti and stayed with a cousin, and Henry William Hughes stayed in the flat above his father's shop, and the day before the wedding Dr Lloyd arrived from the country, saw Mary for tea and had dinner with John William Hughes. I wonder who paid for it, too. Then Dr Lloyd retired to his hotel. I'm giving you these trivial details so that you can see how orderly and ordinary everything was. There the actors were, safe and sure.

"Next day, just before the ceremony was to begin, Mary and her cousin, whose name and character are extraneous, and the two sisters, they were both plain and thirty, waited impatiently for Dr Lloyd to call on them. The minutes passed by, Mary was crying, the sisters were sulking, the cousin was getting in everybody's way, but the doctor didn't come. The cousin telephoned the doctor's hotel, but she was told he hadn't spent the night there. Yes, the clerk in the hotel said, he knew the doctor was going to a wedding. No, his bed hadn't been slept in. The clerk suggested that perhaps he was waiting at the church.

The taxi was ticking away, and that worried Beatrice and Betti, and at last the sisters and the cousin and Mary drove together to the church. A crowd had gathered outside. The cousin poked her head out of the taxi window and asked a policeman to call a churchwarden, and the warden said that Dr Lloyd wasn't there and the groom and the best man were waiting. You can imagine Mary Phillips's feelings when she saw a commotion at the church door and a policeman leading her father out. Mr Phillips had his pockets full of bottles, and how he ever got into the church in the first place no one knew."

"That's the last straw," said Mr Roberts.

"Beatrice and Betti said to her: 'Don't cry, Mary, the policeman's taking him away. Look! He's fallen in the gutter! There's a splash! Don't take on, it'll be all over soon. You'll be Mrs Henry William Hughes.' They were doing their best.

"'You can marry without Dr Lloyd,' the cousin told her, and she brightened through her tears – anybody would be crying – and at that moment another policeman—"

"Another!" said Mr Roberts.

"...made his way through the crowd and walked up to the door of the church and sent a message inside. John William Hughes and Henry William Hughes and the best man came out, and they all talked to the policeman, waving their arms and pointing to the taxi with Mary and the bridesmaids and the cousin in it.

"John William Hughes ran down the path to the taxi and shouted through the window: 'Dr Lloyd is dead! We'll have to cancel the wedding.'

"Henry William Hughes followed him and opened the taxi door and said: 'You must drive home, Mary. We've got to go to the police station.'

"'And the mortuary,' his father said.

"So the taxi drove the bride-to-be home, and the sisters cried worse than she did all the way."

"That's a sad end," said Mr Roberts with appreciation. He poured himself another drink.

"It isn't really the end," Mr Evans said, "because the wedding wasn't just cancelled. It never came off."

"But why?" asked Mr Humphries, who had followed the story with a grave expression, even when Mr Phillips fell in the gutter. "Why should the doctor's death stop everything? She could get someone else to give her away. I'd have done it myself."

"It wasn't the doctor's death, but where and how he died," said Mr Evans. "He died in bed in a bed-sittingroom in the arms of a certain lady. A woman of the town."

"Kiss me!" Mr Roberts said. "Seventy-five years old. I'm glad you asked us to remember his age, Mr Evans."

"But how did Mary Phillips come to live in Bellevue? You haven't told us that," Mr Thomas said.

"The William Hugheses wouldn't have the niece of a man who died in those circumstances—"

"However complimentary to his manhood," Mr Humphries said, stammering.

"...marry into their family, so she went back to live with her father and he reformed at once... oh! She had a temper those days – and one day she met a traveller in grain and pigs' food and she married him out of spite. They came to live in Bellevue, and when Mr Phillips died, he left his money to the chapel, so Mary got nothing after all."

"Nor her husband either. What did you say he travelled in?" asked Mr Roberts.

"Grain and pigs' food."

After that, Mr Humphries read his biography, which was long and sad and detailed and in good prose, and Mr Roberts told a story about the slums, which could not be included in the book.

Then Mr Evans looked at his watch. "It's midnight. I promised Maud not after midnight. Where's the cat? I've got to put him out – he tears the cushions. Not that I mind. Sambo! Sambo!"

"There he is, Mr Evans, under the table."

"Like poor Mary," said Mr Roberts.

Mr Humphries, Mr Roberts and young Mr Thomas collected their hats and coats from the banister.

"Do you know what time it is, Emlyn?" Mrs Evans called from upstairs.

Mr Roberts opened the door and hurried out.

"I'm coming now, Maud, I'm just saying goodnight. Goodnight," Mr Evans said in a loud voice. "Next Friday, nine sharp," he whispered. "I'll polish my story up. We'll finish the second chapter and get going on the third. Goodnight, comrades."

"Emlyn! Emlyn!" called Mrs Evans.

"Goodnight, Mary," said Mr Roberts to the closed door.

The three friends walked down the drive.

Who Do You Wish Was with Us?*

Birds in the Crescent trees were singing; boys on bicycles were ringing their bells and pedalling down the slight slope to make the whirrers in their wheels startle the women gabbing on the sunny doorsteps; small girls on the pavement, wheeling young brothers and sisters in prams, were dressed in their summer best and with coloured ribbons; on the circular swing in the public playground, children from the snot school spun themselves happy and sick, crying "Swing us!" and "Swing us!" and "Ooh! I'm falling!"; the morning was as varied and bright as though it were an international or a jubilee when Raymond Price* and I, flannelled and hatless, with sticks and haversacks, set out together to walk to the Worm's Head.* Striding along, in step, through the square of the residential Uplands, we brushed by young men in knife-creased whites and showing-off blazers, and hockey-legged girls with towels round their necks and celluloid sunglasses, and struck a letterbox with our sticks, and bullied our way through a crowd of day-trippers who waited at the stop of the Gower-bound buses, and stepped over luncheon baskets, not caring if we trod in them.

"Why can't those bus lizards walk?" Ray said.

"They were born too tired," I said.

We went on up Sketty Road at a great speed, our haversacks jumping on our backs. We rapped on every gate to give a terrific walker's benediction to the people in the choking houses. Like a breath of fresh air we passed a man in office pinstripes standing, with a dog lead in his hand, whistling at a corner. Tossing the sounds and smells of the town from us with the swing of our shoulders and loose-limbed strides, halfway up the road we heard women on an outing call "Mutt and Jeff!"* – for Ray was tall and thin and I was short. Streamers flew out of the charabanc. Ray, sucking hard at his bulldog pipe, walked too fast to wave and did not even smile. I wondered whom I had missed among the waving women bowling over the rise. My love to come, with a paper cap on, might have sat at the back of the outing, next to the barrel; but, once away from the familiar roads and swinging towards the coast, I forgot her face and voice, that had been made at night, and breathed the country air in.

"There's a different air here. You breathe. It's like the country," Ray said, "and a bit of the sea mixed. Draw it down – it'll blow off the nicotine."

He spat in his hand. "Still town grey," he said.

He put back the spit in his mouth, and we walked on with our heads high.

By this time we were three miles from the town. The semi-detached houses, with a tin-roofed garage each and a kennel in the back plot and a mowed lawn, with sometimes a hanging coconut on a pole, or a birdbath, or a bush like a peacock, grew fewer when we reached the outskirts of the common.

Ray stopped and sighed and said: "Wait half a sec, I want to fill the old pipe." He held a match to it as though we were in a storm.

Hot-faced and wet-browed, we grinned at each other. Already the day had brought us close as truants: we were running away, or walking with pride and mischief, arrogantly from the streets that owned us into the unpredictable country. I thought it was against our fate to stride in the sun without the shop windows dazzling or the music of mowers rising above the birds. A bird's dropping fell on a fence. It was one in the eye for the town. A sheep cried "Baa!" out of sight, and that would show the Uplands. I did not know what it would show. "A couple of wanderers in wild Wales," Ray said, winking, and a lorry carrying cement drove past us towards the golf links. He slapped my haversack and straightened his shoulders. "Come on, let's be going." We walked uphill faster than before.

A party of cyclists had pulled up on the roadside and were drinking dandelion and burdock from paper cups. I saw the empty bottles in a bush. All the boys wore singlets and shorts, and the girls wore open cricket shirts and boys' long grey trousers, with safety pins for clips at the bottoms.

"There's room for one behind, sonny boy," a girl on a tandem said to me.

"It won't be a stylish marriage,"* Ray said.

"That was quick," I told Ray as we walked away from them and the boys began to sing.

"God, I like this!" said Ray. On the first rise of the dusty road through the spreading heathered common, he shaded his eyes and looked all round him, smoking like a chimney and pointing with his Irish stick at the distant clumps of trees and sights of the sea between them. "Down there is Oxwich, but you can't see it. That's a farm. See the roof? No, there, follow my finger. This is the life," he said.

Side by side, thrashing the low banks, we marched down the very middle of the road, and Ray saw a rabbit running. "You wouldn't think this was near town. It's wild."

We pointed out the birds whose names we knew, and the rest of the names we made up. I saw gulls and crows, though the crows may have been rooks, and Ray said that thrushes and swallows and skylarks flew above us as we hurried and hummed.

He stopped to pull some blades of grass. "They should be straws," he said, and put them in his mouth next to his pipe. "God, the sky's blue! Think of me, in the GWR when all this is about. Rabbits and fields and farms. You wouldn't think I'd suffered to look at me now. I could do anything: I could drive cows, I could plough a field."

His father and sister and brother were dead, and his mother sat all day in a wheelchair, crippled with arthritis. He was ten years older than I was. He had a lined and bony face and a tight, crooked mouth. His upper lip had vanished.

Alone on the long road, the common in the heat mist wasting for miles on either side, we walked on under the afternoon sun, growing thirsty and drowsy but never slowing our pace. Soon the cycling party rode by, three boys and three girls and the one girl on the tandem, all laughing and ringing.

"How's Shanks's pony?"

"We'll see you on the way back."

"You'll be walking still."

"Like a crutch?" they shouted.

Then they were gone. The dust settled again. Their bells rang faintly through the wood around the road before us. The wild common, six miles and a bit from the town, lay back without a figure on it, and, under the trees, smoking hard to keep the gnats away, we leant against a trunk and talked like men, on the edge of an untrodden place, who have not seen another man for years.

"Do you remember Curly Parry?"

I had seen him only two days ago in the snooker room, but his dimpled face was fading, even as I thought of him, into the colours of our walk, the ash-white of the road, the common heathers, the green and blue of fields and fragmentary sea, and the memory of his silly voice was lost in the sounds of birds and unreasonably moving leaves in the lack of wind.

"I wonder what he's doing now? He should get out more in the open air, he's a proper town boy. Look at us here." Ray waved his pipe at the trees and leafy sky. "I wouldn't change this for High Street."

I looked at us there: a boy and a young man, with faces, under the strange sunburn, pale from the cramped town, out of breath and hot-footed, pausing in the early afternoon on a road through a popular wood, and I could see the unaccustomed happiness in Ray's eyes and the impossible friendliness in mine, and Ray protested against his history each time he wondered or pointed in the country scene and I had more love in me than I could ever want or use.

"Yes, look at us here," I said, "dawdling about. Worm's Head is twelve miles off. Don't you want to hear a tramcar, Ray? That's a wood pigeon. See! The boys are out on the streets with the sports special now. Paper! Paper! I bet you Curl's potting the red. Come on! Come on!"

"Eyes right!" said Ray, "I's b———d! Remember that story?"

Up the road and out of the wood, and a double-decker roared behind us.

"The Rhossili bus is coming," I said.

We both held up our sticks to stop it.

"Why did you stop the bus?" Ray said when we were sitting upstairs. "This was a walking holiday."

"You stopped it as well."

We sat in front like two more drivers.

"Can't you mind the ruts?" I said.

"You're wobbling," said Ray.

We opened our haversacks and shared the sandwiches and hard-boiled eggs and meat paste and drank from the thermos in turns.

"When we get home don't say we took a bus," I said. "Pretend we walked all day. There goes Oxwich! It doesn't seem far, does it? We'd have had beards by now."

The bus passed the cyclists crawling up a hill. "Like a tow along?" I shouted, but they couldn't hear. The girl on the tandem was a long way behind the others.

We sat with our lunch on our laps, forgetting to steer, letting the driver in his box beneath drive where and how he liked on the switchback road, and saw grey chapels and weather-worn angels; at the feet of the hills farthest from the sea, pretty, pink cottages – horrible, I thought, to live in, for grass and trees would imprison me more securely than any jungle of packed and swarming streets and chimney-roosting roofs – and petrol pumps and hayricks and a man on a carthorse standing stock-still in a ditch, surrounded by flies.

"This is the way to see the country."

The bus, on a narrow hill, sent two haversacked walkers bounding to the shelter of the hedge, where they stretched out their arms and drew their bellies in.

"That might have been you and me."

We looked back happily at the men against the hedge. They climbed onto the road, slow as snails continued walking, and grew smaller.

At the entrance to Rhossili we pushed the conductor's bell and stopped the bus, and walked, with springing steps, the few hundred yards to the village.

"We've done it in pretty good time," said Ray.

"I think it's a record," I said.

Laughing on the cliff above the very long golden beach, we pointed out to each other, as though the other were blind, the great rock of the Worm's Head. The sea was out. We crossed over on slipping stones and stood, at last, triumphantly on the windy top. There was monstrous, thick grass there that made us spring-heeled, and we laughed and bounced on it, scaring the sheep who ran up and down the battered sides like goats. Even on this calmest day a wind blew along the Worm. At the end of the humped and serpentine body, more gulls than I had ever seen before cried over their new dead and the droppings of ages. On the point, the sound of my quiet voice was scooped and magnified into a hollow shout, as though the wind around me had made a shell or cave, with blue, intangible roof and sides, as tall and wide as all the arched sky, and the flapping gulls were made thunderous. Standing there, legs apart, one hand on my hip, shading my eyes like Raleigh* in some picture, I thought myself alone in the epileptic moment near bad sleep, when the legs grow long and sprout into the night and the heart hammers to wake the neighbours and breath is a hurricane through the elastic room. Instead of becoming small on the great rock poised between sky and sea, I felt myself the size of a breathing building, and only Ray in the world could match my lovely bellow as I said: "Why don't we live here always? Always and always. Build a bloody house and live like bloody kings!" The word bellowed among the squawking birds; they carried it off to the headland in the drums of their wings; like a tower, Ray pranced on the unsteady edge of a separate rock and beat about with his stick, which could turn into snakes or flames; and we sank to the ground, the rubbery, gull-limed grass, the sheep-pilled stones, the pieces of bones and feathers, and crouched at the extreme point of the Peninsula. We were still for so long that the dirty-grey gulls calmed down, and some settled near us.

Then we finished our food.

"This isn't like any other place," I said. I was almost my own size again, five feet five and eight stone, and my voice didn't sweep any longer up to the amplifying sky. "It could be in the middle of the sea. You could think the Worm was moving, couldn't you? Guide it to Ireland, Ray. We'll see W.B. Yeats* and you can kiss the Blarney.* We'll have a fight in Belfast."

Ray looked out of place on the end of the rock. He would not make himself easy and loll in the sun and roll onto his side to stare down a precipice into the sea, but tried to sit upright as though he were in a hard chair and had nothing to do with his hands. He fiddled with his tame stick and waited for the day to be orderly, for the Head to grow paths and for railings to shoot up on the scarred edges.

"It's too wild for a townee," I said.

"Townee yourself! Who stopped the bus?"

"Aren't you glad we stopped it? We'd still be walking, like Felix.* You're just pretending you don't like it here. You were dancing on the edge."

"Only a couple of hops."

"I know what it is: you don't like the furniture. There's not enough sofas and chairs," I said.

"You think you're a country boy – you don't know a cow from a horse."

We began to quarrel, and soon Ray felt at home again and forgot the monotonous out-of-doors. If snow had fallen suddenly, he would not have noticed. He drew down into himself, and the rock, to him, became dark as a house with the blinds drawn. The sky-high shapes that had danced and bellowed at birds crept down to hide, two small town mutterers in a hollow.

I knew what was going to happen by the way Ray lowered his head and brought his shoulders up, so that he looked like a man with no neck, and by the way he sucked his breath in between his teeth. He stared at his dusty white shoes, and I knew what shapes his imagination made of them: they were the feet of a man dead in bed, and he was going to talk about his brother. Sometimes, leaning against a fence when we watched football, I caught him staring at his own thin hand; he was thinning it more and more, removing the flesh, seeing Harry's hand in front of him, with the bones appearing through the sensitive skin. If he lost the world around him for a moment, if I left him alone, if he cast his eyes down, if his hand lost its grip on the hard, real fence or the hot bowl of his pipe, he would be back in ghastly bedrooms, carrying cloths and basins and listening for handbells.

"I've never seen such a lot of gulls," I said. "Have you ever seen such a lot? Such a lot of gulls. You try and count them. Two of them are fighting up there – look, pecking each other like hens in the air. What'll you bet the big one wins? Old dirty beak! I wouldn't like to have had his dinner, a bit of sheep and dead gull." I swore at myself for saying the word "dead".

"Wasn't it gay in town this morning?" I said.

Ray stared at his hand. Nothing could stop him now. "Wasn't it gay in town this morning? Everybody laughing and smiling in their summer outfits. The kids were playing and everybody was happy – they almost had the band out. I used to hold my father down on the bed when he had fits. I had to change the sheets twice a day for my brother, there was blood on everything. I watched him getting thinner and thinner – in the end you could lift him up with one hand. And his wife wouldn't go to see him, because he coughed in her face; Mother couldn't move, and I had to cook as well, cook and nurse and change the sheets and hold Father down when he got mad. It's embittered my outlook," he said.

"But you loved the walk, you enjoyed yourself on the common. It's a wonderful day, Ray. I'm sorry about your brother. Let's explore. Let's climb down to the sea. Perhaps there's a cave with prehistoric drawings, and we can write an article and make a fortune. Let's climb down."

"My brother used to ring a bell for me; he could only whisper. He used to say: 'Ray, look at my legs. Are they thinner today?'"

"The sun's going down. Let's climb."

"Father thought I was trying to murder him when I held him on the bed. I was holding him down when he died, and he rattled. Mother was in the kitchen in her chair, but she knew he was dead, and she started screaming for my sister. Brenda was in a sanatorium in Craig-y-Nos.* Harry rang the bell in his bedroom when Mother started, but I couldn't go to him, and Father was dead in the bed."

"I'm going to climb to the sea," I said. "Are you coming?"

He got up out of the hollow into the open world again and followed me slowly over the point and down the steep side; the gulls rose in a storm. I clung to dry, spiked bushes, but the roots came out; a foothold crumbled, a crevice for the fingers broke as I groped in it; I scrambled onto a black, flat-backed rock whose head, like a little Worm's, curved out of the sea a few perilous steps away from me, and, drenched by flying water, I gazed up to see Ray and a shower of stones falling. He landed at my side.

"I thought I was done for," he said, when he had stopped shaking.

"I could see all my past life in a flash."

"All of it?"

"Well, nearly. I saw my brother's face clear as yours."

We watched the sun set.

"Like an orange."

"Like a tomato."

"Like a goldfish bowl."

We went one better than the other, describing the sun. The sea beat on our rock, soaked our trouser legs, stung our cheeks. I took off my shoes and held Ray's hand and slid down the rock on my belly to trail my feet in the sea. Then Ray slid down, and I held him fast while he kicked up water.

"Come back now," I said, pulling his hand.

"No, no," he said, "this is delicious. Let me keep my feet in a bit more. It's warm as the baths." He kicked and grunted and slapped the rock in a frenzy with his other hand, pretending to drown. "Don't save me!" he cried. "I'm drowning! I'm drowning!"

I pulled him back, and in his struggles he brushed a shoe off the rock. We fished it out. It was full of water.

"Never mind, it was worth it. I haven't paddled since I was six. I can't tell you how much I enjoyed it."

He had forgotten about his father and his brother, but I knew that once his joy in the wild, warm water was over he would return to the painful house and see his brother growing thinner. I had heard Harry die so many times, and the mad father was as familiar to me as Ray himself. I knew every cough and cry, every clawing at the air.

"I'm going to paddle once a day from now on," Ray said. "I'm going to go down to the sands every evening and have a good paddle. I'm going to splash about and get wet up to my knees. I don't care who laughs."

He sat still for a minute, thinking gravely of this. "When I wake up in the mornings, there's nothing to look forward to, except on Saturdays," he said then, "or when I come up to your house for Lexicon.* I may as well be dead. But now I'll be able to wake up and think: 'This evening I'm going to splash about in the sea.' I'm going to do it again now." He rolled up his wet trousers and slid down the rock. "Don't let go."

As he kicked his legs in the sea, I said: "This is a rock at the world's end. We're all alone. It all belongs to us, Ray. We can have anybody we like here and keep everybody else away. Who do you wish was with us?"

He was too busy to answer, splashing and snorting, blowing as though his head were under, making circular commotions in the water or lazily skimming the surface with his toes.

"Who would you like to be here on the rock with us?"

He was stretched out like a dead man, his feet motionless in the sea, his mouth on the rim of a rock pool, his hand clutched round my foot.

"I wish George Gray was with us," I said. "He's the man from London who's come to live in Norfolk Street. You don't know him. He's the most curious man I ever met, queerer than Oscar Thomas, and I thought nobody could ever be queerer than that. George Gray wears glasses, but there's no glass in them, only the frames. You wouldn't know until you came near him. He does all sorts of things. He's a cat's doctor, and he goes to somewhere in Sketty every morning to help a woman put her clothes on. She's an old widow, he said, and she can't dress by herself. I don't know how he came to know her. He's only been in town for a month. He's a BA, too. The things he's got in his pockets! Pincers, and scissors for cats, and lots of diaries. He read me some of the diaries, about the jobs he did in London. He used to go to bed with a policewoman, and she used to pay him. She used to go to bed in her uniform. I've never met such a queer man. I wish he was here now. Who do you wish was with us, Ray?"

Ray began to move his feet again, kicking them out straight behind him and bringing them down hard on the water, and then stirring the water about.

"I wish Gwilym was here, too," I said. "I've told you about him. He could give a sermon to the sea. This is the very place, there isn't anywhere as lonely as this." Oh, the beloved sunset! Oh, the terrible sea! Pity the sailors, pity the sinners, pity Raymond Price and me! Oh, the evening is coming like a cloud! Amen. Amen. "Who do you wish, Ray?"

"I wish my brother was with us," Ray said. He climbed onto the flat of the rock and dried his feet. "I wish Harry was here. I wish he was here now, at this moment, on this rock."

The sun was nearly right down, halved by the shadowed sea. Cold came up, spraying out of the sea, and I could make a body for it, icy antlers, a dripping tail, a rippling face with fishes passing across it. A wind, cornering the Head, chilled through our summer shirts, and the sea began to cover our rock quickly, our rock already covered with friends, with living and dead, racing against the darkness. We did not speak as we climbed. I thought: "If we open our mouths we'll both say: 'Too late, it's too late.'" We ran over the springboard grass and the scraping rock needles, down the hollow in which Ray had talked about blood, up rustling humps and along the ragged flat. We stood on the beginning of the Head and looked down, though both of us could have said, without looking: "The sea is in."

The sea was in. The slipping stepping stones were gone. On the mainland, in the dusk, some little figures beckoned to us. Seven clear figures, jumping and calling. I thought they were the cyclists.

Old Garbo*

Mr Farr* trod delicately and disgustedly down the dark, narrow stairs like a man on ice. He knew, without looking or slipping, that vicious boys had littered the darkest corners with banana peel, and when he reached the lavatory, the basins would be choked and the chains snapped on purpose. He remembered "Mr Farr, no father" scrawled in brown, and the day the sink was full of blood that nobody admitted having lost. A girl rushed past him up the stairs, knocked the papers out of his hand, did not apologize, and the loose meg* of his cigarette burned his lower lip as he failed to open the lavatory door. I heard from inside his protest and rattlings, the sing-song whine of his voice, the stamping of his small patent-leather shoes, his favourite swear words – he swore, violently and privately, like a collier used to thinking in the dark – and I let him in.

"Do you always lock the door?" he asked, scurrying to the tiled wall.

"It stuck," I said.

He shivered, and buttoned.

He was the senior reporter, a great shorthand writer, a chain-smoker, a bitter drinker, very humorous, round-faced and round-bellied, with dart holes in his nose. Once, I thought as I stared at him then in the lavatory of the offices of the *Tawe News*, he might have been a mincing-mannered man, with a strut and a cane to balance it, a watch chain across the waistcoat, a gold tooth, even, perhaps a flower from his own garden in his buttonhole. But now each attempt at a precise gesture was caked and soaked before it began; when he placed the tips of his thumb and forefinger together, you saw only the cracked nails in mourning and the Woodbine stains. He gave me a cigarette and shook his coat to hear matches.

"Here's a light, Mr Farr," I said.

It was good to keep in with him: he covered all the big stories, the occasional murder, such as when Thomas O'Connor used a bottle on his wife (but that was before my time), the strikes, the best fires. I wore my cigarette as he did, a hanging badge of bad habits.

"Look at that word on the wall," he said. "Now, that's ugly. There's a time and a place."

Winking at me, scratching his bald patch as though the thought came from there, he said: "Mr Solomon wrote that."

Mr Solomon was the news editor, and a Wesleyan.*

"Old Solomon," said Mr Farr. "He'd cut every baby in half just for pleasure."

I smiled and said: "I bet he would!" But I wished that I could have answered in such a way as to show for Mr Solomon the disrespect I did not feel. This was a great male moment, and the most enjoyable since I had begun work three weeks before: leaning against the cracked tiled wall, smoking and smiling, looking down at my shoe scraping circles on the wet floor, sharing a small wickedness with an old, important man. I should have been writing up last night's performance of *The Crucifixion** or loitering, with my new hat on one side, through the Christmas Saturday-crowded town in the hopes of an accident.

"You must come along with me one night," Mr Farr said slowly.

"We'll go down the Fishguard on the docks: you can see the sailors knitting there in the public bar. Why not tonight? And there's shilling women in the Lord Jersey. You stick to Woodbines, like me."

He washed his hands as a young boy does, wiping the dirt on the roll towel, stared in the mirror over the basin, twirled the ends of his moustache, and saw them droop again immediately after.

"Get to work," he said.

I walked into the lobby, leaving him with his face pressed to the glass and one finger exploring his bushy nostrils.

It was nearly eleven o'clock, and time for a cocoa or a Russian tea in the Café Royal, above the tobacconist's in High Street, where junior clerks and shop assistants and young men working in their fathers' offices or articled to stockbrokers and solicitors meet every morning for gossip and stories. I made my way through the crowds: the Valley* men, up for the football; the country shoppers, the window gazers; the silent, shabby men at the corners of the packed streets, standing in isolation in the rain; the press of mothers and prams; old women in black, brooched dresses carrying frails,* smart girls with shining mackintoshes and splashed stockings; little, dandy lascars,* bewildered by the weather; businessmen with wet spats; through a mushroom forest of umbrellas, and all the time I thought of the paragraphs I would never write. I'll put you all in a story by and by.

Mrs Constable, laden and red with shopping, recognized me as she charged out of Woolworth's like a bull. "I haven't seen your mother for ages! Oh! This Christmas rush! Remember me to Florrie. I'm going to have a cup of tea at the Modern. There," she said, "I've lost a pan!"

I saw Percy Lewis, who put chewing gum in my hair at school.

A tall man stared at the doorway of a hat shop, resisting the crowds, standing hard and still. All the moving irrelevancies of good news grew and acted around me as I reached the café entrance and climbed the stairs.

"What's for you, Mr Swaffer?"

"The usual, please." Cocoa and free biscuit.

Most of the boys were there already. Some wore the outlines of moustaches, others had sideboards and crimped hair, some smoked curved pipes and talked with them gripped between their teeth; there were pinstripe trousers and hard collars, one daring bowler.

"Sit by here," said Leslie Bird. He was in the boots at Dan Lewis's.*

"Been to the flicks this week, Thomas?"

"Yes. The Regal. *White Lies*. Damned good show, too! Connie Bennett* was great! Remember her in the foam bath,* Leslie?"

"Too much foam for me, old man."

The broad vowels of the town were narrowed in, the rise and fall of the family accent was caught and pressed.

At the top window of the International Stores across the street a group of uniformed girls were standing with teacups in their hands. One of them waved a handkerchief. I wondered if she waved it to me. "There's that dark piece again," I said. "She's got her eye on you."

"They look all right in their working clothes," he said. "You catch them when they're all dolled up, they're awful. I knew a little nurse once, she looked a peach in her uniform, really refined – no, really, I mean. I picked her up on the prom one night. She was in her Sunday best. There's a difference – she looked like a bit of Marks & Spencer's." As he talked he was looking through the window with the corners of his eyes.

The girl waved again, and turned away to giggle.

"Pretty cheap!" he said.

I said: "And little Audrey laughed and laughed."*

He took out a plated cigarette case. "Present," he said. "I bet my uncle with three balls has it in a week. Have a best Turkish."

His matches were marked Allsopps. "Got them from the Carlton," he said. "Pretty girl behind the bar: knows her onions. You've never been there, have you? Why don't you drop in for one tonight? Gil Morris'll be there, too. We usually sink a couple Saturdays. There's a hop at the Melba."

"Sorry," I said. "I'm going out with our senior reporter. Some other time, Leslie. So long!"

I paid my threepence.

"Good morning, Cassie."

"Good morning, Hannen."

The rain had stopped, and High Street shone. Walking on the tramlines, a neat man held his banner high and prominently feared the Lord. I knew him as a Mr Matthews, who had been saved some years ago from British port and who now walked every night, in rubber shoes with a prayer book and a flashlight, through the lanes. There went Mr Evans the Produce through the side door of the Bugle. Three typists rushed by for lunch, poached egg and milkshake, leaving a lavender scent. Should I take the long way through the Arcade and stop to look at the old man with the broken, empty pram who always stood there, by the music store, and who would take off his cap and set his hair alight for a penny? It was only a trick to amuse boys, and I took the short cut down Chapel Street, on the edge of the slum called the Strand, past the enticing Italian chip shop where young men who had noticing parents bought twopennyworth on late nights to hide their breath before the last tram home. Then up the narrow office stairs and into the reporters' room.

Mr Solomon was shouting down the telephone. I heard the last words: "You're just a dreamer, Williams." He put the receiver down. "That boy's a buddy dreamer," he said to no one. He never swore.

I finished my report of *The Crucifixion* and handed it to Mr Farr.

"Too much platitudinous verbosity."

Half an hour later, Ted Williams, dressed to golf, sidled in, smiling, thumbed his nose at Mr Solomon's back and sat quietly in a corner with a nail file.

I whispered: "What was he slanging you for?"

"I went out on a suicide, a tram conductor called Hopkins, and the widow made me stay and have a cup of tea. That's all." He was very winning in his ways, more like a girl than a man who dreamt of Fleet Street and spent his summer fortnight walking up and down past the *Daily Express* office and looking for celebrities in the pubs.

Saturday was my free afternoon. It was one o'clock and time to leave, but I stayed on – Mr Farr said nothing. I pretended to be busy scribbling words and caricaturing with no likeness Mr Solomon's toucan profile and the snub copy boy who whistled out of tune behind the windows of the telephone box. I wrote my name, "Reporters' Room, *Tawe News*, Tawe,* South Wales, England, Europe, the Earth." And a list of books I had not written: "*Land of My Fathers, a Study of the Welsh Character in All Its Aspects*; *Eighteen, a Provincial Autobiography*; *The Merciless Ladies, a*

Novel." Still Mr Farr did not look up. I wrote "*Hamlet*". Surely Mr Farr, stubbornly transcribing his council notes, had not forgotten. I heard Mr Solomon mutter, leaning over his shoulder: "To aitch with Alderman Daniels." Half-past one. Ted was in a dream. I spent a long time putting on my overcoat, tied my Old Grammarian's scarf one way and then another.

"Some people are too lazy to take their half-days off," said Mr Farr suddenly. "Six o'clock in the Lamps back bar." He did not turn round or stop writing.

"Going for a nice walk?" asked my mother.

"Yes, on the common. Don't keep tea waiting."

I went to the Plaza. "Press," I said to the girl with the Tyrolean hat and skirt.

"There's been two reporters this week."

"Special notice."

She showed me to a seat. During the educational film, with the rude seeds hugging and sprouting in front of my eyes and plants like arms and legs, I thought of the bob women and the pansy sailors in the dives. There might be a quarrel with razors, and once Ted Williams found a lip outside the Mission to Seamen.* It had a small moustache. The sinuous plants danced on the screen. If only Tawe were a larger sea town, there would be curtained rooms underground with blue films. The potato's life came to an end. Then I entered an American college and danced with the president's daughter. The hero, called Lincoln, tall and dark with good teeth, I displaced quickly, and the girl spoke my name as she held his shadow; the singing college chorus in sailors' hats and bathing dresses called me "big boy" and "king"; Jack Oakie and I sped up the field, and on the shoulders of the crowd the president's daughter and I brought across the shifting-coloured curtain with a kiss that left me giddy and bright-eyed as I walked out of the cinema into the strong lamplight and the new rain.*

A whole wet hour to waste in the crowds. I watched the queue outside the Empire and studied the posters of *Nuit de Paris*, and thought of the long legs and startling faces of the chorus girls I had seen walking arm in arm, earlier that week, up and down the streets in the winter sunshine, their mouths, I remembered remarking and treasuring for the first page of *The Merciless Ladies* that was never begun, like crimson scars, their hair raven-black or silver; their scent and paint reminded me of the hot and chocolate-coloured East, their eyes were pools. Lola de Kenway, Babs Courcey, Ramona Day would be with me all my life. Until I died, of a wasting, painless disease, and spoke my prepared last words, they would always walk with me, recalling me to my dead youth in the vanished High Street nights when the shop windows were blazing, and singing came out of the pubs, and sirens from the Hafod* sat in the steaming chip shops with their handbags on their knees and their earrings rattling. I stopped to look at the window of Dirty Black's, the Fancy Man, but it was innocent: there were only itching and sneezing powders, stink bombs, rubber pens and Charlie masks* – all the novelties were inside, but I dared not go in for fear a woman should serve me, Mrs Dirty Black with a moustache and knowing eyes, or a thin, dog-faced girl I saw there once, who winked and smelt of seaweed. In the market I bought pink cachous.* You never knew.

The back room of the Three Lamps was full of elderly men. Mr Farr had not arrived. I leant against the bar, between an alderman and a solicitor, drinking bitter, wishing that my father could see me now, and glad, at the same time, that he was visiting Uncle A. in Aberavon. He could not fail to see that I was a boy no longer, nor fail to be angry at the angle of my fag and my hat and the threat of the clutched tankard. I liked the taste of beer, its live, white lather, its brass-bright depths, the sudden world through the wet brown walls of the glass, the tilted rush to the lips and the slow swallowing down to the lapping belly, the salt on the tongue, the foam at the corners.

"Same again, miss." She was middle-aged. "One for you, miss?"

"Not during hours, ta all the same."

"You're welcome."

Was that an invitation to drink with her afterwards, to wait at the back door until she glided out, and then to walk through the night, along the promenade and sands, onto a soft dune where couples lay loving under their coats and looking at the Mumbles Lighthouse?* She was plump and plain, her netted hair was auburn and wisped with grey. She gave me my change like a mother giving her boy pennies for the pictures, and I would not go out with her if she put cream on it.

Mr Farr hurried down High Street, savagely refusing laces and matches, averting his eyes from the shabby crowds. He knew that the poor and the sick and the ugly, unwanted people were so close around him that, with one look of recognition, one gesture of sympathy, he would be lost among them and the evening would be spoilt for ever.

"You're a pint man, then," he said at my elbow.

"Good evening, Mr Farr. Only now and then for a change. What's yours? Dirty night," I said.

Safe in a prosperous house, out of the way of the rain and the unsettling streets, where the poor and the past could not touch him, he took his glass lazily in the company of business and professional men and raised it to the light. "It's going to get dirtier," he said. "You wait till the Fishguard. Here's health! You can see the sailors knitting there. And the old fish girls in the Jersey. Got to go to the w. for a breath of fresh air."

Mr Evans the Produce came in quickly through a side door hidden by curtains, whispered his drink, shielded it with his overcoat, swallowed it in secrecy.

"Similar," said Mr Farr, "and half for his nibs."

The bar was too high-class to look like Christmas. A notice said "No Ladies".

We left Mr Evans gulping in his tent.

Children screamed in Goat Street, and one boy, out of season, pulled my sleeve, crying: "Penny for the guy!" Big women in men's caps barricaded their doorways, and a posh girl gave us the wink at the corner of the green-iron convenience opposite the Carlton Hotel. We entered to music; the bar was hung with ribbons and balloons; a tubercular tenor clung to the piano; behind the counter, Leslie Bird's pretty barmaid was twitting a group of young men, who leant far over and asked to see her garters and invited her to gins and limes and lonely midnight walks and moist adventures in the cinema. Mr Farr sneered down his glass as I watched the young men enviously and saw how much she liked their ways, how she slapped their hands lightly and wriggled back, in pride of her prettiness and gaiety, to pull the beer handles.

"Toop little Twms* from the Valleys. There'll be some puking tonight," he said with pleasure.

Other young men, sleek-haired, pale and stocky, with high cheekbones and deep eyes, bright ties, double-breasted waistcoats and wide trousers, some pocked from the pits, their broad hands scarred and damaged, all exultantly half drunk, stood singing round the piano, and the tenor with the fallen chest led in a clear voice. Oh! To be able to join in the suggestive play or the rocking choir, to shout "Bread of heaven",* with my shoulders back and my arms linked with Little Moscow, or to be called "saucy" and "a one" as I joked and ogled at the counter, making innocent, dirty love that could come to nothing among the spilt beer and piling glasses.

"Let's get away from the bloody nightingales," said Mr Farr.

"Too much bloody row," I said.

"Now we're coming to somewhere." We crawled down Strand alleys by the side of the mortuary, through a gaslit lane where hidden babies cried together and reached the Fishguard door as a man, muffled like Mr Evans, slid out in front of us with a bottle or a blackjack* in one gloved hand. The bar was empty. An old man whose hands trembled sat behind the counter, staring at his turnip watch.*

"Merry Christmas, Pa."

"Good evening, Mr F."

"Drop of rum, Pa."

A red bottle shook over two glasses.

"Very special poison, son."

"This'll make your eyes bulge," said Mr Farr.

My iron head stood high and firm, no sailors' rum could rot the rock of my belly. Poor Leslie Bird the port-sipper, and little Gil Morris, who marked dissipation under his eyes with a blacklead every Saturday night, I wished they could have seen me now, in the dark, stunted room with photographs of boxers peeling on the wall.

"More poison, Pa," I said.

"Where's the company tonight? Gone to the Riviera?"

"They're in the snuggery, Mr F., there's a party for Mrs Prothero's daughter."

In the back room, under a damp royal family, a row of black-dressed women on a hard bench sat laughing and crying, short glasses lined by their Guinnesses. On an opposite bench two men in jerseys drank appreciatively, nodding at the emotions of the women. And on the one chair, in the middle of the room, an old woman, with a bonnet tied under her chins, a feather boa and white gym shoes, tittered and wept above the rest. We sat on the men's bench. One of the two touched his cap with a sore hand.

"What's the party, Jack?" asked Mr Farr. "Meet my colleague, Mr Thomas; this is Jack Stiff, the mortuary keeper."

Jack Stiff spoke from the side of his mouth. "It's Mrs Prothero there. We call her Old Garbo, because she isn't like her,* see. She had a message from the hospital about an hour ago; Mrs Harris's Winifred brought it here, to say her second daughter's died in pod."*

"Baby girl dead, too," said the man at his side.

"So all the old girls came round to sympathize, and they made a big collection for her, and now she's beginning to drink it up and treating round. We've had a couple of pints from her already."

"Shameful!"

The rum burned and kicked in the hot room, but my head felt tough as a hill, and I could write twelve books before morning and roll the Carlton barmaid, like a barrel, the length of Tawe sands.

"Drinks for the troops!"

Before a new audience, the women cried louder, patting Mrs Prothero's knees and hands, adjusting her bonnet, praising her dead daughter.

"What'll you have, Mrs Prothero, dear?"

"No, have it with me, dear, best in the house."

"Well, a Guinness tickles my fancy."

"And a little something in it, dear."

"Just for Margie's sake, then."

"Think if she was here now, dear, singing 'One of the Ruins' or 'Cockles and Mussels'* – she had a proper madam's voice."

"Oh, don't, Mrs Harris!"

"There, we're only bucking you up. Grief killed the cat, Mrs Prothero. Let's have a song together, dear."

"The pale moon was rising above the grey mountain,
The sun was declining beneath the blue sea,
When I strolled with my love to the pure crystal fountain,"

Mrs Prothero sang.

"It was her daughter's favourite song," said Jack Stiff's friend.

Mr Farr tapped me on the shoulder; his hand fell slowly from a great height, and his thin, bird's voice spoke from a whirring circle on the ceiling. "A drop of out-of-doors for you and me." The gamps* and bonnets, the white gym shoes, the bottles and the mildew king, the singing mortuary man, the 'Rose of Tralee',* swam together in the snuggery; two small men, Mr Farr and his twin brother, led me on an ice rink to the door, and the night air slapped me down. The evening happened suddenly. A wall slumped over and knocked off my trilby; Mr Farr's brother disappeared under the cobbles. Here came a wall like a buffalo – dodge him, son. Have a drop of Angostura, have a drop of brandy, Fernet-Branca,* Polly, Ooo! The mother's darling! Have a hair of the dog.

"Feeling better now?"

I sat in a plush chair I had never seen before, sipping a mothball drink and appreciating an argument between Ted Williams and Mr Farr. Mr Farr was saying sternly: "You came in here to look for sailors."

"No, I didn't then," said Ted. "I came for local colour."

The notices on the walls were: "The Lord Jersey. Prop.: Titch Thomas"; "No betting"; "No swearing, b—— you"; "The Lord helps Himself, but you mustn't"; "No ladies allowed, except ladies."

"This is a funny pub," I said. "See the notices?"

"OK now?"

"I'm feeling upsy-daisy."

"There's a pretty girl for you. Look, she's giving you the glad."

"But she's got no nose."

My drink, like winking, had turned itself into beer. A hammer tapped. "Order! Order!" At a sound in a new saloon a collarless chairman with a cigar called on Mr Jenkins to provide 'The Lily of Laguna'.*

"By request," said Mr Jenkins.

"Order! Order! For Katie Sebastopol Street.* What is it, Katie?"

She sang the national anthem.

"Mr Fred Jones will supply his usual dirty one."

A broken baritone voice spoilt the chorus: I recognized it as my own, and drowned it.

A girl of the Salvation Army avoided the arms of two firemen and sold them a *War Cry*.*

A young man with a dazzling handkerchief round his head, black-and-white holiday shoes with holes for the toes and no socks, danced until the bar cried: "Mabel!"

Ted clapped at my side. "That's style! 'Nijinsky* of the Night World', there's a story! Wonder if I can get an interview?"

"Half a crack," said Mr Farr.

"Don't make me cross."

A wind from the docks tore up the street; I heard the rowdy dredger in the bay and a boat blowing to come in; the gas lamps bowed and bent, then again smoke closed about the stained walls with George and Mary dripping above the women's bench, and Jack Stiff whispered, holding his hand in front of him like the paw of an animal: "Old Garbo's gone."

The sad and jolly women huddled together.

"Mrs Harris's little girl got the message wrong. Old Garbo's daughter's right as rain, the baby was born dead. Now the old girls want their money back, but they can't find Garbo anywhere." He licked his hand. "I know where she's gone."

His friend said: "To a boozer over the bridge."

In low voices the women reviled Mrs Prothero – liar, adulteress, mother of bastards, thief.

"She got you know what."
"Never cured it."
"Got Charlie tattooed on her."
"Three and eight she owes me."
"Two and ten."
"Money for my teeth."
"One and a tanner out of my Old Age."*

Who kept filling my glass? Beer ran down my cheek and my collar. My mouth was full of saliva. The bench spun. The cabin of the Fishguard tilted. Mr Farr retreated slowly; the telescope twisted, and his face, with wide and hairy nostrils, breathed against mine.

"Mr Thomas is going to get sick."
"Mind your brolly, Mrs Arthur."
"Take his head."

The last tram clanked home. I did not have the penny for the fare. "You get off here. Careful!" The revolving hill to my father's house reached to the sky. Nobody was up. I crept to a wild bed, and the wallpaper lakes converged and sucked me down.

Sunday was a quiet day, though St Mary's bells, a mile away, rang on, long after church time, in the holes of my head. Knowing that I would never drink again, I lay in bed until midday dinner and remembered the unsteady shapes and far-off voices of the ten o'clock town. I read the newspapers. All news was bad that morning, but an article called 'Our Lord Was a Flower-Lover' moved me to tears of bewilderment and contrition. I excused myself from the Sunday joint and three vegetables.

In the park in the afternoon I sat alone near the deserted bandstand. I caught a ball of waste paper that the wind blew down the gravel path towards the rockery, and, straightening it out and holding it on my knee, wrote the first three lines of a poem without hope. A dog nosed me out where I crouched, behind a bare tree in the cold, and rubbed its nose against my hand. "My only friend," I said. It stayed with me up to the early dusk, sniffing and scratching.

On Monday morning, with shame and hate, afraid to look at them again, I destroyed the article and the poem, throwing the pieces onto the top of the wardrobe, and I told Leslie Bird in the tram to the office: "You should have been with us Saturday, Christ!" Early on Tuesday night, which was Christmas Eve, I walked, with a borrowed half-crown, into the back room of the Fishguard. Jack Stiff was alone. The women's bench was covered with sheets of newspaper. A bunch of balloons hung from the lamp.

"Here's health!"

"Merry Christmas!"

"Where's Mrs Prothero?"

His hand was bandaged now. "Oh! You haven't heard? She spent all the collection money. She took it over the bridge to the Heart's Delight. She didn't let one of the old girls see her. It was over a pound. She'd spent a lot of it before they found her daughter wasn't dead. She couldn't face them then. Have this one with me. So she finished it up by stop-tap* Monday. Then a couple of men from the banana boats saw her walking across the bridge, and she stopped halfway. But they weren't in time."

"Merry Christmas!"

"We got a pair of gym shoes on our slab."

None of Old Garbo's friends came in that night.

When I showed this story a long time later to Mr Farr, he said:

"You got it all wrong. You got the people mixed. The boy with the handkerchief danced in the Jersey. Fred Jones was singing in the Fishguard. Never mind. Come and have one tonight in the Nelson. There's a girl down there who'll show you where the sailor bit her. And there's a policeman who knew Jack Johnson."*

"I'll put them all in a story by and by," I said.

One Warm Saturday*

The young man in a sailor's jersey, sitting near the summer huts to see the brown and white women coming out and the groups of pretty-faced girls with pale vees and scorched backs who picked their way delicately on ugly, red-toed feet over the sharp stones to the sea, drew on the sand a large, indented woman's figure; and a naked child, just out of the sea, ran over it and shook water, marking on the figure two wide wet eyes and a hole in the footprinted middle. He rubbed the woman away and drew a paunched man; the child ran over it, tossing her hair, and shook a row of buttons down its belly and a line of drops, like piddle in a child's drawing, between the long legs stuck with shells.

In a huddle of picnicking women and their children, stretched out limp and damp in the sweltering sun or fussing over paper carriers or building castles that were at once destroyed by the tattered march of other picnickers to different pieces of the beach, among the ice-cream cries, the angrily happy shouts of boys playing ball and the screams of girls as the sea rose to their waists, the young man sat alone with the shadows of his failure at his side. Some silent husbands, with rolled-up trousers and suspenders dangling, paddled slowly on the border of the sea; paddling women, in thick, black picnic dresses, laughed at their own legs; dogs chased stones, and one proud boy rode the water on a rubber seal. The young man, in his wilderness, saw the holiday Saturday set down before him, false and pretty, as a flat picture under the vulgar sun; the disporting families with paper bags, buckets and spades, parasols and bottles, the happy, hot and aching girls with sunburn liniments in their bags, the bronzed young men with chests, and the envious, white young men in waistcoats, the thin, pale, hairy, pathetic legs of the husbands silently walking through the water, the plump and curly, shaven-headed and bowed-backed children up to no sense with unrepeatable delight in the dirty sand, moved him, he thought dramatically in his isolation, to an old shame and pity; outside all holiday, like a young man doomed for ever to the company of his maggots, beyond the high and ordinary, sweating, sun-awakened power and stupidity of the summer flesh on a day and a world out, he caught the ball that a small boy had whacked into the air with a tin tray, and rose to throw it back.

ONE WARM SATURDAY

The boy invited him to play. A friendly family stood waiting some way off, the tousled women with their dresses tucked in their knickers, the barefooted men in shirtsleeves, a number of children in slips and cut-down underwear. He bowled bitterly to a father standing with a tray before the wicket of hats. "The lone wolf playing ball," he said to himself as the tray whirled. Chasing the ball towards the sea, passing undressing women with a rush and a wink, tripping over a castle into a coil of wet girls lying like snakes, soaking his shoes as he grabbed the ball off a wave, he felt his happiness return in a boast of the body, and "Look out, Duckworth,* here's a fast one coming," he cried to the mother behind the hats. The ball bounced on a boy's head. In and out of the scattered families, among the sandwiches and clothes, uncles and mothers fielded the bouncing ball. A bald man, with his shirt hanging out, returned it in the wrong direction, and a collie carried it into the sea. Now it was Mother's turn with the tray. Tray and ball together flew over her head. An uncle in a panama smacked the ball to the dog, who swam with it out of reach. They offered the young man egg-and-cress sandwiches and warm stout, and he and an uncle and a father sat down on the *Evening Post* until the sea touched their feet.

Alone again, hot and unhappy, for the boasting minute when he ran among the unknown people lying and running loudly at peace was struck away, like a ball, he said, into the sea, he walked to a space on the beach where a hellfire preacher on a box marked "Mr Matthews" was talking to a congregation of expressionless women. Boys with pea-shooters sat quietly near him. A ragged man collected nothing in a cap. Mr Matthews shook his cold hands, stormed at the holiday and cursed the summer from his shivering box. He cried for a new warmth. The strong sun shone into his bones, and he buttoned his coat collar. Valley children, with sunken, impudent eyes, quick tongues and singing voices, chests thin as shells, gathered round the Punch and Judy and the Stop Me tricycles,* and he denied them all. He contradicted the girls in their underclothes combing and powdering, and the modest girls cleverly dressing under tents of towels.

As Mr Matthews cast down the scarlet town, drove out the bare-bellied boys who danced around the ice-cream man and wound the girls' sunburnt thighs about with his black overcoat – "Down! Down!" he cried. "The night is upon us" – the young man in dejection stood, with a shadow at his shoulder, and thought of Porthcawl's Coney Beach, where his friends were rocking with girls on the Giant Racer or tearing in the Ghost Train down the skeletons' tunnel. Leslie Bird would have his arms full of coconuts. Brenda was with Herbert at the rifle range. Gil Morris was buying Molly a cocktail with a cherry at the Esplanade. Here he stood, listening to Mr Matthews, the retired drinker, crying darkness on the evening sands, with money hot in his pocket and Saturday burning away.

In his loneliness he had refused their invitations. Herbert, in his low, red sports car, "GB" at the back, a sea-blown nymph on the radiator, called at his father's house, but he said: "I'm not in the mood, old man. I'm going to spend a quiet day. Enjoy yourselves. Don't take too much pop." Only waiting for the sun to set, he stood in the sad circle with the pleasureless women who were staring at a point in the sky behind their prophet, and wished the morning back. Oh, boy! To be wasting his money now on the rings and ranges of the fair, to be sitting in the chromium lounge with a short worth one and six and a Turkish cigarette, telling the latest one to the girls, seeing the sun, through the palms in the lounge window, sink over the promenade, over the Bath chairs,* the cripples and widows, the beach-trousered, kerchiefed, weekend wives, the smart, kiss-curled girls with plain and spectacled girl friends, the innocent, swaggering, loud bad boys, and the Poms at the ankles, and the cycling sweet men. Ronald had sailed to Ilfracombe on the *Lady Moira*, and, in the thick saloon, with a party from Brynhyfryd, he'd be knocking back nips without a thought that on the sands at home his friend was alone and pussyfoot* at six o'clock, and the evening dull as a chapel. All his friends had vanished into their pleasures.

He thought: poets live and walk with their poems; a man with visions needs no other company; Saturday is a crude day; I must go home and sit in my bedroom by the boiler. But he was not a poet living and walking: he was a young man in a sea town on a warm bank holiday, with two pounds to spend; he had no visions, only two pounds and a small body with its feet on the littered sand; serenity was for old men; and he moved away, over the railway points, onto the tramlined road.

He snarled at the flower clock in Victoria Gardens.*

"And what shall a prig do now?" he said aloud, causing a young woman on a bench opposite the white-tiled urinal to smile and put her novel down.

She had chestnut hair arranged high on her head in an old-fashioned way, in loose coils and a bun, and a Woolworth's white rose grew out of it and drooped to touch her ear. She wore a white frock with a red paper flower pinned on the breast, and rings and bracelets that came from a funfair stall. Her eyes were small and quite green.

He marked, carefully and coldly in one glance, all the unusual details of her appearance; it was the calm, unstartled certainty of her bearing before his glance from head to foot, the innocent knowledge, in her smile and the set of her head, that she was defended by her gentleness and accessible strangeness against all rude encounters and picking looks, that made his fingers tremble. Though her frock was long and the collar high, she could as well be naked there on the blistered bench. Her smile confessed her body bare and spotless and willing and warm under the cotton, and she waited without guilt.

How beautiful she is, he thought, with his mind on words and his eyes on her hair and red-and-white skin, how beautifully she waits for me, though she does not know she is waiting and I can never tell her.

He had stopped and was staring. Like a confident girl before a camera, she sat smiling, her hands folded, her head slightly to one side so that the rose brushed her neck. She accepted his admiration. The girl in a million took his long look to herself, and cherished his stupid love.

Midges flew into his mouth. He hurried on shamefully. At the gates of the gardens he turned to see her for the last time on earth. She had lost her calm with his abrupt and awkward going, and stared in confusion after him. One hand was raised as though to beckon him back. If he waited, she would call him. He walked round the corner and heard her voice, a hundred voices, and all hers, calling his name, and a hundred names that were all his, over the bushy walls.

And what shall the terrified prig of a love-mad young man do next? he asked his reflection silently in the distorting mirror of the empty Victoria saloon.* His ape-like hanging face, with "Bass" across the forehead, gave back a cracked sneer.

If Venus came in on a plate, said the two red, melon-slice lips, I would ask for vinegar to put on her.

She could drive my guilt out; she could smooth away my shame; why didn't I stop to talk to her? he asked.

You saw a queer tart in a park, his reflection answered, she was a child of nature, oh my! Oh my! Did you see the dewdrops in her hair? Stop talking to the mirror like a man in a magazine, I know you too well.

A new head, swollen and lop-jawed, wagged behind his shoulder. He spun round to hear the barman say:

"Has the one and only let you down? You look like death warmed up. Have this one on the house. Free beer today. Free Xs."* He pulled the beer handle. "Only the best served here. Straight from the rust. You do look queer," he said, "the only one saved from the wreck and the only wreck saved. Here's looking at you!" He drank the beer he had drawn.

"May I have a glass of beer, please?"

"What do you think this is, a public house?"

On the polished table in the middle of the saloon the young man drew, with a finger dipped in strong, the round head of a girl and piled a yellow froth of hair upon it.

"Ah! Dirty, dirty!" said the barman, running round from behind the counter and rubbing the head away with a dry cloth.

Shielding the dirtiness with his hat, the young man wrote his name on the edge of the table and watched the letters dry and fade.

Through the open bay window, across the useless railway covered with sand, he saw the black dots of bathers, the stunted huts, the jumping dwarfs round the Punch and Judy, and the tiny religious circle. Since he had walked and played down there in the crowded wilderness excusing his despair, searching for company though he refused it, he had found his own true happiness and lost her all in one bewildering and clumsy half a minute by the "Gentlemen" and the flower clock. Older and wiser and no better, he would have looked in the mirror to see if his discovery and loss had marked themselves upon his face in shadows under the eyes or lines about the mouth, were it not for the answer he knew he would receive from the distorted reflection.

The barman came to sit near him, and said in a false voice: "Now you tell me all about it, I'm a regular storehouse of secrets."

"There isn't anything to tell. I saw a girl in Victoria Gardens and I was too shy to speak to her. She was a piece of God help us all right."

Ashamed of his wish to be companionable, even in the depth of love and distress, with her calm face before his eyes and her smile reproving and forgiving him as he spoke, the young man defiled his girl on the bench, dragged her down into the spit and sawdust and dolled her up to make the barman say:

"I like them big myself. Once round Bessy, once round the gasworks.* I missed the chance of a lifetime, too. Fifty lovelies in the rude and I'd left my Bunsen burner* home."

"Give me the same, please."

"You mean similar."

The barman drew a glass of beer, drank it and drew another.

"I always have one with the customers," he said, "it puts us on even terms. Now we're just two heartbroken bachelors together." He sat down again.

"You can't tell me anything I don't know," he said. "I've seen over twenty chorines* from the Empire in this bar, drunk as printers. Oh, les girls! Les limbs!"

"Will they be in tonight?"

"There's only a fellow sawing a woman in half this week."

"Keep a half for me."

A drunk man walked in on an invisible white line, and the barman, reeling in sympathy across the room, served him with a pint. "Free beer today," he said. "Free Xs. You've been out in the sun."

"I've been out in the sun all day," said the man.

"I thought you looked sunburnt."

"That's drink," said the man. "I've been drinking."

"The holiday is drawing to an end," the young man whispered into his glass. Bye-bye blackbird,* the moment is lost, he thought, examining, with an interest he could not forgive, the comic coloured postcards of mountain-buttocked women on the beach and henpecked, pin-legged men with telescopes pasted on the wall beneath the picture of a terrier drinking stout; and now, with a jolly barman and a drunk in a crushed cap, he was mopping the failing day down. He tipped his hat over his forehead, and a lock of hair that fell below the hat tickled his eyelid. He saw, with a stranger's darting eye that missed no single subtlety of the wry grin or the faintest gesture drawing the shape of his death on the air, an unruly-haired young man who coughed into his hand in the corner of a rotting room and puffed the smoke of his doped Weight.*

But as the drunk man weaved towards him on wilful feet, carrying his dignity as a man might carry a full glass around a quaking ship, as the barman behind the counter clattered and whistled and dipped to drink, he shook off the truthless, secret tragedy with a sneer and a blush, straightened his melancholy hat into a hard-brimmed trilby, dismissed the affected stranger. In the safe centre of his own identity, the familiar world about him like another flesh, he sat sad and content in the plain room of the undistinguished hotel at the sea end of the shabby, spreading town, where everything was happening. He had no need of the dark interior world when Tawe pressed in upon him and the eccentric ordinary people came bursting and crawling, with noise and colours, out of their houses, out of the graceless buildings, the factories and avenues, the shining shops and blaspheming chapels, the terminuses and the meeting halls, the falling alleys and brick lanes, from the arches and shelters and holes behind the hoardings, out of the common, wild intelligence of the town.

At last the drunk man had reached him. "Put your hand here," he said, and turned about and tapped himself on the bottom.

The barman whistled and rose from his drink to see the young man touch the drunk on the seat of the trousers.

"What can you feel there?"

"Nothing."

"That's right. Nothing. Nothing. There's nothing there to feel."

"How can you sit down, then?" asked the barman.

"I just sit down on what the doctor left," the man said angrily. "I had as good a bottom as you've got once. I was working underground in Dowlais,* and the end of the world came down on me. Do you know what I got for losing my bottom? Four and three! Two and three ha'pence a cheek. That's cheaper than a pig."

The girl from Victoria Gardens came into the bar with two friends: a blonde young girl almost as beautiful as she was and a middle-aged woman dressed and made up to look young. The three of them sat at the table. The girl he loved ordered three ports and gins.

"Isn't it delicious weather?" said the middle-aged woman.

The barman said: "Plenty of sky about." With many bows and smiles he placed their drinks in front of them. "I thought the princesses had gone to a better pub," he said.

"What's a better pub without you, handsome?" said the blonde girl.

"This is the Ritz and the Savoy, isn't it, *garçon* darling?" the girl from the Gardens said, and kissed her hand to him.

The young man in the window seat, still bewildered by the first sudden sight of her entering the darkening room, caught the kiss to himself and blushed. He thought to run out of the room and through the miracle-making Gardens, to rush into his house and hide his head in the bedclothes and lie all night there, dressed and trembling, her voice in his ears, her green eyes wide awake under his closed eyelids. But only a sick boy with tossed blood would run from his proper love into a dream, lie down in a bedroom that was full of his shames and sob against the feathery, fat breast and face on the damp pillow. He remembered his age and poems, and would not move.

"Tanks a million, Lou," said the barman.

Her name was Lou, Louise, Louisa. She must be Spanish or French or a Gypsy, but he could tell the street that her voice came from; he knew where her friends lived by the rise and fall of their sharp voices, and the name of the middle-aged woman was Mrs Emerald Franklin. She was to be seen every night in the Jew's Harp, sipping and spying and watching the clock.

"We've been listening to Matthews Hellfire on the sands. Down with this and down with that, and he used to drink a pint of biddy* before his breakfast," Mrs Franklin said. "Oh, there's a nerve!"

"And his eye on the fluff all the time," said the blonde girl. "I wouldn't trust him any further than Ramon Novarro* behind the counter."

"Whoops! I've gone up in the world. Last week I was Charley Chase,"* said the barman.

Mrs Franklin raised her empty glass in a gloved hand and shook it like a bell. "Men are deceivers ever," she said. "And a drop of mother's ruin right around."

"Especially Mr Franklin," said the barman.

"But there's a lot in what the preacher says, mind," Mrs Franklin said, "about the carrying on. If you go for a constitutional after stop-tap along the sands, you might as well be in Sodom and Gomorrah."

The blonde girl laughed. "Hark to Mrs Grundy!* I see her with a black man last Wednesday, round by the museum."

"He was an Indian," said Mrs Franklin, "from the university college, and I'd thank you to remember it. Every one's brothers under the skin, but there's no tarbrush in my family."

"Oh, dear! Oh, dear!" said Lou. "Lay off it, there's loves. This is my birthday. It's a holiday. Put a bit of fun in it. Miaow! Miaow! Marjorie, kiss Emerald and be friends." She smiled and laughed at them both. She winked at the barman, who was filling their glasses to the top. "Here's to your blue eyes, *garçon*!" She had not noticed the young man in the corner. "And one for granddad there," she said, smiling at the swaying drunk man. "He's twenty-one today. There! I've made him smile."

The drunk man made a deep, dangerous bow, lifted his hat, stumbled against the mantelpiece, and his full pint in his free hand was steady as a rock. "The prettiest girl in Carmarthenshire," he said.

"This is Glamorganshire, Dad," she said. "Where's your geography? Look at him waltzing! Mind your glasses! He's got that Kruschen feeling.* Come on, faster! Give us the Charleston."

The drunk man, with his pint held high, danced until he fell, and all the time he never spilt a drop. He lay at Lou's feet on the dusty floor and grinned up at her in confidence and affection. "I fell," he said. "I could dance like a trooper when I had a beatyem."

"He lost his bottom at the last trump," the barman explained.

"When did he lose his bottom?" said Mrs Franklin.

"When Gabriel blew his whistle down in Dowlais."

"You're pulling my leg."

"It's a pleasure, Mrs Em. Hoi, you! Get up from the vomitorium."

The man wagged his end like a tail, and growled at Lou's feet.

"Put your head on my foot. Be comfy. Let him lie there," she said.

He went to sleep at once.

"I can't have drunks on the premises."

"You know where to go then."

"Cru-el Mrs Franklin!"

"Go on, attend to your business. Serve the young man in the corner, his tongue's hanging out."

"Cru-el lady!"

As Mrs Franklin called attention to the young man, Lou peered short-sightedly across the saloon and saw him sitting with his back to the window.

"I'll have to get glasses," she said.

"You'll have plenty of glasses before the night's out."

"No, honest, Marjorie, I didn't know anyone was there. I do beg your pardon, you in the corner," she said.

The barman switched on the light. "A bit of *lux in tenebris*."*

"Oh!" said Lou.

The young man dared not move for fear that he might break the long light of her scrutiny, the enchantment shining like a single line of light between them, or startle her into speaking; and he did not conceal the love in his eyes, for she could pierce through to it as easily as she could turn his heart in his chest and make it beat above the noises of the two friends' hurried conversation, the rattle of glasses behind the counter, where the barman spat and polished and missed nothing, and the snores of the comfortable sleeper. Nothing can hurt me. Let the barman jeer. Giggle in your glass, our Em. I'm telling the world, I'm walking in clover, I'm staring at Lou like a fool, she's my girl, she's my lily. O love! O love!

She's no lady, with her sing-song Tontine voice,* she drinks like a deep-sea diver; but Lou, I'm yours, and Lou, you're mine. He refused to meditate on her calmness now and twist her beauty into words. She was nothing under the sun or moon but his. Unashamed and certain, he smiled at her, and, though he was prepared for all, her answering smile made his fingers tremble again, as they had trembled in the Gardens, and reddened his cheeks and drove his heart to a gallop.

"Harold, fill the young man's glass up," Mrs Franklin said.

The barman stood still, a duster in one hand and a dripping glass in the other.

"Have you got water in your ears? Fill the young man's glass!"

The barman put the duster to his eyes. He sobbed. He wiped away the mock tears.

"I thought I was attending a premiere and this was the royal box," he said.

"He's got water on the brain, not in his earhole," said Marjorie.

"I dreamt it was a beautiful tragicomedy entitled *Love at First Sight, or Another Good Man Gone Wrong*. Act one in a boozer by the sea."

The two women tapped their foreheads.

Lou said, still smiling: "Where was the second act?"

Her voice was as gentle as he had imagined it to be before her gay and nervous playing with the overfamiliar barman and the inferior women. He saw her as a wise, soft girl whom no hard company could spoil, for her soft self, bare to the heart, broke through every defence of her sensual falsifiers. As he thought this, phrasing her gentleness, faithlessly running to words away from the real room and his love in the middle, he woke with a start and saw her lively body six steps from him, no calm heart dressed in a sentence, but a pretty girl, to be got and kept. He must catch hold of her fast. He got up to cross to her.

"I woke before the second act came on," said the barman. "I'd sell my dear old mother to see that. Dim lights. Purple couches. Ecstatic bliss. *Là, là, chérie!*"*

The young man sat down at the table, next to her.

Harold, the barman, leant over the counter and cupped his hand to his ear.

The man on the floor rolled in his sleep, and his head lay in the spittoon.

"You should have come and sat here a long time ago," Lou whispered. "You should have stopped to talk to me in the Gardens. Were you shy?"

"I was too shy," the young man whispered.

"Whispering isn't manners. I can't hear a word," said the barman.

At a sign from the young man, a flick of the fingers that sent the waiters in evening dress bustling with oysters about the immense room, the barman filled the glasses with port, gin and Nutbrown.*

"We never drink with strangers," Mrs Franklin said, laughing.

"He isn't a stranger," said Lou. "Are you, Jack?"

He threw a pound note on the table: "Take the damage."

The evening that had been over before it began raced along among the laughter of the charming women, sharp as knives, and the stories of the barman, who should be on the stage, and Lou's delighted smiles and silences at his side. Now she is safe and sure, he thought, after her walking like my doubtful walking around the lonely distances of the holiday. In the warm, spinning middle they were close and alike. The town and the sea and the last pleasure-makers drifted into the dark that had nothing to do with them, and left this one room burning.

One by one, some lost men from the dark shuffled into the bar, drank sadly and went out. Mrs Franklin, flushed and dribbling, waved her glass at their departures. Harold winked behind their backs. Marjorie showed them her long, white legs.

"Nobody loves us except ourselves," said Harold. "Shall I shut the bar and keep the riff-raff out?"

"Lou is expecting Mr O'Brien, but don't let that stop you," Marjorie said. "He's her sugar daddy from old Ireland."

"Do you love Mr O'Brien?" the young man whispered.

"How could I, Jack?"

He could see Mr O'Brien as a witty, tall fellow of middle age, with waved greying hair and a clipped bit of dirt on his upper lip, a flash ring on his marriage finger, a pouched knowing eye, dummy-dressed with a whalebone waist, a broth of a man about Cardiff, Lou's horrible lover tearing towards her now down the airless streets in the firm's car. The young man clenched his hand on the table covered with dead, and sheltered her in the warm strength of his fist. "My round, my round," he said, "up again, plenty! Doubles, trebles, Mrs Franklin is a jibber."

"My mother never had a jibber."

"Oh, Lou!" he said. "I am more than happy with you."

"Coo! Coo! Hear the turtle doves."

"Let them coo," said Marjorie. "I could coo, too."

The barman looked around him in surprise. He raised his hands, palms up, and cocked his head.

"The bar is full of birds," he said.

"Emerald's laying an egg," he said as Mrs Franklin rocked in her chair.

Soon the bar was full of customers. The drunk man woke up and ran out, leaving his cap in a brown pool. Sawdust dropped from his hair. A small, old, round, red-faced, cheery man sat facing the young man and Lou, who held hands under the table and rubbed their legs against each other.

"What a night for love!" said the old man. "On such a night as this did Jessica steal from the wealthy Jew.* Do you know where that comes from?"

"*The Merchant of Venice*," Lou said. "But you're an Irishman, Mr O'Brien."

"I could have sworn you were a tall man with a little tish,"* said the young man gravely.

"What's the weapons, Mr O'Brien?"

"Brandies at dawn, I should think, Mrs Franklin."

"I never described Mr O'Brien to you at all. You're dreaming!" Lou whispered.

"I wish this night could go on for ever."

"But not here. Not in the bar. In a room with a big bed."

"A bed in a bar," said the old man, "if you'll pardon me hearing you, that's what I've always wanted. Think of it, Mrs Franklin."

The barman bobbed up from behind the counter.

"Time, gentlemen and others!"

The sober strangers departed to Mrs Franklin's laughter.

The lights went out.

"Lou, don't you lose me."

"I've got your hand."

"Press it hard, hurt it."

"Break his bloody neck," Mrs Franklin said in the dark. "No offence meant."

"Marjorie smack hand," said Marjorie. "Let's get out of the dark. Harold's a rover in the dark."

"And the Girl Guides."

"Let's take a bottle each and go down to Lou's," she said.

"I'll buy the bottles," said Mr O'Brien.

"It's you don't lose me now," Lou whispered. "Hold on to me, Jack. The others won't stay long. Oh, Mr Christ, I wish it was just you and me!"

"Will it be just you and me?"

"You and me and Mr Moon."

Mr O'Brien opened the saloon door. "Pile into the Rolls, you ladies. The gentlemen are going to see to the medicine."

The young man felt Lou's quick kiss on his mouth before she followed Marjorie and Mrs Franklin out.

"What do you say we split the drinks?" said Mr O'Brien.

"Look what I found in the lavatory," said the barman. "He was singing on the seat." He appeared behind the counter with the drunk man leaning on his arm.

They all climbed into the car.

"First stop, Lou's."

The young man, on Lou's knee, saw the town in a daze spin by them, the funnelled and masted smoke-blue outline of the still, droning docks, the lightning lines of the poor streets growing longer, and the winking shops that were snapped out one by one. The car smelt of scent and powder and flesh. He struck with his elbow, by accident, Mrs Franklin's upholstered breast. Her thighs, like cushions, bore the drunk man's rolling weight. He was bumped and tossed on a lump of woman. Breasts, legs, bellies, hands, touched, warmed and smothered him. On through the night, towards Lou's bed, towards the unbelievable end of the dying holiday, they tore past black houses and bridges, a station in a smoke cloud, and drove up a steep side street with one weak lamp in a circle of railings at the top, and swerved into a space where a tall tenement house stood surrounded by cranes, standing ladders, poles and girders, barrows, brick heaps.

They climbed to Lou's room up many flights of dark, perilous stairs. Washing hung on the rails outside closed doors. Mrs Franklin, fumbling alone with the drunk man behind the others, trod in a bucket, and a lucky black cat ran over her foot. Lou led the young man by the hand through a passage marked with names and doors, lit a match and whispered: "It won't be very long. Be good and patient with Mr O'Brien. Here it is. Come in first. Welcome to you, Jack!" She kissed him again at the door of her room.

She turned on the light, and he walked with her proudly into her own room, into the room that he would come to know, and saw a wide bed, a gramophone on a chair, a washbasin half hidden in a corner, a gas fire and a cooking ring, a closed cupboard and her photograph in a cardboard frame on the chest of drawers with no handles. Here she slept and ate. In the double bed she lay all night, pale and curled, sleeping on her left side. When he lived with her always, he would not allow her to dream. No other men must lie and love in her head. He spread his fingers on her pillow.

"Why do you live at the top of the Eiffel Tower?" said the barman, coming in.

"What a climb!" said Mr O'Brien. "But it's very nice and private when you get here."

"If you get here!" said Mrs Franklin. "I'm dead beat. This old nuisance weighs a ton. Lie down, lie down on the floor and go to sleep. The old nuisance!" she said fondly. "What's your name?"

"Ernie," the drunk man said, raising his arm to shield his face.

"Nobody's going to bite you, Ernie. Here, give him a nip of whisky. Careful! Don't pour it on your waistcoat – you'll be squeezing your waistcoat in the morning. Pull the curtains, Lou, I can see the wicked old moon," she said.

"Does it put ideas in your head?"

"I love the moon," said Lou.

"There never was a young lover who didn't love the moon." Mr O'Brien gave the young man a cheery smile and patted his hand. His own hand was red and hairy. "I could see at the flash of a glance that Lou and this nice young fellow were made for each other. I could see it in their eyes. Dear me, no! I'm not so old and blind I can't see love in front of my nose. Couldn't you see it, Mrs Franklin? Couldn't you see it, Marjorie?"

In the long silence, Lou collected glasses from the cupboard as though she had not heard Mr O'Brien speak. She drew the curtains, shut out the moon, sat on the edge of her bed with her feet tucked under her, looked at her photograph as at a stranger, folded her hands as she folded them, on the first meeting, before the young man's worship in the Gardens.

"A host of angels must be passing by," said Mr O'Brien. "What a silence there is! Have I said anything out of place? Drink and be merry, tomorrow we die. What do you think I bought these lovely shining bottles for?"

The bottles were opened. The dead were lined on the mantelpiece. The whisky went down. Harold the barman and Marjorie, her dress lifted, sat in the one armchair together. Mrs Franklin, with Ernie's head on her lap, sang in a sweet, trained contralto voice 'The Shepherd's Lass'. Mr O'Brien kept rhythm with his foot.

I want Lou in my arms, the young man said to himself, watching Mr O'Brien tap and smile and the barman draw Marjorie down deep. Mrs Franklin's voice sang sweetly in the small bedroom where he and Lou should be lying in the white bed without any smiling company to see them drown. He and Lou could go down together, one cool body weighted with a boiling stone, onto the falling, blank white, entirely empty sea, and never rise. Sitting on their bridal bed, near enough to hear his breath, she was farther from him than before they met. Then he had everything but her body; now she had given him two kisses, and everything had vanished but that beginning. He must be good and patient with Mr O'Brien. He could wipe away the embracing, old smile with the iron back of his hand. Sink lower, lower, Harold and Marjorie, tumble like whales at Mr O'Brien's feet.

He wished that the light would fail. In the darkness he and Lou could creep beneath the clothes and imitate the dead. Who would look for them there, if they were dead still and soundless? The others would shout to them down the dizzy stairs or rummage in the silence about the narrow, obstacled corridors or stumble out into the night to search for them among the cranes and ladders in the desolation of the destroyed houses. He could hear, in the made-up dark, Mr O'Brien's voice cry "Lou, where are you? Answer! Answer!", the hollow answer of the echo – "Answer!" – and hear her lips in the cool pit of the bed secretly move around another name and feel them move.

"A fine piece of singing, Emerald, and very naughty words. That was a shepherd, that was," Mr O'Brien said.

Ernie, on the floor, began to sing in a thick, sulking voice, but Mrs Franklin placed her hand over his mouth, and he sucked and nuzzled it.

"What about this young shepherd?" said Mr O'Brien, pointing his glass at the young man. "Can he sing as well as make love? You ask him kindly, girlie," he said to Lou, "and he'll give us a song like a nightingale."

"Can you sing, Jack?"

"Like a crow, Lou."

"Can't he even talk poetry? What a young man to have who can't spout the poets to his lady!" Mr O'Brien said.

From the cupboard Lou brought out a red-bound book and gave it to the young man, saying: "Can you read us a piece out of here? The second volume's in the hatbox. Read us a dreamy piece, Jack. It's nearly midnight."

"Only a love poem, no other kind," said Mr O'Brien. "I won't hear anything but a love poem."

"Soft and sweet," Mrs Franklin said. She took her hand away from Ernie's mouth and looked at the ceiling.

The young man read, but not aloud, lingering on her name, the inscription on the flyleaf of the first volume of the collected poems of Tennyson: "To Louisa, from her Sunday-school teacher, Miss Gwyneth Forbes. God's in His heaven, all's right with the world."*

"Make it a love poem, don't forget."

The young man read aloud, closing one eye to steady the dancing print, 'Come into the garden, Maud'.* And when he reached the beginning of the fourth verse his voice grew louder:

> "I said to the lily, 'There is but one
>   With whom she has heart to be gay.
> When will the dancers leave her alone?
>   She is weary of dance and play.'

Now half to the setting moon are gone,
    And half to the rising day;
Low on the sand and loud on the stone
    The last wheel echoes away.

"I said to the rose, 'The brief night goes
    In babble and revel and wine.
Oh, young lord-lover, what sighs are those,
    For one that will never be thine?
But mine, but mine,' so I sware to the rose,
    'For ever and ever, mine.'"

At the end of the poem, Harold said, suddenly, his head hanging over the arm of the chair, his hair made wild and his mouth red with lipstick: "My grandfather remembers seeing Lord Tennyson – he was a little man with a hump."

"No," said the young man, "he was tall and he had long hair and a beard."

"Did you ever see him?"

"I wasn't born then."

"My grandfather saw him. He had a hump."

"Not Alfred Tennyson."

"Lord Alfred Tennyson was a little man with a hump."

"It couldn't have been the same Tennyson."

"You've got the wrong Tennyson, this was the famous poet with a hump."

Lou, on the wonderful bed, waiting for him alone of all the men, ugly or handsome, old or young, in the wide town and the small world that would be bound to fall, lowered her head and kissed her hand to him and held her hand in the river of light on the counterpane. The hand, to him, became transparent, and the light on the counterpane glowed up steadily through it in the thin shape of her palm and fingers.

"Ask Mr O'Brien what Lord Tennyson was like," said Mrs Franklin. "We appeal to you, Mr O'Brien – did he have a hump or not?"

Nobody but the young man, for whom she lived and waited now, noticed Lou's little loving movements. She put her glowing hand to her left breast. She made a sign of secrecy on her lips.

"It depends," Mr O'Brien said.

The young man closed one eye again, for the bed was pitching like a ship; a sickening hot storm out of a cigarette cloud unsettled cupboard and chest. The motions of the seagoing bedroom were calmed with the cunning closing of his eye, but he longed for night air. On sailor's legs he walked to the door.

"You'll find the House of Commons on the second floor at the end of the passage," said Mr O'Brien.

At the door, he turned to Lou and smiled with all his love, declaring it to the faces of the company and making her, before Mr O'Brien's envious regard, smile back and say: "Don't be long, Jack. Please! You mustn't be long."

Now everyone knew. Love had grown up in an evening.

"One minute, my darling," he said. "I'll be here."

The door closed behind him. He walked into the wall of the passage. He lit a match. He had three left. Down the stairs, clinging to the sticky, shaking rails, rocking on see-saw floorboards, bruising his shin on a bucket, past the noises of secret lives behind doors, he slid and stumbled and swore and heard Lou's voice in a fresh fever drive him on, call him to return, speak to him with such passion and abandonment that even in the darkness and the pain of his haste he was dazzled and struck still. She spoke, there on the rotting stairs in the middle of the poor house, a frightening rush of love words; from her mouth, at his ear, endearments were burnt out. Hurry! Hurry! Every moment is being killed. Love, adored, dear, run back and whistle to me, open the door, shout my name, lay me down. Mr O'Brien has his hands on my side.

He ran into a cavern. A draught blew out his matches. He lurched into a room where two figures on a black heap on the floor lay whispering, and ran from there in a panic. He made water at the dead end of the passage and hurried back towards Lou's room, finding himself at last on a silent patch of stairway at the top of the house; he put out his hand, but the rail was broken and nothing there prevented a long drop to the ground down a twisted shaft that would echo and double his cry, bring out from their holes in the wall the sleeping or stirring families, the whispering figures, the blind, startled turners of night into day. Lost in a tunnel near the roof, he fingered the damp walls for a door; he found a handle and gripped it hard, but it came off in his hand. Lou had led him down a longer passage than this. He remembered the number of doors: there were three on each side. He ran down the broken-railed flight into another passage and dragged his hand along the wall. Three doors, he counted. He opened the third door, walked into darkness and groped for the switch on the left. He saw, in the sudden light, a bed and a cupboard and a chest of drawers with no handles, a gas fire, a washbasin in the corner. No bottles. No glasses. No photograph of Lou. The red counterpane on the bed was smooth. He could not remember the colour of Lou's counterpane.

He left the light burning and opened the second door, but a strange woman's voice cried, half asleep: "Who is there? Is it you, Tom? Tom, put the light on." He looked for a line of light at the foot of the next door, and stopped to listen for voices. The woman was still calling in the second room.

"Lou, where are you?" he cried. "Answer! Answer!"

"Lou, what Lou? There's no Lou here," said a man's voice through the open door of the first dark room at the entrance to the passage.

He scampered down another flight and counted four doors with his scratched hand. One door opened, and a woman in a nightdress put out her head. A child's head appeared below her.

"Where does Lou live? Do you know where Lou lives?"

The woman and the child stared without speaking.

"Lou! Lou! Her name is Lou!" he heard himself shout "She lives here, in this house! Do you know where she lives?"

The woman caught the child by the hair and pulled her into the room. He clung to the edge of her door. The woman thrust her arm round the edge and brought down a bunch of keys sharply on his hands. The door slammed.

A young woman with a baby in a shawl stood at an open door on the opposite side of the passage, and caught his sleeve as he ran by. "Lou who? You woke my baby."

"I don't know her other name. She's with Mrs Franklin and Mr O'Brien."

"You woke my baby."

"Come in and find her in the bed," a voice said from the darkness behind the young woman.

"He's woken my baby."

He ran down the passage, holding his wet hand to his mouth. He fell against the rails of the last flight of stairs. He heard Lou's voice in his head once more whisper to him to return as the ground floor rose, like a lift full of dead, towards the rails. Hurry! Hurry! I can't, I won't wait, the bridal night is being killed.

Up the rotten, bruising, mountainous stairs he climbed, in his sickness, to the passage where he had left the one light burning in an end room. The light was out. He tapped all the doors and whispered her name. He beat on the doors and shouted, and a woman, dressed in a vest and a hat, drove him out of the passage with a walking stick.

For a long time he waited on the stairs, though there was no love now to wait for and no bed but his own too many miles away to lie in, and only the approaching day to remember his discovery. All around him the disturbed inhabitants of the house were falling back into sleep. Then he walked out of the house onto the waste space and under the leaning cranes and ladders. The light of the one weak lamp in a rusty circle fell across the brick heaps and the broken wood and the dust that had been houses once, where the small and hardly known and never-to-be-forgotten people of the dirty town had lived and loved and died and, always, lost.

EARLY STORIES*

Brember*

From the stairs, the shadows slid gently down into the hall. He could see the dark outline of the banisters reflected across the mirror, and the arc of the chandelier throwing its light. But that was all. Towards the door, the shadows became larger. Then they were lost in the darkness of the floor and ceiling. He fumbled in his pocket for a match, and lit the taper in his hand. Holding the tiny flame above his head, he turned the handle and stepped into the room. There was a smell of dust and old wood. It was curious how sensitive he was to it, how it quickened his imagination. Old ladies making lace by the light of the moon, their thin, pale fingers stealing along the brocade, their ageless cheeks tinted like a little child's. That was what the room always reminded him of, since the days when he had first tiptoed in and gazed with terror at the windows opening onto the grey lawn and the trees beyond. Or when, still a little boy, he had sat at the harpsichord, touching the dusty keys so lightly no one could hear their sound, afraid and yet entranced as the music rose faintly into the air. It was always sad. He could detect the desolate sadness beneath the lightest fugue; as his hand touched the notes, there were tears in his eyes, a great longing for something he had known and had forgotten, loved but had lost.

That was a number of years ago, and now the same sensation of unreality and of longing came over him as he lit the harpsichord's long candles with his taper, and saw in their spreading light the walls crowd closer round him, and the heavy chairs hem him in. The keys were as dusty as ever. He brushed them lightly with his sleeve, then let his fingers wander for a moment over them. How frail their sound was. What curious little melodies they made, so sad and yet so perfect. For a moment he thought he heard the sound of childish footsteps outside the door, running down the corridor into the darkness. But then they were gone, and he could but suppose that they had never been. Now there was a hint of laughter sounding in his ears; now it was gone again. As he played, he seemed to hear the soft, rustling noise of a silk skirt dragged along the ground. Then his music grew louder, and, when it was soft again, there was nothing.

Try as he would, he could not analyse his reasons for coming to the house. It terrified him, and yet he could not draw away from it. Out on the road he had suddenly felt the desire to throw apart the veil of the years, to bring back to him all that old house had meant, the dusk, the soft voices in the corridors, the harpsichord, the stairs that wound interminably up into the dark, the thousand details of the rooms, the soft, insinuating fear that looked out of corners and never went away. He had walked up the drive to the front door. The lion's head on the door-knocker grinned down at him. He lifted it and struck the wood. No one answered. Again and again he knocked, but the house was quiet. He put his shoulder to the door. It swung open. He had tiptoed along the passages, looked into the rooms, touched the familiar objects. Nothing had changed. And then, when the night had crept out of the leaded windows, he had closed the door of the music room softly behind him. He was filled with a great relief. The longing always at the back of his mind was realized, the lost thing found, and the forgotten thing remembered. This was the end of the journey.

Momentarily, the candles became brighter. He was able to see further into the room. Rising, he walked across and picked up a dusty book laid on the table. *The House of Brember*. He brought it over to the light. Each page was familiar to him, the family, generation by generation, men of thought rather than of action, all visionaries who saw the world from the cloud of their own dreaming. He turned over the pages, until he came to the last: George Henry Brember, last of the line, died...

He looked down on his name, and then closed the book.

Jarley's*

On the day that the travelling waxworks came to town, the attendant vanished. Next morning the proprietor called at the employment agency and asked for a smart lad who could talk English. But the smart lads talked Welsh, and the boy from Bristol had a harelip. So the proprietor returned to his lodgings and, passing the canal, saw Eleazar reading on the bank.

"Any luck?" he enquired.

"I'm not fishing," replied Eleazar.

He was immediately engaged.

It was late in the evening, and the last curious visitor had left the tent. The proprietor counted the day's takings and went away, leaving Eleazar alone in the dark, wax world. Eleazar removed the last cigarette end from the ground and brought out a duster from his pocket. Tremblingly he dusted over the lean, brown body of Hiawatha; tremblingly he patted the pale cheeks of Charlie Peace; tremblingly he dusted over the wax neck of Circe.*

"You forgot my left calf," said Hiawatha.

"You forgot my top lip," said Charlie Peace.

"You forgot my right shoulder," said the temptress.

Eleazar looked at the wax figures in amazement.

"You heard me," said Hiawatha.

"You heard me," said Charlie Peace.

"You heard me," said the temptress.

Eleazar stared around him. The entrance to the tent was a long way off. There was no escape.

"Calf," said Hiawatha.

"Lip," said Charlie Peace.

"Shoulder," said Circe.

Tremblingly Eleazar dusted over the strong-muscled calf; tremblingly he patted the snarling lip; tremblingly he dusted over the wax shoulder.

"That is certainly better," said Hiawatha. "You see," he continued in apology, "I used to run a lot – and you want your calves dusted then, don't you?"

"I do a lot of snarling," said Charlie Peace.

"I do a lot of tempting," said the temptress, "though, really, I should be losing my fascination by this time, and my shoulder is not all that it was. I had it bitten in Aberdare once."

"I remember the night well," said Hiawatha. "Somebody put an old hat on me."

"I remember the night," remarked the murderer, "when as a child I stuck a needle into my nurse: it was a darning needle."

"I remember chasing Minnehaha* all over the rapids," said Hiawatha. "She used to be terribly annoyed when I called her Laughing Water."

"I remember the sea-green eyes of Jason,"* said Circe.

Eleazar could remember nothing. His first fears had vanished, to be replaced by a sense of friendly curiosity. He enquired politely if all was well in the state of wax.

"Indeed," said Hiawatha, "I have little to complain of. There is a great deal to be said for being wax. One has few troubles. It is difficult to receive injury. The sharpest arrow could do little to me: a momentary impression soon to be filled in with a farthing's worth of wax from the local stores. It is a perpetual source of wonder to me that more people do not realize the advantages of a wax life."

"How is it with you, ma'am?" asked Eleazar.

"There is still the desire to tempt," replied the temptress, "that I cannot conquer. And I still remember those confounded sea-green eyes."

"Murder as a profession," began Charlie Peace...

"Henry Wadsworth," began Hiawatha...

"The history of temptation," began the temptress...

And suddenly the three wax figures were still.

Eleazar shuffled further along the tent.

"Eleazar," said an ape.

"Sir?" said Eleazar.

"Life," said the ape, "is a never-ending mystery. We are born. Why are we born? We die. The reason is obvious. The life of the body is short, and the veins are incapable of holding an eternal supply of blood."

Eleazar would have continued on his way, but the ape held up its hand. "Stop," said the ape. "Consider the man of flesh and the man of wax. Everything is done for the wax man; he is made painlessly and skilfully; he is found a house in a nice waterproof tent or in the interior of a large and hygienic building; he is clothed, brushed and dusted; he is the cynosure of all eyes. Think of the opportunities he enjoys to study the mentality of his near neighbour – man. Day after day, the faces of men are pressed close to mine; I see into men's eyes; I listen to their conversations. The man of wax is an unchanging, unprejudiced and unemotional observer of the human comedy."

"Sir," said Eleazar, "you talk very well for an ape."

"Eleazar," said the ape, "I have known this frame of wax for two days only. I was the late attendant."

"Tell me," said Eleazar, "do you feel the cold?"

"Neither cold nor warmth."

"Do you feel hunger?"

"Neither hunger nor thirst. I feel nothing. I want nothing. I am perpetually happy."

Eleazar removed his jacket and trousers.

"Make room – move up," said Eleazar.

Next morning the proprietor called at the employment agency and asked for a smart lad.

"He must be careful, too," he explained, "for my waxworks has just been presented with an expensive new figure."

"An historical figure?"

"No, no," said the proprietor, "the figure of a Welsh Druid in a long white shirt."

After the Fair*

The fair was over, the lights in the coconut stalls were put out, and the wooden horses stood still in the darkness, waiting for the music and the hum of the machines that would set them trotting forward. One by one, in every booth, the naphtha jets were turned down and the canvases pulled over the little gaming tables. The crowd went home, and there were lights in the windows of the caravans.

Nobody had noticed the girl. In her black clothes she stood against the side of the roundabouts, hearing the last feet tread upon the sawdust and the last voices die in the distance. Then, all alone on the deserted ground, surrounded by the shapes of wooden horses and cheap fairy boats, she looked for a place to sleep. Now here and now there, she raised the canvas that shrouded the coconut stalls and peered into the warm darkness. She was frightened to step inside, and as a mouse scampered across the littered shavings on the floor, or as the canvas creaked and a rush of wind set it dancing, she ran away and hid again near the roundabouts. Once she stepped on the boards; the bells round a horse's throat jingled and were still; she did not dare breathe again until all was quiet and the darkness had forgotten the noise of the bells. Then here and there she went peeping for a bed, into each gondola, under each tent. But there was nowhere, nowhere in all the fair for her to sleep. One place was too silent, and in another was the noise of mice. There was straw in the corner of the Astrologer's tent, but it moved as she touched it; she knelt by its side and put out her hand; she felt a baby's hand upon her own.

Now there was nowhere, so slowly she turned towards the caravans on the outskirts of the field, and found all but two to be unlit. She waited, clutching her empty bag and wondering which caravan she should disturb. At last she decided to knock upon the window of the little shabby one near her, and, standing on tiptoes, she looked in. The fattest man she had ever seen was sitting in front of the stove, toasting a piece of bread. She tapped three times on the glass, then hid in the shadows. She heard him come to the top of the steps and call out "Who? Who?", but she dare not answer. "Who? Who?" he called again.

She laughed at his voice, which was as thin as he was fat.

He heard her laughter and turned to where the darkness concealed her. "First you tap," he said, "then you hide, then you laugh."

She stepped into the circle of light, knowing she need no longer hide herself.

"A girl," he said. "Come in, and wipe your feet." He did not wait, but retreated into his caravan, and she could do nothing but follow him up the steps and into the crowded room. He was seated again, and toasting the same piece of bread. "Have you come in?" he said, for his back was towards her.

"Shall I close the door?" she asked, and closed it before he replied.

She sat on the bed and watched him toast the bread until it burned.

"I can toast better than you," she said.

"I don't doubt it," said the Fat Man.

She watched him put the charred toast upon a plate by his side, take another round of bread and hold that, too, in front of the stove. It burned very quickly.

"Let me toast it for you," she said. Ungraciously he handed her the fork and the loaf.

"Cut it," he said, "toast it and eat it."

She sat on the chair.

"See the dent you've made on my bed," said the Fat Man. "Who are you to come in and dent my bed?"

"My name is Annie," she told him.

Soon all the bread was toasted and buttered, so she put it in the centre of the table and arranged two chairs.

"I'll have mine on the bed," said the Fat Man. "You'll have it here."

When they had finished their supper, he pushed back his chair and stared at her across the table.

"I am the Fat Man," he said. "My home is Treorchy; the Fortune-Teller next door is Aberdare."

"I am nothing to do with the fair," she said. "I am Cardiff."

"There's a town," agreed the Fat Man. He asked her why she had come away.

"Money," said Annie.

Then he told her about the fair and the places he had been to and the people he had met. He told her his age and his weight and the names of his brothers and what he would call his son. He showed her a picture of Boston Harbour and the photograph of his mother, who lifted weights. He told her how summer looked in Ireland.

"I've always been a fat man," he said, "and now I'm the Fat Man – there's nobody to touch me for fatness." He told her of a heatwave in Sicily and of the Mediterranean Sea. She told him of the baby in the Astrologer's tent.

"That's the stars again," he said.

"The baby'll die," said Annie.

He opened the door and walked out into the darkness. She looked about her, but did not move, wondering if he had gone to fetch a policeman. It would never do to be caught by the policeman again. She stared through the open door into the inhospitable night and drew her chair closer to the stove.

"Better to be caught in the warmth," she said. But she trembled at the sound of the Fat Man approaching, and pressed her hands upon her thin breast as he climbed up the steps like a walking mountain. She could see him smile through the darkness.

"See what the stars have done," he said, and brought in the Astrologer's baby in his arms.

After she had nursed it against her and it had cried on the bosom of her dress, she told him how she had feared his going.

"What should I be doing with a policeman?"

She told him that the policeman wanted her.

"What have you done for a policeman to be wanting you?"

She did not answer, but took the child nearer to her wasted breast. He saw her thinness.

"You must eat, Cardiff," he said.

Then the child began to cry. From a little wail its voice rose into a tempest of despair. The girl rocked it to and fro on her lap, but nothing soothed it.

"Stop it! Stop it!" said the Fat Man, and the tears increased. Annie smothered it in kisses, but it howled again.

"We must do something," she said.

"Sing it a lullaby."

She sang, but the child did not like her singing.

"There's only one thing," said Annie, "we must take it on the roundabouts." With the child's arm around her neck she stumbled down the steps and ran towards the deserted fair, the Fat Man panting behind her.

She found her way through the tents and stalls into the centre of the ground, where the wooden horses stood waiting, and clambered up onto a saddle. "Start the engine," she called out. In the distance the Fat Man could be heard cranking up the antique machine that drove the horses all the day into a wooden gallop. She heard the spasmodic humming of the engines; the boards rattled under the horses' feet. She saw the Fat Man get up by her side, pull the central lever and climb onto the saddle of the smallest horse of all. As the roundabout started, slowly at first and slowly gaining speed, the child at the girl's breast stopped crying and clapped its hands. The night wind tore through its hair, the music jangled in its ears. Round and round the wooden horses sped, drowning the cries of the wind with the beating of their hooves.

And so the men from the caravans found them, the Fat Man and the girl in black with a baby in her arms, racing round and round on their mechanical steeds to the ever-increasing music of the organ.

The Enemies*

It was morning in the green acres of the Jarvis Valley,* and Mr Owen was picking the weeds from the edges of his garden path. A great wind pulled at his beard, the vegetable world roared under his feet. A rook had lost itself in the sky, and was making a noise to its mate, but the mate never came, and the rook flew into the west with a woe in its beak. Mr Owen, who had stood up to ease his shoulders and look at the sky, observed how dark the wings beat against the red sun. In her draughty kitchen Mrs Owen grieved over the soup. Once, in past days, the valley had housed the cattle alone; the farm boys came down from the hills to holla at the cattle and to drive them to be milked; but no stranger set foot in the valley. Mr Owen, walking lonely through the country, had come upon it at the end of a late summer evening when the cattle were lying down still, and the stream that divided it was speaking over the pebbles. Here, thought Mr Owen, I will build a small house with one storey, in the middle of the valley, set around by a garden. And, remembering clearly the way he had come along the winding hills, he returned to his village and the questions of Mrs Owen. So it came about that a house with one storey was built in the green fields; a garden was dug and planted, and a low fence put up around the garden to keep the cows from the vegetables.

That was early in the year. Now summer and autumn had gone over; the garden had blossomed and died; there was frost at the weeds. Mr Owen bent down again, tidying the path, while the wind blew back the heads of the nearby grasses and made an oracle of each green mouth. Patiently he strangled the weeds; up came the roots, making war in the soil around them; insects were busy in the holes where the weeds had sprouted, but, dying between his fingers, they left no stain. He grew tired of their death, and tireder of the fall of the weeds. Up came the roots, down went the cheap, green heads.

Mrs Owen, peering into the depths of her crystal, had left the soup to bubble on unaided. The ball grew dark, then lightened as a rainbow moved within it. Growing hot like a sun, and cooling again like an arctic star, it shone in the folds of her dress, where she held it lovingly. The tea leaves in her cup at breakfast had told of a dark stranger. What would the crystal tell her? Mrs Owen wondered.

Up came the roots, and a crooked worm, disturbed by the probing of the fingers, wriggled blind in the sun. Of a sudden the valley filled all its hollows with the wind, with the voice of the roots, with the breathing of the nether sky. Not only a mandrake screams; torn roots have their cries; each weed Mr Owen pulled out of the ground screamed like a baby. In the village behind the hill the wind would be raging, the clothes on the garden lines would be set to strange dances. And women with shapes in their wombs would feel a new knocking as they bent over the steamy tubs. Life would go on in the veins, in the bones, the binding flesh, that had their seasons and their weathers even as the valley binding the house about with the flesh of the green grass.

The ball, like an open grave, gave up its dead to Mrs Owen. She stared on the lips of women and the hairs of men that wound into a pattern on the face of the crystal world. But suddenly the patterns were swept away, and she could see nothing but the shapes of the Jarvis hills. A man with a black hat was walking down the paths into the invisible valley beneath. If he walked any nearer, he would fall into her lap. "There's a man with a black hat walking on the hills," she called through the window. Mr Owen smiled and went on weeding.

It was at this time that the Reverend Mr Davies lost his way; he had been losing it most of the morning, but now he had lost it altogether, and stood perturbed under a tree on the rim of the Jarvis hills. A great wind blew through the branches, and a great grey-green earth moved unsteadily beneath him. Wherever he looked, the hills stormed up to the sky, and, wherever he sought to hide from the wind, he was frightened by the darkness. The farther he walked, the stranger was the scenery around him; it rose to undreamt-of heights, and then fell down again into a valley no bigger than the palm of his hand. And the trees walked like men. By a divine coincidence he reached the rim of the hills just as the sun reached the centre of the sky. With the wide world rocking from horizon to horizon, he stood under a tree and looked down into the valley. In the fields was a little house with a garden. The valley roared around it, the wind leapt at it like a boxer, but the house stood still. To Mr Davies it seemed as though the house had been carried out of a village by a large bird and placed in the very middle of the tumultuous universe.

But as he climbed over the craggy edges and down the side of the hill, he lost his place in Mrs Owen's crystal. A cloud displaced his black hat, and under the cloud walked a very old phantom, a shape of air with stars all frozen in its beard, and a half-moon for a smile. Mr Davies knew nothing of this as the stones scratched his hands. He was old, he was drunk with the wine of the morning, but the stuff that came out of his cuts was a human blood.

Nor did Mr Owen, with his face near the soil and his hands on the necks of the screaming weeds, know of the transformation in the crystal. He had heard Mrs Owen prophesy the coming of the black hat, and had smiled as he always smiled at her faith in the powers of darkness. He had looked up when she called, and, smiling, had returned to the clearer call of the ground. "Multiply, multiply," he had said to the worms disturbed in their channelling, and had cut the brown worms in half so that the halves might breed and spread their life over the garden and go out, contaminating, into the fields and the bellies of the cattle.

Of this Mr Davies knew nothing. He saw a young man with a beard bent industriously over the garden soil; he saw that the house was a pretty picture, with the face of a pale young woman pressed up against the window. And, removing his black hat, he introduced himself as the rector of a village some ten miles away.

"You are bleeding," said Mr Owen.

Mr Davies's hands, indeed, were covered in blood.

When Mrs Owen had seen to the rector's cuts, she sat him down in the armchair near the window and made him a strong cup of tea.

"I saw you on the hill," she said, and he asked her how she had seen him, for the hills are high and a long way off.

"I have good eyes," she answered.

He did not doubt her. Her eyes were the strangest he had seen.

"It is quiet here," said Mr Davies.

"We have no clock," she said, and laid the table for three.

"You are very kind."

"We are kind to those that come to us."

He wondered how many came to the lonely house in the valley, but did not question her for fear of what she would reply. He guessed she was an uncanny woman loving the dark, because it was dark. He was too old to question the secrets of darkness, and now, with the black suit torn and wet and his thin hands bound with the bandages of the stranger woman, he felt older than ever. The winds of the morning might blow him down, and the sudden dropping of the dark be blind in his eyes. Rain might pass through him as it passes through the body of a ghost. A tired, white-haired old man, he sat under the window, almost invisible against the panes and the white cloth of the chair.

Soon the meal was ready, and Mr Owen came in unwashed from the garden.

"Shall I say grace?" asked Mr Davies when all three were seated around the table.

Mrs Owen nodded.

"O Lord God Almighty, bless this our meal," said Mr Davies. Looking up as he continued his prayer, he saw that Mr and Mrs Owen had closed their eyes. "We thank Thee for the bounties that Thou hast given us." And he saw that the lips of Mr and Mrs Owen were moving softly. He could not hear what they said, but he knew that the prayers they spoke were not his prayers.

"Amen," said all three together.

Mr Owen, proud in his eating, bent over the plate as he had bent over the complaining weeds. Outside the window was the brown body of the earth, the green skin of the grass, and the breasts of the Jarvis hills; there was a wind that chilled the animal earth, and a sun that had drunk up the dews on the fields; there was creation sweating out of the pores of the trees; and the grains of sand on faraway seashores would be multiplying as the sea rolled over them. He felt the coarse foods on his tongue; there was a meaning in the rind of the meat, and a purpose in the lifting of food to mouth. He saw, with a sudden satisfaction, that Mrs Owen's throat was bare.

She, too, was bent over her plate, but was letting the teeth of her fork nibble at the corners of it. She did not eat, for the old powers were upon her, and she dared not lift up her head for the greenness of her eyes. She knew by the sound which way the wind blew in the valley; she knew the stage of the sun by the curve of the shadows on the cloth. Oh, that she could take her crystal and see within it the stretches of darkness covering up this winter light! But there was a darkness gathering in her mind, drawing in the light around her. There was a ghost on her left; with all her strength she drew in the intangible light that moved around him, and mixed it in her dark brains.

Mr Davies, like a man sucked by a bird, felt desolation in his veins, and, in a sweet delirium, told of his adventures on the hills, of how it had been cold and blowing, and how the hills went up and down. He had been lost, he said, and had found a dark retreat to shelter from the bullies in the wind, but the darkness had frightened him, and he had walked again on the hills, where the morning tossed him about like a ship on the sea. Wherever he went, he was blown in the open or frightened in the narrow shades. There was nowhere, he said pityingly, for an old man to go. Loving his parish, he had loved the surrounding lands, but the hills had given under his feet or plunged him into the air. And, loving his God, he had loved the darkness where men of old had worshipped the dark invisible. But now the hill caves were full of shapes and voices that mocked him because he was old.

"He is frightened of the dark," thought Mrs Owen, "the lovely dark." With a smile, Mr Owen thought: "He is frightened of the worm in the earth, of the copulation in the tree, of the living grease in the soil." They looked at the old man, and saw that he was more ghostly than ever. The window behind him cast a ragged circle of light round his head.

Suddenly Mr Davies knelt down to pray. He did not understand the cold in his heart nor the fear that bewildered him as he knelt, but, speaking his prayers for deliverance, he stared up at the shadowed eyes of Mrs Owen and at the smiling eyes of her husband. Kneeling on the carpet at the head of the table, he stared in bewilderment at the dark mind and the gross dark body. He stared and he prayed, like an old god beset by his enemies.

In the Garden*

The boy was more afraid of the dark garden than of anything else in the world. It was frightening enough in the twilight, but when there was blackness above and below and the trees spoke among themselves, the garden was too terrible to think about.

He tried to convince himself that behind the red curtains there lay nothing at all, and that there was nothing at all anywhere, only the bright room, his mother and himself. In the morning, the garden was full of delight: the grass was long and unkempt; there were sunflowers that nobody had planted there. Against the farther wall was a summer house, the home of beetles, where he kept his collection of strange pebbles and his picture postcards. There he would sit for as long as the sunlight lasted, with his back against the wood box on the seat and his feet on an old and mysterious trunk. The trunk was all the more fascinating because there was nothing in it at all. Once he had prised up the rusty padlock with his pocket knife and very fearfully opened the lid, to find only emptiness and the smell of rot. He felt sure that it must have a secret drawer somewhere that held precious stones as bright as the sun, and he planned, when he should discover them, to sell the treasure to a rich merchant, in return for a journey to the parrot-haunted islands.

But as the last rags of the sunset withered away behind the tallest chimney stack, he would hear the warning voices telling him that it was time for him to go, and he knew that somewhere in the approaching shadows were the ugly night tenants of the garden. Then he would close the door of the summer house very slowly and carefully, and walk up the garden path until he reached the three stone steps that led down to the scullery. These he would take at one leap, and run quickly into the house with all the devils of darkness at his heels.

It was a very hot night. The windows were open, and the spinning jinnies whirled into the house to shake their long legs in the glare of the gas. The boy liked to watch them for as long as they kept to the ceiling, but he hated them when they fell dizzily onto the tablecloth or flew blindly into his face, and worst of all he hated the great grey moths that blundered round the room, for he knew they were in league with the things in the garden outside.

"It's hot in here," his mother said suddenly. "Put out the chairs on the lawn."

She left him alone in the kitchen. He picked up a chair, then set it down again and went out into the scullery. He opened the garden door, and a great moth flew into his face. Then he stepped out into the garden and faced the enemies.

Hooded and gloved in black, they lined the paths and stood across the grass. He squared his shoulders and mounted bravely to the top of the steps. He could not see the faces of the shadows, but they could see his face, for he was framed in the light from the open door. He thought of the summer house in the morning, friendly, dusted with light, and of the trunk where the treasure lay. He went out onto the edge of the grass, and he could not hear the warning of the trees for the drumming of his heart. As he advanced, the shadows curtsied and fell back a little, leaving his path clear to the darkness that was most dreadful of all.

Then he stopped, for he was more afraid than he thought he could ever be. The garden writhed about him, and the walls and the trees shot upwards so that he could not see the sky. The pointed roof of the summer house shot up the dark like a steeple hat. The boy dared not look behind him, for he knew that he was surrounded by his foes, and that their arms were linked behind his back. Very, very soon, they would close in upon him, as though they were playing an innocent game of poor Jenny lies a-weeping,* and one of them would throw a hood over his head. He waited and waited, and still nothing happened, only the gradual mounting of the trees, the walls and the wrongly shaped tower to the sky. He could not see them, for now his hands were over his eyes. The ring closed in upon him. He could hear their feet in the ragged grass and the slipping of their robes over the damp soil.

He threw back his head and stared straight into the eyes of the tallest shadow. For a long while he stared. Then he smiled at his friend the shadow, and held out his arms. The door of the summer house swung back in the wind, and he saw that the trunk, lying open on its side, was full of fire. The precious stones poured from it in streams of silver, of gold and of blue. The garden was bright with their colour.

He opened his arms a little wider, and the stones leapt upwards to his breast. He smiled at the silent watchers, and they dared not meet his eyes. Slowly they melted away, and the trees melted with them. He gathered up the jewels, and, slipping onto his knees, he laid them in the lap of his friend. The door of the summer house closed softly with the falling of the latch, the wind dropped, and still the boy smiled and did not move.

His mother called to him. She called to him again, and still he did not answer, so she ran into the garden with his name on her lips. There, in the middle of the grass, she found the boy kneeling, his face in his hands, in the blinding light of the moon.

Gaspar, Melchior, Balthasar*

A flying fleet came out of the shadow, and the arsenal of the iron mist hovered over the island and, hidden in the smoke of the exhausts, dropped death upon the cities. The men in the cities raced for shelter, fixing their leather masks, their trousers unbuttoned as they scampered out of the urinals, their hair uncombed as they climbed out of a purchased sleep, puffed out of tenement offices, cupping their hands for the exploding manna. Two lovers, struck by the same shell, fell into bliss. Down thumped a ripper of women, a woman with rings on her fingers in the levelling gutter. Bullets broke up the hungry ranks. Crow food sliced about them.

The workers in the south and the north of the island, where death had fallen thinly, were provided with guns and shafts of steel. They cocked the guns and laughed up at the shadow above them. Street rose against street, and city against city. In the ruined cities, along the deserted streets where the dead on the pavements fell apart, the dying spoke women's names, the shadow moved. I saw two ghosts in the avenue by the broken park. They moved among the dead, prying into each shot face, each hollow head, and under each folded eye.

The ships were unloaded at the wharves, the engines cold in the stations, the printing presses silent, and the sentries before the island palace stiff in their boxes. In the parks the birds were singing; a new froth was on the trees; the wind blew the waste paper up the paths. I walked all that morning, a ghost. Wherever I walked, in street or under arch, on the grass of the green parks, through alley and slum down to the edge of the corpsy water, I saw the two ghosts searching. They moved among the dead, questioning each dead eye, invisibly touching the hems of the dresses, the young, triangular breasts, the soft heart, the hard loins.

The guns grew quieter in the distance. The last of the first revolution died away in a splutter of fire from the east of the great city. I walked in strange thoroughfares and through the unlit centre of the city, strange itself in its first blindness. As I journeyed through the first stages of the night, coming upon the two ghosts now at a dark corner, now in the shadow of a doorway, and bent for ever over the riddled dead, I held my scarf to my face for the smell of the dead-flowering Black plague would branch from these blacker plants that shot to heaven through the wounds of the unburied fallen. I made my image as I walked, and the hemlock and the upas* sprouted for me from the gutter beds.

It was a minute before midnight that I saw a lantern swinging at the end of a street. It was bright and sweet among the flowers that stank at my side, but, as I moved towards it, I felt the wind of the two ghosts as they drifted past me, and I followed them, calling them by name. There were men at the corner, dark-eyed behind their lantern.

"Who goes there?" they cried.

They swung the lantern before my face.

"Let me pass", I said.

They cried again.

"Where are you going?"

I waited no longer, but knocked the lantern from their hands and plunged into the darkness after the windy ghosts. I ran on and on, with the noise of the revolvers behind me, through a maze of alleys into a moonlit square.

There stood the two ghosts. At their feet lay a dead woman, naked but for her shawl, with a bayonet wound in her breasts. Slowly I stepped towards her. As I watched, a miraculous life stirred in her belly, and the arms of the child in her womb broke, lifted, through the flesh.

The two ghosts bowed down.

Gold, said the first ghost, raising a golden shadow to the light of the moon.

Frankincense, said the second ghost, and his shadowy gift smoked from him.

The noise of the guns grew nearer and still nearer.

I knelt where I stood and felt the new joy of pain as a bullet drove into my breast. I fell upon the pavement near the two lifted arms, and my blood streamed bitterly onto the emerging head.

The End of the River*

Twelve generations of the Quincey family, that dog-faced line, had left their mark upon the manor. The walls remained steadfast, but covered with a green fungus that sprouted upon the Quincey habitations, regardless of pruning. The gardener had not neglected the lawns, and the flower beds, though pale and blowsy, were tended with all his senile care, for Chubb could never die, bound as he was so inextricably to the Quincey bosom. But weeds grew thick where weeds were little expected to grow. Ivy climbed up the walls of the coach house, and, in spite of the daily attentions of the youngest housemaid but one, moss invaded the front steps and rust lay thick upon the knocker. Hens upon the bird-limed patch beyond the kitchen died at a premature age, while the eggs they contrived to lay were rarely oval and often of a withered shape and a rather unpleasant mottled colour. The pigs were fed as heartily as pigs could wish, but they grew thin and died. The cows' milk tasted like vinegar.

The Quincey manor, with its portrait gallery of canine gentlemen, its dining hall furnished in three periods and its perilous verandas from which the bloodless Quinceys, on midsummer nights, would pass their gravish comments on the moon, had resolved to crumble, spurning renovations and improvements, sitting on the camel hill over the disagreeable river, waiting for its end.

And Sir Peregrine, twelfth baron, had nothing but sympathy for it. It had sheltered twelve generations of doggy aristocrats and their litters, had seen small boys grow to be small men, had seen them meet, mate and lie, at last, in the depths of the family vault, their dead paws on their chests. It had entertained near-royalty, and consequently had allotted a royal bedroom to its left wing. Over all the passions of a most impure world it had spread its painted roofs, and, on one notable occasion, had hidden, in a cellar full of stale wine and rats, the murdered body of poor Sir Thomas.

The manor, thought Sir Peregrine, was old enough to die, had pondered enough upon the human follies and felt no fear of death.

Stroking a three days' beard, he placed a deckchair on the safest part of the veranda, looked up into the sun and turned to the year 1889 in the Quincey chronicles.

THE END OF THE RIVER

Somewhere a romantic daughter spelt out her Sunday music. His lady, in the quiet of her room, was writing to an Australian cousin. In his apartment the butler was reading from the literary pages of the *Observer*. Chubb, in the not very far distance, leant on a garden gate and smoked.

Peregrine, read the twelfth baron from the chronicles, took up the title on the death of his father, Belphigor, in 1889. In 1902 he married the Honourable Katerina Hautley, second daughter of Lord and Lady Winch of Alltheway Park, Gloucestershire. From this union were born three daughters: Katerina, who died of influenza in her second year, Astasia and Phoebe Mary. Sir Peregrine was a colonel in the Territorial Army up to the Great War (1914–1918), and an official in the Ministry of War during those troubled years. He was elected Master of the Tidhampton Hunt in 1920, following upon the death of Alderman Alcock, and in 1922 broke his arm while riding with the hounds. In the following year Phoebe Mary married the Honourable Douglas Dougal, son of Sir Douglas and Lady Dougal of Halfandhalf Castle, Perth. In 1924 Phoebe Mary died in childbirth.

That was all. The chronicles of the previous Quincey generations were written in detail and with an ornamentation of style that did credit to the literary accomplishments of the family. But Sir Peregrine dealt in facts, and facts alone. His life until that moment, but shorn of its hopes and foolishness, its strength and weaknesses, delights and dolours, spread over half a page of the ponderous book. This little life set between the eccentricities of the long-winded Belphigor and...

Sir Peregrine put the book down.

Chubb was still leaning and smoking. The smoke rose up vertically into the windless air. Chubb had not moved. His eyes rested on the river, which went Sir Peregrine knew not where, meandering, he supposed, through a world of fields and rushes, making noise over pebbles, till it came to a sudden stop. He had always called it the one river that did not wind safely to the sea.

Astasia had stopped her playing.

Life was good, he found, on most Sunday afternoons. But today he was restless, and could not sit, as he had for so many years, dreamily upon the veranda, feeling the world grow and hum around him, hearing the music of a sweetly untuned piano or the songs of birds.

The day was beautiful. Clouds sailed on the sky. There was a warm sun. He looked down to where the chronicles lay at his feet, and knew, quite suddenly and almost happily, all that was the matter. The time had come for the dissolution of the Quinceys, for the fall of their manor and the end of their dynasty.

Sir Peregrine, lifting the book, took out a pencil used to a stump through the solving of innumerable crossword puzzles.

In 1924, he read again, Phoebe Mary died in childbirth.

Phoebe Mary had been his favourite daughter. He had cried for six nights after she was buried. Then he, too, had buried her, under the clouds and mists of his mind. Once he had forgotten her name. Phoebe Mary? he said, and had fallen to wondering who that could be with such a name.

Phoebe Mary died in childbirth.

The end of the Quinceys, he wrote with the pencil.

Then he added the date.

In the garden he looked around him, at the flowers whose colours were as even as those in a toy paintbox. The little wind there was moved the petals so that they seemed, to him, to breathe for the last time the sweet air of the surrounding beds. He knew they were aware of climax, and loved them for their serenity. Chubb had nurtured them, and the end of the world would see the gardener like a god, waiting in a woman's blue smock for his reward.

The end of the world was the end of the manor. And Chubb, though he would say nothing of it, neither affirm nor contradict, had tended the first bed for the first young baron.

Sir Peregrine found him at the end of the path. The gardener did not move. His arms were resting on the gate that led to the seven fields going down to the river.

Sir Peregrine, wiping a remnant of dinner from his ancient waistcoat, looked down to where the water rolled over the dirty stones. At the end of the water was the end of everything. Today he was to walk over the fields and follow the river where it went, through towns or countries, over hills or under, until the sudden stop.

The garden was humming behind them.

The clouds moved on softly to some stop.

How old are you, Chubb? asked Sir Peregrine. You were the gardener here when Lady Astasia rode to her queen, Elizabeth, over the rocky roads on a piebald horse. You tended the flowers when Quentin, third of the Quinceys, wrote to his lady in an ivory tower, wrapping the verses round a pigeon's throat. At Christmas you made snowmen for me. How many years have you brooded over the dirty river? You always knew the end of all things lay where it stopped. I only knew today. It came to me suddenly, and I knew.

The immortal Chubb made no answer. He tilted his felt hat further back on his head, and sent up a ring of smoke from a white pipe. His face, fringed with a yellowing beard, was as round and expressionless as a saucer. At any time a breath of wind might send another crack along its surface, and make a thousand smiles or frowns. Through a space in his teeth he breathed and whistled, and made a succession of mysterious tunes as he drew at his pipe.

The exterior Chubb belied what was divine beneath. He looked like nothing more than an ancient gardener, with his woman's smock pinned untidily around him.

Chubb, I am going.

Sir Peregrine waited for the words to pierce the gardener's smoky armour.

I am going to follow the river to its end. Tell me one word of cheer before I go. Say goodbye, undying Chubb.

The birds, said the gardener, 'ave 'ad the seeds.

It was enough. Sir Peregrine climbed quickly over the gate and ran down the field. At the end was a stile. He climbed it, and ran again over the uneven grass, his hair leaping about his head and his brass-buttoned waistcoat flapping against his sides. Three fields. Four fields. Sweat ran down his forehead onto his neck and collar. He could hear his heart thundering in his ears. But he kept at the same crazy jog, over another stile, along another field, stopping to climb through a small hole in the hedge, then on again, snorting and blowing.

A crow, perched on a scarecrow's shoulder, suddenly started cawing as the twelfth baron galloped past, then flew above him, spurring him on with harsh cries.

Now he could hear the noise of the river. On the low bank above it, he stared down onto the little fishes and the shining pebbles. The crow, seeing him stop, gave a final sardonic caw and flew back to its lone companion, who was swinging a ragged arm in the wind.

Sir Peregrine felt a great elation surging through him. He turned around and saw the Quincey manor, on its imperial hill, squinting down upon him. He followed the river bank through the dirty fields and through a wood brown with owls' wings. He saw the sun lowering in the sky. Now he no longer ran, but stumbled over the fields, his eyes dim, covered in tears, half unseeing. His clothes were damp about him. His hair, that had, in the mad run down the seven fields, leapt so proudly on his head, straggled onto his wet brow. He was thirsty and tired. But he stumbled on.

Where does the river end? he called out to an old woman driving cows over a green field.

Where does it end? he asked. But the hedges and the ferns and the talking pebbles never replied.

He came at last to a well by the side of a meadow, and there a girl-child was washing clothes. He saw her through his tears and heard her voice singing.

Is this the end?

Yes, said the girl-child.

The end, said Sir Peregrine in a whisper. The end of the manor, the Quinceys and me.

The words made such a nice little rhythm that he started to sing them in his old voice.

The end of the manor, the Quinceys and me.

The child was frightened.

For twelve generations, he said, the Quinceys have lived their little lives up there. And he pointed with a bewildered hand towards the sky. This is the end, he said.

Yes, said the child.

What is the end? he said. What have you to give? What at the end?

He held his arms out.

With a frightened cry, the girl-child thrust an unwashed napkin into his hand. He clasped it, and she ran away. Not looking, but holding it to his breast and making soft, delighted noises in his throat, Sir Peregrine lay down upon the grass. The moon came up. Chubb had not failed.

And that immortal gardener, as the twelfth baron lay down on a bed of grass and soft manure, was smoking a white pipe in the quiet of the Quincey gardens. Sunday was almost passed, and then there would be another day. Contentedly the ancient gardener, in his woman's smock, leant on the garden gate and smoked.

The Tree*

Rising from the house that faced the Jarvis hills in the long distance, there was a tower for the day birds to build in and for the owls to fly around at night. From the village the light in the tower window shone like a glow-worm through the panes, but the room under the sparrows' nests was rarely lit; webs were spun over its unwashed ceilings; it stared over twenty miles of the up-and-down county, and the corners kept their secrets where there were claw marks in the dust.

The child knew the house from roof to cellar; he knew the irregular lawns and the gardener's shed, where flowers burst out of their jars; but he could not find the key that opened the door of the tower.

The house changed to his moods, and a lawn was the sea or the shore or the sky or whatever he wished it. When a lawn was a sad mile of water and he was sailing on a broken flower down the waves, the gardener would come out of his shed near the island of bushes. He too would take a stalk and sail. Straddling a garden broom, he would fly wherever the child wished. He knew every story from the beginning of the world.

"In the beginning," he would say, "there was a tree."

"What kind of a tree?"

"The tree where that blackbird's whistling."

"A hawk, a hawk," cried the child.

The gardener would look up at the tree, seeing a monstrous hawk perched on a bough or an eagle swinging in the wind.

The gardener loved the Bible. When the sun sank and the garden was full of people, he would sit with a candle in his shed, reading of the first love and the legend of apples and serpents. But the death of Christ on a tree he loved most. Trees made a fence around him, and he knew of the changing of the seasons by the hues on the bark and the rushing of sap through the covered roots. His world moved and changed as spring moved along the branches, changing their nakedness; his God grew up like a tree from the apple-shaped earth, giving bud to His children and letting His children be blown from their places by the breezes of winter; winter and death moved in one wind. He would sit in his shed and read of the crucifixion, looking over the jars on his window shelf into the winter nights. He would think that love fails on such nights, and that many of its children are cut down.

The child transfigured the blowsy lawns with his playing. The gardener called him by his mother's name, and seated him on his knee, and talked to him of the wonders of Jerusalem and the birth in the manger.

"In the beginning was the village of Bethlehem," he whispered to the child before the bell rang for tea out of the growing darkness.

"Where is Bethlehem?"

"Far away," said the gardener, "in the East."

To the east stood the Jarvis hills, hiding the sun, their trees drawing up the moon out of the grass.

The child lay in bed. He watched the rocking horse and wished that it would grow wings so that he could mount it and ride into the Arabian sky. But the winds of Wales blew at the curtains, and crickets made a noise in the untidy plot under the window. His toys were dead. He started to cry and then stopped, knowing no reason for tears. The night was windy and cold; he was warm under the sheets; the night was as big as a hill; he was a boy in bed.

Closing his eyes, he stared into a spinning cavern deeper than the darkness of the garden, where the first tree on which the unreal birds had fastened stood alone and bright as fire. The tears ran back under his lids as he thought of the first tree that was planted so near him, like a friend in the garden. He crept out of bed and tiptoed to the door. The rocking horse bounded forward on its springs, startling the child into a noiseless scamper back to bed. The child looked at the horse, and the horse was quiet; he tiptoed again along the carpet and reached the door, and turned the knob around, and ran onto the landing. Feeling blindly in front of him, he made his way to the top of the stairs; he looked down the dark stairs into the hall, seeing a host of shadows curve in and out of the corners, hearing their sinuous voices, imagining the pits of their eyes and their lean arms. But they would be little and secret and bloodless, not cased in invisible armour, but wound around with cloths as thin as a web; they would whisper as he walked, touch him on the shoulder, and say S in his ear. He went down the stairs; not a shadow moved in the hall; the corners were empty. He put out his hand and patted the darkness, thinking to feel some dry and velvet head creep under the fingers and edge, like a mist, into the nails. But there was nothing. He opened the front door, and the shadows swept into the garden.

THE TREE

Once on the path, his fears left him. The moon had lain down on the unweeded beds, and her frosts were spread on the grass. At last he came to the illuminated tree at the long gravel end, older even than the marvel of light, with the woodlice asleep under the bark, with the boughs standing out from the body like the frozen arms of a woman. The child touched the tree; it bent as to his touch. He saw a star, brighter than any in the sky, burn steadily above the first birds' tower and shine on nowhere but on the leafless boughs and the trunk and the travelling roots.

The child had not doubted the tree. He said his prayers to it, with knees bent on the blackened twigs the night wind fetched to the ground. Then, trembling with love and cold, he ran back over the lawns towards the house.

There was an idiot to the east of the county who walked the land like a beggar. Now at a farmhouse and now at a widow's cottage, he begged for his bread. A parson gave him a suit, and it lopped round his hungry ribs and shoulders and waved in the wind as he shambled over the fields. But his eyes were so wide and his neck so clear of the country dirt that no one refused him what he asked. And, asking for water, he was given milk.

"Where do you come from?"

"From the east," he said.

So they knew he was an idiot, and gave him a meal to clean the yards.

As he bent with a rake over the dung and the trodden grain, he heard a voice rise in his heart. He put his hand into the cattle's hay, caught a mouse, rubbed his hand over its muzzle and let it go away.

All day the thought of the tree was with the child; all night it stood up in his dreams as the star stood above its plot. One morning towards the middle of December, when the wind from the farthest hills was rushing around the house and the snow of the dark hours had not dissolved from lawns and roofs, he ran to the gardener's shed. The gardener was repairing a rake he had found broken. Without a word, the child sat on a seed box at his feet and watched him tie the teeth, and knew that the wire would not keep them together. He looked at the gardener's boots, wet with snow, at the patched knees of his trousers, at the undone buttons of his coat and the folds of his belly under the patched flannel shirt. He looked at his hands as they busied themselves over the golden knots of wire: they were hard, brown hands, with the stains of the soil under the broken nails and the stains of tobacco on the tips of the fingers. Now the lines of the gardener's face were set in determination as time upon time he knotted the iron teeth only to feel them shake insecurely from the handle. The child was frightened of the strength and uncleanliness of the old man, but, looking at the long, thick beard, unstained and white as fleece, he soon became reassured. The beard was the beard of an apostle.

"I prayed to the tree," said the child.

"Always pray to a tree," said the gardener, thinking of Calvary and Eden.

"I pray to the tree every night."

"Pray to a tree."

The wire slid over the teeth.

"I pray to that tree."

The wire snapped.

The child was pointing over the glasshouse flowers to the tree that, alone of all the trees in the garden, had no sign of snow.

"An elder," said the gardener, but the child stood up from his box and shouted so loud that the unmended rake fell with a clatter on the floor.

"The first tree. The first tree you told me of. In the beginning was the tree, you said. I heard you," the child shouted.

"The elder is as good as another," said the gardener, lowering his voice to humour the child.

"The first tree of all," said the child in a whisper.

Reassured again by the gardener's voice, he smiled through the window at the tree, and again the wire crept over the broken rake.

"God grows in strange trees," said the old man. "His trees come to rest in strange places."

As he unfolded the story of the twelve stages of the cross, the tree waved its boughs to the child. An apostle's voice rose out of the tarred lungs.

So they hoisted him up on a tree, and drove nails through his belly and his feet.

There was the blood of the noon sun on the trunk of the elder, staining the bark.

* * *

The idiot stood on the Jarvis hills, looking down into the immaculate valley from whose waters and grasses the mists of morning rose and were lost. He saw the dew dissolving, the cattle staring into the stream and the dark clouds flying away at the rumour of the sun. The sun turned at the edges of the thin and watery sky like a sweet in a glass of water. He was hungry for light as the first and almost invisible rain fell on his lips; he plucked at the grass, and, tasting it, felt it lie green on his tongue. So there was light in his mouth, and light was a sound at his ears, and the whole dominion of light in the valley that had such a curious name. He had known of the Jarvis hills; their shapes rose over the slopes of the county to be seen for miles around, but no one had told him of the valley lying under the hills. Bethlehem, said the idiot to the valley, turning over the sounds of the word and giving it all the glory of the Welsh morning. He brothered the world around him, sipped at the air, as a child newly born sips and brothers the light. The life of the Jarvis Valley, steaming up from the body of the grass and the trees and the long hand of the stream, lent him a new blood. Night had emptied the idiot's veins, and dawn in the valley filled them again.

"Bethlehem," said the idiot to the valley.

The gardener had no present to give the child, so he took out a key from his pocket and said: "This is the key to the tower. On Christmas Eve I will unlock the door for you."

Before it was dark, he and the child climbed the stairs to the tower; the key turned in the lock, and the door, like the lid of a secret box, opened and let them in. The room was empty. "Where are the secrets?" asked the child, staring up at the matted rafters and into the spiders' corners and along the leaden panes of the window.

"It is enough that I have given you the key," said the gardener, who believed the key of the universe to be hidden in his pocket along with the feathers of birds and the seeds of flowers.

The child began to cry because there were no secrets. Over and over again he explored the empty room, kicking up the dust to look for a colourless trapdoor, tapping the unpanelled walls for the hollow voice of a room beyond the tower. He brushed the webs from the window, and looked out through the dust into the snowing Christmas Eve. A world of hills stretched far away into the measured sky, and the tops of hills he had never seen climbed up to meet the falling flakes. Woods and rocks, wide seas of barren land, and a new tide of mountain sky sweeping through the black beeches, lay before him. To the east were the outlines of nameless hill creatures and a den of trees.

"Who are they? Who are they?"

"They are the Jarvis hills," said the gardener, "which have been from the beginning."

He took the child by the hand and led him away from the window. The key turned in the lock.

That night the child slept well; there was power in snow and darkness; there was unalterable music in the silence of the stars; there was a silence in the hurrying wind. And Bethlehem had been nearer than he expected.

* * *

On Christmas morning the idiot walked into the garden. His hair was wet, and his flaked and ragged shoes were thick with the dirt of the fields. Tired with the long journey from the Jarvis hills, and weak for the want of food, he sat down under the elder tree where the gardener had rolled a log. Clasping his hands in front of him, he saw the desolation of the flower beds and the weeds that grew in profusion on the edges of the paths. The tower stood up like a tree of stone and glass over the red eaves. He pulled his coat collar round his neck as a fresh wind sprang up and struck the tree; he looked down at his hands and saw that they were praying. Then a fear of the garden came over him, the shrubs were his enemies, and the trees that made an avenue down to the gate lifted their arms in horror. The place was too high, peering down onto the tall hills; the place was too low, shivering up at the plumed shoulders of a new mountain. Here the wind was too wild, fuming about the silence, raising a Jewish voice out of the elder boughs; here the silence beat like a human heart. And as he sat under the cruel hills, he heard a voice that was in him cry out: "Why did you bring me here?"

He could not tell why he had come; they had told him to come and had guided him, but he did not know who they were. The voice of a people rose out of the garden beds, and rain swooped down from heaven.

"Let me be," said the idiot, and made a little gesture against the sky. There is rain on my face, there is wind on my cheeks. He brothered the rain.

So the child found him under the shelter of the tree, bearing the torture of the weather with a divine patience, letting his long hair blow where it would, with his mouth set in a sad smile.

Who was this stranger? He had fires in his eyes, the flesh of his neck under the gathered coat was bare. Yet he smiled as he sat in his rags under a tree on Christmas Day.

"Where do you come from?" asked the child.

"From the east," answered the idiot.

The gardener had not lied, and the secret of the tower was true: this dark and shabby tree, that glistened only in the night, was the first tree of all.

But he asked again:

"Where do you come from?"
"From the Jarvis hills."
"Stand up against the tree."
The idiot, still smiling, stood up with his back to the elder.
"Put out your arms like this."
The idiot put out his arms.

The child ran as fast as he could to the gardener's shed, and, returning over the sodden lawns, saw that the idiot had not moved, but stood, straight and smiling, with his back to the tree and his arms stretched out.

"Let me tie your hands."

The idiot felt the wire that had not mended the rake close round his wrists. It cut into the flesh, and the blood from the cuts fell shining onto the tree.

"Brother," he said. He saw that the child held silver nails in the palm of his hand.

The Visitor*

His hands were weary, though all night they had lain over the sheets of his bed and he had moved them only to his mouth and his wild heart. The veins ran, unhealthily blue streams, into the white sea. Milk at his side steamed out of a chipped cup. He smelt the morning, and knew that cocks in the yard were putting back their heads and crowing at the sun. What were the sheets around him if not the covering sheets of the dead? What was the busy-voiced clock, sounding between photographs of mother and dead wife, if not the voice of an old enemy? Time was merciful enough to let the sun shine on his bed, and merciless to chime the sun away when night came over and even more he needed the red light and the clear heat.

Rhianon was attendant on a dead man, and put the chipped edge of the cup to a dead lip. It could not be heart that beat under the ribs. Hearts do not beat in the dead. While he had lain ready for the inch-tape* and the acid, Rhianon had cut open his chest with a book knife, torn out the heart, put in the clock. He heard her say, for the third time, "Drink the lovely milk." And, feeling it run sour over his tongue, and her hand caress his forehead, he knew he was not dead. He was a living man. For many miles the months flowed into the years, rounding the dry days.

Callaghan today would sit and talk with him. He heard in his brain the voices of Callaghan and Rhianon battle until he slept, and tasted the blood of words. His hands were weary. He brooded over his long, white body, marking the ribs stick through the sides. The hands had held other hands and thrown a ball high into the air. Now they were dead hands. He could wind them about his hair and let them rest untingling on his belly or lose them in the valley between Rhianon's breasts. It did not matter what he did with them. They were as dead as the hands of the clock, and moved to clockwork.

"Shall I close the windows until the sun's warmer?" said Rhianon.

"I'm not cold."

He would tell her that the dead feel neither cold nor warmth: sun and wind could never penetrate his cloths. But she would laugh in her kind way and kiss him on the forehead and say to him, "Peter, what's getting you down? You'll be out and about one day."

One day he would walk on the Jarvis hills like a boy's ghost, and hear the people say: "There walks the ghost of Peter, a poet, who was dead for years before they buried him."

Rhianon tucked the sheets around his shoulders, gave him a morning kiss and carried the chipped cup away.

A man with a brush had drawn a rib of colour under the sun and painted many circles around the circle of the sun. Death was a man with a scythe, but that summer day no living stalk was to be cut down.

The invalid waited for his visitor. Peter waited for Callaghan. His room was a world within a world. A world in him went round and round, and a sun rose in him and a moon fell. Callaghan was the west wind, and Rhianon blew away the chills of the west wind like a wind from Tahiti.

He let his hand rest on his head, stone on stone. Never had the voice of Rhianon been so remote as when it told him that the sour milk was lovely. What was she but a sweetheart talking madly to her sweetheart under a coffin of garments? Somebody in the night had turned him up and emptied him of all but a false heart. That under the ribs' armour was not his, not his the beating of a vein in the foot. His arms could no longer make their movements nor a circle around a girl to shield her from winds and robbers. There was nothing more remote under the sun than his own name, and poetry was a string of words stringed on a beanstalk. With his lips he rounded a little ball of sound into some shape and spoke a word.

There was no tomorrow for dead men. He could not think that after the next night and its sleeping, life would sprout up again like a flower through a coffin's cracks.

His room around him was a vast place. From their frames the lying likenesses of women looked down on him. That was the face of his mother, that nearly yellow oval in its frame of old gold and thinning hair. And, next to her, dead Mary. Though Callaghan blew hard, the walls around Mary would never fall down. He thought of her as she had been, remembered her "Peter, darling, Peter" and her smiling eyes.

He remembered he had not smiled since that night, seven years ago, when his heart had trembled so violently within him that he had fallen to the ground. There had been strengthening in the unbelievable setting of the sun. Over the hills and the roof went the broad moons, and summer came after spring. How had he lived at all when Callaghan had not blown away the webs of the world with a great shout and Millicent spread her loveliness about him? But the dead need no friends. He peered over the turned coffin lid. Stiff and straight, a man of wax stared back. Taking away the pennies from those dead eyes, he looked on his own face.

"Breed, cardboard on cardboard," he had cried, "before I blow down your paste huts with one bellow out of my lungs." When Mary came, there was nothing between the changing of the days but the divinity he had built around her. His child killed Mary in her womb. He felt his body turn to vapour, and men who had been light as air walked, metal-hooved, through and beyond him.

He started to cry: "Rhianon, Rhianon, someone has upped and kicked me in the side. Drip, drip, goes my blood in me. Rhianon," he cried.

She hurried upstairs, and time and time over again wiped away the tears from his cheeks with the sleeve of her dress.

He lay still as the morning matured and grew up into a noble noon. Rhianon passed in and out, her dress, he smelt as she bent over him, smelling of clover and milk. With a new surprise he followed her cool movements around the room, the sweep of her hands as she brushed the dead Mary in her frame. With such surprise, he thought, do the dead follow the movements of the quick, seeing the bloom under the living skin. She should be singing as she moved from mantelpiece to window, putting things right, or should be humming like a bee about her work. But if she had spoken, or laughed, or struck her nails against the thin metal of the candlesticks, drawing forth a bellnote, or if the room had been suddenly crowded with the noises of birds, he would have wept again. It pleased him to look upon the unmoving waves of the bedclothes, and think himself an island set somewhere in the South Sea. Upon this island of rich and miraculous plants, the seeds grown fruits hung from the trees and, smaller than apples, dropped with the Pacific winds onto the ground to lie there and be the harbourers of the summer slugs.

And thinking of the island set somewhere in the south caverns, he thought of water and longed for water. Rhianon's dress, rustling about her, made the soft noise of water. He called her over to him and touched the bosom of her dress, feeling the water on his hands. "Water," he told her, and told her how, as a boy, he had lain on the rocks, his fingers tracing cool shapes on the surfaces of the pools. She brought him water in a glass, and held the glass up level with his eyes so that he could see the room through a wall of water. He did not drink, and she set the glass aside. He imagined the coolness under the sea. Now, on a summer day soon after noon, he wished again for water to close utterly around him, to be no island set above the water, but a green place under, staring around a dizzy cavern. He thought of some cool words, and made a line about an olive tree that grew under a lake. But the tree was a tree of words, and the lake rhymed with another word.

"Sit and read to me, Rhianon."

"After you have eaten," she said, and brought him food.

He could not think that she had gone down into the kitchen and, with her own hands, prepared his meal. She had gone and had returned with food, as simply as a maiden out of the Old Testament. Her name meant nothing. It was a cool sound. She had a strange name out of the Bible. Such a woman had washed the body after it had been taken off the tree, with cool and competent fingers that touched on the holes like ten blessings. He could cry out to her: "Put a sweet herb under my arm. With your spittle make me fragrant."

"What shall I read you?" she asked when at last she sat by his side.

He shook his head, not caring what she read so long as he could hear her speak and think of nothing but the inflections of her voice.

"Ah! Gentle may I lay me down, and gentle rest my head,
And gentle sleep the sleep of death, and gentle hear the voice
Of Him that walketh in the garden in the evening time."*

She read on until the Worm sat on the Lily's leaf.*

Death lay over his limbs again, and he closed his eyes.

There was no ease from pain, nor from the figures of death that went about their familiar business even in the darkness of the heavy lids.

"Shall I kiss you awake?" said Callaghan. His hand was cold on Peter's hand.

"And all the lepers kissed," said Peter, and fell to wondering what he had meant.

Rhianon saw that he was no longer listening to her, and went on tiptoes away.

Callaghan, left alone, leant over the bed and spread the soft ends of his fingers on Peter's eyes. "Now it is night," he said. "Where shall we go tonight?"

Peter opened his eyes again, saw the spreading fingers and the candles glowing like the heads of poppies. A fear and a blessing were on the room.

The candles must not be blown out, he thought. There must be light, light, light. Wick and wax must never be low. All day and all night the three candles, like three girls, must blush over my bed. These three girls must shelter me.

The first flame danced and then went out. Over the second and the third flame Callaghan pursed his grey mouth. The room was dark. "Where shall we go tonight?" he said, but waited for no answer, pulling the sheets back from the bed and lifting Peter in his arms. His coat was damp and sweet on Peter's face.

"Oh, Callaghan, Callaghan," said Peter with his mouth pressed on the black cloth. He felt the movements of Callaghan's body, the tense, the relaxing muscles, the curving of the shoulders, the impact of the feet on the racing earth. A wind from under the clay and the limes of the earth swept up to his hidden face. Only when the boughs of trees scraped on his back did he know that he was naked. So that he might not cry aloud, he shut his lips firmly together over a damp fold of flesh. Callaghan, too, was naked as a baby.

"Are we naked? We have our bones and our organs, our skin and our flesh. There is a ribbon of blood tied in your hair. Do not be frightened. You have a cloth of veins around your thighs." The world charged past them, the wind dropped to nothing, blowing the fruits of battle under the moon. Peter heard the songs of birds, but no such songs as he had heard the birds, on his bedroom sill, fetch out of their throats. The birds were blind.

"Are they blind?" said Callaghan. "They have worlds in their eyes. There is white and black in their whistling. Do not be frightened. There are bright eyes under the shells of their eggs."

He came suddenly to a stop, Peter light as a feather in his arms, and set him gently down on a green globe of soil. Below there was a valley journeying far away with its burden of lame trees and grass into the distance, where the moon hung on a navelstring from the dark. From the woods on either side came the sharp cracks of guns and the pheasants falling like a rain. But soon the night was silent, softening the triggers of the fallen twigs that had snapped out under Callaghan's feet.

Peter, conscious of his sick heart, put a hand to his side, but felt none of the protecting flesh. The tips of his fingers tingled around the driving blood, but the veins were invisible. He was dead. Now he knew he was dead. The ghost of Peter, wound invisible about the ghost of the blood, stood on his globe and wondered at the corrupting night.

"What is this valley?" said Peter's voice.

"The Jarvis Valley," said Callaghan. Callaghan too was dead. Not a bone or a hair stood up under the steadily falling frost.

"This is no Jarvis Valley."

"This is the naked valley."

The moon, doubling and redoubling the strength of her beams, lit up the barks and the roots and the branches of the Jarvis trees, the busy lice in the wood, the shapes of the stones and the black ants travelling under them, the pebbles in the streams, the secret grass, the untiring death worms under the blades. From their holes in the flanks of the hills came the rats and weasels, hairs white in the moon, breeding and struggling as they rushed downward to set their teeth in the cattle's throats. No sooner did the cattle fall sucked onto the earth and the weasels race away than all the flies, rising from the dung of the fields, came up like a fog and settled on the sides. There from the stripped valley rose the smell of death, widening the mountainous nostrils on the face of the moon. Now the sheep fell, and the flies were at them. The rats and the weasels, fighting over the flesh, dropped one by one with a wound for the sheep's fleas staring out of their hair. It was to Peter but a little time before the dead, picked to the symmetrical bone, were huddled in under the soil by the wind that blew louder and harder as the fat flies dropped onto the grass. Now the worm and the death beetle undid the fibres of the animal bones, worked at them brightly and minutely, and the weeds through the sockets and the flowers on the vanished breasts sprouted up with the colours of the dead life fresh on their leaves. And the blood that had flowed flowed over the ground, strengthening the blades of the grass, fulfilling the wind-planted seeds in its course, into the mouth of the spring. Suddenly all the streams were red with blood, a score of winding veins all over the twenty fields, thick with their clotted pebbles.

Peter, in his ghost, cried out with joy. There was life in the naked valley, life in his nakedness. He saw the streams and the beating water, how the flowers shot out of the dead, and the blades and roots were doubled in their power under the stride of the spilt blood.

And the streams stopped. Dust of the dead blew over the spring, and the mouth was choked. Dust lay over the waters like a dark ice. Light, that had been all-eyed and moving, froze in the beams of the moon.

Life in this nakedness mocked Callaghan at his side, and Peter knew that he was pointing, with the ghost of a finger, down onto the dead streams. But as he spoke, and the shape that Peter's heart had taken in the time of the tangible flesh was aware of the knocks of terror, a life burst out of the pebbles like the thousand lives, wrapped in a boy's body, out of the womb. The streams again went on their way, and the light of the moon, in a new splendour, shone on the valley and magnified the shadows of the valley and pulled the moles and the badgers out of their winter into the deathless midnight season of the world.

"Light breaks over the hill," said Callaghan, and lifted the invisible Peter in his arms. Dawn, indeed, was breaking far over the Jarvis wilderness still naked under the descending moon.

As Callaghan raced along the rim of the hills and into the woods and over an exultant country where the trees raced with him, Peter cried out joyfully.

He heard Callaghan's laughter like a rattle of thunder that the wind took up and doubled. There was a shouting in the wind, a commotion under the surface of the earth. Now under the roots and now on the tops of the wild trees, he and his stranger were racing against the cock. Over and under the falling fences of the light they climbed and shouted.

"Listen to the cock," cried Peter, and the sheets of the bed rolled up to his chin.

A man with a brush had drawn a red rib down the east. The ghost of a circle around the circle of the moon spun through a cloud. He passed his tongue over his lips, that had miraculously clothed themselves with skin and flesh. In his mouth was a strange taste, as if last night, three hundred nights ago, he had squeezed the head of a poppy and drunk and slept. There was the old rumour of Callaghan down his brain. From dawn to dark he had talked of death, had seen a moth caught in the candle, had heard the laughter that could not have been his ring in his ears. The cock cried again, and a bird whistled like a scythe through wheat.

Rhianon, with a sweet, naked throat, stepped into the room.

"Rhianon," he said, "hold my hand, Rhianon."

She did not hear him, but stood over his bed and fixed him with an unbreakable sorrow.

"Hold my hand," he said. And then: "Why are you putting the sheet over my face?"

The Dress*

They had followed him for two days over the length of the county, but he had lost them at the foot of the hills, and, hidden in a golden bush, had heard them shouting as they stumbled down the valley. Behind a tree on the ridge of the hills he had peeped down onto the fields, where they hurried about like dogs, where they poked the hedges with their sticks and set up a faint howling as a mist came suddenly from the spring sky and hid them from his eyes. But the mist was a mother to him, putting a coat around his shoulders where the shirt was torn and the blood dry on his blades. The mist made him warm; he had the food and the drink of the mist on his lips; and he smiled through her mantle like a cat. He worked away from the valleywards side of the hill into the denser trees that might lead him to light and fire and a basin of soup. He thought of the coals that might be hissing in the grate, and of the young mother standing alone. He thought of her hair. Such a nest it would make for his hands. He ran through the trees, and found himself on a narrow road. Which way should he walk: towards or away from the moon? The mist had made a secret of the position of the moon, but, in a corner of the sky, where the mist had fallen apart, he could see the angles of the stars. He walked towards the north, where the stars were, mumbling a song with no tune, hearing his feet suck in and out of the spongy earth.

Now there was time to collect his thoughts, but no sooner had he started to set them in order than an owl made a cry in the trees that hung over the road, and he stopped and winked up at her, finding a mutual melancholy in her sounds. Soon she would swoop and fasten on a mouse. He saw her for a moment as she sat screeching on her bough. Then, frightened of her, he hurried on, and had not gone more than a few yards into the darkness when, with a fresh cry, she flew away. Pity the hare, he thought, for the weasel will drink her. The road sloped to the stars, and the trees and the valley and the memory of the guns faded behind.

He heard footsteps. An old man, radiant with rain, stepped out of the mist.

"Goodnight, sir," said the old man.

"No night for the son of woman," said the madman.

The old man whistled, and hurried, half running, in the direction of the roadside trees.

Let the hounds know, the madman chuckled as he climbed up the hill, let the hounds know. And, crafty as a fox, he doubled back to where the misty road branched off three ways. Hell on the stars, he said, and walked towards the dark.

The world was a ball under his feet; it kicked as he ran; it dropped; up came the trees. In the distance a poacher's dog yelled at the trap on its foot, and he heard it and ran the faster, thinking the enemy was on his heels. "Duck, boys, duck," he called out, but with the voice of one who might have pointed to a falling star.

Remembering of a sudden that he had not slept since the escape, he left off running. Now the waters of the rain, too tired to strike the earth, broke up as they fell and blew about in the wind like the sandman's grains. If he met sleep, sleep would be a girl. For the last two nights, while walking or running over the empty county, he had dreamt of their meeting. "Lie down," she would say, and would give him her dress to lie on, stretching herself out by his side. Even as he had dreamt, and the twigs under his running feet had made a noise like the rustle of her dress, the enemy had shouted in the fields. He had run on and on, leaving sleep farther behind him. Sometimes there was a sun, a moon, and sometimes under a black sky he had tossed and thrown the wind before he could be off.

"Where is Jack?" they asked in the gardens of the place he had left. "Up on the hills with a butcher's knife," they said, smiling. But the knife was gone, thrown at a tree and quivering there still. There was no heat in his head. He ran on and on, howling for sleep.

And she, alone in the house, was sewing her new dress. It was a bright country dress with flowers on the bodice. Only a few more stitches were needed before it would be ready to wear. It would lie neat on her shoulders, and two of the flowers would be growing out of her breasts.

When she walked with her husband on Sunday mornings over the fields and down into the village, the boys would smile at her behind their hands, and the shaping of the dress round her belly would set all the widow women talking. She slipped into her new dress, and, looking into the mirror over the fireplace, saw that it was prettier than she had imagined. It made her face paler and her long hair darker. She had cut it low.

A dog out in the night lifted its head up and howled. She turned away hurriedly from her reflection, and pulled the curtains closer.

Out in the night they were searching for a madman. He had green eyes, they said, and had married a lady. They said he had cut off her lips because she smiled at men. They took him away, but he stole a knife from the kitchen and slashed his keeper and broke out into the wild valleys.

From afar he saw the light in the house, and stumbled up to the edge of the garden. He felt, he did not see, the little fence around it. The rusting wire scraped on his hands, and the wet, abominable grass crept over his knees. And once he was through the fence, the hosts of the garden came rushing to meet him, the flower-headed, and the bodying frosts. He had torn his fingers while the old wounds were still wet. Like a man of blood he came out of the enemy's darkness onto the steps. He said in a whisper: "Let them not shoot me." And he opened the door.

She was in the middle of the room. Her hair had fallen untidily, and three of the buttons at the neck of her dress were undone. What made the dog howl as it did? Frightened of the howling, and thinking of the tales she had heard, she rocked in her chair. What became of the woman? she wondered as she rocked. She could not think of a woman without any lips. What became of women without any lips? she wondered.

The door made no noise. He stepped into the room, trying to smile and holding out his hands.

"Oh, you've come back," she said.

Then she turned in her chair and saw him. There was blood even by his green eyes. She put her fingers to her mouth. "Not shoot," he said.

But the moving of her arm drew the neck of her dress apart, and he stared in wonder at her wide, white forehead, her frightened eyes and mouth, and down onto the flowers on her dress. With the moving of her arm, her dress danced in the light. She sat before him, covered in flowers. "Sleep," said the madman. And, kneeling down, he put his bewildered head upon her lap.

The Lemon*

Early one morning, under the arc of a lamp, carefully, silently, in smock and rubber gloves, the doctor grafted a cat's head onto a chicken's trunk. The cat-headed creature, in a house of glass, swayed on its legs; though it stared through the slits of its eyes, it saw nothing; there was the flutter of a strange pulse under its fur and feathers; and, lifting its foot to the right of the glass wall, it rocked again to the left. Change the sex of a dog: it cries like a bitch in a high heat, and sniffs, bewildered, over the blind litter. Such a strange dog, with a grafted ovary, howled in its cage. The doctor put his ear to the glass, hoping for a new sound. The sun blew in through the laboratory windows, and the light of the wind was the colour of the sun. With music in his ears, he moved among the phials and the bottles of life; the mutilated were silent; the newborn in the rabbits' cages drew down the hygienic air delightedly into their lungs. Tomorrow there were to be mastoids* for the ferret by the window, but today it leapt in the sun.

The hill was as big as a mountain, and the house swelled like a hill on the topmost peak. Holding too many rooms, the house had a room for the wild owls and a cellar for the vermin, that multiplied on clean straw and grew fat as rabbits. The people in the house moved like too many ghosts among the white-sheeted tables, met face to face in the corridors and covered their eyes for fear of a new stranger, or suddenly crowded together in the central hall, questioning one another as to the names of the newborn. One by one the faces vanished, but there was always one to take its place, a woman with a child at her breast, or a blind man from the world. All had possession of the keys of the house.

There was one boy among them who had the name of the house, and, son of the house that was called a hill, he played with the shadows in the corridors and slept at night in a high room shuttered from the stars. But the people of the house slept in sight of the moon; they heard the gulls from the sea, the noise of the waves, when the wind blew from the south, breaking on sand, and slept with their eyes open.

The doctor woke up with the birds, seeing the sun rise each morning in a coloured water and the day, like the growths in his jars, grow brighter and stronger as the growing hours let the rain or the shine and the particles of

THE LEMON

winter light fall from them. As was his custom, he turned, this one morning, from the window where the weasel leapt to the life behind glass. He marked with an unmortal calm, with the never-ended beginning of a smile no mother bared with the mouth of her milk, how the young lapped at their mothers and his creatures, and the newly hatched fluttered, and the papped* birds opened their beaks. He was power and the clay knife, he was the sound and the substance, for he made a hand of glass, a hand with a vein, and sewed it upon the flesh, and it strengthened with the heat of the false light, and the glass nails grew long. Life ran from his fingers, in the heat of his acids, on the surface of the boiling herbs; he had death in a thousand powders; he had frozen a crucifix of steam; all the great chemistries of the earth, the mystery of matter – "See," he said aloud, "a brand on a frog's forehead, where there was neither" – in his room at the top of the house had no mystery.

The house was one mystery. Everything happens in a blaze of light; the groping of the boy's blind hands along the walls of the corridors was a movement of light, though the last candle dimmed by the head of the stairs and the lines of light at the feet of the locked doors were suddenly taken away. Nant, the boy, was not alone; he heard a frock rustle, a hand beneath his own scrape on the distemper.* "Whose hand?" he said softly. Then, flying in a panic down the dark carpets, he cried more loudly: "Never answer me." "Your hand," said the dark, and Nant stopped still.

Death was too long for the doctor, and eternity took too much time.

I was that boy in a dream, and I stood stock-still, knowing myself to be alone, knowing that the voice was mine and the dark not the death of the sun, but the dark light thrown back by the walls of the windowless corridors. I put out my arm, and it turned into a tree.

Early that morning, under the arc of a lamp, the doctor made a new acid, turning it round and round with a spoon, seeing it have colour in its beaker and then, by the change of heat, be the colour of water. It was the strongest acid, burning the air, but it struggled through his fingers sweet as a syrup and did not burn at all. Carefully, silently, he raised the beaker and opened the door of a cage. This was a new milk for the cat. He poured the acid into a saucer, and the cat-headed creature slipped down to drink. I was that cat-head in a dream: I drank the acid, and I slept; I woke up in death, but there I forgot the dream and moved on a different being in the image of the boy who was terrified of the dark. And, my arm no longer the branch of a tree, like a mole I hurried from light and to the light; for one blind moment I was a mole with a child's hands digging, up or down, I knew not which, in the Welsh earth. I knew that I was dreaming, but suddenly I awoke to the hard, real lack of light in the corridors of the house. There was nobody to guide me: the doctor, the foreigner in a white coat making a new logic in his tower of birds, was my only friend. Nant raced for the doctor's tower. Up spiral stairs and a broken ladder, reading, by candle, a sign that said "To London and the Sun", he climbed in my image, I in his, and we were two brothers climbing.

The key was on a chain ringed from my waist. Opening the door, I found the doctor as I always found him, staring through the walls of a glass cage. He smiled, but paid no heed to me, who had lusted a hundred seconds for his smile and his white coat. "I gave it my acid, and it died," the doctor said. "And, after ten minutes, the dead hen rose to its feet; it rubbed against glass like a cat, and I saw its cat's head. This was ten minutes' death."

A storm came up, black-bodied, from the sea, bringing rain and twelve winds to drive the hillbirds off the face of the sky; the storm, the black man, the whistler from the sea bottom and the fringe of the fish stones, the thunder, the lightning, the mighty pebbles, these came up, as a sickness, an afterbirth, coming up from the belly of weathers; mad as a mist coming up, the Antichrist from a seaflame or a steam crucifix, coming up the putting on of rain; as the acid was stronger, the multiplying storm, the colour of temper, the whole, the unholy, rock-handed, came up coming up.

This was the exterior world.

And the shadows, that were web- and cloven-footed in the house, with the beaks of birds, the shifted shadows that bore a woman in each hand, had no casting substances; and the foam horses of the exterior sea climbed like foxes on the hills. This that held Nant and the doctor, the bone of a horse head, the ox and black man arising from the clay picture, was the interior world. This was the interior world where the acid grew stronger, and the death in the acid added ten days to the dead time.

Still the doctor did not see me. I who was the doctor in a dream, the foreign logician, the maker of birds, engrossed in the acid strengthening and the search for oblivion, soon raised the beaker to my mouth as the storm came up. There was thunder as I drank – and, as he fell, the lightning crossed on the wind.

"There is a dead man in the tower," a woman said to her companion as they stood by the door of the central hall.

"There is a dead man in the tower," said the corner echoes, and their voices rose through the house. Suddenly the hall was crowded, and the people of the house moved among one another, questioning as to the name of the new dead.

THE LEMON

Nant stood over the doctor. Now the doctor was dead. There was a corridor leading to the tower of ten days' death, and there a woman danced alone, with the hands of a man upon her shoulders. And soon the virgins joined her, bared to the waist, and made the movements of dancing; they danced towards the open doors of the corridors, stood lightly in the doorways; they danced four steps towards the doors, and then danced four steps away. In the long hall they danced in celebration of the dead. This was the dance of the halt* the blind, and the half-dead, this the dance of the abnegation of the dead, this the dance of the children, the grave girls bared to the waist, this the dance of the dreamers, the open-eyed and the naked hopheads, sleeping as they moved. The doctor was dead at my feet. I knelt down to count his ribs, to raise his jaw, to take the beaker of acid from his hand. But the dead hand stiffened.

Said a voice at my elbow: "Unlock the hand." I moved to obey the voice, but a softer voice said at my ear: "Let the hand stiffen." "Strike the second voice." "Strike the first voice." "Unlock the hand." "Let the hand stiffen." I struck at the two voices with my fist, and Nant's hand turned into a tree.

At noon the storm was stronger; all afternoon it shook the tower, pulling the slates from the roof; it came from the sea and the earth from the seabeds and the roots of the forests. I could hear nothing but the voice of the thunder that drowned the two stricken voices; I saw the lightning stride up the hill, a bright, forked man blinding me through the tower windows. And still they danced, into the early evening, the storm increasing, and still the half-naked virgins danced to the doors. This was the dance of the celebration of death in the interior world.

I heard a voice say over the thunder: "The dead shall be buried. This was not everlasting death, but a death of days; this was a sleep with no heart. We bury the dead," said the voice that heard my heart, the brief and the everlasting. The storm up the wind measured off the distances of the voice, but a lull in the rain let the two struggling voices at my side recall me to the hand and the acid. I dragged up the stiffening hand, unlocked the fingers and raised the beaker to my mouth. As the glass burned me, there came a knocking at the door and a cry from the people of the house. They who were seeking the body of the new dead worried the door. My boy's heart was breaking. Swiftly I glanced towards the table, where a lemon lay on a plate. I punctured the skin of the lemon and poured in the acid. Then down came the storm of the dark voices and the knocks, and the tower door broke on its hinges. The dead was found. I fought between the shoulders of the entering strangers and, leaving them to their picking, spiralled down, sped through the corridors, the lemon at my breast.

Nant and I were brothers in this wild world far from the border villages, from the sea that has England in its hand, from the lofty spires and the uneaten graves beneath them. As one, one-headed, two-footed, we ran through the passages and the halls, seeing no shadows, hearing none of the wicked intimacies of the house. The rooms were empty of wickedness. We looked for a devil in the corners, but their secrets were ours. So we ran on, afraid of our footfalls, exulting in the beating of the blood, for death was at our breast, a sharp fruit, a full and yellow tumour shaped to the skin. Nant was a lonely runner in the house; I parted from him, leaving a half-ache and a half-terror, going my own way, the way of the light breaking over Cathmarw* hill and the Black Valley. And, going his own way, he climbed alone up a stone stairs to the last tower. He put his mouth to her cheek and touched her nipple. The storm died as she touched him.

He cut the lemon in half with the scissors dangling from the rope of her skirt.

And the storm came up as they drank.

This was the coming of death in the interior world.

The Burning Baby*

They said that Rhys was burning his baby* when a gorse bush broke into fire on the summit of the hill. The bush, burning merrily, assumed to them the sad white features and the rickety limbs of the vicar's burning baby. What the wind had not blown away of the baby's ashes, Rhys Rhys had sealed in a stone jar. With his own dust lay the baby's dust, and near him the dust of his daughter in a coffin of white wood.

They heard his son howl in the wind. They saw him walking over the hill, holding a dead animal up to the light of the stars. They saw him in the valley shadows as he moved, with the motion of a man cutting wheat, over the brows of the fields. In a sanatorium he coughed his lung into a basin, stirring his fingers delightedly in the blood. What moved with invisible scythe through the valley was a shadow and a handful of shadows cast by the grave sun.

The bush burned out, and the face of the baby fell away with the smoking leaves.

It was, they said, on a fine sabbath morning in the middle of the summer that Rhys Rhys fell in love with his daughter. The gorse that morning had burst into flames. Rhys Rhys, in clerical black, had seen the flames shoot up to the sky, and the bush on the edge of the hill burn red as God among the paler burning of the grass. He took his daughter's hand as she lay in the garden hammock, and told her that he loved her. He told her that she was more beautiful than her dead mother. Her hair smelt of mice, her teeth came over her lip, and the lids of her eyes were red and wet. He saw her beauty come out of her like a stream of sap. The folds of her dress could not hide from him the shabby nakedness of her body. It was not her bone, nor her flesh, nor her hair that he found suddenly beautiful. The poor soil shudders under the sun, he said. He moved his hand up and down her arm. Only the awkward and the ugly, only the barren bring forth fruit. The flesh of her arm was red with the smoothing of his hand. He touched her breast. From the touch of her breast he knew each inch of flesh upon her. Why do you touch me there? she said.

In the church that morning he spoke of the beauty of the harvest, of the promise of the standing corn and the promise in the sharp edge of the scythe as it brings the corn low and whistles through the air before it cuts into the ripeness. Through the open windows at the end of the aisles, he saw the yellow fields upon the hillside and the smudge of heather on the meadow borders. The world was ripe.

The world is ripe for the second coming of the Son of Man, he said aloud.

But it was not the ripeness of God that glistened from the hill. It was the promise and the ripeness of the flesh, the good flesh, the mean flesh, flesh of his daughter, flesh, flesh, the flesh of the voice of thunder howling before the death of man.

That night he preached of the sins of the flesh. O God in the image of our flesh, he prayed.

His daughter sat in the front pew and stroked her arm. She would have touched her breast where he had touched it, but the eyes of the congregation were upon her.

Flesh, flesh, flesh, said the vicar.

His son, scouting in the fields for a mole's hill or the signs of a red fox, whistling to the birds and patting the calves as they stood untimid at their mother's sides, came upon a dead rabbit sprawling on a stone. The rabbit's head was riddled with pellets, the dogs had torn open its belly, and the marks of a ferret's teeth were upon its throat. He lifted it gently up, tickling it behind the ears. The blood from its head dropped on his hand. Through the rip in the belly, its intestines had dropped out and coiled on the stone. He held the little body close to his jacket, and ran home through the fields, the rabbit dancing against his waistcoat. As he reached the gate of the vicarage, the worshippers dribbled out of church. They shook hands and raised their hats, smiling at the poor boy with his long green hair, his ass's ears and death buttoned under his jacket. He was always the poor boy to them.

Rhys Rhys sat in his study, the stem of his pipe stuck between his fly-buttons, the Bible unopened upon his knees. The day of God was over, and the sun, like another sabbath, went down behind the hills. He lit the lamp, but his own oil burned brighter. He drew the curtains, shutting out the unwelcome night. But he opened his own heart up, and the bald pulse that beat there was a welcome stranger. He had not felt love like this since the woman who scratched him, seeing the woman witch in his male eyes, had fallen into his arms and kissed him, and whispered Welsh words as he took her. She had been the mother of his daughter and had died in her pains, stealing, when she was dead, the son of his second love, and leaving the green-haired changeling in its place. Merry with desire, Rhys

Rhys cast the Bible on the floor. He reached for another book, and read, in the lamplit darkness, of the old woman who had deceived the Devil. The Devil is poor flesh, said Rhys Rhys.

His son came in, bearing the rabbit in his arms. The lank, red-coated boy was a flesh out of the past. The skin of the unburied dead patched to his bones, the smile of the changeling on his mouth and the hair of the sea rising from his scalp, he stood before Rhys Rhys. A ghost of his mother, he held the rabbit gently to his breast, rocking it to and fro. Cunningly, from under half-closed lids, he saw his father shrink away from the vision of death. Be off with you, said Rhys Rhys. Who was this green stranger to carry in death and rock it, like a baby under a warm shawl of fur, before him? For a minute the flesh of the world lay still; the old terror set in; the waters of the breast dried up; the nipples grew through the sand. Then he drew his hand over his eyes, and only the rabbit remained, a little sack of flesh, half empty, swaying in the arms of his son. Be off, he said. The boy held the rabbit close and rocked it, and tickled it again.

Changeling, said Rhys Rhys. He is mine, said the boy, I'll peel him and keep the skull. His room in the attic was crowded with skulls and dried pelts, and little bones in bottles.

Give it to me.

He is mine.

Rhys Rhys tore the rabbit away and stuffed it deep in the pocket of his smoking coat. When his daughter came in, dressed and ready for bed, with a candle in her hand, Rhys Rhys had death in his pocket.

She was timid, for his touch still ached on her arm and breast, but she bent unblushing over him. Saying goodnight, she kissed him, and he blew her candle out. She was smiling as he lowered the wick of the lamp.

Step out of your shift, said he. Shiftless, she stepped towards his arms.

I want the little skull, said a voice in the dark.

From his room at the top of the house, through the webs on the windows, and over the furs and the bottles, the boy saw a mile of green hill running away into the darkness of the first dawn. Summer storm in the heat of the rain, flooring the grassy mile, had left some new morning brightness, out of the dead night, in each reaching root.

Death took hold of his sister's legs as she walked through the calf-deep heather up the hill. He saw the high grass at her thighs. And the blades of the upgrowing wind, out of the four windsmells of the manuring dead, might drive through the soles of her feet, up the veins of the legs and stomach, into her womb and her pulsing heart. He watched her climb.

She stood, gasping for breath, on a hill of the wider hill, tapping the wall of her bladder, fondling her matted chest (for the hair grew on her as on a grown man), feeling the heart in her wrist, loving her coveted thinness. She was to him as ugly as the sow-faced woman Llareggub,* who had taught him the terrors of the flesh. He remembered the advances of that unlovely woman. She blew out his candle as he stepped towards her on the night the great hail had fallen and he had hidden in her rotting house from the cruelty of the weather. Now half a mile off his sister stood in the morning, and the vermin of the hill might spring upon her as she stood, uncaring, rounding the angles of her ugliness. He smiled at the thought of the devouring rats, and looked around the room for a bottle to hold her heart. Her skull, fixed by a socket to the nail above his bed, would be a smiling welcome to the first pains of waking.

But he saw Rhys Rhys stride up the hill, and the bowl of his sister's head, fixed invisibly above his sheets, crumbled away. Standing straight by the side of a dewy tree, his sister beckoned. Up went Rhys Rhys through the calf-deep heather, the death in the grass, over the boulders and up through the reaching ferns, to where she stood. He took her hand. The two shadows linked hands and climbed together to the top of the hill. The boy saw them go, and turned his face to the wall as they vanished, in one dull shadow, over the edge and down to the dingle at the west foot of the lovers' alley.

Later, he remembered the rabbit. He ran downstairs and found it in the pocket of the smoking coat. He held death against him, tasting a cough of blood upon his tongue as he climbed, contented, back to the bright bottles and the wall of heads.

In the first dew of light he saw his father clamber for her white hand. She who was his sister walked with a swollen belly over the hill. She touched him between the legs, and he sighed and sprang at her. But the nerves of her face mixed with the quiver in his thighs, and she shot from him. Rhys Rhys, over the bouldered rim, led her to terror. He sighed and sprang at her. She mixed with him in the fourth and the fifth terrors of the flesh. Said Rhys Rhys, Your mother's eyes. It was not her eyes that saw him proud before her, nor the eyes in her thumb. The lashes of her fingers lifted. He saw the ball under the nail.

It was, they said, on a fine sabbath morning in the early spring that she bore him a male child. Brought to bed of her father, she screamed for an anaesthetic as the knocking head burst through. In her gown of blood she slept until twilight, and a star burst bloody through each ear. With a scissors and rag, Rhys Rhys attended her, and, gazing on the shrivelled features and the hands like the hands of a mole, he gently took the child away, and his daughter's breast cried out and ran into the mouth of the surrounding shadow. The shadow pouted for the milk and the binding cottons. The child spat in his arms, the noise of the running air was blind in its ears, and the deaf light died from its eyes.

Rhys Rhys, with the dead child held against him, stepped into the night, hearing the mother moan in her sleep and the deadly shadow, filled sick with milk, flowing around the house. He turned his face towards the hills. A shadow walked close to him, and, silent in the shadow of a full tree, the changeling waited. He made an image for the moon, and the flesh of the moon fell away, leaving a star-eyed skull. Then with a smile he ran back over the lawns and into the crying house. Halfway up the stairs, he heard his sister die. Rhys Rhys climbed on.

On the top of the hill he laid the baby down and propped it against the heather. Death propped the dark flowers. The baby stiffened in the rigor of the moon. Poor flesh, said Rhys Rhys as he pulled at the dead heather and furze. Poor angel, he said to the listening mouth of the baby. The fruit of the flesh falls with the worm from the tree. Conceiving the worm, the bark crumbles. There lay the poor star of flesh that had dropped, like the bead of a woman's milk through the nipples of a wormy tree.

He stacked the torn heathers in the midst of the circle, where the stones still howled on the sabbaths. On the head of the purple stack, he piled the dead grass. A stack of death, the heather grew as tall as he, and loomed at last over his windy hair.

Behind a boulder moved the accompanying shadow, and the shadow of the boy was printed under the fiery flank of a tree. The shadow marked the boy, and the boy marked the bones of the naked baby under their chilly cover, and how the grass scraped on the bald skull, and where his father picked out a path in the cancerous growths of the silent circle. He saw Rhys Rhys pick up the baby and place it on the top of the stack, saw the head of a burning match, and heard the crackle of the bush, breaking like a baby's arm.

The stack burst into flame. Rhys Rhys, before the red eye of the creeping fire, stretched out his arms and beckoned the shadow from the stones. Surrounded by shadows, he prayed before the flaming stack, and the sparks of the heather blew past his smile. Burn, child, poor flesh, mean flesh, flesh, flesh, sick, sorry flesh, flesh of the foul womb, burn back to dust, he prayed.

And the baby caught fire. The flames curled round its mouth and blew upon the shrinking gums. Flame round its red cord lapped its little belly till the raw flesh fell upon the heather.

A flame touched its tongue. Eeeeeh, cried the burning baby, and the illuminated hill replied.

The Horse's Ha*

He saw the plague enter the village on a white horse. It was a cancerous horseman, with a furuncle* for a hat, that galloped the beast over grass and cobble and the coloured hill. Plague, plague, cried Tom Twp as the horse on the horizon, scenting the stars, lifted a white head. Out came the grocer with an egg in his hand, and the butcher in a bloody coat. They followed the line of the lifted finger, but the horse had gone, the trees were no speakers, and the birds who flew criss-cross on the sky said no word of warning to the parson's rookery or the chained starlings in the parlour of ApLlewelyn. As white, said Tom Twp, as the egg in your hand. He remembered the raw head of the horseman, and whispered slyly, As red as mother's rump in your window. The clouds darkened, the sun went in, the suddenly ferocious wind broke down three fences, and the cows, blue-eyed with plague, nibbled at the centres of the marrow beds. The egg fell, and the red yolk struggled between the spaces of the cobbles, the white mixed with the rain that dripped from the scarlet coat. In went the grocer with a stained hand, and the butcher among the hands of veal. Tom Twp, following his finger towards the horizon where the horse of plague had stamped and vanished, reached the dark church as the rain grew sick of the soil and drew back to heaven. He ran between the graves, where the worm rubbed in the tradesman's hands. Mrs ApLlewelyn raised a stone breast above the grass. Softly opening the door, he came upon the parson praying for disarmament in the central aisle. Disarm the forces of the army and the navy, he heard the parson murmur to the Christ of stained glass who smiled like a nanny goat above him, hearing the cries from Cardiff and the smoking west. Disarm the territorial forces, the parson prayed. In anger, God smote him. There is plague, said Tom Twp. ApLlewelyn in the organ loft reached for the bass stops. The white plague drifted through the church to the music of the savage voluntary. Parson and sinner stood beneath the reflections of the Holy Family, marking in each ginger halo the hair of blood. There was to one the voice of an arming God in the echo of each chord, and, to the other, the horse's ha.

One by one the starlings died; the last remaining bird, with a pain in its crop, whistled at the late afternoon. ApLlewelyn, returning from music and marvelling at the sky, heard the last starling's voice as he walked up the drive. Why is there no welcome, wondered the keeper, from my starling charges? Every day of the year they had lost their tempers, tore at the sashes of the window watching on the flying world; they had scraped on the glass and fetched up their wings from the limed bar, signalling before him. On the rug at his feet lay six starlings, cold and stiff, the seventh mourning. Death in his absence had laid six singers low. He who marks the sparrow's* fall has no time for my birds, said ApLlewelyn. He smote big, bloody death, and death, relenting, pulled a last fart from the bodies of the dead birds.

Plague, plague, cried Tom Twp, standing in a new rain. Where the undertaker's house had died in the trees, he holla'd, like ApLlewelyn, of big, bloody death; he heard the rooks cawing in the trees, and saw a galloping shadow. The trees smelt of opium and mice, to Tom two sorts of the hell-headed animal who ran in the skirtings of the grave. There were, on the branches of the trees and hanging upright from the earth, the owls that ate the mice and the mouths of the rosy flowers that fed on opium. To the chimneys of Last House and the one illuminated window he called the plague. Out came the undertaker in a frock coat; distrusting the light of the moon, he carried a candle in his gloved hand, the candle casting three shadows. To the middle shadow Tom Twp addressed his words of the white coming. Shall I measure, said the shadow on the left, the undead of Wales? Plague on a horse, said Tom Twp to the left shadow, and heard the darker shadow on the right reply.

No drug of man works on the dead. The parson, at his pipe, sucked down a dead smoke from the nostrils of the travelling horse, who now, on a far-off mountain, neighed down at Africa. Smitten by God, the parson, as the dark rose deepest where the moon rose in a blaze of light, counted his blessings: the blazing fire, the light in the tobacco and the shape of the deep bowl. Hell was this fire, the dark denial burning like a weed, and the poppy out of the smoking earth. The lines of the bowl, that patterned his grave, were the lines of the weedy world; the light in the tobacco faded; the weed was at the parson's legs, worrying him into a longer fall than the fall from heaven, and, heavier than the poppy, into a long sleep.

Butcher and baker fell asleep that night, their women sleeping at their sides. Butcher and baker took their women in no image; their women broke again for them the accustomed maidenheads, their erected saviours crossing, in my language, the hill of hairs. Over the shops, the cold eggs that had life, the box where the rats worked all night on the high meat, the shopkeepers gave no thought to death. They felt, in the crowded space between hip and belly, the action of a third lover. Death, in the last gristle, broke on the minutes, and, by twelve beneath Cathmarw steeple, the towers fell.

Shall I measure the undead? This, said the undertaker in his parlour, pointing through the uncurtained window to the shape of the night, is the grave for the walking and the breathing. Here lay the sleepy body, the smoking body, the flesh that burned a candle and the lessening manwax. Go home and die, he had told Tom Twp, and, telling it again to the mad moon, he remembered the story of the resurrection men* who had snatched a talking body out of the Cathmarw yards. He heard the dead die round him, and a live man, in his grafted suit, break up the gravel on the drive of Last House. Cathmarw, in a bath of blood, slept still for the light day, Tom twisted in the hedge, butcher and baker stiff by their loves, and parson with a burnt-out pipe loose in his jaws. ApLlewelyn skinned the six starlings; he dropped to the ground at last, holding two handfuls of red and broken feathers; the seventh bird, naked as its dead mates, still shivering, sang on the limed bar. Plague is upon us, said Mr Montgomery, the undertaker, for the wind was resounding with the noise of departure and the smell of the departing flesh crept up the wind. In the skin of this western Wales, through the veins of the county, the rub of the plague transformed into a circle of sick and invisible promise the globe of seeds; swollen in the tubers of the trees, death poisoned the green buds and coloured the birthmarks of the forest with a fresh stain. Mr Montgomery threw his glass of vinegar in the plague's face; the glass broke on the window, and the vinegar ran down the broken panes. He cardboarded each slit and crack, smelling the running acid as he nailed up a cloth to shield night from him; he bolted and barred the doors of his wooden house and stuffed the holes in the parlour corners, until, buried at last in a coffin with chimneys, he took down his mother's book. Cures for the sickness of the body and the sickness of the mind, ingredients for a saucer for resurrection, calls to the dead, said Bronwen Montgomery. The hand that wrote squarely to the crowded planet held a worm, and rain beat down the letters of her living name, and of Cathmarw's plague she said, in a translated tongue, that the horse was a white beast ridden over the hill by a raw-headed horseman. Take, said Bronwen, the blood of a bird, and mix it with the stuff of man. Take, of a dead man and bird, a bowl of death, and pour the bird's blood and the mortal sap through the sockets of the bowl. Stir with a finger, and, if a dead finger, drink my brew by me. He cast her aside. There was a bird and man in the unbolted darkness, plague in the loin and feather tickling the flesh and bone, uplifted fingers in the trees, and an eye in the air. These were his common visions; plague could not cloud the eye, nor the wind in the trees split the fingernail. Unbolting, unbarring the coffin with chimneys, he walked into the single vision of the night; the night was one bird's blood, one pocket of man, one finger lifted in the many and the upward world. He walked through the woods and onto the dusty road that led to Wales all ways, to the left, to the right, to the north, to the south, down through the vegetations, and up through the eye of the air. Looking at the still trees in the darkness, he came at last to the house of ApLlewelyn. He opened the gate and walked up the drive. There, in the parlour, lay ApLlewelyn, six featherless starlings at his side, the seventh mourning. Take, take, said Bronwen out of the Cathmarw yards, the blood of a bird. He gathered a dead bird up, tore at its throat and caught the cold blood in his hands. Drink my brew by me, said Bronwen at his ear. He found a cup on the dresser, and half filled it with the blood of the shrunken starling. Though he rot he must wait, said Mr Montgomery to the organist, till I drink her brew by her. Take, take, said his mother, the stuff of man. He hurried out and on, hearing the last starling mourn for the new departure.

Tom Twp was twisted in the hedge. He did not feel the jackknife at his finger, and the going of the grassy wedding ring around it did not trouble him at all.

Parson, dead in his chair, did not cry aloud as his trousers slid down to his boots, and promise filled the bladder of a fountain pen.

The cup was full. Mr Montgomery stirred it with a wedding finger, and drank from it in the Cathmarw yards by the grave of his mother. Down went the red brew. The graves spun around him, the angels shifted on their stones, and the lids, invisible to the silent drinker, creaked on their hinges. Poison stirred him, and he spun, one foot in his mother's grave. Dead Cathmarw made a movement out of the wooden hamlet towards the hill of hairs. The hair rose on his scalp. Blood in his blood, and the cold ounce of the parson's seed edging to creation, he counted the diminishings of the moon; the stationary sun slipped down, and the system he could not take to the ground broke in half and in a hundred stars. Three days went by in a wind, the fourth rising cloudless and sinking again to too many strokes from the out-counted steeple. The fourth night got up like a man; the vision altering, a woman in the moon lit up the yards. He counted the diminishings of the sun. Too many days, he said, sick of his mother's brew and of the poisoned hours that passed and repassed him, leaving on the gravel path a rag and a bone in a faded frock coat. But as the days passed, so the dead grew tired of waiting. Tom, uneasy in the hedge, raised a four-fingered hand to stifle the yawn that broke up the last remaining skins upon his face. Butcher and baker ached in too long a love, and cursed the beds that bore them. The six naked starlings rose on their wings, the seventh singing, and ApLlewelyn, out of a deep sleep, drifted into a reawakened world where the birds danced about him. So, tired of waiting, the dead rose and sought the undertaker, for the rot had set in, and their flesh fell as they walked, in a strange procession, along the dusty road that led all ways to the graves of Cathmarw.

Mr Montgomery saw them come, and, as a new sunshine descended on the yards, offered them his cup of brew. But the dead refused his hand. Tom Twp hunched, the sterile parson, butcher and baker ungainly in their loves, and ApLlewelyn with his hands around the feathers, clawed at the earth, making a common grave. Far, far above them, the seven naked starlings scratched on the sky. A darkness descended on the yards, but lifted again as Mr Montgomery questioned the parson as to the God of death. What is God's death? Lifting his head from the soil, the parson said, God took my promise. And he smote the earth. I am your tomb-maker, said Mr Montgomery as the unshrouded parson climbed into the grave. I, I took your promise, he said as the soil closed over. What is death's music? One note or many? The chord of contagion? Thus questioned the undertaker, the cup three quarters empty in his gloved hand. He who marks the sparrow's* fall has no time for my birds, said ApLlewelyn. What music is death? What should I know of the music of death who am no longer the keeper of birds? ApLlewelyn vanished into the second quarter of the grave. I, I slew your birds, said the undertaker to the vanishing man. The butcher was dead meat. Let me answer your platitudes, said the butcher's wife, scrubbing the surface of the double hole in the earth. I was love, I am dead, and my man still walks in me. What is death's love? said the undertaker to the woman. Let me answer your platitudes, said the grocer's wife. I was dead, I am love, and my man still treads in me. They who filled and were filled, in a two-backed death, filled the third quarter. And Tom Twp, counting his fingers at the edge of their acre, found a tenth miraculous finger, with a nail red as blood and a clear half-moon. Death is my last finger, said Tom Twp, and dived into the closing grave. So Mr Montgomery was left alone, by the desolate church, under a disappearing moon. One by one the stars went out, leaving a hole in heaven. He looked upon the grave, and slowly removed his coat.

The Orchards*

He had dreamt that a hundred orchards on the road to the sea village had broken into flame; and all the windless afternoon tongues of fire shot through the blossom. The birds had flown up as a small red cloud grew suddenly from each branch; but as night came down with the rising of the moon and the swinging-in of the mile-away sea, a wind blew out the fires and the birds returned. He was an apple farmer in a dream that ended as it began: with the flesh-and-ghost hand of a woman pointing to the trees. She twined the fair and dark tails of her hair together, smiled over the apple fields to a sister figure who stood in a circular shadow by the walls of the vegetable garden; but the birds flew down onto her sister's shoulders, unafraid of the scarecrow face and the cross-wood nakedness under the rags. He gave the woman a kiss, and she kissed him back. Then the crows came down to her arms as she held him close; the beautiful scarecrow kissed him, pointing to the trees as the fires died.

Marlais* awoke that summer morning with his lips still wet from her kiss. This was a story more terrible than the stories of the reverend madmen in the Black Book of Llareggub, for the woman near the orchards and her sister-stick by the wall were his scarecrow lovers for ever and ever. What were the sea-village burning orchards and the clouds at the end of the branches to his love for these bird-provoking women? All the trees of the world might blaze suddenly from the roots to the highest leaves, but he would not sprinkle water on the shortest fiery field. She was his lover, and her sister with birds on her shoulders held him closer than the women of LlanAsia.

Through the top-storey window he saw the pale-blue, cloudless sky over the tangle of roofs and chimneys, and the promise of a lovely day in the rivers of the sun. There, in a chimney's shape, stood his bare, stone boy and the three blind gossips, blowing fire through their skulls, who huddled for warmth in all weathers. What man on a roof had turned his weathercock's head to stare at the red-and-black girls over the town and, by his turning, made them stone pillars? A wind from the world's end had frozen the roof-walkers when the town was a handful of houses; now a circle of coal table-hills, where the children played Indians, cast

THE ORCHARDS

its shadow on the black lots and the hundred streets; and the stone-blind gossips cramped together by his bare boy and the brick virgins under the towering crane-hills.

The sea ran to the left, a dozen valleys away, past the range of volcanoes and the great stack forests and ten towns in a hole. It met the Glamorgan shores, where a half-mountain fell westward out of the clump of villages in a wild wood, and shook the base of Wales. But now, thought Marlais, the sea is slow and cool, full of dolphins; it flows in all directions from a green centre, lapping the land stones; it makes the shells speak on the blazing half-mountain sand, and the lines of time even shall not join the blue sea surface and the bottomless bed.

He thought of the sea running; when the sun sank, a fire went in under the liquid caverns. He remembered, while he dressed, the hundred fires around the blossoms of the apple trees, and the uneasy salt rising of the wind that died with the last pointing of the beautiful scarecrow's hand. Water and fire, sea and apple tree, two sisters and a crowd of birds, blossomed, pointed and flew down all that midsummer morning in a top-storey room in the house on a slope over the black-housed town.

He sharpened his pencil and shut the sky out, shook back his untidy hair, arranged the papers of a devilish story on his desk and broke the pencil point with a too-hard scribble of "sea" and "fire" on a clean page. Fire would not set the ruled lines alight, adventure, burning, through the heartless characters, nor water close over the bogey heads and the unwritten words. The story was dead from the Devil up; there was a white-hot tree with apples where a frozen tower with owls should have rocked in a wind from Antarctica; there were naked girls, with nipples like berries, on the sand in the sun, where a cold and unholy woman should be wailing by the Kara Sea or the Sea of Azov.* The morning was against him. He struggled with his words like a man with the sun, and the sun stood victoriously at high noon over the dead story.

Put a two-coloured ring of two women's hair round the blue world, white and coal-black against the summer-coloured boundaries of sky and grass, four-breasted stems at the poles of the summer sea ends, eyes in the seashells, two fruit trees out of a coal hill: poor Marlais's morning, turning to evening, spins before you. Under the eyelids, where the inward night drove backwards, through the skull's base, into the wide, first world on the faraway eye, two love trees smouldered like sisters. Have an orchard sprout in the night, an enchanted woman with a spine like a railing burn her hand in the leaves, man-on-fire a mile from a sea have a wind put out your heart: Marlais's death in life in the circular going down of the day that had taken no time blows again in the wind for you.

The world was the saddest in the turning world, and the stars in the north, where the shadow of a mock moon spun until a wind put out the shadow, were the ravaged south faces. Only the fork-tree breast of the woman's scarecrow could bear his head like an apple on the white wood where no worm would enter, and her barbed breast alone pierce the worm in the dream under her sweetheart's eyelid. The real round moon shone on the women of LlanAsia and the love-torn virgins of This street.

The word is too much with us.* He raised his pencil so that its shadow fell, a tower of wood and lead, on the clean paper; he fingered the pencil tower, the half-moon of his thumbnail rising and setting behind the leaden spire. The tower fell, down fell the city of words, the walls of a poem, the symmetrical letters. He marked the disintegration of the ciphers as the light failed, the sun drove down into a foreign morning, and the word of the sea rolled over the sun. "Image, all image," he cried to the fallen tower as the night came on. "Whose harp is the sea? Whose burning candle is the sun?" An image of man, he rose to his feet and drew the curtains open. Peace, like a simile, lay over the roofs of the town. "Image, all image," cried Marlais, stepping through the window onto the level roofs.

The slates shone around him, in the smoke of the magnified stacks and through the vapours of the hill. Below him, in a world of words, men on their errands moved to no purpose but the escape of time. Brave in his desolation, he scrambled to the edge of the slates, there to stand perilously above the tiny traffic and the lights of the street signals. The toy of the town was at his feet. On went the marzipan cars, changing gear, applying brake, over the nursery carpets into a child's hands. But soon height had him, and he swayed, feeling his legs grow weak beneath him and his skull swell like a bladder in the wind. It was the image of an infant city that threw his pulses into confusion. There was dust in his eyes; there were eyes in the grains of dust ascending from the street. Once on the leveller roofs, he touched his left breast. Death was the bright magnets of the streets; the wind pulled off the drag of death and the falling visions. Now he was stripped of fear, strong, night-muscled. Over the housetops he ran towards the moon. There the moon came, in a colder glory than before, attended by stars, drawing the tides of the sea. By a parapet he watched her, finding a word for each stage of her journey in the directed sky, calling her same-faced, wondering at her many masks. Death mask and dance mask over her mountainous features transformed the sky; she struggled behind a cloud, and came with a new smile over the wall of wind. Image, and all was image, from Marlais, ragged in the wind, to the appalling town, he on the roofs invisible to the street, the street beneath him blind to his walking word. His hand before him was five-fingered life.

A baby cried, but the cry grew fainter. It is all one, the loud voice and the still voice striking a common silence, the dowdy lady flattening her nose against the panes, and the well-mourned lady. The word is too much with us, and the dead word. Cloud, the last muslin's rhyme, shapes above tenements and bursts in cold rain on the suburban drives. Hail falls on cinder track and the angelled stone. It is all one, the rain and the macadam; it is all one, the hail and cinder, the flesh and the rough dust. High above the hum of the houses, far from the skyland and the frozen fence, he questioned each shadow; man among ghosts, and ghost in clover, he moved for the last answer.

The bare boy's voice through a stone mouth, no longer smoking at this hour, rose up unanswerably: "Who walks, mad among us, on the roofs, by my cold, brick-red side and the weathercock-frozen women, walks over This street, under the image of the Welsh summer heavens walks all night loverless, has two sister lovers ten towns away. Past the great stack forests to the left and the sea his lovers burn for him endlessly by a hundred orchards." The gossips' voices rose up unanswerably: "Who walks by the stone virgins is our virgin Marlais, wind and fire, and the coward on the burning roofs."

He stepped through the open window.

Red sap in the trees bubbled from the cauldron roots to the last spray of blossom, and the boughs, that night after the hollow walk, fell like candles from the trunks but could not die for the heat of the sulphurous head of the grass burned yellow by the dead sun. And flying there, he rounded, half mist, half man, all apple circles on the sea-village road in the high heat of noon as the dawn broke; and as the sun rose like a river over the hills, so the sun sank behind a tree. The woman pointed to the hundred orchards and the black birds who flocked around her sister, but a wind put the trees out and he woke again. This was the intolerable, second waking out of a life too beautiful to break, but the dream was broken. Who had walked by the virgins near the orchards was a virgin, wind and fire, and a coward in the destroying coming of the morning. But after he had dressed and taken breakfast, he walked up This street to the hilltop and turned his face towards the invisible sea.

"Good morning, Marlais," said an old man sitting with six greyhounds in the blackened grass.

"Good morning, Mr David Davies."

"You are up very early," said David Two Times.

"I am walking towards the sea."

"The wine-coloured sea," said Dai Twice.

Marlais strode over the hill to the greener left, and down behind the circle of the town to the rim of Whippet Valley, where the trees, for ever twisted between smoke and slag, tore at the sky and the black ground. The dead boughs prayed that the roots might shoulder up the soil, leaving a dozen channels empty for the leaves and the spirit of the cracking wood, a hole in the valley for the mole-handed sap, a long grave for the last spring's skeleton that once had leapt, when the blunt and forked hills were sharp and straight, through the once-green land. But Whippet's trees were the long dead of the stacked south of the country; who had vanished under the hacked land pointed, thumb-to-hill, these black leaf-nailed and warning fingers. Death in Wales had twisted the Welsh dead into those valley cripples.

The day was a passing of days. High noon, the story-killer and the fire bug (the legends of the Russian seas died as the trees awoke to their burning) passed in all the high noons since the fall of man from the sun and the first sun's pinnacling of the half-made heavens. And all the valley summers, the once monumental red and the now headstone-featured, all that midsummer afternoon were glistening in the seaward walk. Through the ancestral valley where his fathers, out of their wooden dust and full of sparrows, wagged at a hill, he walked steadily; on the brink of the hole that held LlanAsia as a grave holds a town, he was caught in the smoke of the forests and, like a ghost from the clear-cut quarters under the stack roots, climbed down onto the climbing streets.

"Where are you walking, Marlais?" said a one-legged man by a black flower bed.

"Towards the sea, Mr William Williams."

"The mermaid-crowded sea," said Will Peg.

Marlais passed out of the tubercular valley onto a waste mountain, through a seedy wood to a shagged field; a crow, on a molehill, in Prince Price's skull cawed of the breadth of hell in the packed globe; the afternoon broke down, the stumped land heaving, and, like a tree or lightning, a wind, roots up, forked between smoke and slag as the dusk dropped; surrounded by echoes, the red-hot travellers of voices and the devils from

THE ORCHARDS

the horned acres, he shuddered on his enemies' territory as a new night came on in the nightmare of an evening. "Let the trees collapse," the dusty journeymen said, "the boulders flake away and the gorse rot and vanish, earth and grass be swallowed down onto a hill's vee balancing on the grave that proceeds to Eden. Winds on fire, through vault and coffin and fossil we'll blow a manful of dust into the garden. Where the serpent sets the tree alight and the apple falls like a spark out of its skin, a tree leaps up; a scarecrow shines on the cross-boughs, and, by one in the sun, the new trees arise, making an orchard round the crucifix." By midnight two more valleys lay beneath him, dark with their two towns in the palms of the mined mountains; a valley, by one in the morning, held Aberbabel in its fist beneath him. He was a young man no longer, but a legendary walker, a folk man walking, with a cricket for a heart; he walked by Aberbabel's chapel, cut through the graveyard over the unstill headstones, spied a red-cheeked man in a nightshirt two foot above ground.

The valleys passed; out of the water-dipping hills, the moments of mountains, the eleventh valley came up like an hour. And coming out timelessly through the dwarf's eye of the telescope, through the ring of light like a circle's wedding on the last hill before the sea, the shape of the hundred orchards magnified with the immaculate diminishing of the moon. This was the spectacle that met the telescope, and the world Marlais saw in the morning following upon the first of the eleven untold adventures: to his both sides the unbroken walls, taller than the beanstalks that married a story on the roof of the world, of stone and earth and beetle and tree; a graveyard before him the ground came to a stop, shot down and down, was lost with the Devil in bed, rose shakily to the sea-village road where the blossoms of the orchards hung over the wooden walls and sister roads ran off into the four white country points; a rock line thus, straight to the hilltop, and the turning graph scored with trees; dip down the county, deep as the history of the final fire burning through the chamber one storey over Eden, the first green structure after the red downfall; down, down, like a stone stuck with towns, like the river out of a glass of places, fell his foot-holding hill. He was a folk man no longer, but Marlais the poet walking, over the brink into ruin, up the side of doom, over hell in bed to the red left, till he reached the first of the fields, where the unhatched apples were soon to cry fire in a wind from a half-mountain falling westward to the sea. A man-in-a-picture Marlais, by noon's blow to the centre, stood by a circle of apple trees and counted the circles that travelled over the shady miles into a clump of villages. He laid himself down in the grass, and noon fell back bruised to the sun; and he slept till a handbell rang over the fields. It was a windless afternoon in the sisters' orchards, and the fair-headed sister was ringing the bell for tea.

He had come very near to the end of the indescribable journey. The fair girl, in a field sloping seaward three fields and a stile from Marlais, laid out a white cloth on a flat stone. Into one of a number of cups she poured milk and tea, and cut the bread so thin she could see London through the white pieces. She stared hard at the stile and the pruned, transparent hedge, and as Marlais climbed over, ragged and unshaven, his stripped breast burnt by the sun, she rose from the grass and smiled and poured tea for him. This was the end to the untold adventures. They sat in the grass by the stone table like lovers at a picnic, too loved to speak, desireless familiars in the shade of the hedge corner. She had shaken a handbell for her sister, and called a lover over eleven valleys to her side. Her many lovers' cups were empty on the flat stone.

And he who had dreamt that a hundred orchards had broken into flame saw suddenly then in the windless afternoon tongues of fire shoot through the blossom. The trees all around them kindled and crackled in the sun, the birds flew up as a small red cloud grew from each branch, the bark caught like gorse, the unborn, blazing apples whirled down devoured in a flash. The trees were fireworks and torches, smouldered out of the furnace of the fields into a burning arc, cast down their branded fruit like cinders on the charred roads and fields.

Who had dreamt a boy's dream of her flesh-and-ghost hand in the windless afternoon saw then, at the red height, when the wooden step-roots splintered at the orchard entrance and the armed towers came to grief, that she raised her hand heavily and pointed to the trees and birds. There was a flurry in the sky, of wing and fire and near-to-evening wind in the going below of the burnt day. As the new night was built, she smiled as she had done in the short dream eleven valleys old; lame like Pisa, the night leant on the west walls; no trumpet shall knock the Welsh walls down before the last crack of music; she pointed to her sister in a shadow by the disappearing garden, and the dark-headed figure with crows on her shoulders appeared at Marlais's side.

This was the end of a story more terrible than the stories of the quick and the undead in mountainous houses on Jarvis hills, and the unnatural valley that Idris* waters is a children's territory to this eleventh valley in the seaward travel. A dream that was no dream skulked there; the real world's wind came up to kill the fires; a scarecrow pointed to the extinguished trees.

This he had dreamt before the blossom's burning and the putting-out, before the rising and the salt swinging-in, was a dream no longer near these orchards. He kissed the two secret sisters, and a scarecrow kissed him back. He heard the birds fly down onto his lovers' shoulders. He saw the fork-tree breast, the barbed eye and the dry twig hand.

The School for Witches*

On Cader Peak* there was a school for witches where the doctor's daughter, teaching the unholy cradle and the devil's pin, had seven country girls. On Cader Peak, half ruined in an enemy weather, the house with a storey held the seven girls, the cellar echoing, and a cross reversed above the entrance to the inner rooms. Here the doctor, dreaming of illness, in the centre of the tubercular hill, heard his daughter cry to the power swarming under the West roots. She invoked a particular devil, but the Gehenna* did not yawn under the hill, and the day and the night continued with their two departures; the cocks crew and the corn fell in the villages and yellow fields as she taught the seven girls how the lust of man, like a dead horse, stood up to his injected mixtures. She was short and fat-thighed; her cheeks were red; she had red lips and innocent eyes. But her body grew hard as she called to the black flowers under the tide of roots; when she fetched the curdlers out of the trees to bore through the cows' udders, the seven staring stared at the veins hardening in her breast; she stood uncovered, calling the devil, and the seven uncovered closed round her in a ring.

Teaching them the intricate devil, she raised her arms to let him enter. Three years and a day had vanished since she first bowed to the moon, and, maddened by the mid-light, dipped her hair seven times in the salt sea, and a mouse in honey. She stood, still untaken, loving the lost man; her fingers hardened on light as on the breastbone of the unentering devil.

Mrs Price climbed up the hill, and the seven saw her. It was the first evening of the new year; the wind was motionless on Cader Peak, and a half-red, promising dusk floated over the rocks. Behind the midwife the sun sank as a stone sinks in a marsh, the dark bubbled over it, and the mud sucked it down into the bubble of the bottomless fields.

In Bethlehem there is a prison for mad women, and in Cathmarw by the parsonage trees a black girl screamed as she laboured. She was afraid to die like a cow on the straw, and to the noises of the rooks. She screamed for the doctor on Cader Peak as the tumultuous West moved in its grave. The midwife heard her. A black girl rocked in her bed. Her eyes were stones. Mrs Price climbed up the hill, and the seven saw her.

Midwife, midwife, called the seven girls. Mrs Price crossed herself. A chain of garlic hung at her throat. Carefully, she touched it. The seven cried aloud, and ran from the window to the inner rooms, where the doctor's daughter, bent on uncovered knees, counselled the black toad, her familiar, and the divining cat slept by the wall. The familiar moved its head. The seven danced, rubbing the white wall with their thighs until the blood striped the thin symbols of fertility upon them. Hand in hand they danced among dark symbols, under the charts that marked the rise and fall of the satanic seasons, and their white dresses swung around them. The owls commenced to sing, striking against the music of the suddenly awaking winter. Hand in hand the dancers spun around the black toad and the doctor's daughter, seven stags dancing, their antlers shaking, in the confusion of the unholy room.

She is a very black woman, said Mrs Price, and curtsied to the doctor.

He woke to the midwife's story out of a dream of illness, remembering the broken quicked, the black patch and echo, the mutilated shadows of the seventh sense.

She lay with a black scissorman.*

He wounded her deep, said the doctor, and wiped a lancet on his sleeve.

Together they stumbled down the rocky hill.

A terror met them at the foot, the terror of the blind tapping their white sticks and the stumps of the arms on the solid darkness; two worms in the foil of a tree, bellies on the rubber sap and the glues of a wrong-grained forest, they, holding tight to hats and bags, crawled now up the path that led to the black birth. From right, from left, the cries of labour came in under the branches, piercing the dead wood, from the earth, where a mole sneezed, and from the sky, out of the worms' sight.

They were not the only ones caught that night in the torrential blindness; to them, as they stumbled, the land was empty of men, and the prophets of bad weather alone walked in their neighbourhoods. Three tinkers appeared out of silence by the chapel wall. Capel Cader, said the panman. Parson is down on tinkers, said John Bucket. Cader Peak, said the scissorman, and up they went. They passed the midwife close; she heard the scissors clacking, and the branch of a tree drum on the buckets. One, two, three, they were gone, invisibly shuffling as she hugged her skirts. Mrs Price crossed herself for the second time that day, and touched the garlic at her throat. A vampire with a scissors was a Pembroke devil. And the black girl screamed like a pig.

Sister, raise your right hand. The seventh girl raised her right hand. Now say, said the doctor's daughter, Rise up out of the bearded barley. Rise out of the green grass asleep in Mr Griffiths's dingle. Big man, black man, all eye, one tooth, rise up out of Cader marshes. Say the devil kisses me. The devil kisses me, said the girl cold in the centre of the kitchen. Kiss me out of the bearded barley. Kiss me out of the bearded barley. The girls giggled in a circle. Swive* me out of the green grass. Swive me out of the green grass. Can I put on my clothes now? said the young witch, after encountering the invisible evil.

Throughout the hours of the early night, in the smoke of the seven candles, the doctor's daughter spoke of the sacrament of darkness. In her familiar's eyes she read the news of a great and an unholy coming; divining the future in the green and sleepy eyes, she saw, as clearly as the tinkers saw the spire, the towering coming of a beast in stag's skin, the antlered animal whose name read backwards, and the black, black, black wanderer climbing a hill for the seven wise girls of Cader. She woke the cat. Poor Bell, she said, smoothing his fur the wrong way. And, Ding dong, Bell, she said, and swung the spitting cat.

Sister, raise your left hand. The first girl raised her left hand. Now with your right hand put a needle in your left hand. Where is a needle? Here, said the doctor's daughter, is a needle, here in your hair. She made a gesture over the black hair, and drew a needle out from the coil at her ear. Say I cross you. I cross you, said the girl, and, with the needle in her hand, struck at the black cat racked on the daughter's lap.

For love takes many shapes, cat, dog, pig or goat; there was a lover, spellbound in the time of mass, now formed and featured in the image of the darting cat; his belly bleeding, he sped past the seven girls, past parlour and dispensary, into the night, onto the hill; the wind got at his wound, and swiftly he darted down the rocks, in the direction of the cooling streams.

He passed the three tinkers like lightning. Black cat is luck, said the panman. Bloody cat is bad luck, said John Bucket. The scissorman said nothing. They appeared out of silence by the wall of the Peak house, and heard a hellish music through the open door. They peered through the stained-glass window, and the seven girls danced before them. They have beaks, said the panman. Web feet, said John Bucket. The tinkers walked in.

At midnight the black girl bore her baby, a black beast with the eyes of a kitten and a stain at the corner of its mouth. The midwife, remembering birthmarks, whispered to the doctor of the gooseberry on his daughter's arm. Is it ripe yet? said Mrs Price. The doctor's hand trembled, and his lancet cut the baby under the chin. Scream you, said Mrs Price, who loved all babies.

The wind howled over Cader, waking the sleepy rooks who cawed from the trees and, louder than owls, disturbed the midwife's meditations. It was wrong for the rooks, those sleepy birds over the zinc roofs, to caw at night. Who put a spell on the rooks? The sun might rise at ten past one in the morning.

Scream you, said Mrs Price, the baby in her arms, this is a wicked world. The wicked world, with a voice out of the wind, spoke to the baby half smothering under the folds of the midwife's overcoat. Mrs Price wore a man's cap, and her great breasts heaved under the black blouse. Scream you, said the wicked world, I am an old man blinding you, a wicked little woman tickling you, a dry death parching you. The baby screamed, as though a flea were on its tongue.

The tinkers were lost in the house, and could not find the inner room where the girls still danced with the beaks of birds upon them and their web feet bare on the cobblestones. The panman opened the dispensary door, but the bottles and the tray of knives alarmed him. The passages were too dark for John Bucket, and the scissorman surprised him at a corner. Christ defend me, he cried. The girls stopped dancing, for the name of Christ rang in the outer halls. Enter, and, Enter, cried the doctor's daughter to the welcome devil. It was the scissorman who found the door and turned the handle, walking into candlelight. He stood before Gladwys on the threshold, a giant black as ink with a three days' beard. She lifted her face to his, and her sackcloth fell away.

Up the hill, the midwife, cooing as she came, held the newborn baby in her arms, and the doctor toiled behind her with his black bag rattling. The birds of the night flew by them, but the night was empty, and these restless wings and voices, hindering emptiness forever, were the feathers of shadows and the accents of an invisible flying. What purpose there was in the shape of Cader Peak, in the bouldered breast of the hill and the craters poxing the green-black flesh, was no more than the wind's purpose that willy-nilly blew from all corners the odd turfs and stones of an unmoulded world. The grassy rags and bones of the steep hill were, so the doctor pondered as he climbed behind the baby rocking into memory on a strange breast, whirled together out of the bins of chaos by a winter wind. But the doctor's conceits came to nothing, for the black child let out a scream so high and loud that Mr Griffiths heard it in his temple in the dingle. The worshipper of vegetables, standing beneath his holy marrow nailed in four places to the wall, heard the cry come down from the heights. A mandrake cried on Cader. Mr Griffiths hastened in the direction of the stars.

John Bucket and the panman stepped into candlelight, seeing a strange company. Now in the centre circle of the room, surrounded by the unsteady lights, stood the scissorman and a naked girl; she smiled at him, he smiled at her; his hands groped for her body, she stiffened and slackened; he drew her close, smiling she stiffened again, and he licked his lips.

John Bucket had not seen him as a power for evil baring the breasts and the immaculate thighs of the gentlewomen, a magnetic blackman with the doom of women in his smile, forcing open the gates of love. He remembered a black companion on the roads, sharpening the village scissors, and, in the shadows, when the tinkers took the night, a coal-black shadow, silent as the travelling hedges.

Was this tall man, the panman murmured, who takes the doctor's daughter with no how-d'you-do, was he Tom the scissorman? I remember him on the highways in the heat of the sun, a black, three-coated tinker.

And, like a god, the scissorman bent over Gladwys; he healed her wound, she stood his ointment and his fire, she burned at the tower altar, and the black sacrifice was done. Stepping out of his arms, her offering cut and broken, the gut of a lamb, she smiled and cried manfully: Dance, dance, my seven. And the seven danced, their antlers shaking, in the confusion of the unholy room. A coven, a coven, cried the seven as they danced. They beckoned the panman from the door. He edged towards them, and they caught his hands. Dance, dance, my strange man, the seven cried. John Bucket joined them, his buckets drumming, and swiftly they dragged him into the rising fury of the dance. The scissorman in the circle danced like a tower. They sped round and round, none crying louder than the two tinkers in the heart of the swirling company, and lightly the doctor's daughter was among them. She drove them to a faster turn of foot; giddy as weathercocks in a hundred changing winds, they were revolving figures in the winds of their dresses and to the music of the scissors and the metal pans; giddily she spun between the dancing hoops, the wheels of cloth and hair, and the bloody ninepins spinning; the candles grew pale and lean in the wind of the dance; she whirled by the tinker's side, by the scissorman's side, by his dark, damp side, smelling his skin, smelling the seven Furies.

It was then that the doctor, the midwife and the baby entered through the open door as quietly as could be. Sleep well, Pembroke, for your devils have left you. And woe on Cader Peak that the black man dances in my house. There had been nothing for that savage evening but an end of evil. The grave had yawned, and the black breath risen up.

Here danced the metamorphoses of the dusts of Cathmarw. Lie level, the ashes of man, for the phoenix flies from you, woe unto Cader, into my nice, square house. Mrs Price fingered her garlic, and the doctor stood grieving.

The seven saw them. A coven, a coven, they cried. One, dancing past them, snatched at the doctor's hand; another, dancing, caught him around the waist; and, all bewildered by the white flesh of their arms, the doctor danced. Woe, woe on Cader, he cried as he swirled among maidens, and his steps gathered speed. He heard his voice rising; his feet skimmed over the silver cobbles. A coven, a coven, cried the dancing doctor, and bowed in his measures.

Suddenly Mrs Price, hugging the black baby, was surrounded at the entrance of the room. Twelve dancers hemmed her in, and the hands of strangers pulled at the baby on her breast. See, see, said the doctor's daughter, the cross on the black throat. There was blood beneath the baby's chin, where a sharp knife had slipped and cut. The cat, cried the seven, The cat, the black cat. They had unloosed the spellbound devil that dwelt in the cat's shape, the human skeleton, the flesh and heart out of the Gehenna of the valley roots and the image of the creature calming his wound in the far-off streams. Their magic was done; they set the baby down on the stones, and the dance continued. Pembroke, sleep well, whispered the dancing midwife. Lie still, you empty county.

And it was thus that the last visitor that night found the thirteen dancers in the inner rooms of Cader House: a black man and a blushing girl, two shabby tinkers, a doctor, a midwife and seven country girls, swirling hand in hand under the charts that marked the rise and fall of the satanic seasons, among the symbols of the darker crafts, giddily turning, raising their voices to the roofs as they bowed to the cross reversed above the inner entrance.

Mr Griffiths, half blinded by the staring of the moon, peeped in and saw them. He saw the newborn baby on the cold stones. Unseen in the shadow by the door, he crept towards the baby and lifted it to its feet. The baby fell. Patiently Mr Griffiths lifted the baby to its feet. But the little mandrake would not walk that night.

The Mouse and the Woman*

1

In the eaves of the lunatic asylum were birds who whistled the coming in of spring. A madman, howling like a dog from the top room, could not disturb them, and their tunes did not stop when he thrust his hands through the bars of the window near their nests and clawed the sky. A fresh smell blew with the winds around the white building and its grounds. The asylum trees waved green hands over the wall to the world outside.

In the gardens the patients sat and looked up at the sun or upon the flowers or upon nothing, or walked sedately along the paths, hearing the gravel crunch beneath their feet with a hard, sensible sound. Children in print dresses might be expected to play, not noisily, upon the lawns. The building too had a sweet expression, as though it knew only the kind things of life and the polite emotions. In a middle room sat a child who had cut off his double thumb with a scissors.

A little way off the main path leading from house to gate, a girl, lifting her arms, beckoned to the birds. She enticed the sparrows with little movements of her fingers, but to no avail. "It must be spring," she said. The sparrows sang exultantly, and then stopped.

The howling in the top room began again. The madman's face was pressed close to the bars of the window. Opening his mouth wide, he bayed up at the sun, listening to the inflections of his voice with a remorseless concentration. With his unseeing eyes fixed on the green garden, he heard the revolution of the years as they moved softly back. Now there was no garden. Under the sun the iron bars melted. Like a flower, a new room pulsed and opened.

2

Waking up when it was still dark, he turned the dream over and over on the tip of his brain, until each little symbol became heavy with a separate meaning. But there were symbols he could not remember: they came and went so quickly among the rattle of leaves, the gestures of women's hands spelling on the sky, the falling of rain and the humming wind. He remembered the oval of her face and the colour of her eyes. He remembered the pitch of her voice, though not what she said. She moved again wearily up and down the same ruler of turf. What she said fell with the leaves, and spoke in the wind, whose brother rattled the panes like an old man.

There had been seven women, in a mad play by a Greek, each with the same face, crowned by the same hoop of mad, black hair. One by one they trod the ruler of turf, then vanished. They turned the same face to him, intolerably weary with the same suffering.

The dream had changed. Where the women were was an avenue of trees. And the trees leant forward and interlaced their hands, turning into a black forest. He had seen himself, absurd in his nakedness, walk into the depths. Stepping on a dead twig, he was bitten.

Then there was her face again. There was nothing in his dream but her tired face. And the changes of the details of the dream and the celestial changes, the levers of the trees and the toothed twigs, these were the mechanisms of her delirium. It was not the sickness of sin that was upon her face. Rather it was the sickness of never having sinned and of never having done well.

He lit the candle on the little deal table by his bedside. Candlelight threw the shadows of the room into confusion, and raised up the warped men of shadow out of the corners. For the first time he heard the clock. He had been deaf until then to everything except the wind outside the window and the clean winter sounds of the night world. But now the steady tick tock tick sounded like the heart of someone hidden in his room. He could not hear the night birds now. The loud clock drowned their crying, or the wind was too cold for them and made commotion among their feathers. He remembered the dark hair of the woman in the trees and of the seven women treading the ruler of turf.

He could no longer listen to the speaking of reason. The pulse of a new heart beat at his side. Contentedly he let the dream dictate its rhythm. Often he would rise when the sun had dropped down, and, in the lunatic blackness under the stars, walk on the hill, feeling the wind finger his hair and at his nostrils. The rats and the rabbits on his towering hill came out in the dark, and the shadows consoled them for the light of the harsh sun. The dark woman, too, had risen out of darkness, pulling down the stars in their hundreds and showing him a mystery that hung and shone higher in the night of the sky than all the planets crowding beyond the curtains.

He fell to sleep again and woke in the sun. As he dressed, the dog scratched at the door. He let it in and felt its wet muzzle in his hand. The weather was hot for a midwinter day. The little wind there was could not relieve the sharpness of the heat. With the opening of the bedroom window, the uneven beams of the sun twisted his images into the hard lines of light.

He tried not to think of the woman as he ate. She had risen out of the depths of darkness. Now she was lost again. She is drowned, dead, dead. In the clean glittering of the kitchen, among the white boards, the oleographs of old women, the brass candlesticks, the plates on the shelves and the sounds of kettle and clock, he was caught between believing in her and denying her. Now he insisted on the lines of her neck. The wilderness of her hair rose over the dark surface. He saw her flesh in the cut bread; her blood, still flowing through the channels of her mysterious body, in the spring water.

But another voice told him that she was dead. She was a woman in a mad story. He forced himself to hear the voice telling that she was dead. Dead, alive, drowned, raised up. The two voices shouted across his brain. He could not bear to think that the last spark in her had been put out. She is alive, alive, cried the two voices together.

As he tidied the sheets on his bed, he saw a block of paper, and sat down at the table with a pencil poised in his hand. A hawk flew over the hill. Seagulls, on spread, unmoving wings, cried past the window. A mother rat, in a hole in the hillside near the holes of rabbits, suckled its young as the sun climbed higher in the clouds.

He put the pencil down.

3

One winter morning, after the last crowing of the cock, in the walks of his garden, had died to nothing, she who for so long had dwelt with him appeared in all the wonder of her youth. She had cried to be set free, and to walk in his dreams no longer. Had she not been in the beginning, there would have been no beginning. She had moved in his belly when he was a boy, and stirred in his boy's loins. He at last gave birth to her, who had been with him from the beginning. And with him dwelt a dog, a mouse and a dark woman.

4

It is not a little thing, he thought, this writing that lies before me. It is the telling of a creation. It is the story of birth. Out of him had come another. A being had been born, not out of the womb, but out of the soul and the spinning head. He had come to the cottage on the hill that the being within him might ripen and be born away from the eyes of men. He understood what the wind that took up the woman's cry had cried in his last dream. "Let me be born," it had cried. He had given a woman being. His flesh would be upon her, and the life that he had given her would make her walk, talk and sing. And he knew, too, that it was upon the block of paper she was made absolute. There was an oracle in the lead of the pencil.

In the kitchen he cleaned up after his meal. When the last plate had been washed, he looked around the room. In the corner near the door was a hole no bigger than a half-crown. He found a tiny square of tin and nailed it over the hole, making sure that nothing could go in or come out. Then he donned his coat and walked out onto the hill and down towards the sea.

Broken water leapt up from the inrushing tide and fell into the crevices of the rocks, making innumerable pools. He climbed down to the half-circle of beach, and the clusters of shells did not break when his foot fell on them. Feeling his heart knock at his side, he turned to where the greater rocks climbed perilously up to the grass. There, at the foot, the oval of her face towards him, she stood and smiled. The spray brushed her naked body, and the creams of the sea ran unheeded over her feet. She lifted her hand. He crossed to her.

5

In the cool of the evening they walked in the garden behind the cottage. She had lost none of her beauty with the covering up of her nakedness. With slippers on her feet she stepped as gracefully as when her feet were bare. There was a dignity in the poise of her head, and her voice was clear as a bell. Walking by her side along the narrow path, he heard no discord in the crying together of the gulls. She pointed out bird and bush with her finger, illuminating a new loveliness in the wings and leaves, in the sour churning of water over pebbles, and a new life along the dead branches of the trees.

"It is quiet here," she said as they stood looking out to sea and the dark coming over the land. "Is it always as quiet?"

"Not when the storms come in with the tide," he said. "Boys play behind the hill, lovers go down to the shore."

Late evening turned to night so suddenly that, where she stood, stood a shadow under the moon. He took its hand, and they ran together to the cottage.

"It was lonely for you before I came," she said.

As a cinder hissed into the grate, he moved back in his chair, made a startled gesture with his hand.

"How quickly you become frightened," she said. "I am frightened of nothing."

But she thought over her words and spoke again, this time in a low voice.

"One day I may have no limbs to walk with, no hands to touch with. No heart under my breast."

"Look at the million stars," he said. "They make some pattern on the sky. It is a pattern of letters spelling a word. One night I shall look up and read the word."

But she kissed him and calmed his fears.

6

The madman remembered the inflections of her voice, heard, again, her frock rustling, and saw the terrible curve of her breast. His own breathing thundered in his ears. The girl on the bench beckoned to the sparrows. Somewhere a child purred, stroking the black columns of a wooden horse that neighed and then lay down.

7

They slept together on the first night, side by side in the dark, their arms around one another. The shadows in the corner were trimmed and shapely in her presence, losing their old deformity. And the stars looked in upon them and shone in their eyes.

"Tomorrow you must tell me what you dream," he said.

"It will be what I have always dreamt," she said. "Walking on a little length of grass, up and down, up and down, till my feet bleed. Seven images of me walking up and down."

"It is what I dream. Seven is a number in magic."

"Magic?" she said.

"A woman makes a wax man, puts a pin in its chest – and the man dies. Someone has a little devil, tells it what to do. A girl dies, you see her walk. A woman turns into a hill."

She let her head rest on his shoulder and fell to sleep.

He kissed her mouth, and passed his hand through her hair.

She was asleep, but he did not sleep. Wide awake, he stared into darkness. Now he was drowned in terror, and the sucking waters closed over his skull.

"I, I have a devil," he said.

She stirred at the noise of his voice, and then again her head was motionless and her body straight along the curves of the cool bed.

"I have a devil, but I do not tell it what to do. It lifts my hand. I write. The words spring into life. She, then, is a woman of the devil."

She made a contented sound, nestled ever nearer to him. Her breath was warm on his neck, and her foot lay on his like a mouse. He saw that she was beautiful in her sleep. Her beauty could not have sprouted out of evil. God, whom he had searched for in his loneliness, had formed her for his mate as Eve for Adam out of Adam's rib.

He kissed her again, and saw her smile as she slept.

"God at my side," he said.

8

He had not slept with Rachel and woken with Leah.* There was the pallor of dawn on her cheeks. He touched them lightly with a fingernail. She did not stir.

But there had been no woman in his dream. Not even a thread of woman's hair had dangled from the sky. God had come down in a cloud, and the cloud had changed to a snake's nest. Foul hissing of snakes had suggested the sound of water, and he had been drowned. Down and down he had fallen, under green shiftings and the bubbles that fishes blew from their mouths, down and down onto the bony floors of the sea.

Then against a white curtain people had moved and moved to no purpose but to speak mad things.

"What did you find under the tree?"

"I found an airman."

"No, no, under the other tree?"

"I found a bottle of foetus."

"No, no, under the other tree?"

"I found a mousetrap."

He had been invisible. There had been nothing but his voice. He had flown across back gardens, and his voice, caught in a tangle of wireless aerials, had bled as though it were a thing of substance. Men in deckchairs were listening to the loudspeakers speaking:

"What did you find under the tree?"

"I found a wax man."

"No, no, under the other tree?"

He could remember little else except the odds and ends of sentences, the movement of a turning shoulder, the sudden flight or drop of syllables. But slowly the whole meaning edged into his brain. He could translate every symbol of his dreams, and he lifted the pencil so that they might stand hard and clear upon the paper. But the words would not come. He thought he heard the scratching of velvet paws behind a panel. But when he sat still and listened close, there was no sound.

She opened her eyes.

"What are you doing?" she said.

He put down the paper, and kissed her before they rose to dress.

"What did you dream last night?" he asked her, when they had eaten.

"Nothing. I slept, that is all. What did you dream?"

"Nothing," he said.

9

There was creation screaming in the steam of the kettle, in the light making mouths on the china and the floor she swept as a child sweeps the floor of a doll's house. There was nothing to see in her but the ebb and flood of creation, only the transcendent sweep of being and living in the careless fold of flesh from shoulder bone to elbow. He could not tell, after the horror he had found in the translating symbols, why the sea should point to the fruitful and unfailing stars with the edge of each wave, and an image of fruition disturb the moon in its dead course.

She moulded his images that evening. She lent light, and the lamp was dim beside her, who had the oil of life glistening in every pore of her hand.

And now in the garden they remembered how they had walked in the garden for the first time.

"You were lonely before I came."

"How quickly you become frightened."

She had lost none of her beauty with the covering up of her nakedness. Though he had slept at her side, he had been content to know the surface of her. Now he stripped her of her clothes and laid her on a bed of grass.

10

The mouse had waited for this consummation. Wrinkling its eyes, it crept stealthily along the tunnel, littered with scraps of half-eaten paper, behind the kitchen wall. Stealthily, on tiny, padded paws, it felt its way through darkness, its nails scraping on the wood. Stealthily, it worked its way between the walls, screamed at the blind light through the chinks, and filed through the square of tin. Moonlight dropped slowly into the space where the mouse, working its destruction, inched into light. The last barrier fell away. And on the clean stones of the kitchen floor the mouse stood still.

11

That night he told of the love in the Garden of Eden.

"A garden was planted eastward, and Adam lived in it. Eve was made for him, out of him, bone of his bones, flesh of his flesh. They were as naked as you upon the seashore, but Eve could not have been as beautiful. They ate with the Devil, and saw that they were naked, and covered up their nakedness. In their good bodies they saw evil for the first time."

"Then you saw evil in me," she said, "when I was naked. I would as soon be naked as be clothed. Why did you cover up my nakedness?"

"It was not good to look upon," he said.

"But it was beautiful. You yourself said that it was beautiful," she said.

"It was not good to look upon."

"You said the body of Eve was good. And yet you say I was not good to look upon. Why did you cover up my nakedness?"

"It was not good to look upon."

12

"Welcome," said the devil to the madman. "Cast your eyes upon me. I grow and grow. See how I multiply. See my sad, Grecian stare. And the longing to be born in my dark eyes. Oh, that was the best joke of all."

"I am an asylum boy tearing the wings of birds. Remember the lions that were crucified. Who knows that it was not I who opened the door of the tomb for Christ to struggle out?"

But the madman had heard that welcome time after time. Ever since the evening of the second day after their love in the garden, when he had told her that her nakedness was not good to look upon, he had heard the welcome ring out in the sliding rain, and seen the welcome words burnt into the sea. He had known at the ringing of the first syllable in his ears that nothing on the earth could save him, and that the mouse would come out.

But the mouse had come out already.

The madman cried down at the beckoning girl, to whom, now, a host of birds edged closer on a bough.

13

"Why did you cover up my nakedness?"

"It was not good to look upon."

"Why, then, 'No, no, under the other tree'?"

"It was not good, I found a wax cross."

As she had questioned him, not harshly, but with bewilderment, that he whom she loved should find her nakedness unclean, he heard the broken pieces of the old dirge break into her questioning.

"Why, then," she said, "'No, no, under the other tree'?"

He heard himself reply, "It was not good, I found a talking thorn."

Real things kept changing place with unreal, and, as a bird burst into song, he heard the springs rattle far back in its throat.

She left him with a smile that still poised over a question, and, crossing the strip of hill, vanished into the half-dark where the cottage stood like another woman. But she returned ten times, in ten different shapes. She breathed at his ear, passed the back of her hand over his dry mouth and lit the lamp in the cottage room more than a mile away.

It grew darker as he stared at the stars. Wind cut through the new night. Very suddenly a bird screamed over the trees, and an owl, hungry for mice, hooted in the mile-away wood.

There was contradiction in heartbeat and green Sirius, an eye in the east. He put his hand to his eyes, hiding the star, and walked slowly towards the lamp burning far away in the cottage. And all the elements come together, of wind and sea and fire, of love and the passing of love, closed in a circle around him.

She was not sitting by the fire, as he had expected her to be, smiling upon the folds of her dress. He called her name at the foot of the stairs. He looked into the empty bedroom and called her name in the garden. But she had gone, and all the mystery of her presence had left the cottage. And the shadows that he thought had departed when she had come crowded the corners, muttering in women's voices among themselves. He turned down the wick in the lamp. As he climbed upstairs, he heard the corner voices become louder and louder, until the whole cottage reverberated with them, and the wind could not be heard.

14

With tears in his cheeks and with a hard pain in his heart, he fell to sleep, coming at last to where his father sat in an alcove carved in a cloud.

"Father," he said, "I have been walking over the world, looking for a thing worthy to love, but I drove it away and go now from place to place, moaning my hideousness, hearing my own voice in the voices of the corncrakes and the frogs, seeing my own face in the riddled faces of the beasts."

He held out his arms, waiting for words to fall from that old mouth hidden under a white beard frozen with tears. He implored the old man to speak.

"Speak to me, your son. Remember how we read the classic books together on the terraces. Or on an Irish harp you would pluck tunes until the geese, like the seven geese of the Wandering Jew,* rose squawking into the air. Father, speak to me, your only son, a prodigal out of the herbaceous spaces of small towns, out of the smells and sounds of the city, out of the thorny desert and the deep sea. You are a wise old man."

He implored the old man to speak, but, coming closer to him and staring into his face, he saw the stains of death upon mouth and eyes and a nest of mice in the tangle of the frozen beard.

It was weak to fly, but he flew. And it was a weakness of the blood to be invisible, but he was invisible. He reasoned and dreamt unreasonably at the same time, knowing his weakness and the lunacy of flying, but having no strength to conquer it. He flew like a bird over the fields, but soon the bird's body vanished, and he was a flying voice. An open window beckoned him by the waving of its blinds, as a scarecrow beckons a wise bird by its ragged waving, and into the open window he flew, alighting on a bed near a sleeping girl.

"Awake, girl," he said. "I am your lover come in the night."

She awoke at his voice.

"Who called me?"

"I called you."

"Where are you?"

"I am upon the pillow by your head, speaking into your ear."

"Who are you?"

"I am a voice."

"Stop calling into my ear, then, and hop into my hand so that I may touch you and tickle you. Hop into my hand, voice."

He lay still and warm in her palm.

"Where are you?"

"I am in your hand."

"Which hand?"

"The hand on your breast, left hand. Do not make a fist, or you will crush me. Can you not feel me warm in your hand? I am close to the roots of your fingers."

"Talk to me."

"I had a body, but was always a voice. As I truly am, I come to you in the night, a voice on your pillow."

"I know what you are. You are the still, small voice* I must not listen to. I have been told not to listen to that still, small voice that speaks in the night. It is wicked to listen. You must not come here again. You must go away."

"But I am your lover."

"I must not listen," said the girl, and suddenly clenched her hand.

15

He could go into the garden, regardless of rain, and bury his face in the wet earth. With his ears pressed close to the earth, he would hear the great heart, under soil and grass, strain before breaking. In dreams he would say to some figure, "Lift me up. I am only ten pounds now. I am lighter. Six pounds. Two pounds. My spine shows through my breast." The secret of that alchemy that had turned a little revolution of the unsteady senses into a golden moment was lost as a key is lost in undergrowth. A secret was confused among the night, and the confusion of the last madness before the grave would come down like an animal on the brain.

He wrote upon the block of paper, not knowing what he wrote, and dreading the words that looked up at him at last and could not be forgotten.

16

And this is all there was to it: a woman had been born, not out of the womb, but out of the soul and the spinning head. And he who had borne her out of darkness loved his creation, and she loved him. But this is all there was to it: a miracle befell a man. He fell in love with it, but could not keep it, and the miracle passed. And with him dwelt a dog, a mouse and a dark woman. The woman went away, and the dog died.

17

He buried the dog at the end of the garden. "Rest in peace," he told the dead dog. But the grave was not deep enough, and there were rats in the underhanging of the bank who bit through the sack shroud.

18

Upon town pavements he saw the woman step loose, her breasts firm under a coat on which the single hairs from old men's heads lay white on black. Her life, he knew, was only a life of days. Her spring had passed with him. After the summer and the autumn, unhallowed time between full life and death, there would be winter corrugating charm. He who knew the subtleties of every reason and sensed the four together in every symbol of the earth would disturb the chronology of the seasons. Winter must not appear.

19

Consider now the old effigy of time, his long beard whitened by an Egyptian sun, his bare feet watered by the Sargasso Sea. Watch me belabour the old fellow. I have stopped his heart. It split like a chamber pot. No, this is no rain falling. This is the wet out of the cracked heart.

Parhelion* and sun shine in the same sky with the broken moon. Dizzy with the chasing of moon by sun and by the twinkling of so many stars, I run upstairs to read again of the love of some man for a woman. I tumble down to see the half-crown hole in the kitchen wall stabbed open, and the prints of a mouse's pads on the floor.

Consider now the old effigies of the seasons. Break up the rhythm of the old figures' moving, the spring trot, summer canter, sad stride of autumn and winter shuffle. Break, piece by piece, the continuous changing of motion into a spindle-shanked walking.

Consider the sun, for whom I know no image but the old image of a shot eye, and the broken moon.

20

Gradually the chaos became less, and the things of the surrounding world were no longer wrought out of their own substance into the shapes of his thoughts. Some peace fell about him, and again the music of creation was to be heard trembling out of crystal waters, out of the holy sweep of the sky down to the wet edge of the earth, where a sea flowed over. Night came slowly, and the hill rose to the unrisen stars. He turned over the block of paper, and upon the last page wrote in a clear hand:

21

The woman died.

22

There was dignity in such a murder. And the hero in him rose up in all his holiness and strength. It was just that he who had brought her forth from darkness should pack her away again. And it was just that she should die not knowing what hand out of the sky struck upon her and laid her low.

He walked down the hill, his steps slow as in procession, and his lips smiling at the dark sea. He climbed onto the shore, and, feeling his heart knock at his side, turned to where the greater rocks climbed perilously to the grass. There at the foot, her face towards him, she lay and smiled. Sea water ran unheeded over her nakedness. He crossed to her and touched her cold cheek with his nails.

23

Acquainted with the last grief, he stood at the open window of his room. And the night was an island in a sea of mystery and meaning. And the voice out of the night was a voice of acceptance. And the face of the moon was the face of humility.

He knew the last wonder before the grave and the mystery that bewilders and incorporates the heavens and the earth. He knew that he had failed before the eye of God and the eye of Sirius to hold his miracle. The woman had shown him that it was wonderful to live. And now, when at last he knew how wonderful and how pleasant the blood in the trees, and how deep the well of the clouds, he must close his eyes and die. He opened his eyes and looked up at the stars. There were a million stars spelling the same word. And the word of the stars was written clearly upon the sky.

24

Alone in the kitchen, among the broken chairs and china, stood the mouse that had come out of the hole. Its paws rested lightly upon the floor painted all over with the grotesque figures of birds and girls. Stealthily, it crept back into the hole. Stealthily, it worked its way between the walls. There was no sound in the kitchen but the sound of the mouse's nails scraping upon wood.

25

In the eaves of the lunatic asylum the birds still whistled, and the madman, pressed close to the bars of the window near their nests, bayed up at the sun.

Upon the bench some distance from the main path, the girl was beckoning to the birds, while on a square of lawn danced three old women, hand in hand, simpering in the wind, to the music of an Italian organ from the world outside.

"Spring is come," said the warders.

A Prospect of the Sea*

It was high summer, and the boy was lying in the corn. He was happy, because he had no work to do and the weather was hot. He heard the corn sway from side to side above him, and the noise of the birds who whistled from the branches of the trees that hid the house. Lying flat on his back, he stared up into the unbrokenly blue sky falling over the edge of the corn. The wind, after the warm rain before noon, smelt of rabbits and cattle. He stretched himself like a cat and put his arms behind his head. Now he was riding on the sea, swimming through the golden corn waves, gliding along the heavens like a bird; in seven-league boots he was springing over the fields; he was building a nest in the sixth of the seven trees that waved their hands from a bright, green hill. Now he was a boy with tousled hair, rising lazily to his feet, wandering out of the corn to the strip of river by the hillside. He put his fingers in the water, making a mock sea wave to roll the stones over and shake the weeds; his fingers stood up like ten tower pillars in the magnifying water, and a fish with a wise head and a lashing tail swam in and out of the tower gates. He made up a story as the fish swam through the gates into the pebbles and the moving bed. There was a drowned princess from a Christmas book, with her shoulders broken and her two red pigtails stretched like the strings of a fiddle over her broken throat; she was caught in a fisherman's net, and the fish plucked her hair. He forgot how the story ended, if ever there were an end to a story that had no beginning. Did the princess live again, rising like a mermaid from the net, or did a prince from another story tauten the tails of her hair and bend her shoulder bone into a harp and pluck the dead, black tunes for ever in the courts of the royal country? The boy sent a stone skidding over the green water. He saw a rabbit scuttle, and threw a stone at its tail. A fish leapt at the gnats, and a lark darted out of the green earth. This was the best summer since the first seasons of the world. He did not believe in God, but God had made this summer full of blue winds and heat and pigeons in the house wood. There were no chimneys on the hills with no name in the distance, only the trees, which stood like women and men enjoying the sun; there were no cranes or coal tips, only the nameless distance and the hill with seven trees. He could think of no words to say how wonderful the summer was, or the noise of the wood pigeons, or the lazy corn blowing in the half-wind from the sea at the river's end. There were no words for the sky and the sun and the summer country: the birds were nice, and the corn was nice.

He crossed the nice field and climbed the hill. Under the innocent green of the trees, as blackbirds flew out towards the sun, the story of the princess died. That afternoon there was no drowning sea to pull her pigtails: the sea had flowed and vanished, leaving a hill, a cornfield and a hidden house; tall as the first short tree, she clambered down from the seventh and stood in front of him in a torn cotton frock. Her bare brown legs were scratched all over; there were berry stains round her mouth; her nails were black and broken, and her toes poked through her rubber shoes. She stood on a hill no bigger than a house, but the field below and the shining strip of river were as little as though the hill were a mountain rising over a single blade and a drop of water; the trees round the farmhouse were firesticks; and the Jarvis peaks, and Cader Peak beyond them to the edge of England, were molehills and stones' shadows in the still, single yard of the distance. From the first shade, the boy stared down at the river disappearing, the corn blowing back into the soil, the hundred house trees dwindling to a stalk, and the four corners of the yellow field meeting in a square that he could cover with his hand. He saw the many-coloured county shrink like a coat in the wash. Then a new wind sprang from the pennyworth of water at the river-drop's end, blowing the hill field to its full size, and the corn stood up as before, and the one stalk that hid the house was split into a hundred trees. It happened in half a second.

Blackbirds again flew out from the topmost boughs in a cloud like a cone; there was no end to the black, triangular flight of birds towards the sun; from hill to sun the winged bridge mounted silently; and then again a wind blew up, and this time from the vast and proper sea, and snapped the bridge's back. Like partridges, the common birds fell down in a shower.

All of it happened in half a second. The girl in the torn cotton frock sat down on the grass and crossed her legs; a real wind from nowhere lifted her frock, and up to her waist she was brown as an acorn. The boy, still standing timidly in the first shade, saw the broken holiday princess die for the second time, and a country girl take her place on the live hill. Who had been frightened of a few birds flying out of the trees and a sudden daze of the sun that made river and field and distance look so little under the hill? Who had told him the girl was as tall as a tree? She was no taller or stranger than the flowery girls on Sundays who picnicked in Whippet Valley.

"What were you doing up the tree?" he asked her, ashamed of his silence in front of her smiling, and suddenly shy as she moved so that the grass beneath her rose bent and green between her brown legs. "Were you after nests?" he said, and sat down beside her. But on the bent grass in the seventh shade, his first terror of her sprang up again like a sun returning from the sea that sank it, and burned his eyes to the skull and raised his hair. The stain on her lips was blood, not berries; and her nails were not broken, but sharpened sideways, ten black scissor blades ready to snip off his tongue. If he cried aloud to his uncle in the hidden house, she would make new animals, beckon Carmarthen tigers out of the mile-away wood to jump around him and bite his hands; she would make new, noisy birds in the air to whistle and chatter away his cries. He sat very still by her left side, and heard the heart in her breast drown every summer sound; every leaf of the tree that shaded them grew to man-size then, the ribs of the bark were channels and rivers wide as a great ship; and the moss on the tree, and the sharp grass ring round the base, were all the velvet coverings of green county's meadows blown hedge to hedge. Now on the world-sized hill, with the trees like heavens holding up the weathers, in the magnified summer weather she leant towards him so that he could not see the cornfield nor his uncle's house for her thick, red hair; and sky and far ridge were points of light in the pupils of her eyes.

This is death, said the boy to himself, consumption and whooping cough and the stones inside you... and the way your face stays if you make too many faces in the looking glass. Her mouth was an inch from his. Her long forefingers touched his eyelids. This is a story, he said to himself, about a boy on a holiday kissed by a broom-rider; she flew from a tree onto a hill that changes its size like a frog that loses its temper; she stroked his eyes and put her chest against him; and when she had loved him until he died she carried him off inside her to a den in a wood. But the story, like all stories, was killed as she kissed him; now he was a boy in a girl's arms, and the hill stood above a true river, and the peaks and their trees towards England were as Jarvis had known them when he walked there with his lovers and horses for half a century, a century ago.

Who had been frightened of a wind out of the light swelling the small country? The piece of a wind in the sun was like the wind in an empty house: it made the corners mountains and crowded the attics with shadows who broke through the roof; through the country corridors it raced in a hundred voices, each voice larger than the last, until the last voice tumbled down and the house was full of whispers.

"Where do you come from?" she whispered in his ear. She took her arms away, but still sat close, one knee between his legs, one hand on his hands. Who had been frightened of a sunburnt girl no taller or stranger than the pale girls at home who had babies before they were married?

"I come from Amman Valley," said the boy.

"I have a sister in Egypt," she said, "who lives in a pyramid..." She drew him closer.

"They're calling me in for tea," he said.

She lifted her frock to her waist.

If she loves me until I die, said the boy to himself under the seventh tree on the hill that was never the same for three minutes, she will carry me away inside her, run with me rattling inside her to a den in a wood, to a hole in a tree where my uncle will never find me. This is the story of a boy being stolen. She has put a knife in my belly and turned my stomach round.

She whispered in his ear: "I'll have a baby on every hill – what's your name, Amman?"

The afternoon was dying, lazily, namelessly drifting westward through the insects in the shade, over hill and tree and river and corn and grass to the evening shaping in the sea, blowing away, being blown from Wales in a wind, in the slow, blue grains, like a wind full of dreams and medicines, down the tide of the sun onto the grey and chanting shore where the birds from Noah's ark glide by with bushes in their mouths, and tomorrow and tomorrow tower over the cracked sandcastles.

So she stroked her clothes into place and patted back her hair as the day began to die, she rolled over onto her left side, careless of the low sun and the darkening miles. The boy awoke cautiously into a more curious dream, a summer vision broader than the one black cloud poised in the unbroken centre on a tower shaft of light; he came out of love through a wind full of turning knives and a cave full of flesh-white birds onto a new summit, standing like a stone that faces the stars blowing and stands no ceremony from the sea wind, a hard boy angry on a mound in the middle of a country evening; he put out his chest and said hard words to the world. Out of love he came marching, head on high, through a cave between two doors to a vantage hall room with an iron view over the earth. He walked to the last rail before pitch space; though the earth bowled round quickly, he saw every plough crease and beast's print, man track and water drop, comb, crest and plume mark, dust and death groove and signature and time-cast shade, from icefield to icefield, sea rims to sea centres, all over the apple-shaped ball under the metal rails beyond the living doors. He saw through the black thumbprint of a man's city to the fossil thumb of a once-lively man of meadows; through the grass and clover fossil of the country print to the whole hand of a forgotten city drowned under Europe; through the handprint to the arm of an empire broken like Venus; through the arm to the breast, from history to the thigh, through the thigh in the dark to the first and West print between the dark and the green Eden; and the garden was undrowned, to this next minute and for ever, under Asia in the earth that rolled onto its music in the beginning evening. When God was sleeping, he had climbed a ladder, and the room three jumps above the final rung was roofed and floored with the live pages of the book of days; the pages were gardens, the built words were trees, and Eden grew above him into Eden, and Eden grew down to Eden through the lower earth, an endless corridor of boughs and birds and leaves. He stood on a slope no wider than the loving room of the world, and the two poles kissed behind his shoulders; the boy stumbled forward like Atlas, loped over the iron view through the cave of knives and the capsized overgrowths of time to the hill in the field that had been a short mark under the platform in the clouds over the multiplying gardens.

"Wake up," she said into his ear; the iron characters were broken in her smile, and Eden shrank into the seventh shade. She told him to look in her eyes. He had thought that her eyes were brown or green, but they were sea-blue with black lashes, and her thick hair was black. She rumpled his hair, and put his hand deep in her breast so that he knew the nipple of her heart was red. He looked in her eyes, but they made a round glass of the sun, and as he moved sharply away he saw through the transparent trees; she could make a long crystal of each tree, and turn the house wood into gauze. She told him her name, but he had forgotten it as she spoke; she told him her age, and it was a new number. "Look in my eyes," she said. It was only an hour to the proper night; the stars were coming out, and the moon was ready. She took his hand and led him racing between trees over the ridge of the dewy hill, over the flowering nettles and the shut grass flowers, over the silence into sunlight and the noise of a sea breaking on sand and stone.

The hill in a screen of trees: between the in-country fields and the incoming sea, night on the wood and the stained beach yellow in the sun, the vanishing corn through the ten dry miles of farmland and the golden wastes where the split sand lapped over rocks, it stood between time over a secret root. The hill in two searchlights: the back moon shone on seven trees, and the sun of a strange day moved above water in the spluttering foreground. The hill between an owl and a seagull: the boy heard two birds' voices as brown wings climbed through the branches and the white wings before him fluttered on the sea waves. "Tu wit tu woo, do not adventure any more." Now the gulls that swam in the sky told him to race on along the warm sand until the water hugged him to its waves and the spindrift tore around him like a wind and a chain. The girl had her hand in his, and she rubbed her cheek on his shoulder. He was glad of her near him, for the princess was broken, and the monstrous girl was turned into a tree, and the frightening girl who threw the country into a daze of sizes and drove him out of love into the cloudy house was left alone in the moon's circle and the seven shades behind the screen.

It was hot that morning in the unexpected sunshine. A girl dressed in cotton put her mouth to his ear. "I'll run you to the sea," she said, and her breasts jumped up and down as she raced in front of him, with her hair flying wild, to the edge of the sea that was not made of water and the small, thundering pebbles that broke in a million pieces as the dry sea moved in. Along the bright wrack line, from the horizon where the vast birds sailed like boats, from the four compass corners, bellying up through the weed beds, melting from orient and tropic, surging through the ice hills and the whale grounds, through sunset and sunrise corridors, the salt gardens and the herring fields, whirlpool and rock pool, out of the trickle in the mountain, down the waterfalls, a white-faced sea of people, the terrible mortal number of the waves, all the centuries' sea drenched in the hail before Christ, who suffered tomorrow's storm wind, came in with the whole world's voices on the endless beach.

"Come back! Come back!" the boy cried to the girl.

She ran on unheeding over the sand and was lost among the sea. Now her face was a white drop of water in the horizontal rainfall, and her limbs were white as snow and lost in the white, walking tide. Now the heart in her breast was a small red bell that rang in a wave, her colourless hair fringed the spray, and her voice lapped over the flesh-and-bone water.

He cried again, but she had mingled with the people moving in and out. Their tides were drawn by a grave moon that never lost an arc. Their long sea gestures were deliberate, the flat hands beckoning, the heads uplifted, the eyes in the mask faces set in one direction. Oh, where was she now in the sea? Among the white, walking, and the coral-eyed. "Come back! Come back! Darling, run out of the sea." Among the processional waves. The bell in her breast was ringing over the sand.

He ran to the yellow foot of the dunes, calling over his shoulder. "Run out of the sea." In the once-green water where the fishes swam, where the gulls rested, where the luminous stones were rubbed and rocked on the scales of the green bed, when ships puffed over the tradeways and the mad, nameless animals came down to drink the salt. Among the measuring people. Oh, where was she now? The sea was lost behind the dunes. He stumbled on over sand and sandflowers like a blind boy in the sun. The sun dodged round his shoulders.

There was a story once upon a time whispered in the water voice; it blew out the echo from the trees behind the beach in the golden hollows, scraped on the wood until the musical birds and beasts came jumping into sunshine. A raven flew by him, out of a window in the Flood to the blind wind tower shaking in tomorrow's anger like a scarecrow made out of weathers.

"Once upon a time," said the water voice.

"Do not adventure any more," said the echo.

"She is ringing a bell for you in the sea."

"I am the owl and the echo: you shall never go back."

On a hill to the horizon stood an old man building a boat, and the light that slanted from the sea cast the holy mountain of a shadow over the three-storeyed decks and the eastern timber. And through the sky, out of the beds and gardens, down the white precipice built of feathers, the loud combs and mounds, from the caves in the hill, the cloudy shapes of birds and beasts and insects drifted into the hewn door. A dove with a green petal followed in the raven's flight. Cool rain began to fall.

The Holy Six*

The Holy Six of Wales sat in silence. The day was drawing to a close, and the heat of the first discussion grew cooler with the falling sun. All through the afternoon they had talked of nothing but the disappearance of the rector of Llareggub, and now, as the first lack of light moved in a visible shape and colour through the room and their tongues were tired, and they heard the voices in their nerves, they waited only for the first darkness to set in. At the first signs of night they would step from the table, adjust their hats and smiles and walk into the wicked streets. Where the women* smiled under the lamps, and the promise of the old sickness stirred in the fingertips of the girls in the dark doorways, the Six would pass dreaming, to the scrape of their boots on the pavement, of the women throughout the town smiling and doctoring love. To Mr Stul the women drifted in a maze of hair, and touched him in a raw place. The women drifted around Mr Edger. He caught them close to him, holding their misty limbs to his with no love or fire. The women moved again, with the grace of cats, edging down the darker alleys, where Mr Vyne, envious of their slant-eyed beauty, would scrape and bow. To Mr Rafe their beauties, washed in blood, were enemies of the fluttering eyes, and moved, in what image they would, full-breasted, fur-footed, to a massacre of the flesh. He saw the red nails and trembled. There was no purpose in the shaping wombs but the death of the flesh they shaped, and he shrank from the contact of death, and the male nerve was pulled alone. Tugging and tweaking, putting salt on the old love cuts, Mr Lucytre conducted an imaginary attack upon the maidenheads. How here and now there he ripped the women, and, kissing them, he bit into their lips. Spitefully, Mr Stipe watched him. Down fell the women on the sharp blade, and his heart smiled within him as they rose to dress their wounds.

The holy life was a constant erection to these six gentlemen. Miss Myfanwy came in with a letter.

Mr Edger opened the envelope. It contained a square piece of paper that might be a banknote. It was a letter from Mrs Amabel Owen, and was written in a backward hand.

She put malignity in the curves and tails of the characters, a cloven foot, a fork and a snake's sting coming out from the words in a separate life as the words lay back giddy from her revolving pen along the lines.

She, like Peter the poet, wrote of the Jarvis Valley. But while she saw by each bare tree a barer ghost and the ghost of the last spring and summer, he saw the statue of the tree and no ghost but his own that whistled out of the sickbed and raced among seaward fields.

Here in the valley, wrote Mrs Owen, my husband and I live quiet as two mice.

As she writes, thought Mr Stul, she feels the weight of her breasts on her ink-black arm.

Do the holy gentlemen believe in ghosts?

With the chains of cloud and iron suspended from their limbs, thought Mr Rafe, they would drip the deadly nightshade into my ear.

May she bear a vampire's baby, said Mr Stipe. The Reverend Mr Davies of Llareggub is staying with us for an indefinite period, she wrote in her secret hand.

Over the more level roadway on the lower hills, drawn in a jogcart by a sweating pony, the Holy Six journeyed in search of Mrs Owen. Miss Myfanwy, seated uncomfortably between Mr Stul and Mr Lucytre, conscious of the exposure of her calf and the pressure of Mr Lucytre's hand in the small of her back, prayed that the moon might not go in. There in the crowded cart the darkness would conceal the roving of the holy hands, and better Mr Stul's delight.

The wheels of the cart bumped on a boulder.

Over we go, said Mr Rafe, too frightened to brood upon the dissolution of his delicate body as it tumbled down the slope.

Over we go, said Mr Vyne, thinking how hard it was that death should come alone, the common flesh of Miss Myfanwy seated so near him.

As the cart balanced on one wheel and the pony, with the entire weight on one back leg, pawed at the air with its hanging hooves, Mr Stul thrust his hand high up under Miss Myfanwy's skirt, and Mr Lucytre, smiling at destruction, drove his fingers into her back until the knuckles tingled and the invisible flesh reddened with pain. Mr Edger clasped everything within reach, holding tight to his phallic hat. Mr Stipe leant suddenly to one side. The pony slipped on the wet turf, whinnied and fell. God is good, said old Vole the carter, and down he went, gathering speed, a white-haired boulder plunging into the craggy meadow fifty feet below. In one tight, black ball, the rest of the company rolled over the side. Is it blood? Is it blood? cried Miss Myfanwy as they fell. Mr Stul smiled, and fixed his arm more tightly round her.

On the grass below old Vole lay quietly on his back. He looked at the winter moon, that had not slipped, and the peace in the field. As six clerical hats and a draggled bonnet dropped near his feet, he turned on one side and saw the bodies of his passengers tumbling down upon him like a bony manna.

Darkness came for the second time. Now, with the hiding of the moon, the Holy Six arrived at the foot of the hills that separated the Jarvis Valley from the fields of the wild land. The trees on those ridges were taller than any they had seen in their journey from the fatal meadow, greener and straighter than the trees in the town parks. There was a madman in each tree. This they did not know, seeing only the sanity of the trees on the broad back of the upper grasses. The hills, that had curved all day in the circle of light, now straightened out against the sky, in a hundred straight lines ascended to the clouds, and in one stark shadow blocked out the moon. Shifting along the properties of the soil, man's chemic blood, pulled from him by the warring wind, mixed with the dust that the holy gentlemen, like six old horses, stamped into a cloud. The dust lay thick on their black boots; on old Vole's beard it scraped, grey as water, between the ginger and the white; it drifted over Miss Myfanwy's patent boots and was lost in the cracks of her feet. For a minute they stood trembling at the height of the hills. Then they adjusted their hats.

One behind the other they clambered upward, very far from the stars. The roots beneath their feet cried in the voices of the upspringing trees. It was to each member of the expedition a strange and a different voice that sounded along the branches. They reached the top of the hill, and the Jarvis Valley lay before them. Miss Myfanwy smelt the clover in the grass, but Mr Lucytre smelt only the dead birds. There were six vowels in the language of the branches. Old Vole heard the leaves. Their sentimental voice, as they clung together, spoke of the season of the storks and the children under the bushes. The Holy Six went down the hill, and the carter followed on the dark heels.

But before they knew where they were, and before the tenth Jarvis field had groaned beneath them, and before Mrs Owen spelt out their flesh and bone in the big ball on her table, morning suddenly came down; the meadows were oak-sided, standing greener than a sea as a lull came to the early light, lying under the wind as the south-west opened; the ancient boughs had all the birds of Wales upon them, and, from the farms among the trees and the fields on the unseen hillside, the cocks crew and the sheep cried. The wood

THE HOLY SIX

before them, glowing from a bloody centre, burned like cantharides,* a tuft of half-parting blooms and branches erect on the land that spouted up to the summits of the hills, angelically down, through ribbed throats of flowers and rising poisons, to the county's heart. The grass, that was heavy with dew, though the crystals on each blade broke lightly, lay still as they walked, a woman's stillness under the thrust of man lying in the waking furze and the back of the bedded ribs of the hill's half heather, the halves of gold and green by the slope quarries staining a rich shire and a common soil. And it was early morning, and the world was moist, when the crystal-gazer's husband, a freak in knickerbockers with an open coppish and a sabbath gamp,* came over the stones outside his house to meet the holy travellers.

His beard was wagging as he bowed. Your Holiness, said Mr Owen to the Six. Battered and bruised, the soles of their boots dragging like black and muddy wings along the ground, piously the Six responded. Mr Owen bowed to Miss Myfanwy, who, as his shirt wagged like a beard from his open trousers, curtsied low and blushed.

In the parlour, where Mrs Owen had read out the bloody coming, the Six gathered coldly round the fire, and two kettles sang. An old and ragged man dragged in a tub. Where is the mustard, Mr Davies? questioned the crystal-gazer from her chair in the darkest corner. Aware of her presence for the first time, the Holy Six spun round, seeing the big ball move inwardly, the unendurable head of evil, green as the woman's eyes and blacker than the shadows pouched under the lower lids, wriggle over the wet hint of hills at the globe's edges. She was a tidy little body, with plump hands and feet, and a love curl glistened on her forehead; dressed, like a Sunday, in cold and shining black, with a brooch of mother's ivory and a bone-white bangle, she saw the Holy Six reflected as six solid stumps, the amputated limbs of the deadly man who rotted in her as she swayed before his eyes, before his twelve bright eyes and the power of the staring Six.

Her womb and her throat and her hair.

Her green witch's eyes.

Her costly bangle.

The moles on her cheek.

Her young complexion.

The bones of her legs, her nails, her thumb.

The Six stood in front of her and touched her craftily, like the old men with Susanna,* and stared upon her where the unborn baby stirred manfully in the eighth month.

The old man returned with mustard.

This is the Reverend Mr Davies of Llareggub, said Mrs Owen.

The Holy Six rubbed their hands.

These are the Holy Six of Wales.

Mr Davies bowed, took off the kettles, half filled the tin tub and poured the mustard onto the boiling water. Mr Owen, appearing suddenly at his shoulder, gave him a yellow sponge. Bewildered by the yellow water that sucked at the spoon, by the dripping sponge in his fingers and by the silence in the parlour, Mr Davies turned trembling to the holy gentlemen. A timeless voice spoke in his ear, and a hand on his shrouded shoulder sank through the collarbone; a hand was on his heart, and the intolerable blood heat struck on a strong shadow. He knelt down in the wilderness of the tiny parlour, and off came the holy socks and boots. I, Davies, bathed their feet, muttered the grey minister. So that he might remember, the old, mad man said to himself, I, Davies, the poor ghost, washed the six sins in mustard and water.

Light was in the room, the world of light, and the holy Jewish word. On clock and black fire, light brought the inner world to pass, and the shape in his image that changed with the silent changes of the shape of light twisted his last man's-word. The word grew like light. He loved and coveted the last, dark light, turning from his memories to the yellow sea and the prowed beak of the spoon. In the world of love, through the drowning memories, he shifted one lover's smile to the mouth of a naughty lover cruel to the slept-with dead who died before dressing, and slowly turned to the illuminated face and the firer of the dead. Touching Mr Stul on the ankle, his ghost who laboured – now he was three parts ghost, and his manhood withered like the sap in a stick under a scarecrow's tatters – leapt out to marry Mary; all-sexed and nothing, intangible hermaphrodite riding the neuter dead, the minister of God in a grey image mounted dead Mary. Mrs Owen, wise to the impious systems, saw through the inner eye that the round but unbounded earth rotted as she ripened; a circle, not of her witch's making, grew around her; the immaculate circle broadened, taking a generation's shape. Mr Davies touched the generation's edges; up rose the man-stalking seed; and the circle broke. It was Mr Stul, the horny man, the father of Aberystwyth's bastards, who bounded over the broken circle, and, hand in hand with the grey ghost, kissed on divinity until the heavens melted.

The Holy five were not aware of this.

The lank-shanked Mr Edger put out his right foot, and Mr Davies washed it; careful of the temperature of the water rippling round the glassy skin, the minister of God washed the left foot; he remembered poor Davies, poor ghostly Davies, the man of bone and collar, howling, from a religious hill of the infinite curve of matter and the sound of the unspoken word; and, remembering Llareggub, the village with a rotting house, he grasped at the fat memories, the relics of the flesh that hung shabbily from him, and the undeniable desires; he grasped at the last senile hair on the skull as windily the world broke Davies up, and the ghost, having no greed or desire, came undead out of the particles.

Neither were the Holy four aware of this.

It was the foxy-whiskered Mr Vyne who said out of the darkness to the ghost Davies: Beautiful is Mrs Amabel Owen, the near-mother, the generation-bellied, from her teeth to her ten toes. My smile is a red hole, and my toes are like fingers. He sighed behind Mary and caught his breath at the seedy rim of the circle, seeing how beautiful she was as she shifted about him in the mothering middle of the earth. And out of the roots of the earth, lean as trees and whiter than the spring froth, rose her tall attendants. As the crystal-gazer and the virgin walked in one magic over their double grave, dead Davies and dead Vyne cried enviously: Beautiful is Amabel Mary, the ravished maiden, from her skull to her grave-walking feet.

Where but an hour earlier a far sea wind had blown the sun about, black night dropped down. Time on the clock denied the black coming.

Mr Rafe was more frightened of the dark than anything else in the world. He watched, with wide, white eyes, the lighting of the parlour lamp. What would the red lamp disclose? A mouse in a corner playing with an ivory tooth, a little vampire winking at his shoulder, a bed of spiders with a long woman in it.

Suddenly would the beautiful Mrs Owen be a skeleton with a worm inside her? Oh, oh, God's wrath on such small deer, and the dogs as big as your thumb. Mr Owen turned up the wick.

And secretly holding hands in the hour between the seconds, in the life that has no time for time, outside under the dark walked Mr Rafe and the ghost Davies. Was the grass dead under the night, and did the spirit of the grass, greener than Niagara's devil, sprout through the black weather like the flowers through a coffin's cracks? Nothing that was not half the figure of a ghost moved up the miles. And, as the minister had seen his buried squires spin from the system of the dead and, ruddier-cheeked than ever, dance on the orbit of a flower in the last, long acre of Llareggub, so now he saw the buried grass shoot through the new night and move on the hill wind. Were the faces of the west stars the backs of the east? he questioned his dead parishioners. God's wrath, cried Mr Rafe, in the shadow of a voice, nothing that was not half the substance of a man writhing in his shadow as it fell aslant on the hill, on the double-thumbed piksies* about me. Down, down – he slashed at the blades – down, you bald girls from Merthyr. He slashed at a walking echo, Ah, ah, oh, ah, cried the voice of Jerusalem, and Mary, from the moon's arc over the hill, ran like a wolf at the wailing ministers.

Midnight, guessed Mrs Owen. The hours had gone by in a wind.

Mr Stipe put out his right foot and nagged at the water with his left. He crept with ghost Davies through a narrow world; in his hair were the droppings of birds from the boughs of the mean trees; leading the ghost through dark dingles, he sprung the spiked bushes back and pissed against the wind. He hissed at the thirsty dead who bit their lips, and gave them a dry cherry; he whistled through his fingers, and up rose Lazarus like a weasel. And when the virgin gin came on a white ass by his grave, he raised a ragged hand and tickled the ass's belly till it brayed and threw Mary among the corpse eaters and the quarrelling crows.

Mr Lucytre was not aware of this.

The world, for him, rocked on a snapped foot; the shattered and the razor-bedded sea, the green skewered hulk with a stuffing of eyes, the red sea socket itself and the dead ships crawling around the rim, ached through the gristles and the bone, the bitten patch, the scaled and bubbling menses,* the elastic issues of the deep, the barbed, stained and scissored, the clotted-with-mucus, sawn and thorny flesh, ached on a never-ending ache. As on a crucifix, and turning on her nails, the skinny earth, each country pricked to the bladder, each racked sea torn in the ride, hung despairing in a limp space. What should the cruel Lucytre, who drags ghost Davies over a timeless agony, smooth on her wounds? Rust and salt and vinegar and alcohol, the juice of the upas tree,* the scorpion's ointment and a sponge soaked in dropsy.

The Holy Six stood up.

They took the six glasses of milk from Mr Owen's tray.

And will the holy gentlemen honour us for the night?

A life in Mrs Owen was stirring behind the comfortable little wall. She smiled at Mr Davies, this time with an intimate wrinkling of the corners of her mouth; Mr Owen smiled over his shoulder; and, caught between two smiles and understanding neither, he felt his own lips curl. They shared a mysterious smile, and the Six stood silently behind them.

My child, said Mrs Owen from her corner, shall be greater than all great men.

Your child is my child, said Mr Owen.

And Mr Davies, as suddenly as in the first bewilderment he had gone down upon his knees to pray, leant forward and patted the woman's hand. He would have laid his hands upon the fold of her frock from hip to hip, blessing the unborn under the cotton shroud, but the fear of the power of her eyes held his hand.

Your child is my child, said Mr Davies.

The ghost in him had coupled with the virgin, the virgin ghost that all the great stirrings of her husband's love had left as whole as a flower in a cup of milk.

But Mr Owen burst out laughing; he threw back his head and laughed at the matting shadows, at the oil in the clear, glass bag of the lamp. That there could be seed, shuffling to the spring of heat, in the old man's glands. That there could be life in the ancient loins. Father of the jawbones of asses and the hair-thighed camel's fleas, Mr Davies swayed before him in a mist of laughter. He could blow the old man up the sky with a puff of his lungs.

He is your child, said Mrs Owen.

She smiled at the shadow between them, the eunuch shadow of a man that fitted between the curving of their shoulders.

So Mr Davies smiled again, knowing the shadow to be his. And Mr Owen, caring for no shadow but that cast on his veins by the rising and the setting of the blood, smiled at them both.

The holy gentlemen would honour them that night.

And the Six circled the three.

Prologue to an Adventure*

As I walked through the wilderness of this world, as I walked through the wilderness, as I walked through the city* with the loud electric faces and the crowded petrols of the wind dazzling and drowning me that winter night before the West died, I remembered the winds of the high, white world that bore me and the faces of a noiseless million in the busyhood of heaven staring on the afterbirth. They who nudged through the literate light of the city, shouldered and elbowed me, catching my trilby with the spokes of their umbrellas, who offered me matches and music, made me out of their men's eyes into a manshape walking. But take away, I told them silently, the flannel and cotton, the cheap felt and leather, I am the nakedest and baldest nothing between the pinnacle and the base, an alderman of ghosts holding to watch chain and wallet on the wet pavement, the narrator of echoes moving in man's time. I have Old Moore* by the beard, and the news of the world is no world's news, the gossips of heaven and the fallen rumours are enough and too much for a shadow that casts no shadow, I said to the blind beggars and the paperboys who shouted into the rain. They who were hurrying by me on the narrow errands of the world, time bound to their wrists or blinded in their pockets, who consulted the time strapped to a holy tower and dodged between bonnets and wheels, heard in my fellow's footsteps the timeless accents of another walking. On the brilliant pavements under a smoky moon, their man's world turning to the bass roll of the traffic, they saw in the shape of my fellow another staring under the pale lids, and heard the spheres turn as he spoke. This is a strange city, gentlemen on your own, gentlemen arm in arm making a rehearsed salute, gentlemen with ladies; ladies this is a strange city. For them in the friendless houses in the streets of pennies and pleasures a million ladies and gentlemen moved up in bed, time moved with the practised moon over a million roofs that night, and grim policemen stood at each corner in the black wind. O mister lonely, said the ladies on their own, we shall be naked as newborn mice, loving you long in the short sparks of the night. We are not the ladies with feathers between their breasts, who lay eggs on the quilt. As I walked through the skyscraping centre, where the lamps walked at my side like volted men or the trees of a new scripture, I jostled the devil at my elbow, but lust in his city shadows dogged me under the arches, down the black blind streets. Now in the shape of a bald girl smiling, a wailing wanton with handcuffs for earrings, or the lean girls that lived on pickings, now in a ragged woman with a muckrake curtsying in the slime, the tempter of angels whispered over my shoulder, We shall be naked but for garters and black stockings, loving you long on a bed of strawberries and cream, and the nakeder for a ribbon that hides the nipples. We are not the ladies that eat into the brain behind the ear, or feed on the fat of the heart. I remembered the sexless shining women in the first hours of the world that bore me, and the golden sexless men that cried All Praise in the sounds of shape. Taking strength from a sudden shining, I have Old Scratch by the beard, I cried aloud. But the short-time shapes still followed, and the counsellor of an unholy nakedness nagged at my heels. No, not for nothing did the packed thoroughfares confront me at each cross and pavement's turning with these figures in the shapes of sounds, the lamp-chalked silhouettes and the walking frames of dreams, out of a darker allegory than the fictions of the earth could turn in twelve suns' time. There was more than man's meaning to the man-skulled bogeys thumbing the skeletons of their noses, to the marrow-merry andrews scratching their armpits in a tavern light and to the dead man smiling through his bandages, who laid hand on my sleeve, saying in no man's voice, There is more than man's meaning in a stuffed man talking, split from navel to arsehole, and more in the horned ladies at your heels than a pinch of the cloven delights and the tang of sulphur. Heaven and hell shift up and down the city. I have the God of Israel in the image of a painted boy, and Lucifer, in a woman's shirt, pisses from a window in Damaroid Alley.* See now, you shining ones, how the tuner of harps has fallen, and the painter of winds like a bag of henna into the gutter. The high hopes lie broken with broken bottles and suspender belts, the white mud falls like feathers, there out of Pessary Court comes the Bishop of Bumdom, dressed like a rat-catcher, a holy sister in Gamarouche Mews* sharpens her index tooth on a bloodstone, two weasels couple on All Paul's altar. It was an ungodly meaning, or the purpose of the fallen gods whose haloes magnified the wrong-cross-steepled horns on the pointed heads, that windily informed me of man's lower walking, and, as I thrust the dead-and-bandaged and a split-like-cabbage enemy to my right side, up sidled my no-bigger-than-a-thimble friends to the naked left. He who played the sorcerer, appearing all at one time in a dozen sulphurous beckonings, saying, out of a dozen mouths, We shall be naked as the slant-thighed queens of Asia in your dreams, was a symbol in the story of man's journey through the symboled city. And that which shifted with the greased lightning of a serpent from the nest holes in the bases of the cathedral pillars, tracking round the margins of the four cindery winds, was, too, a symbol in that city journey. In a mouse-tailed woman and a holy snake, the symbols of the city writhed before me. But by one red horn I had that double image, tore off the furry stays and leather jacket. We shall be naked, said Old Scratch variously emerging, as a Jewgirl crucified to the bedposts. We are all metaphors of the sound of shape of the shape of sound, break us we take another shape. Sideways the snake and the woman stroked a cross in the air. I saw the starfall that broke a cloud up, and dodged between bonnets and wheels to the iller-lit streets, where I saw Daniel Dom lurching after a painted shadow.

We walked into the Seven Sins. Two little girls danced barefoot in the sawdust, and a bottle splintered on their legs. A Negress loosened the straps of her yellow frock and bared a breast, holding a plate under the black flesh. Buy a pound, she said, and thrust her breast in Daniel's face. He faced the women as they moved, a yellow, noisy sea towards us, and caught the half-naked Negress by the wrist. Like a woman confronted by a tower, You are so strong, my love, she said, and kissed him full on the mouth. But before the sea could circle us, we were out through the swing doors into the street and the midwinter night, where the moonlight, salt-white no longer, hung windlessly over the city. They were night's enemies who made a lamp out of the devil's eye, but we followed a midnight radiance around the corners, like two weird brothers trod in the glittering webprints. In their damp hats and raincoats, in the blaze of shop windows, the people jostled against us on the pavements, and a gutterboy caught me by the sleeve. Buy an almanac, he said. It was the bitter end of the year. Now the starfall had ended, the sky was a hole in space. How long, how long, lord of the hail, shall my city rock on and the seven deadly seas wait tidelessly for the moon, the bitter end the last tide-spinning of the full circle, Daniel lamented, trailing the midnight radiance to the door of the Deadly Virtue, where the light went out and the seven webprints faded. We were forever climbing the steps of a sea tower, crying aloud from the turret that we might warn us, as we clambered, of the rusty rack and the spiked maiden in the turret corners. Make way for Mister Dom and friend. Walking into the Deadly Virtue, we heard our names announced through the loudspeaker trumpet of the wooden image over the central mirror, and, staring in the glass as the oracle continued, we saw two distorted faces grinning through the smoke. Make way, said the loudspeaker, for Daniel, ace of Destruction, old Dom the toper of Doom's kitchen, and for the alderman of ghosts. Is the translator of man's manuscript, his walking chapters, said the trumpet-faced, a member of my Deadly Virtue? What is the colour of the narrator's blood? Put a leech on his forearm. Make way, the image cried, for bald and naked Mister Dreamer of the bluest veins this side of the blood-coloured sea. As the sea of faces parted, the bare-backed ladies scraped back from the counter, and the matchstick-waisted men, the trussed and corseted stilt-walkers with the tits of ladies, sought out the darker recesses of the saloon, we stumbled forward to the fiery bottles. Brandy for the dreamer and the pilgrim, said the wooden voice. Gentlemen, it is my call, said the live loudspeaker, death on my house. It was then, in the tangled hours of a new morning, surrounded by the dead faces of the drinkers, the wail of lost voices and the words of the one electric image, that Daniel, hair on end, lamented first to me of the death on the city and the lost hero of the heart. There can be no armistice for the sexless, golden singers and the sulphurous hermaphrodites, the flying beast and the walking bird that war about us, for the horn and the wing. I could light the voices of the fiery virgins winking in my glass, catch the brandy-brown beast and bird as they fumed before my eyes, and kiss the two-antlered angel. No, not for nothing were these two intangible brandymaids neighbouring Daniel, who cried, syringe in hand, Open your coke-white legs, you ladies of needles, Dom thunder Daniel is the lightning drug and the doctor.

Now a wind sprang through the room from the dead street; from the racked tower, where two men lay in chains and a hole broke in the wall, we heard our own cries travel through the fumes of brandy and the loudspeaker's music; we pawed, in our tower agony, at the club shapes dancing, at the black girls tattooed from shoulder to nipple with a white dancing shape, frocked with snail-headed rushes and capped like antlers. But they slipped from us into the rubber corners, where their black lovers waited invisibly; and the music grew louder until the tower cry was lost among it; and again Daniel lurched after a painted shadow that led him, threading through smoke and dancers, to the stained window.

Beneath him lay the city sleeping, curled in its streets and houses, lamped by its own red-waxed and iron stars, with a built moon above it, and the spires crossed over the bed. I stared down, rocking at his side, onto the unsmoking roofs and the burnt-out candles. Destruction slept. Slowly the room behind us flowed, like four waters, down the seven gutters of the city into a black sea. A wave, catching the live loudspeaker in its mouth, sucked up the wood and music; for the last time a mountainous wave circled the drinkers and dragged them down, out of the world of light, to a crawling seabed; we saw a wave jumping and the last bright eyes go under, the last raw head, cut like a straw, fall crying through the destroying water. Daniel and I stood alone in the city. The sea of destruction lapped around our feet. We saw the starfall that broke the night up. The glass lights on iron went out, and the waves grew down into the pavements.

The Map of Love*

"Here dwell," said Sam Rib, "the two-backed beasts." He pointed to his map of Love, a square of seas and islands and strange continents with a forest of darkness at each extremity. The two-backed island, on the line of the equator, went in like the skin of lupus to his touch, and the blood sea surrounding found a new motion in its waters. Here seed, up the tide, broke on the boiling coasts; the sand grains multiplied; the seasons passed; summer, in a father's heat, went down to the autumn and the first pricks of winter, leaving the island shaping the four contrary winds out of its hollows.

"Here," said Sam Rib, digging his fingers in the hills of a little island, "dwell the first beasts of love." And here the get* of the first loves mixed, as he knew, with the grasses that oiled their green upgoings, with their own wind and sap nurtured the first rasp of love that never, until spring came, found the nerves' answer in the fellowing blades.

Beth Rib and Reuben marked the green sea around the island. It ran through the land cracks like a boy through his first caves. Under the sea they marked the channels, painted in skeleton, that linked the first beasts' island with the boggy lands. For shame of the half-liquid plants sprouting from the bog, the pen-drawn poisons seething in the grass and the copulation in the second mud, the children blushed.

"Here," said Sam Rib, "two weathers move." He traced with his finger the lightly drawn triangles of two winds and the mouths of two cornered cherubs. The weathers moved in one direction. Singly they crawled over the abominations of the swamp, content in the shadow of their own rains and snowings, in the noise of their own sighs and the pleasures of their own green achings. The weathers, like a girl and a boy, moved through the tossing world, the sea storm dragging under them, the clouds divided in many rages of movement as they stared on the raw wall of wind.

"Return, synthetic prodigals, to thy father's laboratory," declaimed Sam Rib, "and the fatted calf in a test tube." He indicated the shift of locations, the pen lines of the separate weathers travelling over the deep sea and the second split between the lovers' worlds. The cherubs blew harder; wind of the two tossing weathers and the sprays of the cohering sea drove on and on; on the single strand of two coupled countries, the weathers stood.

Two naked towers on the two-loves-in-a-grain of the million sands, they mixed, so the map arrows said, into a single strength. But the arrows of ink shot them back; two weakened towers, wet with love, they trembled at the terror of their first mixing, and two pale shadows blew over the land.

Beth Rib and Reuben scaled the hill that cast an eye of stone on the striped valley; hand in hand they ran down the hill, singing as they went, and took off their gaiters at the wet grass of the first of the twenty fields. There was a spirit in the valley that would roll on when all the hills and trees, all the rocks and streams, had been buried under the West death. Here was the first field wherein mad Jarvis, a hundred years before, had sown his seed in the belly of a bald-headed girl who had wandered out of a distant county and lain with him in the pains of love.

Here was the fourth field, a place of wonder, where the dead might spin all drunken-legged out of the dry graves, or the fallen angels battle upon the waters of the streams. Planted deeper in the soil of the valley than the blind roots could burrow after their mates, the spirit of the fourth field rose out of darkness, drawing the deep and the dark from the hearts of all who trod the valley a score or more miles from the borders of the mountainous county.

In the tenth and the central field Beth Rib and Reuben knocked at the doors of the bungalows, asking the location of the first island surrounded by loving hills. They knocked at the back door and received a ghostly admonishment.

Barefooted and hand in hand, they ran through the ten remaining fields to the edge of the Idris Water, where the wind smelt of seaweed and the valley spirit was set with sea rain. But night came down, hand on thigh, and shapes in the farther stretches of the now misty river drew a new shape close to them. An island shape walled round with darkness a half-mile upriver. Stealthily Beth Rib and Reuben tiptoed to the lapping water. They saw the shape grow, unlocked their fingers, took off their summer clothes and, naked, raced into the river.

"Upriver, upriver," she whispered.

"Upriver," he said.

They floated downriver as a current tugged at their legs, but they fought off the current and swam towards the still-growing island. Then mud rose from the bed of the river and sucked at Beth's feet.

"Downriver, downriver," she called, and struggled from the mud.

Reuben, weed-bound, fought with the grey heads that fought his hands, and followed her back to the brink of the seagoing valley.

But, as Beth swam, the water tickled her; the water pressed on her side.

"My love," cried Reuben, excited by the tickling water and the hands of the weeds.

And, as they stood naked on the twentieth field, "My love," she whispered.

First fear shot them back. Wet as they were, they pulled their clothes on them.

"Over the fields," she said.

Over the fields, in the direction of the hills and the hill home of Sam Rib, like weakened towers the children ran, no longer linked, bewildered by the mud and blushing at the first tickle of the misty island water.

"Here dwell," said Sam Rib, "the first beasts of love." In the cool of a new morning the children listened, too frightened to touch hands. He touched again the sagging hill above the island, and pointed the progression of the skeleton channels linking mud with mud, green sea with darker, and all love hills and islands into one territory. "Here the grass mates, the green mates, the grains," said Sam Rib, "and the dividing waters mate and are mated. The sun with the grass and the green, sand with water, and water with the green grass, these mate and are mated for the bearing and fostering of the globe." Sam Rib had mated with a green woman, as Great-Uncle Jarvis with his bald girl; he had mated with a womanly water for the bearing and the fostering of the child who blushed by him. He marked how the boggy lands lay so near the first beast doubling a back, the round of doubled beasts under as high a hill as Great-Uncle's hill that had frowned last night and wrapped itself in stones. Great-Uncle's hill had cut the children's feet, for the daps* and the gaiters were lost for ever in the grass of the first field.

Thinking of the hill, Beth Rib and Reuben sat quiet. They heard Sam say that the hill of the first island grew soft as wool for the descent, or smooth as ice for tobogganing. They remembered the tame descent last night.

"Tame hill," said Sam Rib, "grows wild for the ascending." Lining the adolescents' hill was a white route of stone and ice marked with the sliding foot or sledge of the children going down; another route, at the foot, climbed upwards in a line of red stone and blood marked with the cracking prints of the ascending children. The descent was soft as wool. Fail on the first island, and the ascending hill wraps itself in a sharp thing of stones.

Beth Rib and Reuben, never forgetful of the humpbacked boulders and the flints in the grass, turned to each other for the first time that day. Sam Rib had made her and would mould him, would make and mould the boy and girl together into a double climber that sought the island and melted there into a single strength. He told them again of the mud, but did not frighten them. And the grey heads of the weeds were broken, never to swell again in the hands of the swimmer. The day of ascending was over; the first descent remained, a hill on the map of love, two branches of stone and olive in the children's hands.

Synthetic prodigals returned that night to the room of the hill, through caves and chambers running to the roof, discerning the roof of stars, and happy in their locked hands. There lay the striped valley before them, and the grass of the twenty fields fed the cattle; the night cattle moved by the hedges or lapped at warm Idris Water. Beth Rib and Reuben ran down the hill, and the tender stones lay still under their feet; faster, they ran down the Jarvis flank, the wind at their hair, smells of the sea blown to their quivering nostrils from the north and the south, where there was no sea; and, slowing their speed, they reached the first field and the rim of the valley to find their gaiters placed neatly in a cow-cloven spot in the grass.

They buttoned on their gaiters, and ran through the falling blades.

"Here is the first field," said Beth Rib to Reuben.

The children stopped, the moonlight night went on, a voice spoke from the hedge darkness.

Said the voice: "You are the children of love."

"Where are you?"

"I am Jarvis."

"Who are you?"

"Here, my dears, here in the hedge with a wise woman."

But the children ran away from the voice in the hedge.

"Here in the second field."

They stopped for breath, and a weasel, making his noise, ran over their feet.

"Hold harder."

"I'll hold you harder."

Said a voice: "Hold hard, the children of love."

"Where are you?"

"I am Jarvis."

"Who are you?"

"Here, here, lying with a virgin from Dolgelley."*

In the third field the man of Jarvis lay loving a green girl, and, as he called them the children of love, lay loving her ghost and the smell of buttermilk on her breath. He loved a cripple in the fourth field, for the twist in her limbs made loving longer, and he cursed the straight children who found him with a straight-limbed lover in the fifth field marking the quarter.

A girl from Tiger Bay held Jarvis close, and her lips marked a red, cracked heart upon his throat; this was the sixth and the weather-tracked field, where, turning from the maul of her hands, he saw their innocence, two flowers wagging in a sow's ear. "My rose," said Jarvis, but the seventh love smelt in his hands, his fingering hands that held Glamorgan's canker under the eighth hedge. From the Convent of Bethel's Heart, a holy woman served him the ninth time.

And the children in the central field cried as ten voices came up, came up, came down from the ten spaces of the half-night and the hedging world.

It was full night when they answered, when the voices of one voice compassionately answered the two-voiced question ringing on the strokes of the upward, upward, and the downward air.

"We," said they, "are Jarvis, Jarvis under the hedge, in the arms of a woman, a green woman, a woman bald as a badger, on a nun's thigh."

They counted the numbers of their loves before the children's ears. Beth Rib and Reuben heard the ten oracles, and shyly they surrendered. Over the remaining fields, to the whispers of the last ten lovers, to the voice of ageing Jarvis, grey-haired in the final shadows, they sped to Idris. The island shone, the water babbled, there was a gesture of the limbs in each wind's stroke denting the flat river. He took off her summer clothes, and she shaped her arms like a swan. The bare boy stood at her shoulder; and she turned and saw him dive into the ripples in her wake. Behind them her fathers' voices slipped out of sound.

"Upriver," called Beth, "upriver."

"Upriver," he answered.

Only the warm, mapped waters ran that night over the edges of the first beasts' island white in a new moon.

In the Direction of the Beginning*

In the light tent in the swinging field in the great spring evening, near the sea and the shingled boat with a mast of cedar wood, the hinderwood decked with beaks and shells, a folded salmon sail and two finned oars; with gulls in one flight high over, stork, pelican and sparrow flying to the ocean's end and the first grain of a timeless land that spins on the head of a sand glass, a hoop of feathers down the dark of the spring in a topsy-turvy year; as the rocks in history, by every feature and scrawled limb, eye of a needle, shadow of a nerve, cut in the heart, by rifted fibre and clay thread, recorded for the rant of odyssey the dropping of the bay leaf toppling of the oak tree splintering of the moonstone against assassin avatar undead and numbered waves, a man was born in the direction of the beginning. And out of sleep, where the moon had raised him through the mountains in her eyes and by the strong, eyed arms that fall behind her, full of tides and fingers, to the blown sea, he wrestled over the edge of the evening, took to the beginning as a goose to the sky and called his Furies by their names from the wind-drawn index of the grave and waters. Who was this stranger who came like a hailstone, cut in ice, a snow-leafed seabush for her hair, and taller than a cedar mast, the north white rain descending and the whale-driven sea cast up to the caves of the eye, from a fishermen's city on the floating island? She was salt-white and travelling as the field, on one blade, swung with its birds around her, evening centred in the never-still heart, he heard her hands among the treetops – a feather dived, her fingers flowed over the voices – and the world went drowning down through a siren stranger's vision of grass and water beasts and snow. The world was sucked to the last lake's drop; the cataract of the last particle worried in a lather to the ground, as if the rain from heaven had let its clouds fall turtle-turning like a manna made of the soft-bellied seasons, and the hard hail, falling, spread and flustered in a cloud half flower half ash or the comb-footed scavenger's wind through a pyramid raised high with mud or the soft slow drift of mingling steam and leaves. In the exact centre of enchantment he was a shoreman in deep sea, lashed by his hair to the eye in the cyclop breast, with his swept thighs strung among her voice; white bears swam and sailors drowned to the music she scaled and drew with hands and fables from his upright hair; she plucked his terror by the ears and bore him singing into light through the forest of the serpent-haired and the stone-turning voice. Revelation stared back over its transfixed shoulder. Which was her genesis, the last spark of judgement or the first whale's spout from the waterland? The conflagration at the end, a burial fire jumping, a spent rocket hot on its tail, or, where the first spring and its folly climbed the sea barriers and the garden locks were bruised, capped and douting* water over the mountain candlehead? Whose was the image in the wind, the print on the cliff, the echo knocking to be answered? She was orioled and serpent-haired. She moved in the swallowing salty field, the chronicle and the rocks, the dark anatomies, the anchored sea itself. She raged in the mule's womb. She faltered in the galloping dynasty. She was loud in the old grave, kept a still, quick tongue in the sun. He marked her outcast image, mapped with a nightmare's foot in poison and framed against the wind, print of her thumb that buckled on its hand with a webbed shadow, interrogation of the familiar echo: which is my genesis, the granite fountain extinguishing where the first flame is cast in the sculptured world, or the bonfire maned like a lion in the threshold of the last vault? One voice then in that evening travelled the light and water waves, one lineament took on the sliding moods, from where the gold-green sea cantharis* dyes the trail of the octopus one venom crawled through foam, and from the four map corners one cherub in an island shape puffed the clouds to sea.

An Adventure from a Work in Progress*

The boat tugged its anchor, and the anchor flew up from the seabed like an iron arrow and hung poised in a new wind and pointed over the corkscrew channels of the sea to the dark holes and caves in the horizon. He saw birds searing out of the pitted distance blind by his anchor as he swam with a seal at his side to the boat that stamped the water. He gripped on the bows like a mane, the arrowing anchor shot north, and the boat sped beneath it with winds and invisible fire puffing and licking. His animal boat split the water into a thousand boat-sized seas, bit deep into the flying shoals, halved and multiplied the flying fishes, it dived under waves like a wooden dolphin and wagged the fingering wrack off its stern, it swerved past a black-and-gold buoy with cathedral chimes and kept cold north. Spray turned to ice as it whipped through his hair, and pierced his cheeks and eyelids, and the running blood froze hard. He saw through a coat of red ice that the sea was transparent; under his boat the drowned dead burned in a pale-green, grass-high fire; the sea rained on the flames. But on through the north, between glass hills on which she-bears climbed and saw themselves reflected, eating the sea between the paddling floes, a shell of lightning fibres skimming and darting under an anchor bolt, tossed and magnified among the frozen window weeds, through a slow snowstorm whose flakes fell like hills one at a time down the white air, lost in a round sudden house of the six-year night and slipping through an arch of sleeping birds each roosted on an icicle, the boat came into blue water. Birds with blue feathers set alight by the sun, with live flames for their crests, flew by the hovering anchor to the trees and bushes on the rims of soft sand round the sea that brushed his boat slowly and whispered it like a name in letters of parting water towards a harbour grove and a slowly spinning island with lizards in its lap. The salmon of the still sail turned to the blue of the birds' eggs in the tips of the fringing forest of each wave. The feathers crackled from the birds and drifted down and fell upon bare rods and stalks that fenced the island entrance, the rods and stalks grew into trees with musical leaves still burning. The history of the boat was spelt in knocking water on the hanging harbour bank; each syllable of his adventure struck on grass and stone and rang out in the passages of the disturbed rock plants and was chattered from flame to tree. The anchor dived to rest. He strode through the blazing fence. The print of the ice was melting. The island spun. He saw between trees a tall woman standing on the opposite bank. He ran directly towards her, but the green thighs closed. He ran on the rim towards her, but she was still the same distance from him on the roundabout island. Time was about to fall; it had slept without sound under and over the blaze and spinning; now it was raised ready. Flowers in the centre of the island caught its tears in a cup. It hardened and shouted and shone in dead echoes and pearls. It fell as he ran on the outer rim, and oaks were felled in the acorn and lizards laid in the shell. He held the woman drowning in his arms, her driftwood limbs, her winking ballast head of glass; he fought with her blood like a man with a waterfall turning to fishdust and ash, and her salvaged seaweed hair twisted blindly about his eyes. The boat with anchor hovering and finned oars trembling for water after land, the beaks at the stern gabbling and the shells alive, was blown alongside him by a wind that took a corner on one breath, from the harbour bank where roots of trees drove up the sky and foliage in cinders smouldered down, the lopped leg of a bird scratched against rock, a thundering cave sat upright and bolted mouth-down into the sea; he dipped the gills of the oars, the cedar mast shook like a cloth, warm north the boat sped off again from an island no longer spinning, but split into vanishing caves and contrary trees. Time that had fallen rested in the edges of its knives and the hammock of its fires, the memory of the woman was strong on his hands, her claws and anemones, weed-wrack and urchin hair, the sea was deserted and colourless, direction was dead as the island and north was a circle, a bird above the anchor spurted through a stationary cloud to catch its cry, the boat with gilled oars swimming ploughed through the foam in the wake, her pale brow glistened in the new moon of his nails, and the drenched thread of her nerves sprang up and down behind them, the stern beaks quacked and yawned, crabs clacked from the shells, a mist rose up that dressed and unshaped the sky, and the sea flowed in secret. Through the mist, dragging a black weather with it, a spade-shaped shoal of clouds tacked to its peak, a broken moon, a wind with trumpets, came a mountain in a moment. The boat struck rock. The beaks were still. The shells snapped shut. He leapt into mud as the wind cried his name to the flapping shoals; his name rolled down the mountain, echoed through caves and crevices, ducked in venomous pools, slap on black walls, translated into the voice of dying stone, growling through slime into silence. He gazed at the mountain peak; a cloud obscured it, cords of light from the moon were looped around the tentacles of the crags. Lightning with a horn and bone on, with gristle white as a spine hardening and halving the forked sides, struck through the tacked cloud cap, lit the stone head, scorched the mist-curled fringe, cut through the cords until the moon sailed upwards like a kite. With the turning out of the lightning, the jackknife doubling-up of the limp spine, the weather in tow rocked to work and flight in a sealed air, the mountain vanished, leaving a hole in space to keep the shape of his horror as he sank, as the monuments of the dark mud toppled and his raised arms were cemented against rock with the wet maggot sacks and the mixed, crawling breasts of statues and creatures who once stood on the ledges of the mountain foot or blocked the crying mouths of caves. The wind, blowing matter with a noise, stuck to his cheek. The sea climbed his limbs like a sailor. Bound and drowning in that dismembered masonry, his eyes on a level with the shuffled circle of headpieces floating, he saw the lightning dart to strike again and the horned bone stiffen among the forks; hope, like another muscle, broke the embraces of the nuzzling bodies, thrust off the face that death-masked his, for the mountain appeared on the strike of light, and the hollow shape of his horror was filled with crags and turrets, rock webs and dens, spinning black balconies, the loud, packed smashing of separate seas and the abominable substances of a new colour. The world happened at once. There was the furnished mountain built in a flash and thunderclap colliding. The shapes of rain falling made a new noise and number. And the lightning stayed striking; its charted shaft of sawteeth struck and bit in continual light; one blind flash was a year of mornings. The mummyfolds, the mudpots, the wet masks, the quick casts, the closing sheathes, melted under the frostbite heat of that unwinking lightning. He boxed free from the statues and the caved and toppling watchers. From a man-sized dent in a melting thigh he came up strung with shells and mussed with weed like a child from the roots of the original sea into a dazzling bed. Once on hard land, with shells that swung from his hair ringing from the tail of a weed and shells repeating the sea, he shook away calamity, bounced the weeds off his bare breast, threw back his head until the pealing shells took in their echo the voices of all miscellaneous water and grappled with the mountainside. His shadow led and beckoned; he turned curves of the eel-backed paths, his shadow pointed to the footprints that appeared before his feet; he followed where his footprints led, saw the smudged outline of his hand on a wet stone as he quarrelled with stones and trees towards it up an attacking valley; animals closed their lips round the shout of a wind walking by and scooped his name to welcome it up hollow trunks and walls. He followed the flight of his name: it slipped to a stop at the peak: there a tall woman caught the flying name to her lips. He flourished in the middle of the pain of the mountain, and joy sped with his shadow, the strong memory of the driftwrack woman was dead on his hands digging deep in the soil towards this stranger tall as a pulled tree and whiter at that great shortening distance than the lightning-coloured sea a hundred dangers below. The thighs smooth as groundstone and sensual cleft, limpet eye and mussel mouth, the white boulders bent, blue shadows and pricked berries, the torrential flowers and blacks of the bush on the skull and the muffed pits, the draped cellars, the lashed stones, the creased face on the knees, all for a moment while he stood in love were still and near. Then slowly her peak in a cloud's alcove – carved animals on an abbey, wind in an amice,* arching accusing her – rose with his lovely dashing from stillness. Slowly her peak got up the cloudy arches, the stones he stumbled on followed her at the same speed. Though he hugged like a bear and climbed fast, she kept her distance from him. The mountain in the intervals of his breathing grew many times its size, until time fell and cut and burned it down. The peak collapsed, the mountain folded, he clasped the woman diminishing in his arms; the downpours of her hair were short falls, her limbs stunted, her hands blunt, her teeth were small and square as dice, and the rot marked them. A halo cracked like china, wings were spoked. Blood flapped behind all the windows of the world. And with the wasting of her limbs suddenly she grew young. Holding her small body, he cried in the nightmare of a naked child kissing and blaspheming close, breasts small as pears with milk foaming from them, the innocent holes of the open eyes, the thin, rouged mussel mouth, when the head falls, the eyes loll, the small throat snaps and the headless child lies loving in the dark. The mad bug trotted in at the ear with the whole earth on a feeler. With his cries she caved in younger. He held her hard. The marrow in her bones was soft as syrup. From a scar in the peak came a shadow with black gamp and scarlet basin. She dangled there with bald and monstrous skull, bunched monkey face and soaked abdominal tail. Out of the webbed sea pig and water-nudging fish a white pool spat in his palm. Reeling to run seaward and away, he trod the flats of waves. The splintered claw of a crab struck from the killed hindershells. And, after the anchor burrowing through blind cloud, he rowed and sailed, that the world might happen to him once, past the events of revolving islands and elastic hills, on the common sea.

The True Story*

The old woman upstairs had been dying since Helen could remember. She had lain like a wax woman in her sheets since Helen was a child coming with her mother to bring fresh fruit and vegetables to the dying. And now Helen was a woman under her apron and print frock, and her pale hair was bound in a bunch behind her head. Each morning she got up with the sun, lit the fire, let in the red-eyed cat. She made a pot of tea and, going up to the bedroom at the back of the cottage, bent over the old woman, whose unseeing eyes were never closed. Each morning she looked into the hollows of the eyes and passed her hands over them. But the lids did not move, and she could not tell if the old woman breathed. "Eight o'clock, eight o'clock now," she said. And at once the eyes smiled. A ragged hand came out from the sheets and stayed there until Helen took it in her padded hand and closed it round the cup. When the cup was empty, Helen filled it, and when the pot was dry, she pulled back the white sheets from the bed. There the old woman was, stretched out in her nightdress, and the colour of her flesh was grey as her hair. Helen tidied the sheets and attended to the old woman's wants. Then she took the pot away.

Each morning she made breakfast for the boy who worked in the garden. She went to the back door, opened it and saw him in the distance with his spade. "Half-past eight now," she said. He was an ugly boy, and his eyes were redder than the cat's, two crafty cuts in his head forever spying on the first shadows of her breast. She put his food in front of him. When he stood up, he always said, "Is there anything you want me to do?" She had never said, "Yes." The boy went back to dig potatoes out of the patch or to count the hens' eggs, and if there were berries to be picked off the garden bushes, she joined him before noon. Seeing the redcurrants pile up in the palm of her hand, she would think of the stain of the money under the old woman's mattress. If there were hens to be killed, she could cut their throats far more cleanly than the boy, who let his knife stay in the wound and wiped the blood on the knife along his sleeve. She caught a hen and killed it, felt its warm blood, and saw it run headless up the path. Then she went in to wash her hands.

THE TRUE STORY

It was in the first weeks of spring that she made up her mind to kill the old woman upstairs. She was twenty years old. There was so much that she wanted. She wanted a man of her own and a black dress for Sundays and a hat with a flower. She had no money at all. On the days that the boy took the eggs and the vegetables to market, she gave him sixpence that the old woman gave her, and the money the boy brought back in his handkerchief she put into the old woman's hand. She worked for her food and shelter as the boy worked for his, though she slept in a room upstairs and he slept in a straw bed over the empty sheds.

On a market morning she walked into the garden so that the plan might be cooled in her head. It was a fine May day with no more than two clouds in the sky, two unshapely hands closing round the head of the sun. "If I could fly," she thought, "I could fly in at the open window and fix my teeth in her throat." But the cool wind blew the thought away. She knew that she was no common girl, for she had read books in the winter evenings when the boy was dreaming in the straw and the old woman was alone in the dark. She had read of a god who came down like money, of snakes with the voices of men, and of a man who stood on the top of a hill talking with a piece of fire.

At the end of the garden, where the fence kept out the wild, green fields, she came to a mound of earth. There she had buried the dog she had killed for catching and killing the hens. On a rough cross the date of the death was written backwards, so that the dog had not died yet. "I could bury her here," said Helen to herself, "by the side of the grave, so that nobody could find her." And she patted her hands and reached the back door of the cottage before the two clouds got round the sun.

Inside there was a meal to be prepared for the old woman, potatoes to be mashed up in the tea. With the knife in her hand and the skins in her lap, she thought of the murder she was about to do. The knife made the only sound, the wind had dropped down, her heart was as quiet as though she had wrapped it up. Nothing moved in the cottage; her hand was dead on her lap; she could not think that smoke went up the chimney and out into the still sky. Her mind, alone in the world, was ticking away. Then, when all things were dead, a cock crew, and she remembered the boy who would soon be back from market. She had made up her mind to kill before he returned, but the grave must be dug and the hole filled up. Helen felt her hand die again in her lap. And in the middle of death she heard the boy's hand lift the latch. He came into the kitchen, saw that she was cleaning the potatoes and dropped his handkerchief on the table.

Hearing the rattle of money, she looked up at him and smiled. He had never seen her smile before.

Soon she put his meal in front of him, and sat sideways by the fire. As he raised the knife to his mouth, he felt the full glance of her eyes on the sides of his eyes. "Have you taken up her dinner?" he asked. She did not answer. When he had finished, he stood up from the table and asked, "Is there anything you want me to do?" as he had asked a thousand times. "Yes," said Helen.

She had never said "Yes" to him before. He had never heard a woman speak as she did then. The first shadow of her breast had never been so dark. He stumbled across the kitchen to her, and she lifted her hands to her shoulders. "What will you do for me?" she said, and loosened the straps of her frock so that it fell about her and left her breast bare. She took his hand and placed it on her flesh. He stared at her nakedness, then said her name and caught hold of her. She held him close. "What will you do for me?" She let her frock fall on the floor and tore the rest of her clothes away. "You will do what I want," she said as his hands dropped on her.

After a minute she struggled out of his arms and ran softly across the room. With her naked back to the door that led upstairs, she beckoned him and told him what he was to do. "You help me, we shall be rich," she said. He smiled and nodded. He tried to finger her again, but she caught his fingers and opened the door and led him upstairs. "You stay here quiet," she said. In the old woman's room she looked around her as if for the last time, at the cracked jug, the half-open window, the bed and the text on the wall. "One o'clock now," she said into the old woman's ear, and the blind eyes smiled. Helen put her fingers round the old woman's throat. "One o'clock now," she said, and with a sudden movement knocked the old woman's head against the wall. It needed but three little knocks, and the head burst like an egg.

"What have you done?" cried the boy. Helen called for him to come in. He stared at the naked woman who cleaned her hands on the bed and at the blood that made a round, red stain on the wall, and screamed out in horror. "Be quiet," said Helen, but he screamed again at her quiet voice and scurried downstairs.

"So Helen must fly," she said to herself. "Fly out of the old woman's room." She opened the window wider and stepped out. "I am flying," she said.

But she was not flying.

The Vest*

He rang the bell. There was no answer. She was out. He turned the key.

The hall in the late-afternoon light was full of shadows. They made one almost solid shape. He took off his hat and coat, looking sideways, so that he might not see the shape, at the light through the sitting-room door.

"Is anybody in?"

The shadows bewildered him. She would have swept them up as she swept the invading dust.

In the drawing room the fire was low. He crossed over to it and sat down. His hands were cold. He needed the flames of the fire to light up the corners of the room. On the way home he had seen a dog run over by a motor car. The sight of the blood had confused him. He had wanted to go down on his knees and finger the blood that made a round pool in the middle of the road. Someone had plucked at his sleeve, asking him if he was ill. He remembered that the sound and strength of his voice had drowned the first desire. He had walked away from the blood, with the stained wheels of the car and the soaking blackness under the bonnet going round and round before his eyes. He needed the warmth. The wind outside had cut between his fingers and thumbs.

She had left her sewing on the carpet near the coal scuttle. She had been making a petticoat. He picked it up and touched it, feeling where her breasts would sit under the yellow cotton. That morning he had seen her with her head enveloped in a frock. He saw her, thin in her nakedness, as a bag of skin and henna drifting out of the light. He let the petticoat drop onto the floor again.

Why, he wondered, was there this image of the red and broken dog? It was the first time he had seen the brains of a living creature burst out of the skull. He had been sick at the last yelp and the sudden caving of the dog's chest. He could have killed and shouted, like a child cracking a black beetle* between its fingers.

A thousand nights ago, she had lain by his side. In her arms, he thought of the bones of her arms. He lay quietly by her skeleton. But she rose next morning in the corrupted flesh.

When he hurt her, it was to hide his pain. When he struck her cheek until the skin blushed, it was to break the agony of his own head. She told him of her mother's death. Her mother had worn a mask to hide the illness at her face. He felt the locust of that illness on his own face, in the mouth and the fluttering eyelid.

The room was darkening. He was too tired to shovel the fire into life, and saw the last flame die. A new coldness blew in with the early night. He tasted the sickness of the death of the flame as it rose to the tip of his tongue, and swallowed it down. It ran around the pulse of the heart, and beat until it was the only sound. And all the pain of the damned. The pain of a man with a bottle breaking across his face, the pain of a cow with a calf dancing out of her, the pain of the dog, moved through him from his aching hair to the flogged soles of his feet.

His strength returned. He and the dripping calf, the man with the torn face and the dog on giddy legs rose up as one, in one red brain and body, challenging the beast in the air. He heard the challenge in his snapping thumb and finger, as she came in.

He saw that she was wearing her yellow hat and frock.

"Why are you sitting in the dark?" she said.

She went into the kitchen to light the stove. He stood up from his chair. Holding his hands out in front of him as though they were blind, he followed her. She had a box of matches in her hand. As she took out a dead match and rubbed it on the box, he closed the door behind him. "Take off your frock," he said.

She did not hear him, and smiled.

"Take off your frock," he said.

She stopped smiling, took out a live match and lit it.

"Take off your frock," he said.

He stepped towards her, his hands still blind. She bent over the stove. He blew the match out.

"What is it?" she said.

His lips moved, but he did not speak.

"Why?" she said.

He slapped her cheek quite lightly with his open hand.

"Take off your frock," he said.

He heard her frock rustle over her head, and her frightened sob as he touched her. Methodically his blind hands made her naked.

He walked out of the kitchen and closed the door.

In the hall, the one married shadow had broken up. He could not see his own face in the mirror as he tied his scarf and stroked the brim of his hat. There were too many faces. Each had a section of his features, and each a stiffened lock of his hair. He pulled up the collar of his coat. It was a wet winter night. As he walked, he counted the lamps. He pushed a door open and stepped into the warmth. The room was empty. The woman behind the bar smiled as she rubbed two coins together.

"It's a cold night," she said.

He drank up the whisky and went out.

He walked on through the increasing rain. He counted the lamps again, but they reached no number.

The corner bar was empty. He took his drink into the saloon, but the saloon was empty.

The Rising Sun was empty.

Outside, he heard no traffic. He remembered that he had seen nobody in the streets. He cried aloud in a panic of loneliness:

"Where are you, where are you?"

Then there was traffic, and the windows were blazing. He heard singing from the house on the corner.

The bar was crowded. Women were laughing and shouting. They spilt their drinks over their dresses and lifted their dresses up. Girls were dancing on the sawdust. A woman caught him by the arm and rubbed his face on her sleeve, and took his hand in hers and put it on her throat. He could hear nothing but the voices of the laughing women and the shouting of the girls as they danced. Then the ungainly women from the seats and the corners rocked towards him. He saw that the room was full of women. Slowly, still laughing, they gathered close to him.

He whispered a word under his breath, and felt the old sickness turn sour in his belly. There was blood before his eyes.

Then he, too, burst into laughter. He stuck his hands deep in the pockets of his coat, and laughed into their faces.

His hand clutched around a softness in his pocket. He drew out his hand, the softness in it.

The laughter died. The room was still. Quiet and still, the women stood watching him.

He raised his hand up level with his eyes. It held a piece of soft cloth.

"Who'll buy a lady's vest?" he said. "Going, going, ladies, who'll buy a lady's vest?"

The meek and ordinary women in the bar stood still, their glasses in their hands, as he leant with his back to the counter and shouted with laughter and waved the bloody cloth in front of them.

ADVENTURES
IN THE SKIN TRADE*

A Fine Beginning*

I

That early morning, in January 1933, only one person was awake in the street, and he was the quietest. Call him Samuel Bennet. He wore a trilby hat that had been lying by his bedside in case the two housebreakers, a man and a woman, came back for the bag they had left.

In striped pyjamas tight under the arms and torn between the legs, he padded barefoot downstairs and opened the breakfast-room door of his parents' six-room house. The room smelt strong of his father's last pipe before bed. The windows were shut fast, and the curtains drawn, the back door was bolted: the housebreaking night could not enter anywhere. At first he peered uneasily into the known flickering corners of the room, as though he feared that the family might have been sitting there in silence in the dark; then he lit the gaslight from the candle. His eyes were still heavy from a dream of untouchable city women and falling, but he could see that Tinker, the aunt-faced Pom, was sleeping before the burnt-out fire, and that the mantelpiece clock between hollow, mock-ebony, pawing horses showed five to two. He stood still and listened to the noises of the house: there was nothing to fear. Upstairs the family breathed and snored securely. He heard his sister sleeping in the boxroom under the signed photographs of actors from the repertory theatre and the jealous pictures of the marriages of friends. In the biggest bedroom overlooking the field that was called "the back", his father turned over the bills of the month in his one dream; his mother in bed mopped and polished through a wood of kitchens. He closed the door: now there was nobody to disturb him.

But all the noises of the otherwise dead or sleeping dark early morning, the intimate breathing of three invisible relations, the loud old dog, could wake up the neighbours. And the gaslight, bubbling, could attract to his presence in the breakfast room at this hour Mrs Probert next door, disguised as a she-goat in a nightgown, butting the air with her kirby grips;* her dapper, commercial son, with a watch chain tattooed across his rising belly; the tubercular lodger, with his neat umbrella up and his basin in his hand. The regular tide of the family breath could beat against the wall of the house on the other side and bring the Baxters out. He turned the gas low and stood for a minute by the clock, listening to sleep and seeing Mrs Baxter climb naked out of her widow's bed with a mourning band round her thigh.

Soon her picture died; she crawled back grieving to her lovebird's mirror under the blankets, and the proper objects of the room slowly returned as he lost his fear that the strangers upstairs he had known since he could remember would wake and come down with pokers and candles.

First there was the long strip of snapshots of his mother propped against the cut glass of the window sill. A professional under a dicky-bird hood had snapped her as she walked down Chapel Street in December, and developed the photographs while she waited looking at the thermos flasks and the smoking sets in the nearest shop window, calling "Good morning" across the street to the shopping bags she knew, and the matron's outside costumes, and the hats like flowerpots and chambers on the crisp, permed heads. There she was, walking down the street along the window sill, step by step, stout, safe, confident, buried in her errands, clutching her handbag, stepping aside from the common women blind and heavy under a week's provisions, prying into the looking glasses at the doors of furniture shops.

"Your photograph has been taken." Immortalized in a moment, she shopped along for ever between the cut-glass vase with the permanent flowers and the box of hairpins, buttons, screws, empty shampoo packets, cotton reels, flypapers, cigarette cards. At nearly two in the morning she hurried down Chapel Street against a backcloth of trilbies and Burberries* going the other way, umbrellas rising to the first drops of the rain a month ago, the sightless faces of people who would always be strangers hanging half developed behind her, and the shadows of the shopping centre of the sprawling, submerged town. He could hear her shoes click on the tramrails. He could see, beneath the pastelled silk scarf, the round metal badge of Mrs Rosser's Society, and the grandmother's cameo brooch on the vee of the knitted clover jumper.

The clock chimed and struck two. Samuel put out his hand and took up the strip of snaps. Then he tore it into pieces. The whole of her dead, comfortable face remained on one piece, and he tore it across the cheeks, up through the chins and into the eyes.

The Pom growled in a nightmare, and showed his little teeth. "Lie down, Tinker. Go to sleep, boy." He put the pieces in his pyjama pocket.

Then there was the framed photograph of his sister by the clock. He destroyed her in one movement, and, with the ripping of her set smile and the crumpling of her bobbed head into a ball, down went the Girls' School and the long-legged, smiling colts with their black knickers and bows; the hockey-legged girls who laughed behind their hands as they came running through the gates when he passed went torn and ruined into his pyjama pocket; they vanished, broken, into the porch and lay in pieces against his heart. Stanley Road, where the Girls' School stood, would never know him again. Down you go, Peggy, he whispered to his sister, with all the long legs and the Young Liberals' dances, and the boys you brought home for supper on Sunday evenings and Lionel you kissed in the porch. He is a solicitor now. When I was eleven years old and you were seventeen I heard you, from my bedroom, playing *The Desert Song*.* People were downstairs all over the world.

Most of the history sheets on the table were already marked and damned in his father's violet writing. With a lump of coal from the dead fire, Samuel marked them again, rubbing the coal hard over the careful corrections, drawing legs and breasts in the margins, smudging out the names and form numbers. History is lies. Now take Queen Elizabeth. Go ahead, take Alice Phillips, take her into the shrubbery. She was the headmaster's daughter. Take old Bennet and whip him down the corridors, stuff his mouth with dates, dip his starched collar in his marking ink and hammer his teeth back into his prim, bald, boring head with his rap-across-the-knuckle ruler. Spin Mr Nicholson on his tellurion* until his tail drops off. Tell Mr Parsons his wife has been seen coming out of the Compass piggyback on a drunk sailor, catching pennies in her garters. It's as true as History.

On the last sheet he signed his name several times under a giant pin man with three legs. He did not scribble on the top sheet. At a first glance there was no sign of interference. Then he threw the coal into the grate. Dust drifted up in a cloud and settled down again on the Pom's back.

If only he could shout at the ceiling now, at the dark circle made by the gas, at the cracks and lines that had always been the same faces and figures, two bearded men chasing an animal over a mountain edge, a kneeling woman with faces on her knees: Come and look at Samuel Bennet destroying his parents' house in Mortimer Street, off Stanley's Grove; he will never be allowed to come back. Mrs Baxter, have a dekko* from under the cold sheets; Mr Baxter, who worked in the Harbour Trust Office, can never come back either. Mrs Probert Chestnuts, your billy goat is gone, leaving a hairy space in the bed; Mr Bell the lodger coughs all night under his gamp; your son cannot sleep, he is counting his gentlemen's three-and-eleven-three half-hose* jumping over the tossed blankets. Samuel shouted under his breath, "Come and see me destroying the evidence, Mrs Rosser; have a peep from under your hairnet. I have seen your shadow on the blind as you undressed, I was watching by the lamp-post next to the dairy: you disappeared under a tent and came out slim and humped and black. I am the only gooseberry in Stanley's Grove who knows that you are a black woman with a hump. Mr Rosser married to a camel; everyone is mad and bad in his box when the blinds are pulled; come and see me break the china without any noise so that I can never come back."

"Hush," he said to himself, "I know you."

He opened the door of the china pantry. The best plates shone in rows, a willow tree next to an ivied castle, baskets of solid flowers on top of fruits and flower-coiled texts. Tureens were piled on one shelf, on another the salad bowls, the finger bowls, the toast racks spelling Porthcawl and Baby, the trifle dishes, the heirloom moustache cup.* The afternoon-tea service was brittle as biscuits and had gold rims. He cracked two saucers together, and the horn-curved spout of the teapot came off in his hand. In five minutes he had broken the whole set. Let all the daughters of Mortimer Street come in and see me, he whispered in the close pantry: the pale young girls who help at home, calculating down the pavement to the rich-smelling shops, screwing up their straight, dry hair in their rooms at the top of the house; their blood is running through them like salt. And I hope the office girls knock on the door with the stubs of their fingers, tap out "Sir" or "Madam" on the glass porch, the hard, bright babies who never go too far. You can hear them in the lane behind the post office as you tiptoe along: they are saying "So he said and I said and he said and Oh yeah I said", and the just male voices are agreeing softly. Shoo them in out of snoring Stanley's Grove, I know they are sleeping under the sheets up to their fringes in wishes. Beryl Gee is marrying the Chamber of Commerce in a pepper-and-salt church. Mrs Mayor's Chain, Madame Cocked Hat, Lady Settee, I am breaking tureens in the cupboard under the stairs.

A tureen cover dropped from his hand and smashed.

He waited for the sound of his mother waking. No one stirred upstairs. "Tinker did it," he said aloud, but the harsh noise of his voice drove him back into silence. His fingers became so cold and numb he knew he could not lift up another plate to break it.

"What are you doing?" he said to himself at last, in a cool, flat voice. "Leave the Street alone. Let it sleep."

Then he closed the pantry door.

"What are you doing, ranting away?"

Even the dog had not been wakened.

"Ranting away," he said.

He would have to be quick now. The accident in the cupboard had made him tremble so much that he could hardly tear up the bills he found in the sideboard drawer and scatter them under the sofa. His sister's crochet work was too difficult to destroy, the doilies and the patterned tea cosies were hard as rubber. He pulled them apart the best he could, and wedged them up the chimney.

"These are such small things," he said. "I should break the windows and stuff the cushions with the glass." He saw his round soft face in the mirror under the *Mona Lisa*. "But you won't," he said, turning away. "You're afraid of the noise." He turned back to his reflection. "It isn't that. You're afraid she'll cut her hands."

He burned the edge of his mother's sunshade at the gas mantle, and felt the tears running down his cheeks and dropping onto his pyjama collar.

Even in the first moment of his guilt and shame, he remembered to put out his tongue and taste the track of the tears. Still crying, he said, "It's salt. It's very salt. Just like in my poems."

He went upstairs in the dark, with the candle shaking, past the boxroom to his own room, and locked the door on the inside. He put out his hands and touched the walls and his bed. Good morning and goodbye, Mrs Baxter. His window, facing her bedroom, was open to the windless, starless early morning, but he could not hear her breathe or sleep. All the houses were quiet. The street was a close grave. The Rossers and the Proberts and the Bennets were still and safe and deep in their separate silences. His head touched the pillow, but he knew that he could not sleep again. His eyes closed.

Come down into my arms, for I shan't sleep, girls asleep on all sides in the attics and spare rooms of the square, red houses with the bay windows looking out on the trees behind the railings. I know your rooms like the backs of my hands, like the backs of your heads in the pictures when you are leaning over onto the next-door shoulders. I shan't sleep again. Tomorrow, today, I am going away by the 7.15 train, with ten pounds and a new suitcase. Lay your curling pins on my pillow, the alarm at six thirty will hurry you back to draw the blinds and light the fires before the rest come down. Come down quickly, the Bennets' house is melting. I can hear you breathe, I can hear Mrs Baxter turn in a dream. Oh, the milkmen are waking!

He was asleep with his hat on still, and his hands clenched.

2

The family awoke before six o'clock. He heard them, from a sunken half-sleep, bothering on the landing. They would be in dressing gowns, stale-eyed and with ragged hair. Peggy might have put two blushes on her cheeks. The family rushed in and out of the bathroom, never stopping to wash, and collided on the narrow top of the stairs as they nagged and bustled to get him ready. He let himself sink deeper until the waves broke round his head again, and the lights of a city spun and shone through the eyes of women walking in his last remembered dream. From the lapping distance he heard his father shout like a man on the opposite shore:

"Have you put the sponge bag in, Hilda?"

"Of course I have," she answered from the kitchen.

Don't let her look in the china pantry, Samuel prayed among the women walking like lamp-posts. She never uses the best china for breakfast.

"All right, all right – I just asked."

"Where's his new hairbrush?"

"That's right, shout my head off. Here it is. How can I give it to you if you're in the kitchen? It's the brush with the initials S.B."

"I know his initials."

"Mother, does he want all these vests? You know he never uses them."

"It's January, Peggy."

"She knows it's January, Hilda. You haven't got to tell the neighbours. Can you smell something burning?"

"It's only Mother's sunshade," Samuel said in the locked bedroom.

He dressed and went down. The gas in the breakfast room was on again. His mother was boiling an egg for him on the gas stove. "We'll have our breakfast later," she said. "You mustn't miss the train. Did you sleep well?"

"No burglars last night, Sam," his father said.

His mother brought the egg in. "You can't expect them every night."

Peggy and his father sat down in front of the empty grate.

"What do you think you'll do first when you get there, Sam?" said Peggy.

"He'll get himself a nice room, of course, not too central. And don't have an Irish landlady." His mother brushed his collar as he ate. "Go and get yourself settled straight away – that's the important thing."

"I'll get myself settled."

"Don't forget to look under the wallpaper for bugs."

"That's enough of that, Peggy. Sam knows a clean place when he sees one."

He saw himself knocking at a lodging house in the very centre of the city, and an Irishwoman appearing at the door. "Good morning, madam. Have you a cheap room?" "Cheaper than sunlight to you, Danny Boy." She would not be more than twenty-one. "Has it got bugs?" "All over the walls, praise be to God." "I'll take it."

"I'll know what I'm doing," he said to his mother.

"Jenkins's motor isn't here yet," Peggy said. "Perhaps there's a puncture."

If he doesn't come soon, they'll notice everything. I'll cut my throat on a piece of china.

"Remember to call on Mrs Chapman. Give her all our love from forty-two."

"I'll call on her tomorrow, Mother."

The taxi drew up outside. The corners of bedroom blinds would be lifted all over the street.

"Here's your wallet. Don't put it in your handkerchief pocket now. You never know when you'll be wanting to blow your nose."

"You'll be scattering largesse," Peggy said. She kissed him on the forehead.

Remind me to wipe it off in the cab.

"You're kissing the editor of *The Times* now," said his mother.

"Well, not quite that, Sam. Not yet, eh?" His father said, "Rungs of the ladder" and then looked away.

"Write tomorrow morning sharp. Send us the news."

"You send me your news, too. Mr Jenkins is blowing his horn."

"Better than blowing your trumpet," Peggy said. "And there's never any news in Mortimer Street."

You wait, slyboots. Wait till the flames touch the doily with the herons on it.

He came down to pat Tinker.

"Come on, don't fuss over the old dog – he's all fleas. It's gone seven."

Peggy was opening the door of the taxi for him. His father shook him by the hand. His mother kissed him on the mouth.

"Goodbye, Mortimer Street," he said, and the cab was off. "Goodbye, Stanley's Grove."

Through the back window he saw three strangers waving. He pulled down the blind.

3

Sitting with his bag in the lavatory of the moving train, for all the compartments were full, he read through his notebook and tore out the pages in order. He was dressed in a brand-new brown tweed overcoat, a brown town suit, a white starched shirt with a woollen tie and a tiepin and black, shining shoes. He had put his hard brown hat in the washbasin. Here was Mrs Chapman's address next to the telephone number of a Mr Hewson who was going to introduce him to a man who worked on a newspaper, and under these the address of the Literary Institute that had once awarded him a guinea for a poem in a competition: 'Will Shakespeare at the Tomb of the Unknown Warrior'. He tore the page out. Then the name and address, in red ink, of a collected poet who had written him a letter thanking him for a sonnet sequence. And a page of names that might help.

The lavatory door half opened, and he shut it quickly with his foot.

"I beg your pardon."

Hear her apologizing down the corridor, full as an egg. She could turn every handle the whole length of the train, and in every closet a fully clothed man would be sitting with his foot against the door, lost and alone in the long, moving house on wheels, travelling in silence with no windows, at sixty miles an hour racing to another place that did not want him, never at home wherever the train stopped. The handle turned again, and Samuel coughed somebody away.

The last page of the notebook was the only one he kept. Under a drawing of a girl with long hair dancing into an address, he had written: Lucille Harris. A man he met on the promenade had said as they sat on a bench, looking at the legs passing: "She's OK. She's a girl I know. She's the best in the world – she'll take care of you. Give her a call when you're up. Tell her you're Austin's friend." That page he placed in his wallet between two one-pound notes.

The rest of the pages he picked up from the floor, bunched together, and threw down between his legs into the bowl. Then he pulled the chain. Down went the helping names, the influential numbers, the addresses that could mean so much, into the round, roaring sea and onto the rails. Already they were lost a mile behind, blowing over the track now, over the glimpses of hedges into the lightning-passing fields.

Home and help were over. He had eight pounds ten and Lucille Harris's address. Many people have begun worse, he said aloud. I am ignorant, lazy, dishonest and sentimental: I have the pull over nobody.

The handle turned again.

"I bet you're dancing," he said to the person the other side of the locked door.

Footsteps pattered away down the train.

First of all, when I reach there, I'll have a Bass* and a stale sandwich, he decided. I'll take them to a table in a corner, brush off the cake crumbs with my hat and prop my book against the cruet. I must have all the details right at the beginning. The rest must come by accident. I'll be sitting there before noon, cool and calm, my hat on my knees, my glass in my hand, looking not a day under twenty, pretending to read and spying from the corners of my eyes at the waiting, drinking, restless people busily alone at the counter. The other tables will be crowded. There will be women, beckoning without moving, over their cold coffee; old, anonymous men with snuff on their cheeks, trembling over tea; quiet men expecting no one from the trains they wait for eagerly every hour; women who have come to run away, to take a train to St Ives or Liverpool or anywhere, but who know they will never take any train and are drinking cups of tea and saying to themselves, "I could be catching the twelve o'clock, but I'll wait for the quarter past"; women from the country with dozens of children coming undone; shop girls, office girls, street girls, people who have nothing worse to do, all the unhappy, happy in chains, bewildered foreign men and women in the station buffet of the city I know from cover to cover.

The door rattled. "You there," a voice said outside. "You've been there for hours."

He turned on the hot-water tap. It spurted cold water into the basin before he could take his hat out. "I'm a director of the company," he said, but his voice sounded weak to him and without assurance.

When the footsteps had faded again, he gathered up his cases and walked out of the lavatory and down the corridor. Standing outside a first-class compartment, he saw a man and a ticket inspector come to the door and hammer on it. They did not try the handle.

"Ever since Neath," the man said.

Now the train was losing speed, running out of the lost country into the smoke and a tunnel of factories, puffing past the district platforms and the high houses with broken windows and underclothes dancing in the dirty yards. Children at the windows never waved their hands to the train. It might have been the wind passing.

A crowd of people stood arguing outside the door as the train drew up under a great glass roof.

4

"Nip of Bass, please, and a ham sandwich." He took them to a table in a corner, brushed off the crumbs with his wet hat and sat down just before noon. He counted his money: eight pound nine and a penny, nearly three pounds more than he had ever seen. Some people had this every week. It had to last him until he was dead. At the next table sat a plump, middle-aged man with a chocolate-brown birthmark over his cheek and chin like the half of a beard. He was propping his book against an empty bottle when a young man walked over from the counter.

"Hullo, Sam."

"Hullo, Ron. Fancy seeing you."

He was Ronald Bishop, who used to live in the Crescent off Stanley's Grove.

"Been up in the smoke for long, Sam?"

"Just arrived. How's tricks?"

"Same as me, we must have been on the same train. Oh, so-so. Still at the old game, Sam?"

"Yeah, up on a bit of business. You at the usual?"

"Yeah."

They had never had anything to say to each other.

"Where you staying, Ron?"

"Usual. Strand Palace."

"Dare say I'll be seeing you, then."

"OK, make it tomorrow in the bar, about seven thirty."

"OK."

"It's a date, don't forget."

"No fear."

They both forget it at once.

"Well, be seeing you."

"Be good."

As Ronald Bishop walked off, Samuel said silently into his glass: A fine beginning. If I go out of the station and turn round the corner, I'll be back in forty-two. The little Proberts will be playing doctor outside the Load of Hay. The only stranger anywhere near me is a businessman with a stained face, reading the palms of his hands. No, here comes a woman in a fur coat; she's going to sit next to me. Yes, no, no. I smelt her as she passed; eau de Cologne and powder and bed.

The woman sat down two tables away, crossed her legs, powdered her nose.

This is the beginning of an advance. Now she is pretending not to notice that her knees are uncovered. There's a lynx in the room, lady. Button your overcoat. She's rattling her spoon on her saucer to attract my attention, but when I stare at her hard, without smiling, I see she is looking down gently and innocently into her lap as though she had a baby there. He was glad she was not brazen.

Dear Mother, he wrote with his finger on the back of an envelope, looking up, between every few invisible words, at the unnoticing woman opposite, this is to tell you that I arrived safely and that I am drinking in the buffet with a tart. I will tell you later if she is Irish. She is about thirty-eight years old and her husband left her five years ago because of her carryings-on. Her child is in a home, and she visits him every other Sunday. She always tells him that she is working in a hat shop. You need not worry that she will take all my money, as we liked each other on first sight. And you need not worry that I shall break my heart trying to reform her, because I have always been brought up to believe that Mortimer Street is what is right, and I would not wish that on anybody. Besides, I do not want to reform her. Not that I think she is nasty. Her business is very hard on stockings, so I am going to pay the first week's rent for our little room in Pimlico. Now she is going across to the counter to buy another cup of coffee. I hope you will notice that she is buying her own. Everybody in the buffet is unhappy except me.

As she came back to her table, he tore up the envelope and stared at her, unsmiling, for a full minute by the Bovril clock. Once she raised her eyes to his, then looked away. She was tapping her spoon on the side of her cup, then opening and closing the clasp of her handbag, then turning her head round slowly to face him and then looking away again quickly through the window. She must be new, he thought with a sudden compassion, but he did not stop staring. Should I wink? He tilted his hard, wet hat over one eye and winked: a long, deliberate wink that screwed up his face and made his burning cigarette nearly touch the blunt end of his nose. She snapped her handbag, pushed two pennies under the saucer and walked right out of the room, never looking at him as she passed.

She's left her coffee, he thought. And then: My God, she was blushing. A fine beginning.

"Did you speak?" asked the man with the birthmark, spying up. His face was red and purple where it was not brown, faintly shabby and unshaved, shiftily angry about the eyes, as though his cunning were an irritation impossible to bear.

"I think I said it was a fine day."

"Stranger in town?"

"Yes, I've just come up."

"How do you like it?" He did not appear to care at all.

"I haven't been outside the station yet."

Now the woman in the fur coat would be telling a policeman, "I have just been winked at by a short boy wearing a wet hat." "But it isn't raining, madam." That would settle her.

He put his hat under the table.

"There's plenty to see," the man said, "if that's what you want. Museums, art galleries." Without speaking, he went through a list of names of other attractions, but rejected them all. "Museums," he said after a long pause. "There's one at South Kensington, and there's the British Museum, and there's one at Whitehall with guns. I've seen them all," he said.

Now every table was occupied. Cold, stiff people with time to kill sat staring at their tea and the clock, inventing replies to questions that would not be asked, justifying their behaviour in the past and the future, drowning every present moment as soon as it began to breathe, lying and wishing, missing all the trains in the terror of their minds, each one alone at the terminus. Time was dying all over the room. And then all the tables except the one next to Samuel's were unoccupied again. The lonely crowd went out in a funeral procession, leaving ash and tea leaves and newspapers.

"You must move out of the station sometime, you know," the man said, returning to a conversation that held no interest for him. "If you want to see around. It's only fair. It's not fair to come up in a train and sit in the buffet and then go back and say you've seen London, is it?"

"I'm going out now, quite soon."

"That's right," the man said, "give London a chance."

He is so tired of talking to me that he is nearly losing his temper, Samuel thought.

He looked around him again, at the mourners fidgeting to the counter, at the quick whisky drinkers in a knot by the tea urn, at the waitresses listlessly busy with cardboard cakes and small change.

"Otherwise, it's like not getting out of bed, isn't it?" the man said. "You've got to walk round, you know, you've got to move sometime. Everybody does it," he said in a sudden, dull passion.

Samuel bought another nip of Bass from a girl like Joan Crawford.*

"This is the last one, then I'm going," he said when he had returned to his table.

"Do you think I care how many more you have? You can stay here all day, why should I mind?" The man was looking at the palms of his hands again as his temper mounted. "Am I my brother's keeper?"*

Ronald Bishop still stood at the counter.

Mortimer Street has tracked me down, Samuel thought bitterly, even into this lopsided quarrel with a palmist in a station restaurant. There was no escape. But it was not escape he wanted. The Street was a safe hole in a wall behind the wind in another country. He wanted to arrive and be caught. Ronald stood there like a Fury with a rolled umbrella. Come in, Mrs Rosser, in your fawn and beige antimacassar coat, with your tribal hat on your waves, and scream the news of the Street across the table in your whist-drive voice. I could not escape your fury on a birds' rock, you would be mincing and pinching down to the fishy sea with your beak gaped open like a shopping bag.

"I hate a nosy parker," the man said, and got up. On his way to the counter he passed the table where the Irish prostitute had sat and removed the pennies from under the plate.

"Stop, thief!" Samuel said softly. No one could hear. There is a waitress with a consumptive husband who needs those pennies. And two children, Tristram and Eve. He changed the names quickly. Tom and Marge. Then he walked over and put a sixpence under the plate just as a waitress came to the table.

"It fell on the floor," he said.

"Oh yeah?"

As he walked back, he saw that the waitress was talking to three men at the counter and nodding her head in his direction. One man was Ronald Bishop. One was the man with the birthmark.

Oh, fine, fine! If he had not broken the china, he would have caught the next train back. The pieces would be swept up by now, but the tears would be running all over the house. "Mother, Mother, he's put my crochet work up the chimney," he heard his sister scream in a guard's whistle. Herons, flower baskets, palm trees, windmills, Red Riding Hoods, stuffed up in the flames and soot. "Get me a rubber to rub out coal, Hilda. I shall of course lose my position. That is only to be expected." "Oh, my teapot, oh, my blue set, oh, my poor boy." He refused to look at the counter, where Ronald Bishop inaudibly reviled him. The waitress knew as soon as she saw him that he stole from the begging tins of the blind and led them by the arm into thick traffic. The birthmarked man said that he had shown a certain postcard to a customer in a fur coat. The voices of his parents condemned above the clattering of the cups. He stared hard at his book, though the print climbed and staggered as if the tears of the left house had run down after him along the rails and flowed into this hot, suspicious room over the tea-stained air into his eyes. But the image was false, and the book was chosen for strangers. He did not like or understand it.

"My bills." "My doilies." "My willow plate."

Ronald Bishop went out onto the platform.

"Be seeing you, Ron."

Ronald Bishop's face was flushed with the embarrassment of not noticing him.

One pleasure is, Samuel said to himself, that I do not know what I expect to happen to me. He smiled at the waitress behind the counter, and she stared away at once as guiltily as though he had discovered her robbing the till. I am not so innocent as I make out, he thought. I do not expect any old cobwebbed Fagin, reeking of character and stories, to shuffle out of a corner and lead me away into his grand, loud, filthy house; there will not be any Nancy* to tickle my fancy in a kitchen full of handkerchiefs and beckoning, unmade beds. I did not think a choir of loose women immediately would sing and dance around the little tables, in plush cloths and advertised brassieres, as I walked into London for the first time, rattling my fortune, fresh as Copperfield.* I could count the straws in my hair with one hand.

Hush! I know you, he said, cheater at patience, keyhole peeper, keeper of nail clippings and earwax, lusting after silhouettes on Laburnum's blind, searching for thighs in the Library of Classical Favourites, Sam Thumb in the manhole prying up on windy days.

I am not like that at all, he said, as the man with the birthmark came over to his table and sat down opposite him.

"I thought you were going," the man said. "You told me you were going. You've been here an hour now."

"I saw you," Samuel said.

"I know you saw me. You must have seen me, mustn't you, because you were looking at me," the man said. "Not that I want the twopence, I've got a house full of furniture. Three rooms full to the ceiling. I've got enough chairs for everyone in Paddington to have a sit-down. Twopence is twopence," he said.

"But it was twopence to the waitress, too."

"She's got sixpence now, hasn't she? She's made fourpence clear. It doesn't do any harm to you just because she thinks you were trying to nip it off her."

"It was my sixpence."

The man raised his hands. The palms were covered with calculations in ink. "And they talk about equality. Does it matter whose sixpence it was? It might have been mine or anybody's. There was talk of calling the manageress," he said, "but I put my foot down there."

They were both silent for several minutes.

"Made up your mind where you're going when you move out of here?" the man said at last. "Because move you must, sometime, you know."

"I don't know where I'm going. I haven't any idea in the world. That's why I came up to London."

"Look here," the man said, controlling his voice, "there's sense in everything. There's bound to be. Otherwise we wouldn't be able to carry on, would we? Everybody knows where he's going, especially if he's come by train. Otherwise he wouldn't move from where he took the train from. That's elementary."

"People run away."

"Have you run away?"

"No."

"Then don't say it. Don't say it." His voice trembled; he looked at the figures on his palms. Then gently and patiently he began again. "Let's get the first thing straight. People who have come must go. People must know where they're going, otherwise the world could not be conducted on a sane basis. The streets would be full of people just wandering about, wouldn't they? Wandering about and having useless arguments with people who know where they're going. My name is Allingham, I live in Sewell Street off Praed Street, and I'm a furniture dealer. That's simple, isn't it? There's no need to complicate things if you keep your head and know who you are."

"I'm Samuel Bennet. I don't live anywhere at all. I don't do any work, either."

"Where are you going to go, then? I'm not a nosy parker, I told you my business."

"I don't know."

"He doesn't know," Mr Allingham said. "Don't think you're anywhere now, mind. You can't call this place anywhere, can you? It's breathing space."

"I've been wondering what was going to happen. That's what I've been discussing with myself. I came up really to see what would happen to me. I don't want to make anything happen myself."

"He was discussing it with himself. With a boy of twenty. How old are you?"

"Twenty."

"That's right. Discussing a question like that with a boy just out of his teens. What did you expect to happen?"

"I don't know. Perhaps people would come up and talk to me at the beginning. Women," Samuel said.

"Why should they talk to you? Why should I talk to you? You're not going anywhere. You're not doing anything. You don't exist," he said.

But all Samuel's strength was in his belly and his eyes. He should veil his eyes, or the marble-topped counter might melt and all the clothes of the girls behind them peel away and all the cups chip on the shelves.

"Anyone might come up," he said. Then he thought of his fine beginning. "Anyone," he said without hope.

A clerk from the Crescent a dozen doors away; a cold, ordinary woman from Birmingham, driven off by a wink; anybody, anybody; a deacon from the Valleys on a mean blind, with his pocketbook sewn in his combs; an elderly female assistant on holiday from a flannel and calico shop, where the change hums on wires. Nobody he had ever wanted.

"Oh, anyone of course. Janet Gaynor," Mr Allingham said. "Marion Davies and Kay Francis* and—"

"You don't understand. I don't expect that kind of person. I don't know what I do expect at all, but it isn't that."

"Modest."

"No, I'm not modest either. I don't believe in modesty. It's just that here I am and I don't know where to go. I don't want to know where to go."

Mr Allingham began to plead, leaning across the table, pulling softly at Samuel's collar, showing the sums on his hands. "Don't say you don't want to know where to go. Please. There's a good boy. We must take things easy, mustn't we? We mustn't complicate things. Take one simple question. Now, don't rush it. Take your own time." He gripped a teaspoon with one hand. "Where will you be tonight?"

"I don't know. I'll be somewhere else, but it won't be anywhere I've chosen, because I'm not going to choose anything."

Mr Allingham put the knotted teaspoon down.

"What do you want, Samuel?" he whispered.

"I don't know." Samuel touched his breast pocket, where his wallet was. "I know I want to find Lucille Harris," he said.

"Who's Lucille Harris?"

Then Mr Allingham looked at him.

"He doesn't know," he said. "Oh, he doesn't know!"

A man and a woman sat down at the next table.

"But you promised you'd destroy him," the woman said.

"I'll do it, I'll do it," the man said. "Don't you worry. You drink your tea. Don't you worry."

They had lived a long time together, and had grown to resemble one another with their dry, bunched faces and their nibbling mouths. The woman scratched herself as she drank, as she gripped the edge of the cup with her grey lips and shook it.

"Twopence she's got a tail," Samuel said in a low voice, but Mr Allingham had not noticed them arrive.

"That's right," he said. "You have it your own way. And she's covered all over with fur."

Samuel put his little finger in the neck of the empty bottle.

"I resign myself," Mr Allingham said.

"But you don't understand, Mr Allingham."

"I understand enough," he said loudly. The couple at the next table stopped talking. "You don't want to make things happen, don't you? I'll make them happen all right. You can't come in here and talk to me like you've been talking. Lucille Harris. Lucy da monk!"

The man and the woman began whispering. "And it's only half-past one," the woman said. She shook her cup like a rat.

"Come on. We're going." Mr Allingham scraped back his chair.

"Where to?"

"Never you mind. It's I'm making things happen, isn't it?"

"I can't get my finger out of the bottle," Samuel said.

Mr Allingham lifted up the suitcases and stood up. "What's a little bottle?" he said. "Bring it with you, son."

"Father and son, too," the woman said as Samuel followed him out.

The bottle hung heavily on his finger.

"Where now?" Outside in the roaring station.

"You follow me. And put your hand in your pocket. It looks silly."

As they walked up the slope to the street, Mr Allingham said, "I've never been with anybody with a bottle on his finger before. Nobody else has ever had a bottle on his finger. What'd you want to put your finger in the bottle for?"

"I just pushed it in. I'll be able to get it off with soap, there's no need to make a fuss."

"Nobody else has ever had to get a bottle off with soap, that's all I'm saying. This is Praed Street."

"It's dull, isn't it?"

"All the horses have gone away," Mr Allingham said. "This is my street. This is Sewell Street. It's dull, isn't it?"

"It's like the streets at home."

A boy passed them and shouted "Ikey Mo"* to Mr Allingham.

"This is twenty-three. See? There's the sign, twenty-three."

Mr Allingham opened the front door with a key. "Second floor, first on the right."

He gave three knocks. "Mr Allingham," he said, and they walked in.

The room was full of furniture.

Plenty of Furniture*

I

Every inch of the room was covered with furniture. Chairs stood on couches that lay on tables; mirrors nearly the height of the door were propped, back to back, against the walls, reflecting and making endless the hills of desks and chairs with their legs in the air, sideboards, dressing tables, chests of drawers, more mirrors, empty bookcases, washbasins, clothes cupboards. There was a double bed, carefully made, with the ends of the sheets turned back, lying on top of a dining table on top of another table; there were electric lamps and lampshades, trays and vases, lavatory bowls and basins, heaped in the armchairs that stood on cupboards and tables and beds, touching the ceiling. The one window, looking out on the road, could just be seen through the curved legs of sideboards on their backs. The walls behind the standing mirrors were thick with pictures and picture frames.

Mr Allingham climbed into the room over a stack of mattresses, then disappeared.

"Hop in, boy." His voice came up from behind a high kitchen dresser hung with carpets; and, climbing over, Samuel looked down to see him seated on a chair on a couch, leaning back comfortably, his elbow on the shoulder of a statue.

"It's a pity we can't cook here," Mr Allingham said. "There's plenty of stoves, too. That's a meat safe," he said, pointing to one corner. "Just under the bedroom suite."

"Have you got a piano?"

"There used to be one," he said. "I think it's in the other room. She put a carpet over it. Can you play?"

"I can vamp. You can tell what tunes I'm doing, easily. Is the other room like this?"

"Two more rooms, but I think the piano's locked. Yes, there's plenty of furniture," Mr Allingham said, looking round with distaste. "Whenever I say 'That's enough now', in she comes with her 'Plenty more room, plenty more room'. She'll find she can't get in one day, that's what'll happen.

Or she can't get out – I don't know which would be the worst. It gets you sometimes, you know," he said, "all this furniture."

"Is she your wife, Mr Allingham?"

"She'll find there's a limit to everything. You get to feel kind of trapped."

"Do you sleep here?"

"Up there. It's nearly twelve foot high. I've measured. I can touch the ceiling when I wake up."

"I like this room," Samuel said. "I think it's perhaps the best room I've ever seen."

"That's why I brought you. I thought you'd like it. Proper little den for a man with a bottle on his finger, isn't it? I told you, you're not like anybody else. Nobody else can bear the sight of it. Got your cases safe?"

"They're there. In the bath."

"You keep your eye on them, that's all. I've lost a sofa. One more suite and I'll lose my bed. And what happens when a customer comes? I'll tell you. He takes one peek through the door and off he trots. You can only buy what's on the top at the moment, see."

"Can you get into the other rooms?"

"You can," Mr Allingham said. "She takes a dive in, head first. I've lost all interest in the other rooms, myself. You could live and die in there and nobody'd know. There's some nice Chippendale, too. Up by the skylight."

He rested his other elbow on a hallstand.

"I got to feel lost," he said. "That's why I go down to the buffet – there's only tables and chairs there."

Samuel sat on his perch, swinging the bottle and drumming his feet against the side of a bath mounted yards above the floor of mattresses. A carpet behind him, laid out flat and wide along the air, having no visible support, bore a great earthenware jar dangerously upon the backs of its patterned birds. High over his head, in the tall room, a rocking chair balanced on a card table, and the table's thin legs rested on the top of a cupboard standing up straight among pillows and fenders, with its mirrored door wide open.

"Aren't you frightened of things falling? Look at that rocking chair. One little prod and over she comes."

"Don't you dare. Of course I'm frightened," Mr Allingham said. "If you open a drawer over there, a washstand falls down over here. You've got to be quick as a snake. There's nothing on the top you'd like to buy, is there?"

"I like a lot of the things, but I haven't any money."

"No, no, you wouldn't have money. That's right. Other people have money."

"I like the big jar. You could hide a man in that. Have you got any soap for my finger?"

"Of course there's no soap, there's only washbasins. You can't have a bath, either, and there's five baths. Why do you want a jar big enough to hide a man in? Nobody I've ever met wants to hide a man in a jar. Everybody else says that jar's too big for anything. Why do you want to find Lucille Harris, Sam?"

"I didn't mean I wanted to hide a man in it. I mean that you could if you wanted to. Oh, a man I know told me about Lucille, Mr Allingham. I don't know why I want to find her, but that's the only London address I kept. I put the others down the lavatory in the train. When the train was moving."

"Good, good." Mr Allingham put his hand on the thick white neck of the naked statue and tightened his fingers.

The door opened onto the landing. Two people came in and climbed up the mattresses without a word. The first, a fat, short woman with black hair and a Spanish comb, who had painted her face as though it were a wall, took a sudden dive towards the corner behind Samuel and disappeared between two columns of chairs. She must have landed on cushions or a bed, for she made no sound. The second visitor was a tall, youngish man with a fixed smile; his teeth were large, like a horse's, but very white; his glistening fair hair was done in tight curls, and it smelt across the room. He stood on a spring mattress just inside the door, bouncing up and down. "Come on, Rose, don't be sulky," he said. "I know where you've gone." Then, pretending to see Samuel for the first time, "Good gracious, you look like a bird up there," he said. "Is Donald hiding anywhere?"

"I'm not hiding," Mr Allingham said. "I'm by the statue. Sam Bennet, George Ring."

George Ring bowed and bounced, rising a foot from the mattress.

He and Mr Allingham could not see each other. Nobody could see the woman with the Spanish comb.

"I hope you've excused the room to Mr Bennet," George Ring said. He bounced a few steps in the direction of the hidden statue.

"I don't think it needs any excusing, Mr Ring," Samuel said. "I've never seen such a comfortable room."

"Oh, but it's terrible." George Ring was moving up and down rapidly now. "It's very kind of you to say it's comfortable, but look at the confusion. Just think of living here. You've got something on your finger, did you know that? Three guesses. It's a bottle." He shook his curls and laughed as he bounced.

"You don't know anything yet," said Mr Allingham's voice. The heavy bouncing had shaken down a carpet onto the hallstand, and he was hidden as though in another, lower room. "You don't know anything about him. You wait. What are you bouncing for, George? People don't go bouncing about like a ball as soon as they come into a room."

"What don't I know about you?" In one leap George Ring was standing directly below Samuel, craning up his curls.

"He doesn't know where he's going, for one thing. And he's looking for a girl he doesn't know called Lucille."

"Why are you looking for her?" George Ring's head touched the bath. "Did you see her picture in the paper?"

"No, I don't know anything about her, but I want to see her because she's the only person I know by name in London."

"Now you know two more, don't you? Are you sure you don't love her?"

"Of course I'm sure."

"I thought perhaps she might be a sort of Holy Grail. You know what I mean. A sort of ideal."

"Go on, you big pussycat," Mr Allingham said. "Get me out of here."

"Is this the first time you've come to London? I felt like that when I came up first, too. Years and years ago. I felt there was something I must find, I can't explain it. Something just round the corner. I searched and searched. I was so innocent. I felt like a sort of knight."

"Get me out of here," Mr Allingham said. "I feel like the whole room's on top of me."

"I never found it." George Ring laughed and sighed and stroked the side of the bath. "Perhaps you'll be lucky," he said. "You'll walk round the corner and there she'll be. Lucille. Lucille. Is she on the telephone?"

"Yes. I've got her number in my book."

"Oh, that makes it easier, doesn't it? Come on, Rose," he said. "I know exactly where you are. She's in a pet."

Samuel rocked softly on his box in the middle of the furniture. This was the fullest room in England. How many hundreds of houses had been spilt in here, tables and chairs coming in on a wooden flood, chests and cupboards soaring on ropes through the window and settling down like birds? The other rooms, beyond that jostled door, would be taller and darker even than this, with the mute, black shape of the locked piano mountainous under a shroud of carpets and Rose, with her comb like the prow of a ship, driving into their darkness and lying all night motionless and silent where she struck. Now she was dead still on a sunk bed between the column of chairs, buried alive, soft and fat and lost in a grave in a house.

"I'm going to buy a hammock," George Ring said. "I can't bear sleeping under all this furniture."

Perhaps the room was crowded at night with people who could not see each other, stretched under chairs, under sofas, dizzily asleep on the tops of raised tables, waking up every morning and crying out, "Earthquake, earthquake!"

"And then I'll go to bed like a sailor."

"Tell Rose to come and get me out of here," Mr Allingham said, behind the cloaked hallstand. "I want to eat."

"She's sulking, Donald. She's mad about a Japanese screen now."

"Do you hear that, Sam? Isn't there enough privacy in this room? Anybody can do anything, nobody can see you. I want to eat. I want to have a snack at Dacey's. Are you sleeping here tonight?"

"Who?" Samuel asked. "Me?"

"You can doss down in one of the other rooms, if you think you can get up again. There's enough beds for a harem."

"Harem," George Ring said, pronouncing it another way. "You've got company, Rose darling. Do come out and be introduced."

"Thank you, Mr Allingham," Samuel said.

"Didn't you really have any idea at all?" George Ring bounced, and for a moment his scented head was level with Samuel's. One wide, bright, horse-toothed smile, and the head was gone. "About sleeping and things. I think it's awfully brave. You might have fallen in with all kinds of people. "He fell among thieves." Do you know Sir Henry Newbolt's poem?"*

"He flung his empty revolver down the slope," Samuel said.

The day was moving carelessly on to a promised end and in a dark room full of furniture, where he'd lie down with his bunch of wives in a crow's-nest bed or rock them in a hammock under the ceiling.

"Goodie goodie! It's so exciting to find someone who knows about poetry. 'The voices faded and the hills slept.'* Isn't that beautiful? The voices faded?... I can read poetry for hours, can't I, Donald? I don't care what kind of poetry it is, I love it all. Do you know 'Is there anybody there, said the traveller?'* Where do you put the emphasis, Mr Bennet? Can I call you Sam? Do you say 'Is there *anybody* there' or 'Is there anybody *there*'?"

"It isn't natural," Mr Allingham said, "for a man not to be able to see anybody when he's sitting right next to them. I'm not grumbling, but I can't see anything, that's all. It's like not being in the room."

"Oh, do be quiet, Donald. Sam and I are having a perfectly serious discussion. Of course you're in the room, don't be morbid."

"I think I'd put about the same emphasis on all the words," Samuel said.

"But don't you find it tends to make the line rather flat? '*Is* there anybody there, said the traveller,'" George Ring murmured, pacing the mattresses, his head on one side. "I feel you do want a stress somewhere."

Will I be alone tonight in the room with the piano? Samuel wondered. Alone like a man in a warehouse, lying on each bed in turn, opening cupboards and putting my hand in, looking at myself in mirrors in the dark.

"Don't you call me morbid, George Ring," Mr Allingham said. He tried to move, but the statue fell against his chair. "I remember once I drank forty-nine Guinnesses straight off and I came home on the top of a bus. There's nothing morbid about a man who can do that. Right on the top of the bus, too, not just in the upper deck."

Or will the room be full as a cemetery, but with the invisible dead breathing and snoring all around me, making love in the cupboards, drunk as tailors in the dry baths? Suddenly a warm body might dive in through the door and lie in my bed all night without a name or a word.

"I think forty-nine Guinnesses is piggish," said George Ring.

"It was raining," Mr Allingham said, "and I never get truculent. I may sing and I may have a bit of a dance, but I never get nasty. Give me a hand, Sam."

Samuel took the carpet off the hallstand and pushed the statue away. It had fallen between Mr Allingham's legs. He came up slowly into sight and rubbed his eyes like a man waking.

"I told you," he said, "you get trapped. Coming to Dacey's, George?"

"I'll have to stay for hours, you know that," George Ring said. "You know I'm the only person who can humour Rosie when she's in one of her states. Oh, come on, Rosie, don't be temperamental. It's ninety per cent temper and ten per cent mental. Just because you're an actress you think you can stay under the furniture all the afternoon. I'll count five..."

Samuel followed Mr Allingham to the door.

"Five, six, seven," George Ring said, as Mr Allingham slammed the door hard, and his voice was lost in the noise of furniture falling. They went down the stairs into the hallway that smelt of cabbage, and out onto the grey street.

"I think it must have been the rocking chair," Samuel said.

"Mrs Dacey's is just round the corner," Mr Allingham said. "There you are. See the Cadbury sign?"

2

Mrs Dacey's front window was whitewashed from inside, and the words "High Class" had been scrawled across it. "'Susan Dacey, licensed to sell tobacco,'" Samuel read aloud. "Is it a restaurant too?"

"You must tell her that," Mr Allingham said, opening the door. A bell rang. "It hasn't been called that before." He held his foot against the door so that the bell kept ringing. "She's a woman in a thousand."

A tall, thin, dignified woman came through the private door at the back of the shop, her hands clasped in front of her. She was dressed in black almost down to the ankles, with a severe white collar, and she held her head primly as though it might spill. God help the other nine hundred and ninety-nine. But she smiled then, and her eyes were sharp and light; the dullness raced from her mouth, leaving it cruel and happy.

"Take your trotter off the door," she said.

The bell stopped.

"That's better. You made enough noise to wake the dead." She was a well-spoken woman, clear and precise, like a schoolmistress.

"Keeping well, Mrs Dacey? This is a new friend, Sam Bennet. Two pies and two coffees, please. Where's Polly?"

"Up to no good," said Mrs Dacey, stepping behind the counter. Her grand dress floated around her. "You're from the country," she said over her shoulder, as she turned the coffee tap on the brass urn. "How did you find Ikey Mo?"

"That's me." Mr Allingham blushed on one side of his face.

"I'm not from the country, really." Samuel told her where he came from. "I met Mr Allingham in the station. I'm going to sleep in his flat tonight."

"I'd sooner sleep in an ashpit," she said.

The coffee was thick and white and tasteless. They took their cups to a cubicle, and Samuel brushed off the crumbs from his chair with his sleeve. His hat was gone. There were small pellets of dirt in the dust at his feet.

"You've got a bottle on your finger," she said.

"There, you see, everybody notices. Why don't you take it off, Sam? It isn't a decoration, it isn't useful, it's just a bottle."

"I think my finger must have swollen, Mr Allingham. The bottle's much tighter now."

"Let me have a look at you again." Mrs Dacey put on a pair of spectacles with steel rims and a hanging chain. "He's only a baby."

"I'm twenty."

"Ikey Mo, the baby farmer." She walked carefully to the back of the shop and called, "Polly, come down here. Polly. Polly."

A girl's voice called back from high up the house, "What for, Ma?"

"Come and get a gentleman's bottle off."

"It sounds like a Russian composer, doesn't it, darling?" George Ring said, at the door. "What a marvellous dress, you look like a murderess."

He sat down next to Samuel.

"I couldn't get Rose to move. She's going to lie there all day in a tantrum. Do tell me what's happening, everybody."

"It's that bottle again," Mr Allingham said. "Why didn't he put his finger in a glass or something? I don't know what he was poking his finger about for in the first place. It's an enigma to me."

"Everything's an enigma to you. You can't understand the slightest touch of originality. I think it must be awful not to have any imagination. It's like a sense of humour."

"I'm just saying that not to be able to go in and buy a bottle of Bass without having to leave with the bottle on your finger seems to me like a kind of nightmare. That's all I'm saying."

Samuel heard Mrs Dacey's daughter running downstairs. Then he saw her hand on the edge of the door. In the second she took to push the door open and come in, he made her a hundred faces; he made her talk and walk in all the disguises of his loves at night; he gave her golden hair, black hair, he knew that she would be Gypsy-skinned and white as milk. Polly come and put the kettle on* with your white, slender, brown, broad hands, and see me waiting like a grenadier or a caliph in the mousy cubicle.

"It's like one of those nightmares when you're playing billiards and the cue's made of elastic," Mr Allingham said.

In came a girl with a long, pale face and glasses. Her hair was not any of Samuel's colours, but only dark and dull.

"Go and help to pull his bottle off," said Mrs Dacey.

Polly sat down on the table and took his hand. "Does it hurt? I've never done it before." She pulled at his finger.

"I hope you won't ever have to do it again, either," Mr Allingham said. "I don't care if I haven't got any imagination. I'm glad I'm like I am without anything on my finger."

Polly bent over Samuel's hand, and he saw down her dress. She knew that he was looking, but she did not start back or spread her hand across the neck of her dress; she raised her head and stared at his eyes. I shall always remember this, he said to himself. In 1933 a girl was pulling at a bottle on the little finger of my left hand while I looked down her dress. It will last longer than all my poems and troubles.

"I can't get it off," she said.

"Take him up to the bathroom then, and put some soap on it," said Mrs Dacey, in her dry, neat voice. "And mind it's only his bottle."

George Ring said as they got up to go, "Scream if you want me, I'll be up in a wink. She's the most terrible person, aren't you, darling? You wouldn't catch little George going up there all alone."

Polly led the way upstairs.

"I'm not complaining," Mr Allingham said, "I'm just making a statement. I'm not saying it isn't all as it should be. He's got a bottle on his finger and I've got a tooth in my pie."

His voice faded.

3

Someone had drawn the ragged curtains in the bathroom to shut out the damp old day, and the bath was half full of water with a rubber duck floating on it. As Polly closed and locked the door, birds began to sing.

"It's only the birds," she said. She put the key down her dress. "You needn't be frightened."

Two cages hung from the ceiling.

But Samuel had looked frightened when she turned the key and put it away where he never wanted to find it, not when the room grew suddenly like a wood in the tangled shadows of the green curtains.

"It's a funny place to have birds," he said.

"They're mine." Polly let the hot water run, and the birds sang more loudly, as though they heard a waterfall. "Mr Allingham comes here for a bath on Wednesdays, and he says they sneer at him and blow little raspberries all the time he's washing. But I don't think he washes very much. Doesn't Mr Allingham make you laugh too?"

He expected her to be smiling when she turned to him, but her face was still and grave, and all at once he saw that she was prettier than any of the girls he had made up in his mind before she opened the door downstairs. He distrusted her prettiness because of the key. He remembered what Mrs Dacey had said when Mr Allingham asked where Polly was. "Up to no good." He did not think she was going to put her arms around him. That would have been different. If she tried to put his head under the water, he'd shout for George Ring, and up he'd come like a horse, neighing and smelling of scent.

"I only locked the door because I don't want George Ring to come in. He's queer. He puts scent all over his underclothes – did you know that? The Passing Cloud, that's what we call him. The Passing Cloud."

"You didn't have to put the key where you put it, though," Samuel said. "I might push you down and fish for it, I might be that sort."

"I don't care."

If only she would have smiled at him when she said that! But she looked as though she really did not care whether he pushed her down or whether he sat on the edge of the bath and touched the duck with his bottle.

The duck floated in circles on the used, greasy water.

"What's your name?"

"Sam."

"Mine's Mary. But they call me Polly for short."

"It isn't much shorter, is it?"

"No, it's exactly the same length."

She sat by his side on the edge of the bath. He could not think of anything to say. Here was the locked door he had often made up in stories and in his head, in bed in Mortimer Street, and the warm, hidden key, and the girl who was willing for anything. The bathroom should be a bedroom, and she should not be wearing glasses.

"Will you take off your glasses, Polly?"

"If you like. But I won't be able to see very far."

"You don't have to see very far, it's only a little room," he said. "Can you see me?"

"Of course I can. You're right next to me. Do you like me better now?"

"You're very pretty, I suppose, Polly."

"Pretty Polly," she said, without a smile.

Well, he said to himself, here you are, here she is without any glasses on.

"Nothing ever happens in Sewell Street." She took his hand and let his finger with the bottle on it lie in her lap.

Here you are, he said, with your hand in her lap.

"Nothing ever happens where I come from, either. I think things must be happening everywhere except where one is. All kinds of things happen to other people. So they say," he said.

"The man who was lodging next door but one cut his throat like this," she said, "before breakfast."

On his first free days since he was born Samuel sat with a loose girl in a locked bathroom over a tea shop, the dirty curtains were drawn, and his hand lay on her thighs. He did not feel any emotion at all. O God, he thought, make me feel something, make me feel as I ought to, here is something happening and I'm cool and dull as a man in a bus. Make me remember all the stories. I caught her in my arms, my heart beat against hers, her body was trembling, her mouth opened like a flower. The lotus of Osiris was opening to the sun.

"Listen to the old birds," she said, and he saw that the hot water was running over the rim of the washbasin.

I must be impotent, he thought.

"Why did he cut his throat like that, Polly? Was it love? I think if I was crossed in love I'd drink brandy and whisky and crème de menthe and that stuff that's made with eggs."

"It wasn't love with Mr Shaw. I don't know why he did it. Mrs Bentley said there was blood everywhere, everywhere, and all over the clock. He left a little note in the letter rack, and all it said was that he'd been meaning to do it ever since October. Look, the water'll drip right through into the kitchen."

He turned it off. The birds stopped singing.

"Perhaps it was love, really. Perhaps he loved you, Polly, but he wouldn't say so. From a distance."

"Go on, he had a limp," she said. "Old Dot and Carry.* How old are you?"

"Twenty."

"No, you're not."

"Well, nearly."

"No, you're not."

Then they were silent, sitting on the bath, his hand in her lap. She trailed her pale hand in the water. The birds began again.

"Pale hands I love," he said.

"Beside the Shalimar.* Do you, Sam? Do you love my hands? That's a funny thing to say." She looked dully at the long, floating weed in the water and made a wave. "It's like the evening here."

"It's like evening in the country," he said. "Birds singing and water. We're sitting on a bank by the river now."

"Having a picnic."

"And then we're going to take our clothes off and have a swim. Gee, it'll be cold. You'll be able to feel all the fish swimming about."

"I can hear the 47 bus, too," she said. "People are going home to tea. It's cold without any clothes on, isn't it? Feel my arm, it's like snow, only not so white. Pale hands I love," she began to sing. "Do you love me altogether?"

"I don't know. I don't think I feel anything like that at all. I never do feel much until afterwards, and then it's too late."

"Now it isn't too late. It isn't too late, Sam. We're alone. Polly and Sam. I'll come and have a swim with you, if you like. In the dirty old river with the duck."

"Don't you ever smile, Polly? I haven't seen you smile once."

"You've only known me for twenty minutes. I don't like smiling much; I think I look best when I'm serious, like this." She saddened her eyes and mouth. "I'm a tragedienne. I'm crying because my lover's dead."

Slowly tears came to her eyes.

"His name was Sam, and he had green eyes and brown hair. He was ever so short. Darling, darling, darling Sam, he's dead." The tears ran down her cheeks.

"Stop crying now, Polly. Please. Stop crying. You'll hurt yourself."

But she was crying pitifully.

"Stop it, Polly, pretty Polly." He put his arm round her shoulders. He kissed her on the cheek. It was warm and wet. "Nobody's dead, Polly darling," he said. She cried and moaned his name in the abandon of her made grief, tore at the loose, low neck of her dress, threw back her hair and raised her damp eyes to the birds in their cages and the cracked heavens of the ceiling.

"You're doing it fine," he said in despair, shaking her shoulders. "I've never seen such fine crying. Stop now, please, Polly, please, while you can stop."

Ninety-eight per cent of the human body is water, he thought. Polly Dacey is all salt water. She sat by his side like a flood in an apron.

"I'll do anything you like if you'll only stop," he said. "You'll drown yourself, Polly. I'll promise to do anything in the world."

She dried her eyes on her bare arm.

"I wasn't really breaking my heart, silly. I was only depicting. What'll you do, then? Anything? I can depict being glad because my lover's not really dead, too. The War Office made a mistake."

"Anything," he said. "I want to see you being glad tomorrow. You mustn't do one after the other."

"It's nothing to me, I can do them all in a row. I can do childbirth and being tight and—"

"You do being quiet. Do being a quiet lady sitting on a bath, Polly."

"I will if you'll come and have a swim with me. You promised." She patted her hair into place. "Where?"

"In the bath. You get in first, go on. You can't break your promise."

George Ring, he whispered, gallop upstairs now and bite your way through the door. She wants me to sit with my overcoat on and my bottle on my finger in the cold, greasy bath, in the half-dark bathroom, under the sneering birds.

"I've got a new suit," he said.

"Take it off, silly. I don't want you to go in the bath with your clothes on. Look, I'll put something over the window so you can undress in the dark. Then I'll undress too. I'll come in the bath with you. Sam, are you frightened?"

"I don't know. Couldn't we take our clothes off and not go in the bath? I mean, if we want to take them off at all. Someone might come in. It's terribly cold, Polly. Terribly cold."

"You're frightened. You're frightened to lie in the water with me. You won't be cold for long."

"But there's no sense in it. I don't want to go in the bath. Let's sit here and you do being glad, Polly."

He could not move his hand, she had caught the bottle between her legs.

"You don't want to be frightened. I'm not any older than you are," she said, and her whispering mouth was close to his ear. "As soon as you get in the bath, I'll jump on top of you in the dark. You can pretend I'm somebody you love if you don't like me properly. You can call me any name." She dug her nails into his hand. "Give me your coat, I'll hang it over the window. Dark as midnight," she said, as she hung the coat up, and her face in the green light through the curtains was like a girl's under the sea. Then all the green went out, and he heard her fumbling. I do not want to drown. I do not want to drown in Sewell Street off Circe Street, he whispered under his breath.

"Are you undressing? I can't hear you. Quick, quick, Sam."

He took off his jacket and pulled his shirt over his head. Take a good look in the dark, Mortimer Street, have a peek at me in London.

"I'm cold," he said.

"I'll make you warm, beautifully warm, Sam." He could not tell where she was, but she was moving in the dark and clinking a glass. "I'm going to give you some brandy. There's brandy, darling, in the medicine cupboard. I'll give you a big glass. You must drink it right down."

Naked, he slipped one leg over the edge of the bath and touched the icy water.

Come and have a look at impotent Samuel Bennet from Mortimer Street off Stanley's Grove trembling to death in a cold bath in the dark near Paddington Station. I am lost in the metropolis with a rubber duck and a girl I cannot see pouring brandy into a tooth glass. The birds are going mad in the dark. It's been such a short day for them, Polly.

"I'm in the bath now."

"I'm undressing too. Can you hear me?" she said softly. "That's my dress rustling. Now I'm taking my petticoat off. Now I'm naked." A cold hand touched him on the face. "Here's the brandy, Sam. Sam, my dear, drink it up, and then I'll climb in with you. I'll love you, Sam, I'll love you up. Drink it all up, then you can touch me."

He felt the glass in his hand, and he lifted it up and drank all that was in it.

"Christ!" he said in a clear, ordinary voice. "Christ!"

Then the birds flew down and kicked him on the head, carefully between the eyes, brutally on each temple, and he fell back in the bath.

That was all the birds singing under the water, and the sea was full of feathers that swam up his nostrils and into his mouth. A duck as big as a ship sailed up on a drop of water as big as a house and smelt his breath as it spurted out from broken, bleeding lips, like flames and waterspouts. Here came a wave of brandy and birds, and Mr Allingham, naked as a baby, riding on the top with his birthmark like a rainbow, and George Ring swimming breaststroke through the open door, and three Mrs Daceys gliding in yards above the flowing ground.

The darkness drowned in a bright ball of light, and the birds stopped.

4

Voices began to reach him from a great distance, travelling in lavatories in racing trains along a liquid track, diving from the immeasurably high ceiling into the cold sea in the enormous bath.

"Do you see what I see?" That was the voice of the man called Allingham, who slept under the furniture. "He's taking a little dip."

"Don't let me look, Donald, he's bare all over." I know him, Samuel thought. That's George Ring the horse. "And he's ill too. Silly Sam."

"Lucky Sam. He's drunk, George. Well, well, well, and he hasn't even got his bottle off. Where's Polly?"

"You look over there," Mrs Dacey said. "Over there on the shelf. He's drunk all the eau de Cologne."

"He must have been thirsty."

Large, bodiless hands came over the bath and lifted him out.

"He's eccentric," Mr Allingham said, as they laid him on the floor, "that's all I'm saying. I'm not preaching, I'm not condemning. I'm just saying that other people get drunk in the proper places."

The birds were singing again in the electric dawn as Samuel fell quietly to sleep.

Four Lost Souls*

I

He sank into the ragged green water for the second time, and, rising naked with seaweed and a woman under each arm and a mouthful of broken shells, he saw the whole of his dead life standing trembling before him, indestructible and unsinkable, on the brandy-brown waves. It looked like a hallstand.

He opened his mouth to speak, but a warm wave rushed in.

"Tea," said Mrs Dacey. "Tea with plenty of sugar every five minutes. That's what I always gave him, and it didn't do a bit of good."

"Not too much Worcester, George – don't bury the egg."

"I won't," Samuel said.

"Oh, listen to the birds. It's been such a short night for the birds, Polly."

"Listen to the birds," he said clearly, and a burning drink drowned his tongue.

"They've laid an egg," Mr Allingham said.

"Try some Coca-Cola, Donald. It can't do any harm – he's had tea and a prairie oyster and Angostura* and Oxo and everything."

"I used to pour the tea down by the pint," Mrs Dacey said affectionately, "and up it came, lump sugar and all."

"He doesn't want a Coca-Cola. Give him a drop of your hair oil. I knew a man who used to squeeze boot-blacking* through a veil."

"You know everybody piggish. He's trying to sit up, the poor darling."

Samuel wrestled into the dry world and looked around a room in it, at Mrs Dacey, now miraculously divided into one long woman, folding her black silk arms in the doorway, at George Ring arching his smile and hair towards the rusty taps, at Mr Allingham resigned above him.

"Polly's gone," he said.

It was then that he understood why the three persons in the bathroom were so tall and far. I am on the floor, looking up, he said to himself. But the others were listening.

"You're naked too," Mr Allingham said, "under the blanket."

"Here's a nice wet sponge." George Ring dabbed and smoothed. "Keep it on your forehead. There, like that. That better?"

"Eau de Cologne is for outside the body," said Mrs Dacey without disapproval, "and I'll give our Polly such a clip. I'll clip her on the earhole every time she opens her mouth."

Mr Allingham nodded. "Whisky I can understand," he said. "But eau de Cologne! You put that on handkerchiefs. You don't put whisky on handkerchiefs." He looked down at Samuel. "I don't."

"No, mustn't suck the sponge, Sam."

"I suppose he thinks red biddy's* like bread and milk," Mr Allingham said.

They gathered his clothes from the side of the bath and hurriedly dressed him. And not until he was dressed and upright, shivering along the landing to the dark stairs, did he try to speak again. George Ring and Mr Allingham held his arms and guided him towards the top of that winding grave. Mrs Dacey, the one mourner, followed with a rustle of silk.

"It was the brandy from the medicine cupboard," he said, and down they went into the coarse, earth-like silence of the stairs.

"Give me furniture polish," Mr Allingham said. "Crack. Mind your head. Especially when I'm out of sorts in the bath."

The darkness was settling like more dirt and dust over the silent shop. Someone had hung up a sign, "Closed", on the inside of the window not facing the street. "Meths is finicky," Mr Allingham said.

They sat Samuel down on a chair behind the counter, and he heard Mrs Dacey, still on the stairs, calling for Polly up into the dark, dirty other floors and caves of the drunken house. But Polly did not answer.

She would be in her locked bedroom now, crying for Sam gone, at her window staring out onto the colourless, slowly disappearing street and the tall houses down at heel; or depicting, in the kitchen, the agony of a woman in childbirth, writhing and howling round the crowded sink; or being glad at a damp corner of the landing.

"Silly goose," said George Ring, sitting long-legged on the table and smiling at Samuel with a ferocious coyness. "You might have been drownded. Drownded," he said again, looking slyly up from under the spider line of his eyebrows.

"Lucky you left the door open," Mr Allingham said. He lit a cigarette and looked at the match until it burned his finger. "I suppose," he said, his finger in his mouth.

"Our maid at home always said 'drownded'," said George Ring.

"But I saw Polly lock the door. She put the key down her dress." Samuel spoke with difficulty from behind the uncertain counter. The words came out in a rush, then reversed and were lost, tumbling among the sour bushes under his tongue. "She put it down her dress," he said, and paused at the end of each word to untie the next. Now the shop was almost entirely dark.

"And chimbley. You know, for chimney. Well, my dear, the door was open when we went up. No key, no Polly."

"Just a boy in the bath," Mr Allingham said. "Do you often get like that, Sam? The water was up to your chin."

"And the dirt!"

"It wasn't my dirt. Someone had been in the bath before. It was cold," Samuel said.

"Yes, yes." Samuel could see Mr Allingham's head nodding. "That alters the situation, doesn't it? Dear God," he said, "you should have gone in with your clothes on like everybody else."

"Polly's gone," said Mrs Dacey. She appeared out of nowhere in the wall and stood behind the counter at Samuel's side. Her rustling dress brushed against his hands, and he drew them sharply back. I touched a funeral, he said to the dazed boy in his chair. Her corpse-cold hand fell against his cheek, chilling him out of a moment's sleep. The coffin has walked upright into my sitting bed.

"Oooh," he said aloud.

"Still cold, baby?" Mrs Dacey bent down, creaking like a door, and mothered him about the hair and mouth.

There had been little light all day, even at dawn and noon, mostly the close, false light of bedroom and restaurant. All day he had sat in small, dark places, bathroom and travelling lavatory, a jungle of furniture, a stuffed shop where no one called except these voices saying:

"You looked so defenceless, Sam, lying there all cold and white."

"Where was Moses when the light went out,* Mrs Dacey?"

"Like one of those cherubs in the Italian primitives,* only with a bottle on your finger, of course."

"In the dark. Like this."

"What did our Polly do to you, the little tart?" Mrs Dacey said in her tidy, lady's voice.

Mr Allingham stood up. "I'm not listening. Don't you say a word, Sam, even if you could. No explanations. There he was, gassed in the bath, at half-past four in the afternoon. I can stand so much."

"I want to go out," Samuel said.

"Out the back?"

"Out."

Out of the blind, stripping hole in a wall, aviary and menagerie, cold-water shop, into the streets without locks. I don't want to sleep with Polly in a drawer. I don't want to lie in a cellar with a wet woman, drinking polish. London is happening everywhere; let me out, let me go. Mrs Dacey is all cold fingers.

"Out then. It's six o'clock. Can you walk, son?"

"I can walk OK – it's my head."

Mrs Dacey, unseen, stroked his hair. Nobody can see, he said silently, but Mrs Susan Dacey, licensed to sell tobacco, is stroking my hair with her lizards; and he gave a cry.

"I've got no sympathy," said Mr Allingham. "Are you coming, Sue?"

"Depends where you're going."

"Taking the air down the Edgware Road. He's got to see around, hasn't he? You don't come up from the provinces to drink eau de Cologne in the bath."

They all went out, and Mrs Dacey locked the shop.

It was raining heavily.

2

"Fun!" George Ring said.

They walked out of Sewell Street into Praed Street arm in arm.

"I'm a fool for the rain." He shook his clinging curls and danced a few steps on the pavement.

"My new brown overcoat's in the bathroom," Samuel said, and Mrs Dacey covered him with her umbrella.

"Go on, you're not the sort that puts a coat on in the rain, are you? Stop dancing, George."

But George Ring danced down the pavement in the flying rain and pulled the others with him; unwillingly they broke into a dancing run under the lamp-posts' drizzle of light, Mrs Dacey, black as a deacon, jumping high over the puddles with a rustle and creak, Mr Allingham, on the outside, stamping and dodging along the gutter, Samuel gliding light and dizzy with his feet hardly touching the ground.

"Look out. People," cried Mr Allingham, and dragged them, still dancing, out onto the slippery street. Caught in a circle of headlights and chased by horns, they stamped and scampered onto the pavement again, clinging fast to each other, their faces glistening, cold and wet.

"Where's the fire, George? Go easy, boy, go easy." But Mr Allingham, one foot in the gutter, was hopping along like a rabbit and tugging at George Ring's arm to make him dance faster. "It's all Sam's fault," he said as he hopped, and his voice was high and loud like a boy's in the rain.

Look at London flying by me, buses and glow-worms, umbrellas and lamp-posts, cigarettes and eyes under the water doorways, I am dancing with three strangers down Edgware Road in the rain, cried Samuel to the gliding boy around him. Light and without will as a suit of feathers, he held on to their arms, and the umbrella rode above them like a bird.

Cold and unsmiling, Mrs Dacey skipped by his side, seeing nothing through her misted glasses.

And George Ring sang as he bounced, with his drenched hair rising and falling in level waves, "Here we go gathering nuts and may,* Donald and Mrs Dacey and George and Sam."

When they stopped, outside the Antelope, Mr Allingham leant against the wall and coughed until he cried. All the time he coughed, he never removed his cigarette.

"I haven't run for forty years," he said, his shoulders shaking, and his handkerchief like a flag to his mouth. He led them into the saloon bar, where three young women sat with their shoes off in front of the electric log fire.

"Three whiskies. What's yours, Sam? Nice drop of Kiwi?"

"He'll have whisky, too," Mrs Dacey said. "See, he's got his colour back."

"Kiwi's boot polish," one of the young women whispered, and she bent, giggling, over the grate. Her big toe came out of a hole in her stocking, suddenly, like a cold inquisitive nose, and she giggled again.

This was a bar in London. Dear Peggy, Samuel wrote with his finger on the counter, I am drinking in a bar called the Antelope in Edgware Road with a furniture dealer, the proprietress of a tea shop, three young women and George Ring. I have put these facts down clearly because the scent I drank in the bath is still troublesome, and people will not keep still. I am quite well, but I do not know for how long.

"What're you doing, Sam? Looks like you're drawing. I've got a proper graveyard in my chest, haven't I? Cough, cough," Mr Allingham said, angrily between each cough.

"It wasn't the cough that carried him off,"* the young woman said. Her whole plump body was giggling.

Everything is very trivial, Samuel wrote. Mr Allingham is drunk on one whisky. All his face goes pale except his mark.

"Here we are," Mr Allingham said, "four lost souls. What a place to put a man in."

"The Antelope's charming," said George Ring. "There's some real hunting prints in the private bar." He smiled at Sam and moved his long, blunt fingers rapidly along the counter as though he were playing a piano. "I'm all rhythm. It's like a kind of current in me."

"I mean the world. This is only a little tiny bit in it. This is all right, it's got regular hours; you can draw the curtains, you know what to expect here. But look at the world. You and your currents," Mr Allingham said.

"No, really it's rippling out of me." George Ring tap-danced with one foot and made a rhythmical kissing noise with his tongue against the roof of his mouth.

"What a place to drop a man in. In the middle of streets and houses and traffic and people."

The young woman wagged her finger at her toe. "You be still." Her friends were giggling now, covering their faces and peeping out at Mr Allingham between their fingers, telling each other to go on, saying "Hotcha" and "Hi de ho" and "Minnie the Moocher's Wedding Day"* as George Ring tapped one narrow, yellow buckskin shoe and strummed on the counter. They rolled their eyes and said "Swing it, sister", then hissed again into a giggle.

"I've been nibbling away for fifty years now," Mr Allingham said, "and look at me. Look at me." He took off his hat.

"There's hair," whispered the young woman with the hole in her stocking.

His hair was the colour of ferrets and thin on the crown; it stopped growing at the temples, but came out again from the ears. His hat made him a deep, white wrinkle on his forehead.

"Here we are nibbling away all day and night, Mrs Dacey. Nibble nibble." His brown teeth came over his lip. "No sense, no order, no nothing – we're all mad and nasty. Look at Sam there. There's a nice harmless boy, curly hair and big eyes and all. What's he do? Look at his bloody bottle."

"No language," said the woman behind the bar. She looked like a duchess, riding, rising and sinking slowly as she spoke, as though to the movements of a horse.

"Tantivy,"* Samuel said, and blushed as Mr Allingham pointed a stained finger.

"That's right. Always the right word in the right place. Tantivy! I told you, people are all mad in the world. They don't know where they're going, they don't know why they're where they are – all they want is love and beer and sleep."

"I wouldn't say no to the first," said Mrs Dacey. "Don't pay any attention to him," she said to the woman behind the counter, "he's a philosopher."

"Calling everybody nasty," said the woman, rising. "There's people live in glass houses." Over the hurdle she goes, thought Samuel idly, and she sank again onto the hidden saddle. She must do miles in a night, he said to his empty glass.

"People think about all kinds of other things." George Ring looked at the ceiling for a vision. "Music," he said, "and dancing." He ran his fingers along the air and danced on his toes.

"Sex," said Mr Allingham.

"Sex, sex, sex, it's always sex with you, Donald. You must be repressed or something."

"Sex," whispered the young woman by the fire.

"Sex is all right," Mrs Dacey said. "You leave sex alone."

"Of course I'm repressed. I've been repressed for fifty years."

"You leave sex out of it." The woman behind the counter rose in a gallop. "And religion," she said.

Over she goes, clean as a whistle, over the hedge and the water jump.

Samuel took a pound out of his wallet and pointed to the whisky on the shelf. He could not trust himself yet to speak to the riding woman with the stuffed, enormous bosom and two long milk-white loaves for arms. His throat was still on fire; the heat of the room blazed up his nostrils into his head, and all the words at the tip of his tongue caught like petrol and gorse; he saw three young women flickering by the metal logs, and his three new friends thundered and gestured before him with the terrible exaggeration of people of flesh and blood moving like dramatic prisoners on a screen, doomed for ever to enact their pettiness in a magnified exhibition.

He said to himself: Mrs Antelope, pouring the whisky as though it were four insults, believes that sex is a bed. The act of love is an act of the bed itself; the springs cry "Tumble", and over she goes, horse and all. I can see her lying like a log on a bed, listening with hate and disgust to the masterly voice of the dented sheets.

He felt old and all-knowing and unsteady. His immediate wisdom weighed so heavily that he clutched at the edge of the counter and raised one arm, like a man trapped in the sea, to signal his sinking.

"You may," Mrs Dacey said, and the room giggled like a girl.

Now I know, thought Samuel beneath his load, as he struggled to the surface, what is meant by a pillar of the Church. Long, cold Mrs Dacey could prop Bethesda* on the remote top of her carved head and freeze with her eyes the beetle-black sinners where they scraped below her. Her joke boomed in the roof.

"You've dropped a fiver, Sam." Mr Allingham picked up a piece of paper and held it out on the sun-stained palm of his hand.

"It's Lucille Harris's address," Samuel said.

"Why don't you give her a ring? The phone's on the stairs, up there." George Ring pointed. "Outside the Ladies."

Samuel parted a curtain and mounted.

"*Outside* the Ladies," a voice said from the sinking room.

He read the instructions above the telephone, put in two pennies, dialled and said, "Miss Harris? I'm a friend of Austin's.

"I am a friend of nobody's. I am detached," he whispered into the buzzing receiver. "I am Lopo the outlaw, loping through the night, companion of owls and murderers. Tu wit to woo," he said aloud into the mouthpiece.

She did not answer, and he shuffled down the stairs, swung open the curtain and entered the bright bar with a loping stride.

The three young women had gone. He looked at the grate to see if their shoes were still there, but they had gone too. People leave nothing.

"She must have been out," he said.

"We heard," said Mr Allingham. "We heard you talking to her owl." He raised his glass and stared at it, standing sadly and savagely in the middle of the room, like a man with oblivion in his hand. Then he made his choice and drank.

"We're going places," he said. "We're taking a taxi, and Sam is going to pay for it. We're going to the West End to look for Lucille."

"I knew she was a kind of Holy Grail," George Ring said when they were all in the darkness of the taxi rattling through the rain.

Samuel felt Mrs Dacey's hand on his knee.

"Four knights at arms, it's terribly exciting. We'll call at the Gayspot first, then the Cheerioh, then the Neptune."

"Four lost souls."

The hand ached on along the thigh, five dry fishes dying on a cloth.

"Marble Arch," Mr Allingham said. "This is where the fairies come out in the moon."

And the hurrying crowd in the rain might have had no flesh or blood.

"Park Lane."

The crowd slid past the bonnet and the windows, mixed their faces with no features and their liquid bodies under a sudden blaze, or vanished into the streaming light of a tall door that led into the bowels of rich night London, where all the women wore pearls and pricked their arms with needles.

A car backfired.

"Hear the champagne corks?"

Mr Allingham is listening to my head, Samuel thought as he drew away from the fingers in the corner.

"Piccadilly. Come on Allingham's tour. That's the Ritz. Stop for a kipper, Sam?"

The Ritz is closed for ever. All the waiters would be bellowing behind their hands. Gustave, Gustave, cried a man in an opera hat, he is using the wrong fork. He is wearing a tie with elastic at the back. And a woman in evening dress cut so low he could see her navel with a diamond in it leant over his table and pulled his bow tie out and let it fly back again to his throat.

"The filthy rich," he said. My place is among the beggars and the outlaws. With power and violence Samuel Bennet destroys the whole artifice of society in his latest novel, *In the Bowels*.

"Piccadilly Circus. Centre of the world. See the man picking his nose under the lamp-post? That's the prime minister."

3

The Gayspot was like a coal cellar with a bar at one end, and several coalmen were dancing with their sacks. Samuel, at the door, swaying between Mrs Dacey and George Ring, felt his thigh, still frightened. He did not dare look down at it, in case even the outside of the trouser leg bore the inexcusable imprint of his terror in the taxi.

"It's cosmopolitan," George Ring whispered. "Look at the nigger."

Samuel rubbed the night out of his eyes and saw the black men dancing with their women, twirling them among the green cane chairs, between the fruit machine and the Russian billiard table. Some of the women were white, and smoked as they danced. They pussed and spied around the room, unaware of their dancing, feeling the arms around them as though around the bodies of different women: their eyes were for the strangers entering; they went through the hot movements of the dance like women in the act of love, looking over men's shoulders at their own remote and unconniving faces in a looking glass. The men were all teeth and bottom, flashers and shakers, with little waists and wide shoulders, in double-breasted pinstripe and sleek, licked shoes, all ageless and unwrinkled, waiting for the fleshpot, proud and silent and friendly and hungry – jerking round the smoking cellar under the centre of the world to the music of a drum and a piano played by two pale white cross boys whose lips were always moving.

As George Ring weaved Samuel through the dancers to the bar, they passed a machine, and Samuel put in a penny for a lemon. Out came one and sixpence.

"Who's going to win the Derby,* Sam?" said Mr Allingham behind them.

"Isn't he a lucky poet?" George Ring said.

Mrs Dacey, in half a minute, had found a partner as tall as herself and was dancing through the smoke like a chapel. He had powdered his face to hide a scar from the corner of his eye to his chin.

"Mrs Dacey's dancing with a razor-man,"* Samuel said.

This was a breath and a scar of the London he had come to catch. Look at the knickerless women enamouring from the cane tables, waiting in the fumes for the country cousins to stagger in, all savings and haywisps, or the rosy-cheeked old men with buttonholes whose wives at home were as lively as bags of sprouts. And the dancing cannibal-mouthed black razor kings shaking their women's breasts and blood to the stutter of the drums, snakily tailored in the shabby sweat-smelling jungle under the wet pavement. And a crimped boy danced like a girl, and the two girls serving were as harsh as men.

Mr Allingham bought four white wines. "Go on. He did it on a pin table.* You could bring your auntie here, couldn't you, Monica?" he said to the girl with the bow tie pouring their drinks.

"Not my auntie," Samuel said. Auntie Morgan Pont-Neath-Vaughan in her elastic-sided boots. "She doesn't drink," he said.

"Show Monica your bottle. He's got a bottle on his finger."

Samuel dug his hand deep in his jacket pocket. "She doesn't want to see an old bottle." His chest began to tickle as he spoke, and he slipped two fingers of his right hand between the buttons of his shirt onto his bare flesh. "No vest," he said in surprise, but the girl had turned away.

"It's a Sunday school," Mr Allingham said. "Tasted your wine yet, Sam? This horse's unfit to work. A regular little bun dance. You could bring the vicar's wife in here."

Mrs Cotmore-Richards, four foot one and a squeak in her stockinged trotters.

"A regular little vestry," Mr Allingham said. "See that woman dancing? The one who fell in the flour bin. She's a bank manager's niece."

The woman with the dead white face smiled as she passed them in the arms of a padded boy.

"Hullo, Ikey."

"Hullo, Lola. She's pretendin', see. Thinks she's Starr Faithfull."*

"Is she a prostitute, Mr Allingham?"

"She's a manicurist, Sammy. How's your cuticles? Don't you believe everything you see, especially after it's dark. This is all pretending. Look at Casanova there with the old girls. The last time he touched a woman he had a dummy in his mouth."

Samuel turned around. George Ring whinnied in a corner with several women. Their voices shrilled and rasped through the cross noise of the drums.

"Lucy got a beating the last time I see her," said a woman with false teeth and a bald fur. "He said he was a chemist."

"Lucille," George Ring said, impatiently shaking his curls. "Lucille Harris."

"With a clothes brush. He had it in a little bag."

"There's a chemist," said a woman wearing a picture hat.

"He doesn't mean Lucy Wakefield," another woman said.

"Lucy Wakefield's in the Feathers with a man from Crouch End," said the bank manager's niece, dancing past. The boy who danced with her was smiling with his eyes closed.

"Perhaps he got a leather belt in his little bag," said the woman with the fur.

"It's all the same in a hundred years," said the woman in the picture hat. She went down to her white wine, widening her legs like an old mule at a pool, and came up gasping. "They put hair oil in it."

This was all wrong. They spoke like the women who wore men's caps and carried fish-frails full of empties in the Jug and Bottle of the Compasses at home.

"Keeps away the dandruff."

He did not expect that the nightclub women under the pavement should sing and twang like sirens or lure off his buttons with their dangerous, fringed violet eyes. London is not under the bedclothes, where all the company is grand and vile by a flick of the cinema eye, and the warm linen doors are always open. But these women with the shabby faces and the comedians' tongues, squatting and squabbling over their mother's ruin, might have lurched in from Llanelly on a football night, on the arms of short men with leeks. The women at the tables, whom he had seen as enamouring shapes when he first came in dazed from the night, were dull as sisters, red-eyed and thick in the head with colds; they would sneeze when you kissed them or hiccup and say "Manners" in the dark traps of the hotel bedrooms.

"Good as gold," he said to Mr Allingham. "I thought you said this was a low place, like a speakeasy."

"Speak easy yourself. They don't like being called low down here." Mr Allingham leant close, speaking from the side of his mouth. "They're too low for that. It's a regular little hellhole," he whispered. "It's just warming up. They take their clothes off soon and do the hula hula – you'll like that."

"Nobody knows Lucille," George Ring said. "Are you sure she isn't Lucy? There's a lovely Lucy."

"No, Lucille."

"'She dwells beside the springs of Dove.' I think I like Wordsworth better than Walter de la Mare sometimes. Do you know 'Tintern Abbey'?"*

Mrs Dacey appeared at Samuel's shoulder. "Doesn't baby dance?" He shuddered at the cold touch of her hand on his neck. Not here. Not now. That terrible impersonal Bethesda rape of the fingers. He remembered that she had carried her umbrella even while she danced.

"I got a sister in Tintern," said a man behind them.

"Tintern Abbey." George Ring pouted and did not turn round.

"Not in the abbey, she's a waitress."

"We were talking about a poem."

"She's not a bloody nun," the man said.

The music stopped, but the two boys on the little platform still moved their hands and lips, beating out the dance in silence.

Mr Allingham raised his fist. "Say that again and I'll knock you down."

"I'll blow you down," the man said. He puffed up his cheeks and blew. His breath smelt of cloves.

"Now, now." Mrs Dacey levelled her umbrella.

"People shouldn't go around insulting nuns, then," Mr Allingham said as the ferrule tapped his waistcoat.

"I'll blow you down," the man said. "I never insulted any nun. I've never spoken to a nun."

"Now, now." The umbrella drove for his eyes, and he ducked.

"You blow again," said Mrs Dacey politely, "I'll push it up your snout and open it."

"Don't you loathe violence?" George Ring said. "I've always been a terrible pacifist. One drop of blood and I feel slimy all over. Shall we dance?"

He put his arm round Samuel's waist and danced him away from the bar. The band began again, though none of the couples had stopped dancing.

"But we're two men," Samuel said. "Is this a waltz?"

"They never play waltzes here, it's just self-expression. Look, there's two other men dancing."

"I thought they were girls."

"My friend thought you were a couple of girls," George Ring said in a loud voice as they danced past them. Samuel looked at the floor, trying to follow the movements of George Ring's feet. One, two, three, turn around, tap.

One of the young men squealed, "Come up and see my Aga cooker."

One, two, three, swirl and tap.

"What sort of a girl is Polly Dacey, really? Is she mad?"

I'm like thistledown, thought Samuel. Swirl about and swirl again, on the toes now, shake those hips.

"Not so heavy, Sam. You're like a little jumbo. When she went to school she used to post mice in the pillar box, and they ate up all the letters. And she used to do things to boys in the scullery. I can't tell you. You could hear them screaming all over the house."

But Samuel was not listening any more. He circled and stumbled to a rhythm of his own among the flying legs, dipped and retreated, hopped on one leg and spun, his hair falling over his eyes and his bottle swinging. He clung to George Ring's shoulder and zigzagged away from him, then bounced up close again.

"Don't swing the bottle. Don't swing it. Look out. Sam. Sam."

Samuel's arm flew back, and a small woman went down. She grabbed at his legs, and he brought George Ring with him. Another man fell, catching fast to his partner's skirt. A long rip and she tumbled among them, her legs in the air, her head in a heave of bellies and arms.

Samuel lay still. His mouth pressed on the curls at the nape of the neck of the woman who had fallen first. He put out his tongue.

"Get off my head – you've got keys in your pocket."

"Oh, my leg!"

"That's right. Easy does it. Upsadaisy."

"Someone's licking me," cried the woman at the bottom.

Then the two girls from behind the bar were standing over them, slapping and kicking, pulling them up by the hair.

"It was that one's fault. He crowned her with a bottle. I saw him," said the bank manager's niece.

"Where'd he get the bottle from, Lola?"

The girl with the bow tie dragged Samuel up by the collar and pointed to his left hand. He tried to slip it in his pocket, but a hand like a black boxing glove closed over the bottle. A large black face bent down and stared into his. He saw only the whites of the eyes and the teeth.

I don't want a cut on my face. Don't cut my lips open. They only use razors in stories. Don't let him have read any stories.

"Now, now," said Mrs Dacey's voice. The black face jerked back as she thrust out her opened umbrella, and Samuel's hand was free.

"Throw him out, Monica."

"He was dancing like a monkey, throw him out."

"If you throw him out, you can throw me out too," Mr Allingham said from the bar. He raised his fists.

Two men walked over to him.

"Mind my glasses." He did not wear any.

They opened the door and threw him up the steps.

"Bloody nun," a voice shouted.

"Now you."

"And the old girl. Look out for her brolly, Dodie."

Samuel fell on the area* step below Mr Allingham, and Mrs Dacey came flying after with her umbrella held high.

It was still raining heavily.

4

"Just a passing call," said Mr Allingham. As though he were sitting indoors at a window, he put out his hand to feel the rain. Shoes slopped past on the pavement above his head. Wet trousers and stockings almost touched the brim of his hat. "Just in and out," he said. "Where's George?"

I've been bounced, Samuel thought.

"It reminds me of my old man." Mrs Dacey's face was hidden under the umbrella, as though in a private, accompanying thundercloud. "In and out, in and out. Just one look at him, and out he went like clockwork."

Oh, the Gayspot? Can't go there, old man. Samuel winked seriously in the dark. Oh, carrying a cargo. Swinging a bottle around. One look at me, out I went.

"He used to carry a little book with all the places he couldn't go to, and he went to them every Saturday."

Fool, fool, fool, Samuel said to himself.

The steps were suddenly lit up as the door opened for George Ring. He came out carefully and tidily, to a rush of music and voices that faded at once with the vanishing of the smoky light, and stood on Mrs Dacey's step, his mane of curls golden against the fanlight, a god or a half-horse emerging from the underworld into the common rain.

"They're awfully cross," he said. "Mrs Cavanagh ripped her skirt, and she didn't have anything on underneath. My dear, it's like ancient Rome down there, and now she's wearing a man's trousers and he's got legs exactly like a spider's. All black and hairy. Why are you sitting in the rain?"

"It's safe," Mr Allingham said. "It's nice and safe in the rain. It's nice and rational sitting on the steps in the rain. You can't knock a woman down with a bottle here. See the stars? That's Arcturus. That's the Great Bear. That's Sirius, see, the green one. I won't show you where Venus is. There's some people can't enjoy themselves unless they're knocking women down and licking them on the floor. They think the evening's wasted unless they've done that. I wish I was home. I wish I was lying in bed by the ceiling. I wish I was lying under the chairs like Rosie."

"Who started to fight, anyway? Let's go round the corner to the Cheerioh."

"That was ethical."

They climbed up the street, George Ring first, then Mr Allingham, then Samuel and Mrs Dacey. She tucked his arm in hers.

"Don't you worry. You hold on to me. Cold? You're shivering."

"It'll be Cheerioh all right."

The Cheerioh was a bad blaze, an old hole of lights. In the dark, open a cupboard full of cast-off clothes moving in a wind from nowhere, the smell of mothballs and damp furs, and find a lamp lit, candles burning, a gramophone playing.

"No dancing for you," Mr Allingham said. "You need space. You want the Crystal Palace."

Mrs Dacey still held Samuel by the arm. "You're safe with me. I've taken a fancy," she said. "Once I take a fancy, I never let go."

"And never trust a woman who can't get up." Mr Allingham pointed to a woman sitting in a chair by the Speedboat pin table. "She's trying to get up all the time." The woman made a sudden movement of her shoulders. "No, no, legs first."

"This used to be the cowshed," George Ring said, "and there was real straw on the floor."

Mrs Dacey never lets go. Samuel saw the fancy shining behind her glasses, and in her hard mousetrap mouth. Her cold hand hooked him. If he struggled and ran, she would catch him in a corner and open her umbrella inside his nose.

"And real cows," Mr Allingham said.

The men and women drinking and dancing looked like the older brothers and sisters of the drinkers and dancers in the club round the corner, but no one was black. There were deep-green faces, dipped in a sea dye, with painted cockles for mouths and lichenous hair, sealed on the cheeks; red and purple, slate-grey, tidemarked, rat-brown and stickily whitewashed, with violet-inked eyes or lips the colour of Stilton; pink-chopped, pink-lidded, pink as the belly of a newborn monkey, nicotine-yellow with mustard-flecked eyes, rust scraping through the bleach, black hairs axle-greased down among the peroxide; squashed-fly stubbles, salt-cellared necks thick with pepper powder; carrot heads, yolk heads, black heads, heads bald as sweetbreads.

"All white people here," Samuel said.

"The salt of the earth," Mr Allingham said. "The foul salt of the earth. Drunk as a pig. Ever seen a pig drunk? Ever seen a monkey dancing like a man? Look at that king of the animals. See him? The one who's eaten his lips. That one smiling. That one having his honeymoon on her feet."

LATE STORIES*

Memories of Christmas*

One Christmas was so much like another, in those years, around the sea-town corner now, and out of all sound except the distant speaking of the voices I sometimes hear a moment before sleep, that I can never remember whether it snowed for six days and six nights when I was twelve or whether it snowed for twelve days and twelve nights when I was six; or whether the ice broke and the skating grocer vanished like a snowman through a white trapdoor on that same Christmas Day that the mince pies finished Uncle Arnold and we tobogganed down the seaward hill, all the afternoon, on the best tea tray, and Mrs Griffiths complained, and we threw a snowball at her niece, and my hands burned so, with the heat and the cold, when I held them in front of the fire, that I cried for twenty minutes and then had some jelly.

All the Christmases roll down the hill towards the Welsh-speaking sea, like a snowball growing whiter and bigger and rounder, like a cold and headlong moon bundling down the sky that was our street; and they stop at the rim of the ice-edged, fish-freezing waves, and I plunge my hands in the snow and bring out whatever I can find: holly or robins or pudding, squabbles and carols and oranges and tin whistles, and the fire in the front room, and bang go the crackers, and holy, holy, holy, ring the bells, and the glass bells shaking on the tree, and Mother Goose, and Struwwelpeter – oh! the baby-burning flames and the clacking scissor-man! – Billy Bunter and Black Beauty, *Little Women* and boys who have three helpings, Alice and Mrs Potter's badgers,* penknives, teddy bears – named after a Mr Theodore Bear,* their inventor, or father, who died recently in the United States – mouth organs, tin soldiers and blancmange, and Auntie Bessie playing 'Pop Goes the Weasel' and 'Nuts in May' and 'Oranges and Lemons'* on the untuned piano in the parlour all through the thimble-hiding, musical-chairing, blind-man's-buffing party at the end of the never-to-be-forgotten day at the end of the unremembered year.

In goes my hand into that wool-white, bell-tongued ball of holidays resting at the margin of the carol-singing sea, and out come Mrs Prothero and the firemen.

It was on the afternoon of the day of Christmas Eve, and I was in Mrs Prothero's garden, waiting for cats, with her son Jim. It was snowing. It was always snowing at Christmas: December, in my memory, is white as Lapland, though there were no reindeers. But there were cats. Patient, cold and callous, our hands wrapped in socks, we waited to snowball the cats. Sleek and long as jaguars and terrible-whiskered, spitting and snarling they would slink and sidle over the white back-garden walls, and the lynx-eyed hunters, Jim and I, fur-capped and moccasined trappers from Hudson's Bay off Eversley Road, would hurl our deadly snowballs at the green of their eyes. The wise cats never appeared. We were so still, Eskimo-footed Arctic marksmen in the muffling silence of the eternal snows – eternal, ever since Wednesday – that we never heard Mrs Prothero's first cry from her igloo at the bottom of the garden. Or, if we heard it at all, it was, to us, like the far-off challenge of our enemy and prey, the neighbour's Polar Cat. But soon the voice grew louder. "Fire!" cried Mrs Prothero, and she beat the dinner gong. And we ran down the garden, with the snowballs in our arms, towards the house, and smoke, indeed, was pouring out of the dining room, and the gong was bombilating,* and Mrs Prothero was announcing ruin like a town crier in Pompeii. This was better than all the cats in Wales standing on the wall in a row. We bounded into the house, laden with snowballs, and stopped at the open door of the smoke-filled room. Something was burning all right; perhaps it was Mr Prothero, who always slept there after midday dinner with a newspaper over his face; but he was standing in the middle of the room, saying "A fine Christmas!" and smacking at the smoke with a slipper.

"Call the fire brigade," cried Mrs Prothero as she beat the gong.

"They won't be there," said Mr Prothero, "it's Christmas."

There was no fire to be seen, only clouds of smoke and Mr Prothero standing in the middle of them, waving his slipper as though he were conducting.

"Do something," he said.

And we threw all our snowballs into the smoke – I think we missed Mr Prothero – and ran out of the house to the telephone box.

"Let's call the police as well," Jim said.

"And the ambulance."

"And Ernie Jenkins, he likes fires."

But we only called the fire brigade, and soon the fire engine came and three tall men in helmets brought a hose into the house and Mr Prothero got out just in time before they turned it on. Nobody could have had a noisier

MEMORIES OF CHRISTMAS

Christmas Eve. And when the firemen turned off the hose and were standing in the wet and smoky room, Jim's aunt, Miss Prothero, came downstairs and peered in at them. Jim and I waited, very quietly, to hear what she would say to them. She said the right thing, always. She looked at the three tall firemen in their shining helmets, standing among the smoke and cinders and dissolving snowballs, and she said: "Would you like something to read?"

Now out of that bright-white snowball of Christmas gone comes the stocking, the stocking of stockings, that hung at the foot of the bed with the arm of a golliwog dangling over the top and small bells ringing in the toes. There was a company, gallant and scarlet but never nice to taste, though I always tried when very young, of belted and busbied* and musketed lead soldiers so soon to lose their heads and legs in the wars on the kitchen table after the tea things, the mince pies and the cakes that I helped to make by stoning the raisins and eating them, had been cleared away; and a bag of moist and many-coloured jelly babies and a folded flag and a false nose and a tram conductor's cap and a machine that punched tickets and rang a bell; never a catapult; once, by a mistake that no one could explain, a little hatchet; and a rubber buffalo, or it may have been a horse, with a yellow head and haphazard legs; and a celluloid duck that made, when you pressed it, a most unducklike noise, a mewing moo that an ambitious cat might make who wishes to be a cow; and a painting book in which I could make the grass, the trees, the sea and the animals any colour I pleased – and still the dazzling sky-blue sheep are grazing in the red field under a flight of rainbow-beaked and pea-green birds.

Christmas morning was always over before you could say Jack Frost. And look! Suddenly the pudding was burning! Bang the gong and call the fire brigade and the book-loving firemen! Someone found the silver threepenny bit with a currant on it; and the someone was always Uncle Arnold. The motto in my cracker read:

Let's all have fun this Christmas Day,
Let's play and sing and shout hooray!

And the grown-ups turned their eyes towards the ceiling, and Auntie Bessie, who had already been frightened, twice, by a clockwork mouse, whimpered at the sideboard and had some elderberry wine. And someone put a glass bowl full of nuts on the littered table, and my uncle said, as he said once every year: "I've got a shoe nut here. Fetch me a shoehorn to open it, boy."

And dinner was ended.

And I remember that on the afternoon of Christmas Day, when the others sat around the fire and told each other that this was nothing, no, nothing, to the great snowbound and turkey-proud yule-log-crackling holly-berry-bedizened and kissing-under-the-mistletoe Christmas when *they* were children, I would go out, school-capped and gloved and mufflered, with my bright new boots squeaking, into the white world onto the seaward hill, to call on Jim and Dan and Jack and to walk with them through the silent snowscape of our town.

We went padding through the streets, leaving huge deep footprints in the snow, on the hidden pavements.

"I bet people'll think there's been hippos."

"What would you do if you saw a hippo coming down Terrace Road?"

"I'd go like this, bang! I'd throw him over the railings and roll him down the hill and then I'd tickle him under the ear and he'd wag his tail..."

"What would you do if you saw *two* hippos?..."

Iron-flanked and bellowing he-hippos clanked and blundered and battered through the scudding snow towards us as we passed by Mr Daniel's house.

"Let's post Mr Daniel a snowball through his letter box."

"Let's write things in the snow."

"Let's write 'Mr Daniel looks like a spaniel' all over his lawn."

"Look," Jack said, "I'm eating snow pie."

"What's it taste like?"

"Like snow pie," Jack said.

Or we walked on the white shore.

"Can the fishes see it's snowing?"

"They think it's the sky falling down."

The silent one-clouded heavens drifted on to the sea. "All the old dogs have gone."

Dogs of a hundred mingled makes yapped in the summer at the sea rim and yelped at the trespassing mountains of the waves.

"I bet St Bernards would like it now."

And we were snow-blind travellers lost on the north hills, and the great dewlapped dogs, with brandy flasks round their necks, ambled and shambled up to us, baying "Excelsior".*

We returned home through the desolate, poor sea-facing streets where only a few children fumbled with bare red fingers in the thick wheel-rutted snow and catcalled after us, their voices fading away, as we trudged uphill, into the cries of the dock birds and the hooters of ships out in the white and whirling bay.

Bring out the tall tales now that we told by the fire as we roasted chestnuts and the gaslight bubbled low. Ghosts with their heads under their arms trailed their chains and said "whooo" like owls in the long nights when I dared not look over my shoulder; wild beasts lurked in the cubbyhole under the stairs, where the gas meter ticked. "Once upon a time," Jim said, "there were three boys, just like us, who got lost in the dark in the snow, near Bethesda Chapel, and this is what happened to them…" It was the most dreadful happening I had ever heard.

And I remember that we went singing carols once, a night or two before Christmas Eve, when there wasn't the shaving of a moon to light the secret, white-flying streets. At the end of a long road was a drive that led to a large house, and we stumbled up the darkness of the drive that night, each one of us afraid, each one holding a stone in his hand in case, and all of us too brave to say a word. The wind made through the drive trees noises as of old and unpleasant and maybe web-footed men wheezing in caves. We reached the black bulk of the house.

"What shall we give them?" Dan whispered.

"'Hark the Herald'? 'Christmas Comes But Once a Year'?"*

"No," Jack said. "We'll sing 'Good King Wenceslas'. I'll count three."

One, two, three, and we began to sing, our voices high and seemingly distant in the snow-felted darkness round the house that was occupied by nobody we knew. We stood close together, near the dark door.

> Good King Wenceslas looked out
> On the feast of Stephen.

And then a small, dry voice, like the voice of someone who has not spoken for a long time, suddenly joined our singing: a small, dry voice from the other side of the door – a small, dry voice through the keyhole. And when we stopped running, we were outside *our* house; the front room was lovely and bright; the gramophone was playing; we saw the red and white balloons hanging from the gas bracket;* uncles and aunts sat by the fire; I thought I smelt our supper being fried in the kitchen. Everything was good again, and Christmas shone through all the familiar town.

"Perhaps it was a ghost," Jim said.

"Perhaps it was trolls," Dan said, who was always reading.

"Let's go in and see if there's any jelly left," Jack said. And we did that.

Quite Early One Morning*

Quite early one morning in the winter in Wales, by the sea that was lying down still and green as grass after a night of tar-black howling and rolling, I went out of the house, where I had come to stay for a cold unseasonable holiday, to see if it was raining still, if the outhouse had been blown away, potatoes, shears, rat-killer, shrimp nets and tins of rusty nails aloft on the wind, and if all the cliffs were left. It had been such a ferocious night that someone in the smoky ship-pictured bar had said he could feel his tombstone shaking even though he was not dead, or at least was moving; but the morning shone as clear and calm as one always imagines tomorrow will shine.

The sun lit the sea town, not as a whole – from topmost down – reproving zinc-roofed chapel to empty but for rats and whispers grey warehouse on the harbour, but in separate bright pieces. There, the quay shouldering out, nobody on it now but the gulls and the capstans like small men in tubular trousers. Here, the roof of the police station, black as a helmet, dry as a summons, sober as Sunday. There, the splashed church, with a cloud in the shape of a bell poised above it, ready to drift and ring. Here the chimneys of the pink-washed pub, the pub that was waiting for Saturday night as an over-jolly girl waits for sailors.

The town was not yet awake. The milkman lay still lost in the clangour and music of his Welsh-spoken dreams, the wish-fulfilled tenor voices more powerful than Caruso's, sweeter than Ben Davies's,* thrilling past Cloth Hall and Manchester House up to the frosty hills. The town was not yet awake. Babies in upper bedrooms of salt-white houses dangling over water, or of bow-windowed villas squatting prim in neatly treed but unsteady hill streets, worried the light with their half-in-sleep cries. Miscellaneous retired sea captains emerged for a second from deeper waves than ever tossed their boats, then drowned again, going down down into a perhaps Mediterranean-blue cabin of sleep, rocked to the sea beat of their ears. Landladies, shawled and bloused and aproned with sleep in the curtained, bombazined* black of their once-spare rooms, remember their loves, their bills, their visitors – dead, decamped or buried in English deserts till the trumpet of next expensive August roused them again to the world of holiday rain, dismal cliff and sand seen through the weeping windows of front parlours, tasselled tablecloths, stuffed pheasants, ferns in pots, fading photographs of the bearded and censorious dead, autograph albums with a lock of limp and colourless beribboned hair lolling out between the thick black boards.

The town was not yet awake. Birds sang in eaves, bushes, trees, on telegraph wires, rails, fences, spars and wet masts, not for love or joy, but to keep other birds away. The landlords in feathers disputed the right of even the flying light to descend and perch.

The town was not yet awake, and I walked through the streets like a stranger come out of the sea, shrugging off wood and wave and darkness with each step, or like an inquisitive shadow, determined to miss nothing – not the preliminary tremor in the throat of the dawn-saying cock or the first whirring nudge of arranged time in the belly of the alarm clock on the trinketed chest of drawers under the knitted text and the done-by-hand watercolours of Porthcawl or Trinidad.

I walked past the small sea-spying windows, behind whose trim curtains lay mild-mannered men and women not yet awake and, for all I could know, terrible and violent in their dreams. In the head of Miss Hughes, "the Cosy", clashed the cymbals of an Eastern court. Eunuchs struck gongs the size of Bethesda Chapel. Sultans with voices fiercer than visiting preachers demanded a most un-Welsh dance. Everywhere there glowed and rayed the colours of the small, slate-grey woman's dreams, purple, magenta, ruby, sapphire, emerald, vermilion, honey. But I could not believe it. She knitted in her tidy sleep-world a beige woollen shroud with "thou shalt not" on the bosom.

I could not imagine Cadwallader Davies the grocer in his near-to-waking dream riding on horseback, two-gunned and Cody-bold,* through the cactus prairies. He added, he subtracted, he receipted, he filed a prodigious account with a candle dipped in dried egg.

What big seas of dreams ran in the captain's sleep? Over what blue-whaled waves did he sail through a rainbow hail of flying fishes to the music of Circe's swinish island? Do not let him be dreaming of dividends and bottled beer and onions.

Someone was snoring in one house. I counted ten savage and indignant grunts and groans like those of a pig in a model and mudless farm which ended with a window rattler, a washbasin shaker, a trembler of tooth glasses, a waker of dormice. It thundered with me to the chapel railings, then brassily vanished.

The chapel stood grim and grey, telling the day there was to be no nonsense. The chapel was not asleep – it never catnapped nor nodded nor closed its long cold eye. I left it telling the morning off and the seagull hung rebuked above it.

And climbing down again and up out of the town I heard the cocks crow from hidden farmyards, from old roosts above waves where fabulous seabirds might sit and cry: "Neptune!" And a faraway clock struck from another church in another village in another universe, though the wind blew the time away. And I walked in the timeless morning past a row of white cottages almost expecting that an ancient man with a great beard and an hourglass and a scythe under his night-dressed arm might lean from the window and ask me the time. I would have told him: "Arise, old counter of the heartbeats of albatrosses, and wake the cavernous sleepers of the town to a dazzling new morning." I would have told him: "You unbelievable Father of Eva and Dai Adam, come out, old chicken, and stir up the winter morning with your spoon of a scythe." I would have told him – I would have scampered like a scalded ghost over the cliffs and down to the bilingual sea.

Who lived in these cottages? I was a stranger to the sea town, fresh or stale from the city where I worked for my bread and butter, wishing it were laver bread* and country salty butter yolk-yellow. Fishermen certainly; no painters but of boats; no man-dressed women with shooting sticks and sketchbooks and voices like macaws to paint the reluctant heads of critical and sturdy natives who posed by the pint against the chapel-dark sea which would be made more blue than the bay of Naples – though shallower.

I walked on to the cliff path again, the town behind and below waking up now so very slowly; I stopped and turned and looked. Smoke from one chimney – the cobbler's, I thought, but from that distance it may have been the chimney of the retired male nurse who had come to live in Wales after many years' successful wrestling with the mad rich of southern England. He was not liked. He measured you for a straitjacket carefully with his eye; he saw you bounce from rubber walls like a sorbo* ball. No behaviour surprised him. Many people of the town found it hard to resist leering at him suddenly around the corner, or convulsively dancing, or pointing with laughter and devilish good humour at invisible dog fights merely to prove to him that they were normal.

Smoke from another chimney now. They were burning their last night's dreams. Up from a chimney came a long-haired wraith like an old politician. Someone had been dreaming of the Liberal Party. But no, the smoky figure wove, attenuated into a refined and precise grey comma. Someone had been dreaming of reading Charles Morgan.* Oh! The town was waking now, and I heard distinctly insistent over the slow-speaking sea the voices of the town blown up to me. And some of the voices said:

I am Miss May Hughes "the Cosy", a lonely lady,
Waiting in her house by the nasty sea,
Waiting for her husband and pretty baby
To come home at last from wherever they may be.

I am Captain Tiny Evans, my ship was the *Kidwelly*,
And Mrs Tiny Evans has been dead for many a year.
"Poor Captain Tiny all alone," the neighbours whisper,
But I like it all alone, and I hated her.

Clara Tawe Jenkins, "Madam" they call me,
An old contralto with her dressing gown on,
And I sit at the window and I sing to the sea,
For the sea does not notice that my voice has gone.

Parchedig* Thomas Evans making morning tea,
Very weak tea, too, you mustn't waste a leaf.
Every morning making tea in my house by the sea,
I am troubled by one thing only, and that, belief.

Open the curtains, light the fire, what are servants for?
I am Mrs Ogmore Pritchard, and I want another snooze.
Dust the china, feed the canary, sweep the drawing-room floor;
And before you let the sun in, mind he wipes his shoes.

I am only Mr Griffiths, very short-sighted, BA, Aber.*
As soon as I finish my egg I must shuffle off to school.
O patron saint of teachers, teach me to keep order,
And forget those words on the blackboard: "Griffiths Bat is a fool."

Do you hear that whistling? It's me, I am Phoebe,
The maid at the King's Head, and I am whistling like a bird.
Someone spilt a tin of pepper in the tea.
There's twenty for breakfast, and I'm not going to say a word.

Thus some of the voices of a cliff-perched town at the far end of Wales moved out of sleep and darkness into the newborn, ancient and ageless morning, moved and were lost.

Holiday Memory*

August bank holiday. A tune on an ice-cream cornet. A slap of sea and a tickle of sand. A fanfare of sunshades opening. A wince and whinny of bathers dancing into deceptive water. A tuck of dresses. A rolling of trousers. A compromise of paddlers. A sunburn of girls and a lark of boys. A silent hullabaloo of balloons.

I remember the sea telling lies in a shell held to my ear for a whole harmonious, hollow minute by a small, wet girl in an enormous bathing suit marked "Corporation Property".

I remember sharing the last of my moist buns with a boy and a lion. Tawny and savage, with cruel nails and capacious mouth, the little boy tore and devoured. Wild as seed cake, ferocious as a hearthrug, the depressed and verminous lion nibbled like a mouse at his half a bun and hiccuped in the sad dusk of his cage.

I remember a man like an alderman or a bailiff, bowlered and collarless, with a bag of monkey nuts* in his hand, crying "Ride 'em, cowboy!" time and again as he whirled in his chairoplane giddily above the upturned laughing faces of the town girls bold as brass and the boys with padded shoulders and shoes sharp as knives; and the monkey nuts flew through the air like salty hail.

Children all day capered or squealed by the glazed or bashing sea, and the steam organ wheezed its waltzes in the threadbare playground and the waste lot, where the dodgems dodged, behind the pickle factory.

And mothers loudly warned their proud pink daughters or sons to put that jellyfish down; and fathers spread newspapers over their faces; and sand fleas hopped on the picnic lettuce; and someone had forgotten the salt.

In those always radiant, rainless, lazily rowdy and sky-blue summers departed, I remember August Monday from the rising of the sun over the stained and royal town to the husky hushing of the roundabout music and the dowsing of the naphtha jets in the seaside fair – from bubble and squeak to the last of the sandy sandwiches.

There was no need, that holiday morning, for the sluggardly boys to be shouted down to breakfast; out of their jumbled beds they tumbled, scrambled into their rumpled clothes; quickly at the bathroom basin they catlicked their hands and faces, but never forgot to run the water loud and long as though they washed like colliers; in front of the cracked looking glass bordered with cigarette cards, in their treasure-trove bedrooms, they whisked a gap-tooth comb through their surly hair; and with shining cheeks and noses and tidemarked necks, they took the stairs three at a time.

But for all their scramble and scamper, clamour on the landing, catlick and toothbrush flick, hair whisk and stair jump, their sisters were always there before them. Up with the lady lark, they had prinked and frizzed and hot-ironed; and smug in their blossoming dresses, ribboned for the sun, in gym shoes white as the blancoed* snow, neat and silly with doilies and tomatoes they helped in the higgledy kitchen. They were calm; they were virtuous; they had washed their necks; they did not romp or fidget; and only the smallest sister put out her tongue at the noisy boys.

And the woman who lived next door came into the kitchen and said that her mother, an ancient uncertain body who wore a hat with cherries, was having "one of her days" and had insisted, that very holiday morning, in carrying all the way to the tram stop a photograph album and the cut-glass fruit bowl from the front room.

This was the morning when Father, mending one hole in the thermos flask, made three; when the sun declared war on the butter, and the butter ran; when dogs, with all the sweet-binned backyards to wag and sniff and bicker in, chased their tails in the jostling kitchen, worried sandshoes, snapped at flies, writhed between legs, scratched among towels, sat smiling on hampers.

And if you could have listened at some of the open doors of some of the houses in the street you might have heard:

"Uncle Owen says he can't find the bottle opener..."

"Has he looked under the hallstand?"

"Willy's cut his finger..."

"Got your spade?"

"If somebody doesn't kill that dog..."

"Uncle Owen says why should the bottle opener be under the hallstand?"

"Never again, never again..."

"I know I put the pepper somewhere..."

"Willy's bleeding..."

"Look, there's a bootlace in my bucket..."

"Oh come *on*, come on..."

"Let's have a look at the bootlace in your bucket..."

"If I lay my hands on that dog..."

"Uncle Owen's found the bottle opener..."

"Willy's bleeding over the cheese..."

And the trams that hissed like ganders took us all to the beautiful beach.

There was cricket on the sand, and sand in the sponge cake, sandflies in the watercress, and foolish, mulish, religious donkeys on the unwilling trot. Girls undressed in slipping tents of propriety; under invisible umbrellas, stout ladies dressed for the male and immoral sea. Little naked navvies dug canals; children with spades and no ambition built fleeting castles; wispy young men, outside the bathing huts, whistled at substantial young women and dogs who desired thrown stones more than the bones of elephants. Recalcitrant uncles huddled over luke* ale in the tiger-striped marquees. Mothers in black, like wobbling mountains, gasped under the discarded dresses of daughters who shrilly braved the goblin waves. And fathers, in the once-a-year sun, took fifty winks. Oh, think of all the fifty winks along the paper-bagged sand.

Liquorice allsorts, and Welsh hearts, were melting, and the sticks of rock, that we all sucked, were like barbers' poles made of rhubarb.

In the distance, surrounded by disappointed theoreticians and an ironmonger with a drum, a cross man on an orange box shouted that holidays were wrong.

And the waves rolled in, with rubber ducks and clerks upon them.

I remember the patient, laborious and enamouring hobby, or profession, of burying relatives in sand.

I remember the princely pastime of pouring sand, from cupped hands or buckets, down collars and tops of dresses; the shriek, the shake, the slap.

I can remember the boy by himself, the beachcombing lone wolf, hungrily waiting at the edge of family cricket; the friendless fielder, the boy uninvited to bat or to tea.

I remember the smell of sea and seaweed, wet flesh, wet hair, wet bathing dresses, the warm smell as of a rabbity field after rain, the smell of pop and splashed sunshades and toffee, the stable-and-straw smell of hot, tossed, tumbled, dug and trodden sand, the swill-and-gas lamp smell of Saturday night, though the sun shone strong, from the bellying beer tents, the smell of the vinegar on shelled cockles, winkle smell, shrimp smell, the dripping-oily backstreet winter smell of chips in newspapers, the smell of ships from the sun-dazed docks round the corner of the sandhills, the smell of the known and paddled-in sea moving, full of the drowned and herrings, out and away and beyond and further still towards the antipodes that hung their koala bears and Maoris, kangaroos and boomerangs, upside down over the backs of the stars.

And the noise of pummelling Punch and Judy falling, and a clock tolling or telling no time in the tenantless town; now and again a bell from a lost tower or a train on the lines behind us clearing its throat, and always the hopeless, ravenous swearing and pleading of the gulls, donkey bray and hawker cry, harmonicas and toy trumpets, shouting and laughing and singing, hooting of tugs and tramps, the clip of the chair attendant's puncher, the motorboat coughing in the bay, and the same hymn and washing of the sea that was heard in the Bible.

"If it could only just, if it could only just," your lips said again and again as you scooped, in the hob-hot sand, dungeons, garages, torture chambers, train tunnels, arsenals, hangars for Zeppelins, witches' kitchens, vampires' parlours, smugglers' cellars, trolls' grog shops, sewers, under a ponderous and cracking castle, "if it could only just be like this for ever and ever, amen." August Monday all over the earth, from Mumbles, where the aunties grew like ladies on a seaside tree, to brown, bear-hugging Henty-land and the turtled Ballantyne Islands.*

"Could donkeys go on the ice?"

"Only if they got snowshoes."

We snowshoed a meek, complaining donkey and galloped him off in the wake of the ten-foot-tall and Atlas-muscled Mounties, rifled and pemmicanned, who always, in the white gold-rush wastes, got their black-oathed-and-bearded man.*

"Are there donkeys on desert islands?"

"Only sort-of donkeys."

"What d'you mean, 'sort-of donkeys'?"

"Native donkeys. They hunt things on them!"

"Sort-of walruses and seals and things?"

"Donkeys can't swim!"

"These donkeys can. They swim like whales, they swim like anything, they swim like—"

"Liar."

"Liar yourself."

And two small boys fought fiercely and silently in the sand, rolling together in a ball of legs and bottoms.

Then they went and saw the pierrots, or bought vanilla ices.

Lolling or larrikin* that unsoiled, boiling beauty of a common day, great gods with their braces over their vests sang, spat pips, puffed smoke at wasps, gulped and ogled, forgot the rent, embraced, posed for the dicky bird, were coarse, had rainbow-coloured armpits, winked, belched, blamed the radishes, looked at Ilfracombe,* played hymns on paper-and-comb, peeled bananas, scratched, found seaweed in their panamas, blew up paper bags and banged them, wished for nothing.

But over all the beautiful beach I remember most the children playing, boys and girls tumbling, moving jewels, who might never be happy again. And "happy as a sandboy" is true as the heat of the sun.

Dusk came down, or grew up out of the sands and the sea, or curled around us from the calling docks and the bloodily smoking sun. The day was done, the sands brushed and ruffled suddenly with a sea broom of cold wind.

And we gathered together all the spades and buckets and towels, empty hampers and bottles, umbrellas and fish-frails, bats and balls and knitting, and went – oh, listen, Dad! – to the fair in the dusk on the bald seaside field.

Fairs were no good in the day; then they were shoddy and tired; the voices of hoop-la girls were crimped as elocutionists'; no cannon ball could shake the roosting coconuts; the gondolas mechanically repeated their sober lurch; the Wall of Death* was safe as a governess cart; the wooden animals were waiting for the night.

But in the night, the hoop-la girls, like operatic crows, croaked at the coming moon; whizz, whirl, and ten for a tanner, the coconuts rained from their sawdust like grouse from the Highland sky; tipsy the griffin-prowed gondolas weaved on dizzy rails, and the Wall of Death was a spinning rim of ruin, and the neighing wooden horses took, to a haunting hunting tune, a thousand Becher's Brooks* as easily and breezily as hooved swallows.

Approaching, at dusk, the fair field from the beach, we scorched and gritty boys heard above the belabouring of the batherless sea the siren voices of the raucous, horsy barkers.

"Roll up, roll up!"

In her tent and her rolls of flesh, the Fattest Woman in the World sat sewing her winter frock, another tent, and fixed her little eyes, blackcurrants in blancmange, on the skeletons who filed and sniggered by.

"Roll up, roll up, roll up to see the Largest Rat on Earth, the Rover or Bonzo of vermin."

Here scampered the smallest pony, like a Shetland shrew. And here "the Most Intelligent Fleas", trained, reined, bridled and bitted, minutely cavorted in their glass corral.

Round galleries and shies and stalls, pennies were burning holes in a hundred pockets.

Pale young men with larded hair and Valentino-black* side whiskers, fags stuck to their lower lips, squinted along their swivel-sighted rifles and aimed at ping-pong balls dancing on fountains.

In knife-creased, silver-grey, skirt-like Oxford bags* and a sleeveless, scarlet, zip-fastened shirt with yellow horizontal stripes, a collier at the strength machine spat on his hands, raised the hammer and brought it Thor-ing down. The bell rang for Blaina.*

Outside his booth stood a bitten-eared and barndoor-chested pug with a nose like a twisted swede and hair that started from his eyebrows and three teeth yellow as a camel's inviting any sportsman to a sudden and sickening basting in the sandy ring or a quid if he lasted a round; and wiry, cocky, bow-legged, coal-scarred, boozed sportsmen by the dozen strutted in and reeled out; and still those three teeth remained, chipped and camel-yellow in the bored teak face.

Draggled and stout-wanting mothers, with haphazard hats, hostile hatpins, buns awry, bursting bags and children at their skirts like pop-filled and jam-smeared limpets, screamed before distorting mirrors at their suddenly tapering or tubular bodies and huge ballooning heads, and the children gaily bellowed at their own reflected bogeys withering and bulging in the glass.

Old men, smelling of Milford Haven* in the rain, shuffled, badgering and cadging, round the edges of the swaggering crowd, their only wares a handful of damp confetti.

A daring dash of schoolboys, safely, shoulder to shoulder, with their father's trilbies cocked at a desperate angle over one eye, winked at and whistled after the procession past the swings of two girls arm in arm – always one pert and pretty, and always one with glasses.

Girls in skulled and cross-boned tunnels shrieked, and were comforted.

Young men, heroic after pints, stood up on the flying chairoplanes, tousled, crimson and against the rules.

Jaunty girls gave sailors sauce.

All the fun of the fair in the hot, bubbling night. The man in the sand-yellow moon over the hurdy of gurdies. The swing boats swimming to and fro like slices of the moon. Dragons and hippogriffs at the prows of the gondolas breathing fire and Sousa.* Midnight roundabout riders tantivying under the fairy lights, huntsmen on billy goats and zebras hallooing under a circle of glow-worms.

And as we climbed home, up the gaslit hill, to the still homes over the mumbling bay, we heard the music die and the voices drift like sand. And we saw the lights of the fair fade. And, at the far end of the seaside field, they lit their lamps, one by one, in the caravans.

The Crumbs of One Man's Year*

Slung as though in a hammock, or a lull, between one Christmas for ever over and a New Year nearing full of relentless surprises, waywardly and gladly I pry back at those wizening twelve months and see only a waltzing snippet of the tipsy-turvy times, flickers of vistas, flashes of queer fishes, patches and chequers of a bard's-eye view.

Of what is coming in the New Year I know nothing, except that all that is certain will come like thunderclaps or like comets in the shape of four-leaved clovers, and that all that is unforeseen will appear with the certainty of the Sun, who every morning shakes a leg in the sky; and of what has gone I know only shilly-shally snatches and freckled plaids, flecks and dabs, dazzle and froth; a simple second caught in coursing snow-light, an instant, gay or sorry, struck motionless in the curve of flight like a bird or a scythe; the spindrift leaf and stray-paper whirl, canter, quarrel and people-chase of everybody's street; suddenly the way the grotesque wind slashes and freezes at a corner the clothes of a passer-by so that she stays remembered, cold and still until the world like a night light in a nursery goes out; and a waddling couple of the small occurrences, comic as ducks, that quack their way through our calamitous days; whits and dots and tittles.

"Look back, back," the big voices clarion, "look back at the black colossal year," while the rich music fanfares and dead-marches.

I can give you only a scattering of some of the crumbs of one man's year; and the penny music whistles.

Any memory, of the long, revolving year, will do, to begin with.

I was walking, one afternoon in August, along a riverbank, thinking the same thoughts that I always think when I walk along a riverbank in August. As I was walking, I was thinking – now it is August and I am walking along a riverbank. I do not think I was thinking of anything else. I should have been thinking of what I should have been doing, but I was thinking only of what I was doing then, and it was all right – it was good, and ordinary, and slow, and idle, and old, and sure, and what I was doing I could have been doing a thousand years before, had I been alive then and myself or any other man. You could have thought the river was ringing – almost you could hear the green, rapid bells sing in it: it could have been the River Elusina, "that dances at the noise of music, for with music it bubbles, dances and growes sandy, and so continues till the music ceases..." or it could have been the river "in Judea that runs swiftly all the six days of the week, and stands still and rests all their sabbath".* There were trees blowing, standing still, growing, knowing, whose names I never knew. (Once, indeed, with a friend I wrote a poem beginning, "All trees are oaks, except fir trees.") There were birds being busy, or sleep-flying, in the sky. (The poem had continued: "All birds are robins, except crows, or rooks.") Nature was doing what it was doing, and thinking just that. And I was walking and thinking that I was walking, and for August it was not such a cold day. And then I saw, drifting along the water, a piece of paper, and I thought: "Something wonderful may be written on this paper." I was alone on the gooseberry earth, or alone for two green miles, and a message drifted towards me on that tabby-coloured water that ran through the middle of the cow-patched, mooing fields. It was a message from multitudinous nowhere to my solitary self. I put out my stick and caught the piece of paper and held it close to the riverbank. It was a page torn from a very old periodical. That I could see. I leant over and read, through water, the message on the rippling page. I made out, with difficulty, only one sentence: it commemorated the fact that, over a hundred years ago, a man in Worcester had, for a bet, eaten, at one sitting, fifty-two pounds of plums.

And any other memory, of the long evolving year, will do, to go on with.

Here now, to my memory, come peaceful blitz and pieces of the fifth of November, guys in the streets and forks in the sky, when Catherine wheels and jacky-jumps* and good bombs burst in the blistered areas. The rockets are few, but they star between roofs and up to the wall of the warless night. "A penny for the guy?" "No, that's my father." The great joke brocks* and sizzles. Sirius explodes in the backyard by the shelter. Timorous ladies sit in their back rooms, with the eighth programme* on very loud. Retiring men snarl under their blankets. In the unkempt gardens of the very rich, the second butler lights a squib. In everybody's street the fearless children shout, under the little homely raids. But I was standing on a signalling country hill, where they fed a hungry bonfire guy with brushwood, sticks and crackerjacks; the bonfire guy whooped for more; small sulphurous puddings banged in his burning belly, and his thorned hair caught. He lurched, and made common noises. He was a long time dying on the hill over the starlit fields, where the tabby river, without a message, ran on, with bells and trout and tins and bangles and literature and cats in it, to the sea never out of sound.

And on one occasion, in this long dissolving year, I remember that I boarded a London bus from a district I have forgotten, and where I certainly could have been up to little good, to an appointment that I did not want to keep.

It was a shooting green spring morning, nimble and crocus, with all the young women treading on naked flower stalks, the metropolitan sward, swinging their milk-pail handbags, gentle, fickle, inviting, accessible, forgiving each robustly abandoned gesture of salutation before it was made or imagined, assenting, as they revelled demurely towards the manicure salon or the typewriting office, to all the ardent unspoken endearments of shaggy strangers and the winks and pipes of cloven-footed sandwichmen. The sun shrilled, the buses gambolled, policemen and daffodils bowed in the breeze that tasted of buttermilk. Delicate carousal plashed and babbled from the public houses, which were not yet open. I felt like a young god. I removed my collar studs and opened my shirt. I tossed back my hair. There was an aviary in my heart, but without any owls or eagles. My cheeks were cherried warm, I smelt, I thought, of sea pinks.* To the sound of madrigals sung by slim sopranos in waterfalled valleys where I was the only tenor, I leapt onto a bus. The bus was full. Carefree, open-collared, my eyes alight, my veins full of the spring as a dancer's shoes should be full of champagne, I stood, in love and at ease and always young, on the packed lower deck. And a man of exactly my own age – or perhaps he was a little older – got up and offered me his seat. He said, in a respectful voice, as though to an old Justice of the Peace, "Please, won't you take my seat?" And then he added: "Sir."

How many variegations of inconsiderable defeats and disillusionments I have forgotten! How many shades and shapes from the polychromatic zebra house! How many Joseph coats I have left uncalled for in the Gentlemen's Cloakrooms of the year!

And one man's year is like the country of a cloud, mapped on the sky, that soon will vanish into the watery, ordered wastes into the spinning rule, into the dark which is light. Now the cloud is flying, very slowly, out of sight, and I can remember of all that voyaging geography, no palaced morning hills or huge plush valleys in the downing sun, forests simmering with birds, stagged moors, merry legendary meadowland, bullish plains, but only... the street near Waterloo station where a small boy, wearing cut-down khaki and a steel helmet, pushed a pram full of firewood and shouted, in a dispassionate voice, after each passer-by: "Where's your tail?"

The estuary pool under the collapsed castle, where the July children rolled together in original mud, shrieking and yawping, and low life, long before newts, twitched on their hands.

The crisp path through the field in this December snow, in the deep dark, where we trod the buried grass like ghosts on dry toast.

The single-line run along the spring-green riverbank where water voles went Indian file to work, and where the young impatient voles, in their sleek vests, always in a hurry, jumped over the threadbare backs of the old ones.

The razor-scarred backstreet café bar where a man with cut cheeks and chewed ears huskily and furiously complained, over tarry tea, that the new baby panda in the zoo was not floodlit.

The gully sands in March, under the flayed and flailing clifftop trees, when the wind played old Harry,* or old Thomas, with me, and cormorants, far off, sped like motorboats across the bay, as I weaved towards the toppling town and the black, loud Lion where the cat, who purred like a fire, looked out of two cinders at the gently swilling retired sea captains in the snug-as-a-bug back bar.

And the basement kitchen in nipping February, with napkins on the line slung across from door to chock-a-block corner, and a bicycle by the larder very much down at wheels, and hats and toy engines and bottles and spanners on the broken rocking chair, and billowing papers and half-finished crosswords stacked on the radio always turned full tilt, and the fire smoking, and onions peeling, and chips always spitting on the stove, and small men in their overcoats talking of self-discipline and the ascetic life until the air grew woodbine-blue and the clock choked and the traffic died.

And then the moment of a night in that cavorting spring, rare and unforgettable as a bicycle clip found in the middle of the desert. The lane was long and soused and dark that led to the house I helped to fill and bedraggle.

"Who's left this in this corner?"

"What, where?"

"Here, this."

A doll's arm, the chitterlings of a clock, a saucepan full of hatbands.

The lane was rutted as though by bosky watercarts, and so dark you couldn't see your front in spite of you. Rain barrelled down. On one side you couldn't hear the deer that lived there, and on the other side... voices began to whisper, muffled in the midnight sack. A man's voice and a woman's voice. "Lovers," I said to myself. For at night the heart comes out, like a cat on the tiles. Discourteously I shone my torch. There, in the thick rain, a young man and a young woman stood, very close together, near the hedge that whirred in the wind. And a yard from them, another young man sat staidly, on the grass verge, holding an open book from which he appeared to read. And in the very rutted and puddly middle of the lane, two dogs were fighting, with brutish concentration and in absolute silence.

The Followers*

It was six o'clock on a winter's evening. Thin, dingy rain spat and drizzled past the lighted street lamps. The pavements shone long and yellow. In squeaking galoshes, with mackintosh collars up and bowlers and trilbies weeping, youngish men from the offices bundled home against the thistly wind –

"Night, Mr Macey."

"Going my way, Charlie?"

"Ooh, there's a pig of a night!"

"Goodnight, Mr Swan."

– and older men, clinging on to the big, black circular birds of their umbrellas, were wafted back, up the gaslit hills, to safe, hot, slippered, weatherproof hearths, and wives called Mother, and old, fond, fleabag dogs, and the wireless babbling.

Young women from the offices, who smelt of scent and powder and wet pixie hoods and hair, scuttled, giggling, arm in arm, after the hissing trams, and screeched as they splashed their stockings in the puddles rainbowed with oil between the slippery lines.

In a shop window, two girls undressed the dummies.

"Where you going tonight?"

"Depends on Arthur. Up she comes."

"Mind her camiknicks,* Edna…"

The blinds came down over another window.

A newsboy stood in a doorway, calling the news to nobody, very softly:

"Earthquake. Earthquake in Japan."*

Water from a chute dripped onto his sacking. He waited in his own pool of rain.

A flat, long girl drifted, snivelling into her hanky, out of a jeweller's shop, and slowly pulled the steel shutters down with a hooked pole. She looked, in the grey rain, as though she were crying from top to toe.

A silent man and woman, dressed in black, carried the wreaths away from the front of their flower shop into the scented deadly darkness behind the window lights. Then the lights went out.

A man with a balloon tied to his cap pushed a shrouded barrow up a dead end.

A baby with an ancient face sat in its pram outside the wine vaults, quiet, very wet, peering cautiously all round it.

It was the saddest evening I had ever known.

A young man, with his arm round his girl, passed by me, laughing, and she laughed back, right into his handsome, nasty face. That made the evening sadder still.

I met Leslie at the corner of Crimea Street. We were both about the same age: too young and too old.* Leslie carried a rolled umbrella, which he never used, though sometimes he pressed doorbells with it. He was trying to grow a moustache. I wore a check, ratting cap at a Saturday angle. We greeted each other formally:

"Good evening, old man."

"Evening, Leslie."

"Right on the dot, boy."

"That's right," I said. "Right on the dot."

A plump, blonde girl, smelling of wet rabbits, self-conscious even in that dirty night, minced past on high-heeled shoes. The heels clicked, the soles squelched. Leslie whistled after her, low and admiring.

"Business first," I said.

"Oh, boy!" Leslie said.

"And she's too fat as well."

"I like them corpulent," Leslie said. "Remember Penelope Bogan? A Mrs too."

"Oh, come *on*. That old bird of Paradise Alley? How's the exchequer, Les?"

"One and a penny. How you fixed?"

"Tanner."

"What'll it be, then? The Compasses?"

"Free cheese at the Marlborough."

We walked towards the Marlborough, dodging umbrella spokes, smacked by our windy macs, stained by steaming lamplight, seeing the sodden, blown scourings and street-wash of the town, papers, rags, dregs, rinds, fag ends, balls of fur, flap, float and cringe along the gutters, hearing the sneeze and rattle of the bony trams and a ship hoot like a fog-ditched owl in the bay, and Leslie said:

"What'll we do after?"

"We'll follow someone," I said.

"Remember following that old girl up Kitchener Street? The one who dropped her handbag?"

"You should have given it back."

"There wasn't anything in it, only a piece of bread and jam."

"Here we are," I said.

The Marlborough saloon was cold and empty. There were notices on the damp walls: No Singing. No Dancing. No Gambling. No Pedlars.

"You sing," I said to Leslie, "and I'll dance, then we'll have a game of nap and I'll peddle my braces."

The barmaid, with gold hair and two gold teeth in front, like a well-off rabbit's, was blowing on her nails and polishing them on her black marocain.* She looked up as we came in, then blew on her nails again and polished them without hope.

"You can tell it isn't Saturday night," I said. "Evening, Miss. Two pints."

"And a pound from the till," Leslie said.

"Give us your one and a penny, Les," I whispered, and then said aloud: "Anybody can tell it isn't Saturday night. Nobody sick."

"Nobody here to *be* sick," Leslie said.

The peeling, liver-coloured room might never have been drunk in at all. Here, commercials told jokes and had Scotches and sodas with happy, dyed, port-and-lemon women; dejected regulars grew grand and muzzy in the corners, inventing their pasts, being rich, important and loved; reprobate grannies in dustbin-black cackled and nipped; influential nobodies revised the earth; a party, with earrings, called "Frilly Willy" played the crippled piano, which sounded like a hurdy-gurdy playing under water, until the publican's nosy wife said, "No." Strangers came and went, but mostly went. Men from the valleys dropped in for nine or ten; sometimes there were fights; and always there was something doing, some argy-bargy, giggle and bluster, horror or folly, affection, explosion, nonsense, peace, some wild goose flying in the boozy air of that comfortless, humdrum nowhere in the dizzy, ditchwater town at the end of the railway lines. But that evening it was the saddest room I had ever known.

Leslie said, in a low voice: "Think she'll let us have one on tick?"

"Wait a bit, boy," I murmured. "Wait for her to thaw."

But the barmaid heard me and looked up. She looked clean through me, back through my small history to the bed I was born in, then shook her gold head.

"I don't know what it is," said Leslie as we walked up Crimea Street in the rain, "but I feel kind of depressed tonight."

"It's the saddest night in the world," I said.

We stopped, soaked and alone, to look at the stills outside the cinema we called the Itch Pit. Week after week, for years and years, we had sat on the edges of the springless seats there, in the dank but snug, flickering dark, first with toffees and monkey nuts that crackled for the dumb guns, and then with cigarettes – a cheap special kind that would make a fire-swallower cough up the cinders of his heart. "Let's go in and see Lon Chaney," I said, "and Richard Talmadge and Milton Sills and... and Noah Beery," I said, "and Richard Dix... and Slim Summerville and Hoot Gibson."*

We both sighed.

"Oh, for our vanished youth," I said.

We walked on heavily, with wilful feet, splashing the passers-by.

"Why don't you open your brolly?" I said.

"It won't open. You try."

We both tried, and the umbrella suddenly bellied out; the spokes tore through the soaking cover; the wind danced its tatters; it wrangled above us in the wind like a ruined, mathematical bird. We tried to tug it down: an unseen new spoke sprang through its ragged ribs. Leslie dragged it behind him, along the pavement, as though he had shot it.

A girl called Dulcie, scurrying to the Itch Pit, sniggered "Hallo", and we stopped her.

"A rather terrible thing has happened," I said to her. She was so silly that, even when she was fifteen, we had told her to eat soap to make her straw hair crinkle, and Les took a piece from the bathroom, and she did.

"I know," she said, "you broke your gamp."

"No, you're wrong there," Leslie said. "It isn't *our* umbrella at all. It fell off the roof. *You* feel," he said. "You can feel it fell off the roof." She took the umbrella gingerly by its handle.

"There's someone up there throwing umbrellas down," I said. "It may be serious."

She began to titter, and then grew silent and anxious as Leslie said: "You never know. It might be walking sticks next."

"Or sewing machines," I said.

"You wait here, Dulce, and we'll investigate," Leslie said.

We hurried on down the street, turned a blowing corner and then ran.

Outside Rabaiotti's café, Leslie said: "It isn't fair on Dulcie." We never mentioned it again.

A wet girl brushed by. Without a word, we followed her. She cantered, long-legged, down Inkerman Street and through Paradise Passage, and we were at her heels.

"I wonder what's the point in following people," Leslie said. "It's kind of daft. It never gets you anywhere. All you do is follow them home and then try to look through the window and see what they're doing, and mostly there's curtains anyway. I bet nobody else does things like that."

"You never know," I said. The girl turned into St Augustus Crescent, which was a wide lamplit mist. "People are always following people. What shall we call her?"

"Hermione Weatherby," Leslie said. He was never wrong about names. Hermione was fey and stringy, and walked like a long gym mistress, full of love, through the stinging rain.

"You never know. You never know what you'll find out. Perhaps she lives in a huge house with all her sisters..."

"How many?"

"Seven. All full of love. And when she gets home they all change into kimonos and lie on divans with music and whisper to each other, and all they're doing is waiting for somebody like us to walk in, lost, and then they'll all chatter round us like starlings and put us in kimonos too, and we'll never leave the house until we die. Perhaps it's so beautiful and soft and noisy – like a warm bath full of birds..."

"I don't want birds in my bath," said Leslie. "Perhaps she'll slit her throat if they don't draw the blinds. I don't care what happens, so long as it's interesting."

She slip-slopped round a corner into an avenue where the neat trees were sighing and the cosy windows shone.

"I don't want old feathers in the tub," Leslie said.

Hermione turned in at number thirteen, Beach View.

"You can see the beach all right," Leslie said, "if you got a periscope."

We waited on the pavement opposite, under a bubbling lamp, as Hermione opened her door, and then we tiptoed across and down the gravel path and were at the back of the house, outside an uncurtained window.

Hermione's mother, a round, friendly, owlish woman in a pinafore, was shaking a chip pan on the kitchen stove.

"I'm hungry," I said.

"Ssh!"

We edged to the side of the window as Hermione came into the kitchen. She was old, nearly thirty, with a mouse-brown shingle* and big earnest eyes. She wore horn-rimmed spectacles and a sensible tweed costume, and a white shirt with a trim bow tie. She looked as though she tried to look like a secretary in domestic films, who had only to remove her spectacles and have her hair cherished, and be dressed like a silk dog's dinner, to turn into a dazzler and make her employer, Warner Baxter,* gasp, woo and marry her; but if Hermione took off her glasses, she wouldn't be able to tell if he was Warner Baxter or the man who read the meters.

We stood so near the window we could hear the chips spitting.

"Have a nice day in the office, dear? There's weather," Hermione's mother said, worrying the chip pan.

"What's *her* name, Les?"

"Hetty."

Everything there in the warm kitchen, from the tea caddy and the grandmother clock to the tabby that purred like a kettle was good, dull and sufficient.

"Mr Truscott was something awful," Hermione said as she put on slippers.

"Where's her kimono?" Leslie said.

"Here's a nice cup of tea," said Hetty.

"Everything's nice in that old hole," said Leslie, grumbling. "Where's the seven sisters like starlings?"

It began to rain much more heavily. It bucketed down on the black backyard, and the little comfy kennel of a house, and us, and the hidden, hushed town, where, even now, in the haven of the Marlborough, the submarine piano would be tinning 'Daisy',* and the happy hennaed women squealing into their port.

Hetty and Hermione had their supper. Two drowned boys watched them enviously.

"Put a drop of Worcester on the chips," Leslie whispered – and by God she did.

"Doesn't anything happen anywhere?" I said. "In the whole wide world? I think the *News of the World* is all made up. Nobody murders no one. There isn't any sin any more, or love, or death, or pearls and divorces and mink coats or anything, or putting arsenic in the cocoa..."

"Why don't they put on some music for us," Leslie said, "and do a dance? It isn't every night they got two fellows watching them in the rain. Not *every* night, anyway!"

All over the dripping town, small lost people with nowhere to go and nothing to spend were gooseberrying in the rain outside wet windows, but nothing happened.

"I'm getting pneumonia," Leslie said.

The cat and the fire were purring, grandmother time tick-tocked our lives away. The supper was cleared, and Hetty and Hermione, who had not spoken for many minutes, they were so confident and close in their little lighted box, looked at one another and slowly smiled.

They stood still in the decent, purring kitchen, facing one another.

"There's something funny going to happen," I whispered very softly.

"It's going to begin," Leslie said.

We did not notice the sour, racing rain any more.

The smiles stayed on the faces of the two still, silent women.

"It's going to begin."

And we heard Hetty say in a small secret voice: "Bring out the album, dear."

Hermione opened a cupboard and brought out a big, stiff-coloured photograph album, and put it in the middle of the table. Then she and Hetty sat down at the table, side by side, and Hermione opened the album.

"That's Uncle Eliot, who died in Porthcawl, the one who had the cramp," said Hetty.

They looked with affection at Uncle Eliot, but we could not see him.

"That's Martha the Woolshop, you wouldn't remember her, dear, it was wool, wool, wool with her all the time – she wanted to be buried in her jumper, the mauve one, but her husband put his foot down. He'd been in India. That's your Uncle Morgan," Hetty said, "one of the Kidwelly Morgans, remember him in the snow?"

Hermione turned a page. "And that's Myfanwy, she got queer all of a sudden, remember. It was when she was milking. That's your cousin Jim, the minister, until they found out. And that's our Beryl," Hetty said.

But she spoke all the time like somebody repeating a lesson: a well-loved lesson she knew by heart.

We knew that she and Hermione were only waiting.

Then Hermione turned another page. And we knew, by their secret smiles, that this was what they had been waiting for.

"My sister Katinka," Hetty said.

"Auntie Katinka," Hermione said. They bent over the photograph.

"Remember that day in Aberystwyth, Katinka?" Hetty said softly. "The day we went on the choir outing."

"I wore my new white dress," a new voice said.

Leslie clutched at my hand.

"And a straw hat with birds," said the clear, new voice.

Hermione and Hetty were not moving their lips.

"I was always a one for birds on my hat. Just the plumes, of course. It was August the third, and I was twenty-three."

"Twenty-three come October, Katinka," Hetty said.

"That's right, love," the voice said. "Scorpio I was. And we met Douglas Pugh on the prom, and he said: 'You look like a queen today, Katinka,' he said. 'You look like a queen, Katinka,' he said. Why are those two boys looking in at the window?"

We ran up the gravel drive, and around the corner of the house, and into the avenue and out onto St Augustus Crescent. The rain roared down to drown the town. There we stopped for breath. We did not speak or look at each other. Then we walked on through the rain. At Victoria corner, we stopped again.

"Goodnight, old man," Leslie said.

"Goodnight," I said.

And we went our different ways.

A Story*

If you can call it a story. There's no real beginning or end, and there's very little in the middle. It is all about a day's outing, by charabanc, to Porthcawl, which, of course, the charabanc never reached, and it happened when I was so high and much nicer.

I was staying at the time with my uncle and his wife. Although she was my aunt, I never thought of her as anything but the wife of my uncle, partly because he was so big and trumpeting and red-hairy and used to fill every inch of the hot little house like an old buffalo squeezed into an airing cupboard, and partly because she was so small and silk and quick and made no noise at all as she whisked about on padded paws, dusting the china dogs, feeding the buffalo, setting the mousetraps that never caught her; and once she sleaked out of the room, to squeak in a nook or nibble in the hayloft, you forgot she had ever been there.

But there he was, always, a steaming hulk of an uncle, his braces straining like hawsers, crammed behind the counter of the tiny shop at the front of the house, and breathing like a brass band; or guzzling and blustery in the kitchen over his gutsy supper, too big for everything except the great black boats of his boots. As he ate, the house grew smaller; he billowed out over the furniture, the loud check meadow of his waistcoat littered, as though after a picnic, with cigarette ends, peelings, cabbage stalks, birds' bones, gravy; and the forest fire of his hair crackled among the hooked hams from the ceiling. She was so small she could hit him only if she stood on a chair, and every Saturday night at half-past ten he would lift her up, under his arm, onto a chair in the kitchen so that she could hit him on the head with whatever was handy, which was always a china dog. On Sundays, and when pickled, he sang high tenor, and had won many cups.

The first I heard of the annual outing was when I was sitting one evening on a bag of rice behind the counter, under one of my uncle's stomachs, reading an advertisement for sheep dip, which was all there was to read. The shop was full of my uncle, and when Mr Benjamin Franklyn, Mr Weazley, Noah Bowen and Will Sentry came in, I thought it would burst. It was like all being together in a drawer that smelt of cheese and turps, and twist tobacco and sweet biscuits and snuff and waistcoat. Mr Benjamin

Franklyn said that he had collected enough money for the charabanc and twenty cases of pale ale and a pound apiece over that he would distribute among the members of the outing when they first stopped for refreshment, and he was about sick and tired, he said, of being followed by Will Sentry.

"All day long, wherever I go," he said, "he's after me like a collie with one eye. I got a shadow of my own *and* a dog. I don't need no Tom, Dick or Harry pursuing me with his dirty muffler on."

Will Sentry blushed and said: "It's only oily. I got a bicycle."

"A man has no privacy at all," Mr Franklyn went on. "I tell you he sticks so close I'm afraid to go out the back in case I sit in his lap. It's a wonder to me," he said, "he don't follow me into bed at night."

"Wife won't let," Will Sentry said.

And that started Mr Franklyn off again, and they tried to soothe him down by saying: "Don't you mind Will Sentry..." "No harm in old Will..." "He's only keeping an eye on the money, Benjie."

"Aren't *I* honest?" asked Mr Franklyn in surprise. There was no answer for some time, then Noah Bowen said: "You know what the committee is. Ever since Bob the Fiddle they don't feel safe with a new treasurer."

"Do you think *I'm* going to drink the outing funds, like Bob the Fiddle did?" said Mr Franklyn.

"You *might*," said my uncle slowly.

"I resign," said Mr Franklyn.

"Not with our money you won't," Will Sentry said.

"Who put dynamite in the salmon pool?" said Mr Weazley, but nobody took any notice of him. And, after a time, they all began to play cards in the thickening dusk of the hot, cheesy shop, and my uncle blew and bugled whenever he won, and Mr Weazley grumbled like a dredger, and I fell to sleep on the gravy-scented mountain meadow of Uncle's waistcoat.

On Sunday evening, after Bethesda, Mr Franklyn walked into the kitchen, where my uncle and I were eating sardines with spoons from the tin, because it was Sunday and his wife would not let us play draughts. She was somewhere in the kitchen, too. Perhaps she was inside the grandmother clock, hanging from the weights and breathing. Then, a second later, the door opened again and Will Sentry edged into the room, twiddling his hard, round hat. He and Mr Franklyn sat down on the settee, stiff and mothballed and black in their chapel and funeral suits.

"I brought the list," said Mr Franklyn. "Every member fully paid. You ask Will Sentry."

My uncle put on his spectacles, wiped his whiskery mouth with a handkerchief big as a Union Jack, laid down his spoon of sardines, took Mr Franklyn's list of names, removed the spectacles so that he could read and then ticked the names off one by one.

"Enoch Davies. Aye. He's good with his fists. You never know. Little Gerwain. Very melodious bass. Mr Cadwalladwr. That's right. He can tell opening time better than my watch. Mr Weazley. Of course. He's been to Paris. Pity he suffers so much in the charabanc. Stopped us nine times last year between the Beehive and the Red Dragon. Noah Bowen, ah, very peaceable. He's got a tongue like a turtle dove. Never a argument with Noah Bowen. Jenkins Loughor. Keep him off economics. It cost us a plate-glass window. And ten pints for the sergeant. Mr Jervis. Very tidy."

"He tried to put a pig in the charra," Will Sentry said.

"Live and let live," said my uncle.

Will Sentry blushed.

"Sinbad the Sailor's Arms. Got to keep in with him. Old O. Jones."

"Why old O. Jones?" said Will Sentry.

"Old O. Jones always goes," said my uncle.

I looked down at the kitchen table. The tin of sardines was gone. By Gee, I said to myself, Uncle's wife is quick as a flash.

"Cuthbert Johnny Fortnight. Now, there's a card," said my uncle.

"He whistles after women," Will Sentry said.

"So do you," said Mr Benjamin Franklyn, "in your mind."

My uncle at last approved the whole list, pausing only to say, when he came across one name: "If we weren't a Christian community, we'd chuck that Bob the Fiddle in the sea."

"We can do that in Porthcawl," said Mr Franklyn, and soon after that he went, Will Sentry no more than an inch behind him, their Sunday-bright boots squeaking on the kitchen cobbles.

And then, suddenly, there was my uncle's wife standing in front of the dresser, with a china dog in one hand. By Gee, I said to myself again, did you ever see such a woman, if that's what she is. The lamps were not lit yet in the kitchen, and she stood in a wood of shadows, with the plates on the dresser behind her shining – like pink-and-white eyes.

"If you go on that outing on Saturday, Mr Thomas," she said to my uncle in her small, silk voice, "I'm going home to my mother's."

Holy Mo, I thought, she's got a mother. Now, that's one old bald mouse of a hundred and five I won't be wanting to meet in a dark lane.

"It's me or the outing, Mr Thomas."

I would have made my choice at once, but it was almost half a minute before my uncle said: "Well, then, Sarah, it's the outing, my love." He lifted her up, under his arm, onto a chair in the kitchen, and she hit him on the head with the china dog. Then he lifted her down again, and then I said goodnight.

For the rest of the week my uncle's wife whisked quiet and quick round the house with her darting duster, my uncle blew and bugled and swole,* and I kept myself busy all the time being up to no good. And then at breakfast time on Saturday morning, the morning of the outing, I found a note on the kitchen table. It said: "There's some eggs in the pantry. Take your boots off before you go to bed." My uncle's wife had gone, as quick as a flash.

When my uncle saw the note, he tugged out the flag of his handkerchief and blew such a hubbub of trumpets that the plates on the dresser shook. "It's the same every year," he said. And then he looked at me. "But this year it's different. *You*'ll have to come on the outing, too, and what the members will say I dare not think."

The charabanc drew up outside, and when the members of the outing saw my uncle and me squeeze out of the shop together, both of us catlicked and brushed in our Sunday best, they snarled like a zoo.

"Are you bringing a *boy*?" asked Mr Benjamin Franklyn as we climbed into the charabanc. He looked at me with horror.

"Boys is nasty," said Mr Weazley.

"He hasn't paid his contributions," Will Sentry said.

"No room for boys. Boys get sick in charabancs."

"So do you, Enoch Davies," said my uncle.

"Might as well bring *women*."

The way they said it, women were worse than boys.

"Better than bringing grandfathers."

"Grandfathers is nasty too," said Mr Weazley.

"What can we do with him when we stop for refreshments?"

"I'm a grandfather," said Mr Weazley.

"Twenty-six minutes to opening time," shouted an old man in a panama hat, not looking at a watch. They forgot me at once.

"Good old Mr Cadwalladwr," they cried, and the charabanc started off down the village street.

A few cold women stood at their doorways, grimly watching us go. A very small boy waved goodbye, and his mother boxed his ears. It was a beautiful August morning.

We were out of the village, and over the bridge, and up the hill towards Steeplehat Wood when Mr Franklyn, with his list of names in his hand, called out loud: "Where's old O. Jones?"

"Where's old O?"

"We've left old O behind."

"Can't go without old O."

And though Mr Weazley hissed all the way, we turned and drove back to the village, where, outside the Prince of Wales, old O. Jones was waiting patiently and alone with a canvas bag.

"I didn't want to come at all," old O. Jones said as they hoisted him into the charabanc and clapped him on the back and pushed him on a seat and stuck a bottle in his hand, "but I always go." And over the bridge and up the hill and under the deep-green wood and along the dusty road we wove, slow cows and ducks flying by, until "Stop the bus!" Mr Weazley cried. "I left my teeth on the mantelpiece."

"Never you mind," they said, "you're not going to bite nobody." And they gave him a bottle with a straw.

"I might want to smile," he said.

"Not you," they said.

"What's the time, Mr Cadwalladwr?"

"Twelve minutes to go," shouted back the old man in the panama, and they all began to curse him.

The charabanc pulled up outside the Mountain Sheep, a small, unhappy public house with a thatched roof like a wig with ringworm. From a flag-pole by the gents fluttered the flag of Siam. I knew it was the flag of Siam because of cigarette cards. The landlord stood at the door to welcome us, simpering like a wolf. He was a long, lean, black-fanged man with a greased love curl and pouncing eyes.

"What a beautiful August day!" he said, and touched his love curl with a claw. That was the way he must have welcomed the Mountain Sheep before he ate it, I said to myself. The members rushed out, bleating, and into the bar.

"You keep an eye on the charra," my uncle said. "See nobody steals it now."

"There's nobody to steal it," I said, "except some cows." But my uncle was gustily blowing his bugle in the bar. I looked at the cows opposite, and they looked at me. There was nothing else for us to do. Forty-five minutes passed, like a very slow cloud. The sun shone down on the lonely road, the lost, unwanted boy and the lake-eyed cows. In the dark bar they were so happy they were breaking glasses. A Shoni-Onion Breton man,* with a beret and a necklace of onions, bicycled down the road and stopped at the door.

"*Quelle un grand matin, Monsieur,*"* I said.

"There's French, boy bach!"* he said.

I followed him down the passage, and peered into the bar. I could hardly recognize the members of the outing. They had all changed colour. Beetroot, rhubarb and puce, they hollered and rollicked in that dark, damp hole like enormous ancient bad boys, and my uncle surged in the middle, all red whiskers and bellies. On the floor was broken glass and Mr Weazley.

"Drinks all round," cried Bob the Fiddle, a small, absconding man with bright-blue eyes and a plump smile.

"Who's been robbing the orphans?"

"Who sold his little babby to the Gyppoes?"

"Trust old Bob, he'll let you down."

"You will have your little joke," said Bob the Fiddle, smiling like a razor, "but I forgive you, boys."

Out of the fug and babel I heard: "Come out and fight."

"No, not now, later."

"No, now when I'm in a temper."

"Look at Will Sentry, he's proper snobbled."

"Look at his wilful feet."

"Look at Mr Weazley lording it on the floor."

Mr Weazley got up, hissing like a gander. "That boy pushed me down deliberate," he said, pointing to me at the door, and I slunk away down the passage and out to the mild, good cows. Time clouded over, the cows wondered, I threw a stone at them and they wandered, wondering, away. Then out blew my uncle, ballooning, and one by one the members lumbered after him in a grizzle. They had drunk the Mountain Sheep dry. Mr Weazley had won a string of onions that the Shoni-Onion man raffled in the bar. "What's the good of onions if you left your teeth on the mantelpiece?" he said. And when I looked through the back window of the thundering charabanc, I saw the pub grow smaller in the distance. And the flag of Siam, from the flagpole by the gents, fluttered now at half mast.

The Blue Bull, the Dragon, the Star of Wales, the Twll in the Wall, the Sour Grapes, the Shepherd's Arms, the Bells of Aberdovey – I had nothing to do in the whole, wild August world but remember the names where the outing stopped and keep an eye on the charabanc. And whenever it passed a public house, Mr Weazley would cough like a billy goat and cry: "Stop the bus, I'm dying of breath!" And back we would all have to go.

Closing time meant nothing to the members of that outing. Behind locked doors, they hymned and rumpused all the beautiful afternoon. And, when a policeman entered the Druid's Tap by the back door and found them all choral with beer, "Sssh!" said Noah Bowen. "The pub is shut."

"Where do you come from?" he said in his buttoned, blue voice.

They told him.

"I got a auntie there," the policeman said. And very soon he was singing 'Asleep in the Deep'.*

Off we drove again at last, the charabanc bouncing with tenors and flagons, and came to a river that rushed along among willows.

"Water!" they shouted.

"Porthcawl!" sang my uncle.

"Where's the donkeys?" said Mr Weazley.

And out they lurched, to paddle and whoop in the cool, white, winding water. Mr Franklyn, trying to polka on the slippery stones, fell in twice. "Nothing is simple," he said with dignity as he oozed up the bank.

"It's cold!" they cried.

"It's lovely!"

"It's smooth as a moth's nose!"

"It's *better* than Porthcawl!"

And dusk came down warm and gentle on thirty wild, wet, pickled, splashing men without a care in the world at the end of the world in the west of Wales. And "Who goes there?" called Will Sentry to a wild duck flying.

They stopped at the Hermit's Nest for a rum to keep out the cold. "I played for Aberavon in 1898," said a stranger to Enoch Davies.

"Liar," said Enoch Davies.

"I can show you photos," said the stranger.

"Forged," said Enoch Davies.

"And I'll show you my cap at home."

"Stolen."

"I got friends to prove it," the stranger said in a fury.

"Bribed," said Enoch Davies.

On the way home, through the simmering moon-splashed dark, old O. Jones began to cook his supper on a Primus stove in the middle of the charabanc. Mr Weazley coughed himself blue in the smoke. "Stop the bus," he cried, "I'm dying of breath!" We all climbed down into the moonlight. There was not a public house in sight. So they carried out the remaining cases, and the Primus stove, and old O. Jones himself, and took them into a field, and sat down in a circle in the field and drank and sang while old O. Jones cooked sausage and mash and the moon flew above us. And there I drifted to sleep against my uncle's mountainous waistcoat, and, as I slept, "Who goes there?" called out Will Sentry to the flying moon.

Abbreviations

AST   *Adventures in the Skin Trade* (1955; London: Dent, 1965 [Aldine Paperback edn])

EPW   *Early Prose Writings*, ed. Walford Davies (London: Dent, 1971)

ML   *The Map of Love* (London: Dent, 1939)

POA   *Portrait of the Artist as a Young Dog* (1940; London: Dent, 1965 [Aldine Paperback edn])

PS   *A Prospect of the Sea and Other Stories and Prose Writings*, ed. Daniel Jones (London: Dent, 1955)

QEOM *Quite Early One Morning: Broadcasts by Dylan Thomas* (London: Dent, 1954)

Note on the Texts

The stories in this collection are taken from the volumes indicated in the endnotes and listed opposite. Typographical errors have been corrected silently where the correct reading is obvious. On a small number of occasions, where there is ambiguity, a judgement has been made and the change annotated. In the story 'Gaspar, Melchior, Balthasar', which was transcribed from a manuscript known as the "Red Notebook" for inclusion in *EPW*, superior additions (indicated by italics in *EPW*) have been silently accepted, and deletions (indicated by square brackets in *EPW*) have been silently deleted. Spelling and punctuation have been standardized, modernized and made consistent throughout.

Notes

p. 3, *Portrait of the Artist as a Young Dog*: A collection first published in 1940 which includes stories that were composed or appeared in magazines and journals between March 1938 and December 1939. For the publication details of the individual stories, see the relevant note to each title in the collection. The text in this volume is from the Aldine Paperback edition of 1965 (*POA*).

p. 5, *The Peaches*: First published in *Life and Letters Today* (October 1938).

p. 5, *J. Jones, Gorsehill*: During the 1920s Thomas enjoyed extended stays with his aunt Annie and her husband Jim Jones at Fernhill, their home, called here "Gorsehill", near the village of Llangain in Carmarthenshire, south-west Wales. These childhood experiences were also the inspiration for 'Fern Hill' (1945), one of Thomas's most famous poems.

p. 7, *Mrs Jesus*: Apparently Uncle Jim's irreverent name for his wife, Annie.

p. 7, *shaggy*: "Shappy" in *POA*, likely a compositor's error.

p. 8, *my cousin Gwilym's*: Gwilym is Thomas's cousin Idris Jones, seventeen years his senior.

NOTES

p. 9, *Diu*: A non-standard spelling of the Welsh *Duw*, meaning "God", used as an interjection to mean "Well, I never" and so on – even by non-Welsh speakers.

p. 11, *mun*: A variation of "man" found in several English dialects, including Welsh English, used to address a person parenthetically and in a familiar manner.

p. 14, *ten-notched Gwilym*: That is, Gwilym is so slender that he fastens the belt around his waist at the tenth notch.

p. 17, *Corinne Griffith*: The American film actress Corinne Griffith (1894–1979), considered one of the most beautiful actresses of silent cinema.

p. 18, *swaying like a Kelly*: Perhaps a reference to the Australian outlaw Ned Kelly (1855–80), the leader of a gang of horse and cattle thieves and bank robbers who operated in Victoria. He was eventually hanged for his crimes.

p. 20, *A Visit to Grandpa's*: First published in the *New English Weekly* (10th March 1938).

p. 20, *lariats*: Lassos.

p. 21, *governess cart*: A small, two-wheeled horse-drawn cart.

p. 22, *Towy gulls*: That is, gulls from the River Towy, one of the longest rivers in Wales, which flows south-westwards through Carmarthenshire.

p. 24, *coracle*: A small wickerwork boat covered with watertight material, used especially by Welsh and Irish fishermen.

p. 25, *Patricia, Edith and Arnold*: First published in *Seven* (Christmas 1939).

p. 25, *Cwmdonkin Special*: From the name of the street where Thomas grew up, Cwmdonkin Drive in Swansea, located near Cwmdonkin Park.

p. 25, *Flying Welshman*: An allusion to the Flying Scotsman, an express passenger train service between Edinburgh and London.

p. 25, *on the randy*: "Randy" is a colloquial term for a rowdy merry-making.

p. 28, *moochin*: A colloquial Welsh English term for a difficult or disagreeable person, often a child. The word is a borrowing from Welsh (*mochyn*).

p. 29, *the Uplands*: A suburb of Swansea, around a mile west of the city centre.

p. 30, *Brynmill*: Another Swansea suburb, around two miles west of the city centre.

p. 33, *You won't call the king your uncle in a minute*: In other words, he will be so happy that not even being elevated to royalty would improve his mood.

p. 34, *The Fight*: First published in *Life and Letters Today* (December 1939).

p. 34, *a strange boy*: Thomas's childhood friend and schoolfellow Daniel Jones (1912–93) – called Daniel Jenkyn in the story – who went on to become a successful composer and produced song settings for Thomas's play *Under Milk Wood* (1954). He also edited collections of Thomas's poetry and prose, including *The Poems* (1971), in which several of the juvenile poems quoted in this story were published for the first time.

p. 35, *Tunney*: The American boxer Gene Tunney (1897–1978).

p. 35, *blue bag*: A bag containing laundry blue, a blue powder used to preserve the whiteness of laundry.

p. 35, *the Sandbanks*: Possibly Thomas's name for Sandfields, an area of Swansea immediately west of the city centre. It originally extended to the West Pier by the mouth of the River Tawe.

p. 36, *Pendine Sands*: A beach on the shores of Carmarthen Bay on the south coast of Wales. In the early twentieth century it was a venue for car and motorcycle races, notably, from 1922, the annual Welsh TT motorcycle event.

p. 36, *the Melba Pavilion*: In reality the Patti Pavilion, a theatre in Swansea's Victoria Park. Originally built in the grounds of Craig-y-Nos Castle in the Welsh county of Powys for the estate's then owner, the Italian opera singer Adelina Patti (1843–1919), the pavilion was relocated to Victoria Park in 1918 after Patti donated it to the city of Swansea.

p. 36, *My father went to Salonika in the war*: During the First World War, the Greek seaport of Thessaloníki, also known as Salonika, was the base for Allied operations against the Bulgarians.

p. 36, *Walter de la Mare... Watts's Hope*: The *Bookman* was a monthly literary magazine published in London by Hodder & Stoughton between 1891 and 1934. The writers named are the English poet Walter de la Mare (1873–1956), remembered for his verse for children, including 'The Listeners' (1912); the English poet Robert Browning (1812–89), best known for dramatic monologues like 'My Last Duchess' (1842) and 'Fra Lippo Lippi' (1855); the English author Stacy Aumonier (1877–1928), renowned for short stories including 'Miss Bracegirdle Does Her Duty' (1916) and 'The Octave of Jealousy' (1922); the English wartime poet

Rupert Brooke (1887–1915), author of the collection *1914 and Other Poems* (1915), including the sonnet 'The Soldier'; and the American Quaker poet and abolitionist John Greenleaf Whittier (1807–92), remembered for his long narrative poem *Snow-Bound* (1866). The allegorical painting *Hope* (1886) by the English Symbolist artist George Frederic Watts (1817–1904) depicts a blindfolded woman sitting on a globe, holding a single-stringed lyre.

p. 36, *A poem I had had printed... had died*: In January 1927 a poem apparently by Thomas, entitled 'War Requiem', appeared in the *Western Mail*, a Welsh daily newspaper. The young poet had, however, plagiarized a poem published in the *Boy's Own Paper* in 1923.

p. 37, '*Grass Blade's Psalm*': Written in around 1929 and first published in *The Poems* (1971), edited by Daniel Jones.

p. 38, *Sketty*: A suburb of Swansea, around two miles west of the city centre.

p. 38, *Pom*: A Pomeranian, a small dog.

p. 39, *Waller's... Vino*: Waller's Rum-and-Butter was a brand of toffee. Charlotte russe is a pudding consisting of custard encased in sponge cake. Cydrax was a brand of apple-flavoured fizzy drink. Vino is presumably also a branded soft drink of some kind.

p. 39, *Would the "Swans" beat the "Spurs"?*: That is, "Would Swansea City beat Tottenham Hotspur?"

p. 39, *Was Arnott's average last year better than Clay's?*: The boys are comparing the batting averages of the Welsh cricketer Trevor Arnott (1902–75) and his Glamorgan teammate Johnnie Clay (1898–1973).

p. 39, '*Warp*': Written in around 1929 and first published in *The Poems* (1971), edited by Daniel Jones.

p. 40, *The school... Mount Pleasant hill*: A reference to Swansea Grammar School for Boys, located in the Mount Pleasant area of Swansea, north of the city centre, which Thomas attended, and where his father, David John Thomas (1876–1952), known as D.J. Thomas, was the senior English master. Established in 1682 in Sketty, the school was originally named Bishop Gore School after its founder, the Anglican bishop Hugh Gore (1613–91). It relocated to Mount Pleasant in 1853.

p. 40, "*Warmley*": The name of the Joneses' house on Eversley Road in the Sketty area of Swansea.

p. 40, *a Cape Horner*: That is, he has sailed around Cape Horn, the southernmost point of South America, as the captain of a sailing ship.

NOTES

p. 40, *the Kardomah*: One of a chain of coffee shops in England and Wales. In the 1930s, the Kardomah in Swansea became the meeting place of the Kardomah Gang, a group of artists, musicians and writers that, as well as Thomas and Jones, included the poets Vernon Watkins (1906–67) and Charles Fisher (1914–2006).

p. 41, *The Meistersingers*: *Die Meistersinger von Nürnberg* (*The Mastersingers of Nuremberg*), an opera by the German composer Richard Wagner (1813–83), first performed in 1868.

p. 41, *Glanrhyd*: The name chosen for the family home, 5 Cwmdonkin Drive, by Thomas's father. It was originally that of the farm owned by D.J. Thomas's uncle, the minister and poet William Thomas (1834–79), also known by his bardic name of Gwilym Marles.

p. 42, *Jack Holt in Richard Dix's place*: The American film actors Jack Holt (1888–1951) and Richard Dix (1893–1949), both archetypal rugged leading men, particularly in Westerns.

p. 42, *the Messiah*: An oratorio written in 1741 by the German-born composer George Frideric Handel (1685–1759).

p. 43, *Frivolous is my hate*: Written in around 1929 and first published in *The Poems* (1971), edited by Daniel Jones.

p. 43, *Break, break, break... O sea*: The opening lines of the elegy 'Break, Break, Break' by the English poet Alfred, Lord Tennyson (1809–92), written in 1835, which describes the poet's grief following the loss of his friend, the poet Arthur Henry Hallam (1811–33).

p. 45, *Extraordinary Little Cough*: First published in *Life and Letters Today* (September 1939).

p. 45, *the Peninsula*: The Gower Peninsula in south-west Wales.

p. 45, *"N.T."... my sister*: The author's sister Nancy (1906–53).

p. 45, *a Primus stove*: A portable cooking stove powered by paraffin.

p. 45, *Rhossili*: A village at the south-western extremity of the Gower Peninsula.

p. 46, *combinations*: A close-fitting undergarment combining chemise and drawers.

p. 47, *Dempsey*: The American boxer Jack Dempsey (1895–1983), known as "Kid Blackie" and the "Manassa Mauler", world heavyweight champion from 1919 to 1926.

p. 48, *cow pads*: Deposits of cow dung.

p. 50, *Ben Evans's stores*: Ben Evans was a famous department store in Swansea, founded in 1863. Its destruction by the Luftwaffe during the "Three Nights' Blitz" of 19th–21st February 1941, in which hundreds of buildings in the city centre were destroyed and 230 people were killed, was referred to by Thomas in 'Return Journey', a talk for the BBC Home Service broadcast in May 1947.

p. 51, *Valentino*: The Italian-born American film actor Rudolph Valentino (1895–1926), famous as the romantic lead in silent films such as *The Sheikh* (1921).

p. 51, *Porthcawl*: A town on the south coast of Wales, nineteen miles south-east of Swansea.

p. 52, *No, No, Nanette*: A musical comedy with music by the American composer Vincent Youmans (1898–1946) and lyrics by Irving Caesar (1895–1996) and Otto Harbach (1873–1963), first performed in 1924. It was based on a play by the American dramatist Frank Mandel (1884–1958) and contained the famous songs 'Tea for Two' and 'I Want to Be Happy'.

p. 53, *Just Like Little Dogs*: First published in *Wales* (October 1939).

p. 54, *Rabaiotti's all-night café*: A café on Swansea's High Street.

p. 54, *Mannesmann Hall*: A boxing venue adjacent to the British Mannesmann Company tube factory in the Landore district of Swansea.

p. 56, *Gracie's*: A reference to the English singer and comedian Gracie Fields (1898–1979), a music-hall star.

p. 56, *shananacking*: Apparently Thomas's coinage, likely a variation of "shenanigans".

p. 56, *St Thomas*: A suburban area of Swansea east of the city centre.

p. 57, *was a caution*: That is, behaved in an amusing manner.

p. 57, *Now the storytelling night*: "Night" appears as "htnig" in *POA*, an obvious compositor's error. This has been changed to "thing" in other editions, but "night" seems more likely due to the resulting parallelism of "storytelling night" and "loving night".

p. 59, *Where Tawe Flows*: Completed by early December 1939 and first published in *POA*. The name refers to the Tawe, a river in South Wales that reaches the sea at Swansea.

p. 59, *a bodysnatcher... Burke and Hare*: Before the Anatomy Act of 1832, the only cadavers that could be legally dissected were those of criminals sentenced to death and dissection. However, due to the dwindling number of executions in the early nineteenth century and the expansion of the medical schools, demand far outstripped supply, forcing doctors to rely on the services of bodysnatchers, or "resurrection men", who illegally disinterred corpses from graveyards. The most notorious of the bodysnatchers were William Burke (1792–1829) and William Hare (1792 or

1804–c.1858), who went a stage further and sold bodies of people they themselves had murdered to the Scottish surgeon and anatomist Robert Knox (1791–1862), who ran an Edinburgh anatomy school.

p. 59, *Ogpu*: The Joint State Political Directorate (known by the Russian acronym OGPU, commonly rendered as "Ogpu"), the Soviet secret police from 1923 to 1934, when it was incorporated into the NKVD.

p. 59, *Saunders Lewis*: The Welsh politician and writer Saunders Lewis (1893–1985), a passionate supporter of Welsh independence and a co-founder in 1925 of Plaid Genedlaethol Cymru (the National Party of Wales), now known as Plaid Cymru.

p. 60, *G.B.S.*: The Irish playwright and writer George Bernard Shaw (1856–1950), a famous socialist and a prominent member of the democratic-socialist Fabian Society.

p. 60, *No clean Shavianism... birds and beasts*: Shaw was a committed vegetarian, declaring that "a man of my spiritual intensity does not eat corpses".

p. 60, *on the knocker*: That is, Roberts goes from door to door collecting for the insurance company for which he works.

p. 61, *John O'London's Society*: A real-life Swansea literary club, named after *John O'London's Weekly*, a literary magazine published between 1919 and 1954.

p. 61, *Jack London*: The American novelist Jack London (1876–1916), best known for *The Call of the Wild* (1903) and *White Fang* (1906), adventure stories set against the backdrop of the Klondike gold rush of 1896–99.

p. 61, *W.J. Locke... 'Bevagged Loveabond'*: The British novelist, dramatist and short-story writer William John Locke (1863–1930) was the author of the novel *The Beloved Vagabond* (1906).

p. 61, *grass widow in Manselton*: A grass widow is a woman whose husband is often away from home. Manselton is a suburb of Swansea.

p. 62, *a Mosleyite*: A follower of Oswald Mosley (1896–1980), founder and leader of the British Union of Fascists, known as the "blackshirts".

p. 62, *Ramsay Mac*: The Scottish statesman Ramsay MacDonald (1866–1937), who served as Britain's first Labour prime minister from January to November 1924, then in 1929–31 and 1931–35.

p. 62, *the grapes of wrath*: A phrase taken from the patriotic song 'The Battle Hymn of the Republic', also known as 'Mine Eyes Have Seen the Glory' or 'Glory, Glory Hallelujah', written during the American Civil War by the abolitionist writer Julia Ward Howe (1819–1910): "Mine eyes have seen the glory of the coming of the Lord; / He is trampling out the vintage where the grapes of wrath are stored." The expression echoes the language of Revelation 14:19: "And the angel thrust in his sickle into the earth, and gathered the vine of the earth, and cast it into the great winepress of the wrath of God."

p. 63, *Go to bed, plain Maud*: A comical reworking of Tennyson's lyric 'Come into the garden, Maud' from his long poem *Maud* (1855).

p. 63, *Tempus is fugiting*: A reference to the Latin phrase "tempus fugit" ("time flies"), derived from the *Georgics* (III, l. 84) of the Roman poet Virgil (70–19 BC): "fugit inreparabile tempus" ("irretrievable time is flying").

p. 65, *Tomorrow and Tomorrow*: The title of Humphries's book alludes to Macbeth's famous soliloquy from Act V, Sc. 5 of Shakespeare's play: "Tomorrow, and tomorrow, and tomorrow, / Creeps in this petty pace from day to day, / To the last syllable of recorded time" (ll. 19–21).

p. 66, *nasturtiums*: A deliberate malapropism for "aspersions".

p. 68, *TTs*: Teetotallers.

p. 69, *Caradoc Evans*: The Welsh writer Caradoc Evans (1878–1945), who grew up in rural Cardiganshire, west Wales. He was known as "the best hated man in Wales" as a result of his controversial fiction, notably the collection *My People: Stories of the Peasantry of West Wales* (1915), which, in addition to shining a light on the stark realities of rural poverty in the country, was caustically critical of the Welsh people themselves, as well as of the hypocrisies of Nonconformist religion.

p. 73, *Who Do You Wish Was with Us?*: Completed by early December 1939 and first published in *POA*.

p. 73, *Raymond Price*: Based on Thomas's friend Trevor Hughes, a clerk for the railway company Great Western Railway (GWR). The title of the story refers to Hughes's grief following the loss of his brother. However, although the incident described in the story is based on an actual excursion made by the young Thomas, he was unaccompanied.

p. 73, *the Worm's Head*: A headland at Rhossili, named for its dragon-like appearance. It is the westernmost point of the Gower Peninsula, and is accessible to pedestrians for only two and a half hours either side of low tide.

p. 73, *Mutt and Jeff!*: The name of a US newspaper comic strip that ran between 1907 and 1983, created by cartoonist Bud Fisher (1885–1954), about two comically mismatched characters: the tall Augustus Mutt and the dwarfish Jeff.

NOTES

p. 74, *It won't be a stylish marriage*: A line from the 1892 song 'Daisy Bell (Bicycle Built for Two)' by the British songwriter Harry Dacre (1857–1922). Its famous chorus is as follows: "Daisy, Daisy, / Give me your answer, do! / I'm half crazy, / All for the love of you. / It won't be a stylish marriage, / I can't afford a carriage, / But you'll look sweet upon the seat / Of a bicycle built for two."

p. 77, *Raleigh*: The English explorer Sir Walter Raleigh (c.1552–1618), remembered as a favourite of Elizabeth I and for numerous voyages of exploration to the New World.

p. 78, *W.B. Yeats*: The Irish poet and dramatist William Butler Yeats (1865–1939), a major figure of the Irish Literary Revival and regarded as one of the greatest writers of the twentieth century. His key works include the plays *The Countess Kathleen* (1892) and *Cathleen ni Houlihan* (1902) and the poetry collections *The Tower* (1928) and *The Winding Stair* (1929).

p. 78, *kiss the Blarney*: According to legend, anyone who kisses the Blarney Stone, a block of limestone incorporated into the battlements of Blarney Castle, outside Cork in the south of Ireland, is thereby granted the "gift of the gab".

p. 78, *We'd still be walking, like Felix*: A reference to the song 'Felix Kept on Walking' (1924), with lyrics by Ed E. Bryant and music by the English songwriter Hubert W. David (1904–99), which contains the refrain "Felix keeps on walking, keeps on walking still". It was based on the silent-era cartoon character Felix the Cat, created in 1919 by animators Pat Sullivan (1885–1933) and Otto Messmer (1892–1983).

p. 79, *a sanatorium in Craig-y-Nos*: After the death of its owner, Adelina Patti (see second note to p. 36), Craig-y-Nos Castle became a sanatorium for patients suffering from tuberculosis.

p. 80, *Lexicon*: A word game created in 1932 and originally published by the British games manufacturer Waddingtons. It was played with a deck of cards marked with the letters of the alphabet.

p. 82, *Old Garbo*: First published in *Life and Letters Today* (July 1939).

p. 82, *Mr Farr*: Freddie "Half-Hook" Farr was chief reporter on the *South Wales Daily Post* (which changed its name to the *South Wales Evening Post* in April 1932) and acted as a mentor to Thomas, who began as a junior reporter on the paper in August 1931, aged seventeen.

p. 82, *meg*: Perhaps a slang term derived from the French word "*mégot*", meaning "cigarette butt".

p. 83, *a Wesleyan*: That is, a Methodist. Methodism is a Nonconformist Protestant denomination founded in Oxford by brothers Charles (1707–88) and John Wesley (1703–91) and George Whitefield (1714–70) in 1729.

p. 83, *The Crucifixion*: Possibly a reference to one of the York Mystery Plays, otherwise known as the York Corpus Christi Plays, a cycle of forty-eight plays or pageants depicting biblical history from the creation of the world to the Last Judgement that were performed on the feast day of Corpus Christi (the Thursday after Trinity Sunday, between 23rd May and 24th June) in the English city of York from the mid-fourteenth century. The pageants were traditionally performed by members of trade guilds, with the crucifixion being the responsibility of the pinners, painters and latoners (workers in or makers of latten, an alloy of copper and zinc resembling brass). The York cycle remained relatively unknown in the modern period after its suppression by the Tudors, but a performance as part of the "York Historic Pageant" in 1909 rekindled interest, sparking further revivals.

p. 83, *the Valley*: Swansea Valley, the valley of the Tawe, which stretches from the Brecon Beacons in the north to Swansea in the south.

p. 83, *frails*: Baskets made of rushes.

p. 83, *lascars*: Sailor from India or South East Asia.

p. 84, *in the boots at Dan Lewis's*: Perhaps meaning that he works in the boots section at Lewis Lewis, a department store located on High Street, Swansea.

p. 84, *White Lies... Bennett*: Although this may be an anachronistic reference to the 1934 film *White Lies*, directed by the Russian-born Leo Bulgakov (1899–1948) – which does not feature the American actor Constance Bennett (1904–65) – it is more likely that Thomas is mischievously fabricating a non-existent film.

p. 84, *Remember her in the foam bath*: Perhaps an anachronistic reference to the 1937 short film *Daily Beauty Rituals*, in which Constance Bennett revealed her morning skincare regime, including a bubble bath.

p. 84, *And little Audrey laughed and laughed*: The beginning of a punchline to a number of ribald jokes popular in the 1920s and 1930s. In extended use, according to Eric Partridge's *Dictionary of Catch Phrases: American and British, from the Sixteenth Century to the Present Day* (1977), the phrase "is applied to a fit of laughter arising for a reason either inadequate or not immediately apparent to others".

p. 85, *Tawe*: A shortened version of the Welsh name for Swansea, Abertawe.

p. 86, *Mission to Seamen*: An Anglican charity dedicated to the welfare of merchant sailors. It is known today as the Mission to Seafarers.

p. 86, *Then I entered... new rain*: The film described here corresponds in some respects to the 1932 comedy *Million Dollar Legs*, directed by Edward F. Cline (1891–1961), in which Migg Tweeny, a salesman played by the American actor Jack Oakie (1903–78), falls in love with Angela, played by the American actress Susan Fleming (1908–2002), the daughter of the president of the near-bankrupt country of Klopstokia. The plot concerns Tweeny's plan to secure the blessing of the president, played by comedian W.C. Fields (1880–1946), by persuading him to enter the Olympics as a weightlifter and win the cash prize offered to medallists by his own employer, thereby solving Klopstokia's financial woes.

p. 87, *the Hafod*: A district of Swansea north of the city centre, home of the Hafod Copperworks, established in 1810.

p. 87, *Charlie masks*: Likely masks resembling the features of the English film actor Charlie Chaplin (1889–1977) in the guise of "the Tramp" – complete with toothbrush moustache and bowler hat – the character he portrayed in a number of silent comedies.

p. 87, *cachous*: Lozenges sucked to disguise halitosis.

p. 87, *Mumbles Lighthouse*: A lighthouse in Mumbles, a headland on the western edge of Swansea Bay.

p. 88, *Toop little Twms*: That is, "stupid little Toms". "Toop" is a phonetic spelling of the Welsh *twp*, meaning "stupid", and "Twm" is the Welsh equivalent of the name Tom.

p. 88, *"Bread of heaven"*: A refrain in the lyric 'Guide Me, O Thou Great Redeemer' by the Welsh hymnist William Williams Pantycelyn (1717–91), usually sung to 'Cwm Rhondda', a hymn tune by the Welsh composer John Hughes (1873–1932). The first verse is as follows: "Guide me, O Thou great Redeemer, / Pilgrim through this barren land; / I am weak, but Thou art mighty; / Hold me with Thy powerful hand: / Bread of heaven, bread of heaven, / Feed me till I want no more, / Feed me till I want no more."

p. 89, *blackjack*: A tar-coated leather container used to hold beer.

p. 89, *turnip watch*: A slang term for a pocket watch, particularly a large one.

p. 89, *We call her Old Garbo, because she isn't like her*: That is, she does not resemble the Swedish-born US actress Greta Garbo (1905–90).

p. 89, *in pod*: The phrase "in pod" usually means "pregnant", but Jack Stiff means that the woman has died in labour.

p. 90, *'One of the Ruins'* or *'Cockles and Mussels'*: Respectively, 'One of the Ruins That Cromwell Knocked About a Bit', a song by Harry Bedford (1873–1939) and Terry Sullivan (d. 1950) that was famously sung by the English music-hall singer Marie Lloyd (1870–1922), and 'Cockles and Mussels', also known as 'Molly Malone', a music-hall song of unknown origin about "Dublin's fair city".

p. 90, *gamps*: Umbrellas.

p. 90, *'Rose of Tralee'*: An Irish ballad traditionally attributed to the lyricist Edward Mordaunt Spencer (d. 1888) and the English composer Charles William Glover (1806–63).

p. 90, *Angostura... Fernet-Branca*: Angostura Bitters and Fernet-Branca are two brands of bitters, alcoholic drinks flavoured with bitter plant extracts and taken medicinally.

p. 91, *'The Lily of Laguna'*: A music-hall song imitative of African American musical styles written in 1896 by the English composer Leslie Stuart (1863–1928). It was generally performed in blackface.

p. 91, *Katie Sebastopol Street*: Sebastopol Street is a street in Swansea.

p. 91, *War Cry*: The official news publication of the Salvation Army.

p. 91, *Nijinsky*: The Russian ballet dancer Vaslav Nijinsky (1890–1950).

p. 92, *One and a tanner out of my Old Age*: That is, one shilling and sixpence (a "tanner") out of her old-age pension.

p. 93, *stop-tap*: The time at which drinks cease to be served in a pub.

p. 93, *Jack Johnson*: The American boxer Jack Johnson (1878–1946), known as the "Galveston Giant".

p. 94, *One Warm Saturday*: Completed by July 1938 and first published in *POA*.

p. 95, *Duckworth*: The English cricketer George Duckworth (1901–66).

p. 95, *Stop Me tricycles*: A reference to a kind of tricycle ridden by an ice-cream salesman, with, at the front, a large box containing the rider's wares and bearing the legend "Stop me and buy one".

p. 96, *Bath chairs*: A "Bath chair" was a kind of wheelchair, named after the city due to its popularity with invalids who came to experience the supposed healing properties of the hot springs.

p. 96, *pussyfoot*: Abstinent, sober.

p. 96, *Victoria Gardens*: Thomas's name for Victoria Park in Swansea.

p. 97, *Victoria saloon*: Based on the Bay View Hotel, at the junction of Oystermouth Road and St Helen's Road in Swansea.

p. 97, *free Xs*: That is, free medium- and high-quality beer, designated "XX" and "XXX", respectively.

NOTES

p. 98, *Once round Bessy, once round the gasworks*: A humorous phrase used to describe an overweight woman, that is, one with a very large circumference.

p. 98, *Bunsen burner*: Possibly a humorous term for a condom.

p. 98, *chorines*: Chorus girls.

p. 99, *Bye-bye blackbird*: A 1926 song by the American composer Ray Henderson (1896–1970), with words by the American lyricist Mort Dixon (1892–1956).

p. 99, *Weight*: Player's Weights were a brand of cigarettes.

p. 100, *working underground in Dowlais*: In other words, he was the victim of an accident at the Abercynon Colliery, known as the Dowlais Cardiff Colliery, a coal mine eleven miles south of Dowlais, opened in 1889.

p. 101, *Mrs Grundy*: Originally the name of an unseen character in the 1798 play *Speed the Plough* by the English dramatist Thomas Morton (1764–1838), Mrs Grundy became a byword for priggishness and unthinking adherence to conventional propriety.

p. 101, *biddy*: Also known as "red biddy", an alcoholic concoction consisting of inferior red wine and methylated spirits.

p. 101, *Ramon Novarro*: The Mexican-American screen actor and sex symbol José Ramón Gil Samaniego (1899–1968), known professionally as Ramon Novarro.

p. 101, *Charley Chase*: The American comedian and comic actor Charles Joseph Parrott (1893–1940), known professionally as Charley Chase.

p. 101, *He's got that Kruschen feeling*: A reference to Kruschen Salts, a cure-all popular in the first half of the twentieth century, which was advertised under the slogan "Get that Kruschen feeling".

p. 102, *lux in tenebris*: "Light in darkness" (Latin). The phrase is taken from the Vulgate (the medieval Latin Bible): "*Et lux in tenebris lucet et tenebræ eam non comprehenderunt*", rendered in the King James Bible as follows: "And the light shineth in darkness; and the darkness comprehended it not" (John 1:5).

p. 102, *Tontine voice*: A reference to Tontine Street in Swansea.

p. 103, *Là, là, chérie!*: "There, there, dear!" (French).

p. 103, *Nutbrown*: Evidently a brand of "nut-brown" ale.

p. 104, *On such a night as this did Jessica steal from the wealthy Jew*: As is acknowledged, the quotation is from *The Merchant of Venice*: "In such a night / Did Jessica steal from the wealthy Jew, / And with an unthrift love did run from Venice / As far as Belmont" (Act V, Sc. 1, ll. 18–21). The quotation refers to events earlier in the play (Act II, Sc. 6), when Jessica, daughter of the moneylender Shylock, steals gold and jewels from her father in order to elope with her lover, Lorenzo.

p. 105, *tish*: A humorous variation of the word "tash", moustache.

p. 108, *'Come into the garden, Maud'*: See first note to p. 63.

p. 108, *God's in His heaven, all's right with the world*: A famous line from a song from Act I of the verse drama *Pippa Passes* (1841) by the English poet Robert Browning (1812–89).

p. 113, *Early Stories*: The stories in this section are arranged in order of publication (if published during Thomas's life) or composition (if published posthumously). For the publication or composition details of the individual stories, see the relevant note to each title.

p. 115, *Brember*: First published in the *Swansea Grammar School Magazine* (Vol. 28, No. 1, April 1931) and collected in *EPW*, from where the text is taken.

p. 117, *Jarley's*: First published in the *Swansea Grammar School Magazine* (Vol. 30, No. 3, December 1933) and collected in *EPW*, from where the text is taken.

p. 117, *Hiawatha... Circe*: Hiawatha was a legendary fifteenth- or sixteenth-century chief of the North American Onondaga tribe and the hero of the epic poem *The Song of Hiawatha* (1855) by the American poet Henry Wadsworth Longfellow (1807–82). Charles Peace (1832–79) was a notorious English burglar and murderer. Circe is a sorceress in Greek mythology, best known for the episode in Homer's *Odyssey* in which she turns Odysseus's crew into swine (X, ll. 133–399).

p. 118, *Minnehaha*: The lover of Hiawatha in Longfellow's poem. The name means "laughing water".

p. 118, *I remember the sea-green eyes of Jason*: In the *Argonautica*, an epic poem written by the Greek poet Apollonius Rhodius (*fl*. third century BC), Jason and his Argonauts, who are on a mission to retrieve the Golden Fleece from the land of Colchis, visit Circe on her island of Aeaea, seeking purification for their murder of Apsyrtus, brother of the sorceress Medea, Jason's lover (IV).

p. 120, *After the Fair*: First published in the *New English Weekly* (15th March 1934) and collected in *PS*, from where the text is taken.

p. 124, *The Enemies*: First published in *New Stories* (June–July 1934) and collected in *ML* and *PS*, from where the text is taken.

p. 124, *the Jarvis Valley*: A fictionalized version of Carmarthenshire that features in several of Thomas's early stories.

NOTES

p. 129, *In the Garden*: First published in the *Swansea Grammar School Magazine* (Vol. 31, No. 2, July 1934) and collected in *EPW*, from where the text is taken.

p. 130, *poor Jenny lies a-weeping*: A children's game in which one child is chosen to be "Jenny" and must kneel in the centre of a circle made by the other players, and then perform the actions described in a nursery rhyme recited by the others; for instance: "Stand up and choose your loved one, / Your loved one, your loved one, / Stand up and choose your loved one, / On a bright summer's day."

p. 132, *Gaspar, Melchior, Balthasar*: Completed on 8th August 1934 and collected in *EPW*, from where the text is taken.

p. 133, *upas*: The upa is a tropical tree whose poisonous sap has traditionally been used in Asia in poison arrows and darts.

p. 134, *The End of the River*: First published in the *New English Weekly* (22nd November 1934) and collected in *EPW*, from where the text is taken.

p. 139, *The Tree*: First published in the *Adelphi* (December 1934) and collected in *ML* and *PS*, from where the text is taken.

p. 146, *The Visitor*: First published in *The Criterion* (January 1935) and collected in *ML* and *PS*, from where the text is taken.

p. 146, *inch-tape*: A tape measure.

p. 149, *Ah! Gentle... time*: From *The Book of Thel* (I, ll. 12–14), an allegorical poem by the English artist and poet William Blake (1757–1827).

p. 149, *the Worm sat on the Lily's leaf*: The conclusion of the second part of Blake's *The Book of Thel* (see previous note): "The helpless worm arose, and sat upon the Lily's leaf, / And the bright cloud sailed on, to find his partner in the vale" (II, ll. 30–31).

p. 153, *The Dress*: First published in *Comment* (4th January 1936) and collected in *ML* and *PS*, from where the text is taken.

p. 156, *The Lemon*: First published in *Life and Letters Today* (Spring 1936) and collected in *PS*, from where the text is taken.

p. 156, *mastoids*: An informal name for mastoiditis, an infection of the mastoid process, the posterior part of the temporal bone, one of the bones of the skull.

p. 157, *papped*: That is, fed with pap.

p. 157, *distemper*: A glue-based paint used on walls.

p. 159, *the halt*: The disabled.

p. 160, *Cathmarw*: A name meaning "dead cat" in Welsh. Cathmarw is also the setting for the story 'The Horse's Ha'.

NOTES

p. 161, *The Burning Baby*: First published in *Contemporary Poetry and Prose* (May 1936) and collected in *EPW*, from where the text is taken.

p. 161, *They said that Rhys was burning his baby*: Rhys is based on the Welsh physician and neo-Druid William Price (1800–93) from the town of Llantrisant in South Wales, who, in January 1884, burned the body of his illegitimate son, Iesu Grist (the Welsh equivalent of "Jesus Christ"), who had died at the age of five months. Price was subsequently arrested and tried, but succeeded in arguing that, despite popular belief, cremation was not illegal. His case paved the way for the passing of the Cremation Act 1902. Thomas was told the story by the Welsh writer Glyn Jones (1905–95) while on a visit to Caradoc Evans (see note to p. 69) in Aberystwyth in 1934.

p. 164, *Llareggub*: "Bugger all" spelt backwards. Llareggub is also the name of the fictional Welsh fishing town that is the setting for *Under Milk Wood*.

p. 167, *The Horse's Ha*: First published in *Janus* (May 1936) and collected in *EPW*, from where the text is taken.

p. 167, *furuncle*: A boil.

p. 168, *sparrow's*: Appears as "sparrows" (without an apostrophe) in *EPW*.

p. 169, *resurrection men*: See second note to p. 59.

p. 171, *sparrow's*: Appears as "sparrows" (without an apostrophe) in *EPW*.

p. 172, *The Orchards*: First published in *The Criterion* (July 1936) and collected in *ML* and *PS*, from where the text is taken.

p. 172, *Marlais*: Thomas's middle name.

p. 173, *the Kara Sea or the Sea of Azov*: Respectively, an arm of the Arctic Ocean located off western Siberia and an inland sea in southern Russia and Ukraine.

p. 174, *The word is too much with us*: A pun on the title of the sonnet 'The World Is Too Much with Us' by the English Romantic poet William Wordsworth (1770–1850), composed in around 1802.

p. 178, *Idris*: Idris Gawr ("Idris the Giant") is a giant in Welsh folklore.

p. 180, *The School for Witches*: First published in *Contemporary Poetry and Prose* (August–September 1936) and collected in *EPW*, from where the text is taken.

p. 180, *Cader Peak*: The name of this fictional mountain echoes that of Cader Idris, Welsh for "Idris's chair", a mountain in Snowdonia, North Wales. For Idris, see note to p. 178.

NOTES

p. 180, *Gehenna*: Hell.

p. 181, *scissorman*: A tailor. The name alludes to a character from Heinrich Hoffmann's (1809–94) *Struwwelpeter* – see second note to p. 291.

p. 182, *Swive*: An archaic or humorous term meaning "have sex with".

p. 186, *The Mouse and the Woman*: First published in *Transition* (Fall 1936) and collected in *ML* and *PS*, from where the text is taken.

p. 191, *He had not slept with Rachel and woken with Leah*: A reference to a story in the Book of Genesis (29), in which the Hebrew patriarch Jacob wishes to marry the beautiful Rachel, but, after working for her father Laban for seven years, is tricked by him into marrying Rachel's older and less attractive sister, Leah. Laban then tells Jacob that he may marry Rachel in return for a further seven years of labour.

p. 195, *the seven geese of the Wandering Jew*: Apparently a conflation of two legends: that of the Jew who taunted Jesus on the way to the crucifixion and was doomed to walk the earth until the Second Coming as punishment, and that of the "seven whistlers", a mysterious flock of birds that, in British folklore, represented the reincarnated souls of the seven Jews who assisted in the crucifixion of Christ, and whose unearthly cries were believed – particularly by miners and seamen from northern England in the nineteenth century – to be an omen of impending disaster.

p. 195, *still, small voice*: "And after the earthquake a fire; but the Lord was not in the fire: and after the fire a still small voice" (1 Kings 19:12).

p. 197, *Parhelion*: A bright point in the sky, often occurring on either side of the sun, caused by sunlight's reflection by ice crystals in the atmosphere. Also known as a "mock sun" or a "sun dog".

p. 199, *A Prospect of the Sea*: First published in *Life and Letters Today* (Spring 1937) and collected in *PS*, from where the text is taken.

p. 206, *The Holy Six*: First published in *Contemporary Poetry and Prose* (Spring 1937) and collected in *EPW*, from where the text is taken.

p. 206, *women*: "Woman" in *EPW*.

p. 209, *cantharides*: A species of emerald-green beetle, also known as Spanish fly.

p. 209, *an open coppish and a sabbath gamp*: Respectively, an open fly (that is, the opening at the crotch of a pair of trousers) and an umbrella – presumably one that is sober in colour and design, and therefore suitable to be carried to and from church on Sunday.

NOTES

p. 209, *like the old men with Susanna*: A reference to a story in the apocryphal book of Susanna (part of the Old Testament book of Daniel in some versions of the Bible) about a young woman named Susanna who, while bathing in a walled garden, is spied upon by two lecherous and elderly voyeurs. Becoming aware of each other's presence, the two men conspire to accuse her of adultery if she does not agree to have sex with them. Susanna is subsequently arrested, but is saved from being put to death by the intervention of Daniel, who has been sent by God to expose the mendacity of her accusers. The story was a popular subject in Renaissance and baroque art.

p. 212, *piksies*: That is, pixies. Thomas's spelling resembles "piskies", common in Cornwall in south-west England.

p. 212, *upas tree*: See note to p. 133.

p. 212, *menses*: Blood and other matter discharged during menstruation.

p. 214, *Prologue to an Adventure*: First published in *Wales* (Summer 1937) and collected in *EPW*, from where the text is taken.

p. 214, *the city*: The city described is London. The story was conceived as part of a longer work, designed to be a reversal of the religious allegory *The Pilgrim's Progress* (1678) by the English writer and preacher John Bunyan (1628–88), in which a man called Christian goes on a journey from the "City of Destruction", which stands for this world, to the "Celestial City", which stands for heaven. Thomas's version features an "anti-Christian" who "travels from the City of Zion to the City of Destruction", as he wrote in a letter to a friend in summer 1935.

p. 214, *Old Moore*: A reference to *Old Moore's Almanack*, an astrological almanac first published in 1697. Originally written by the English physician and astrologer Francis Moore (1657–1715), it is still published annually, containing predictions of world and sporting events.

p. 215, *Damaroid Alley*: "Damaroid" pills were a quack remedy aimed at men that promised to boost virility and were claimed to have aphrodisiac properties. They were sold in the sex shops on and around Charing Cross Road in the West End of London.

p. 215, *Gamarouche Mews*: "Gamarouche" is a slang term meaning oral sex.

p. 219, *The Map of Love*: First published in *Wales* (Autumn 1937) and collected in *ML* and *PS*, from where the text is taken.

p. 219, *get*: Offspring.

p. 221, *daps*: Rubber-soled shoes; plimsolls.

p. 222, *Dolgelley*: An Anglicized spelling of the name of Dolgellau, a town in Gwynedd in the north-west of Wales.

p. 224, *In the Direction of the Beginning*: First published in *Wales* (March 1938) and collected in *PS*, from where the text is taken.

p. 225, *douting*: Extinguishing.

p. 225, *cantharis*: The singular form of "cantharides" – see first note to p. 209.

p. 226, *An Adventure from a Work in Progress*: First published in *Seven* (Spring 1939) and collected in *EPW*, from where the text is taken.

p. 229, *amice*: A liturgical vestment of white linen, worn around the neck and shoulders and over the alb.

p. 230, *The True Story*: First published in *Yellowjacket* (May 1939) and collected in *EPW*, from where the text is taken.

p. 233, *The Vest*: First published in *Yellowjacket* (May 1939) and collected in *EPW*, from where the text is taken.

p. 233, *a black beetle*: A cockroach.

p. 237, *Adventures in the Skin Trade*: Three chapters of an unfinished novel mainly written in May–June 1941 and first published posthumously in 1953. For the publication details of the individual stories, see the relevant note to each title in the collection. The text in this volume is from the Aldine Paperback edition of 1965 (*AST*).

p. 239, *A Fine Beginning*: First published in *Folios of New Writing* (Autumn 1941).

p. 239, *kirby grips*: Hairgrips.

p. 240, *Burberries*: Lightweight, beige-coloured raincoats with a tartan lining, produced by the fashion house Burberry.

p. 241, *The Desert Song*: A 1926 operetta by the Hungarian-born American composer Sigmund Romberg (1887–1951) and the librettist Oscar Hammerstein II (1895–1960), inspired by the 1925 uprising of the Riffs, a group of Berber fighters, against French colonial rule in Morocco, as well as by the story of the British soldier and writer T.E. Lawrence (1888–1935), known as Lawrence of Arabia, remembered for his role in the Arab revolt against the Ottomans during the First World War.

p. 241, *tellurion*: A mechanical model used to illustrate the way in which day, night and the seasons are caused by the rotation of the Earth on its axis and its orbit around the sun.

p. 241, *have a dekko*: That is, have a look – an army-slang term derived from the Hindi imperative "*dekho*", meaning "look!"

p. 241, *three-and-eleven-three half-hose*: That is, socks costing three shillings and elevenpence, plus three farthings (three quarter-pennies).

p. 242, *moustache cup*: A cup containing a small ledge, itself containing a small semicircular opening to allow the passage of liquid, designed to protect the moustache of the drinker.

p. 247, *Bass*: A beer produced by Bass Brewery in Burton-upon-Trent, Staffordshire.

p. 250, *Joan Crawford*: The American film actress Joan Crawford (c.1904–77), one of the biggest movie stars of the era.

p. 251, *Am I my brother's keeper?*: The reply of the fratricide Cain to God's question "Where is Abel thy brother?" See Genesis 4:1–18.

p. 252, *Nancy*: One of Fagin's criminal gang in Dickens's 1838 novel *Oliver Twist*. Nancy is generally regarded as a prostitute, although this is not explicit in the text.

p. 252, *Copperfield*: David Copperfield, the titular hero of Dickens's semi-autobiographical *Bildungsroman* of 1849–50.

p. 254, *Janet Gaynor... Kay Francis*: The Hollywood actors Janet Gaynor (1906–84), known for films including *7th Heaven* (1927) and *A Star Is Born* (1937), Marion Davies (1897–1961), a popular screen star in the 1920s who was perhaps best known as the wife of the newspaper mogul William Randolph Hearst (1863–1951), and Kay Francis (1905–68), known as the "Queen of Warner Brothers", star of the films *Trouble in Paradise* (1932) and *Mandalay* (1934), among many others.

p. 256, *Ikey Mo*: A derogatory term for a Jew.

p. 257, *Plenty of Furniture*: First published in *New World Writing* (November 1952).

p. 261, *He fell... Newbolt's poem?*: The patriotic poem 'He Fell among Thieves' by the English poet Sir Henry Newbolt (1862–1938) is an account of the death of the English explorer George W. Hayward (c.1839–70), who, in July 1870, was murdered by tribesmen near the Darkot Pass in Ghizer in modern Pakistan while journeying to explore the Pamir Mountains in modern Tajikistan. In the two stanzas that precede the line quoted by Samuel in the next paragraph (l. 9), the unnamed explorer (Hayward) succeeds in persuading his assassins to delay his murder until dawn.

p. 261, *The voices faded and the hills slept*: A slight misquotation of the concluding two lines of Newbolt's poem: "Over the pass the voices one by one / Faded, and the hill slept."

p. 261, *Is there anybody there, said the traveller?*: The famous opening line of 'The Listeners' (1912) by the English poet Walter de la Mare (1873–1956): "'Is there anybody there?' said the traveller, / Knocking on the moonlit door; / And his horse in the silence champed the grasses / Of the forest's ferny floor."

p. 264, *Polly come and put the kettle on*: 'Polly Put the Kettle On' is the name of an English nursery rhyme.

p. 267, *Old Dot and Carry*: "Dot and carry one" is an old-fashioned colloquial term for a person with a limp.

p. 267, *Pale hands... the Shalimar*: The opening line of the poem 'Kashmiri Song' (1901) by the English poet Violet Nicolson (1865–1904), who wrote under the pseudonym Laurence Hope: "Pale hands I loved beside the Shalimar, / Where are you now? Who lies beneath your spell?" The poem, which was hugely popular in its day, epitomizing for its audience the spirit of the oriental, was famously set to music by the English composer Amy Woodforde-Finden (1860–1919) in 1902. The "Shalimar" of the title is probably Shalimar Bagh, an ornamental garden in the city of Srinagar in the Indian region of Jammu and Kashmir.

p. 272, *Four Lost Souls*: First published in *New World Writing* (May 1953).

p. 272, *a prairie oyster and Angostura*: Hangover cures. A prairie oyster is a drink made with raw egg and seasoning. For Angostura Bitters, see fourth note to p. 90.

p. 272, *boot-blacking*: Black shoe polish.

p. 273, *red biddy's*: See second note to p. 101.

p. 274, *Where was Moses when the light went out*: A riddle popular in the late nineteenth and early twentieth centuries, to which the implied answer is "in the dark", although other common nonsensical replies included: "Down in the cellar eating sauerkraut."

p. 274, *primitives*: Pre-Renaissance paintings.

p. 276, *Here we go gathering nuts and may*: The first line and refrain of a traditional children's rhyme, which accompanied a game whose result was the pairing of a boy and a girl from two teams of players. The wording "nuts in May" is more common, although since the refrain is a corruption of "Here we go gathering knots of may", that is, knots of hawthorn blossom, George's version represents something of a hybrid.

p. 276, *It wasn't the cough that carried him off*: The beginning of a well-known proverb: "It wasn't the cough that carried him off, but the coffin they carried him off in."

NOTES

p. 277, *Hotcha... Wedding Day*: 'Minnie the Moocher's Wedding Day' is a song by the American jazz singer and bandleader Cab Calloway (1907–94). Like Calloway's similarly titled 'Minnie the Moocher', it is notable for its nonsensical, semi-improvised "scat" lyrics, including the phrases "Hi-de-hi-de-hi" and "Ho-de-ho-de-ho", which the audience would be invited to repeat.

p. 277, *Tantivy*: A rapid gallop.

p. 279, *Bethesda*: A Nonconformist chapel.

p. 281, *the Derby*: An annual flat race (one with no jumps) for three-year-old horses (both colts and fillies) that takes place at Epsom Downs in Surrey in late May or early June. It was devised by a group including Edward Smith-Stanley, 12th Earl of Derby (1752–1834), who, it is said, won the honour of naming the race in a coin toss with Sir Charles Bunbury (1740–1821), another of the co-founders. It was first run in 1780.

p. 281, *razor-man*: A member of a "razor gang", a violent gang armed with razors.

p. 281, *pin table*: A pinball machine.

p. 282, *Starr Faithfull*: The American socialite and model Starr Faithfull (1906–31), whose mysterious death by drowning caused a media sensation.

p. 283, *She dwells... Tintern Abbey*: George combines the first two lines of 'She dwelt among the untrodden ways', one of Wordsworth's five "Lucy" poems, composed between 1798 and 1801: "She dwelt among the untrodden ways / Beside the springs of Dove, / A maid whom there were none to praise / And very few to love." "Dove" is the River Dove in the Peak District, Derbyshire. Four of the "Lucy" poems were first published in the second edition (1800) of the seminal collection *Lyrical Ballads*, which contained poems by both Wordsworth and Samuel Taylor Coleridge (1772–1834). The concluding poem of *Lyrical Ballads* was Wordsworth's 'Lines Written a Few Miles above Tintern Abbey', inspired by a walking tour made by the poet of the Welsh Marches. The medieval ruins of Tintern Abbey are located on the Welsh bank of the River Wye in Monmouthshire, adjacent to the village of Tintern.

p. 285, *the area*: A court below street level, accessed via a flight of steps, providing access to the basement of a building.

p. 289, *Late Stories*: The stories in this section are arranged in order of publication (if published during Thomas's life) or composition (if published posthumously). For the publication or composition details of the individual stories, see the relevant note to each title.

p. 291, *Memories of Christmas*: First broadcast as part of the Welsh edition of the programme *Children's Hour* on the BBC's Home Service on 16th December 1945; first published in *The Listener* (20th December 1945). In 1950, Thomas expanded the text of the original broadcast with material from a separate piece titled 'Conversation about Christmas' (1947), with the result appearing in *Harper's Bazaar* under the title 'A Child's Memories of a Christmas in Wales'. This was subsequently printed in the US edition of *QEOM* (1954), and then as a free-standing book, under the title *A Child's Christmas in Wales* (1955). The text reproduced here is that of the original BBC talk, as collected in the British edition of *QEOM*.

p. 291, *Struwwelpeter... Mrs Potter's badgers*: Struwwelpeter ("shock-headed Peter", sometimes translated as "slovenly Peter") is a character from a collection of cautionary tales for children by the German physician, and later psychiatrist, Heinrich Hoffmann, first published in 1845. (The collection has also come to be known as *Struwwelpeter*, although this was not the original title.) The title character, Struwwelpeter, is a boy with long, uncut fingernails and wild, untamed hair. Other stories include one about a girl who plays with matches and accidentally burns to death, and another about a thumb-sucking boy whose thumbs are cut off by a tailor known as the "Scissorman". Billy Bunter is a fictional schoolboy, a pupil at Greyfriars School in Kent (also fictional), created by the English writer Charles Hamilton (1876–1961), who wrote under the pseudonym Frank Richards. Bunter originally appeared in the children's story paper *The Magnet* between 1908 and 1940, and would later, from 1947, feature in a series of novels. Black Beauty is a horse from a novel for children of the same name by the English author Anna Sewell (1820–78), published in 1877. *Little Women* (1868–69) is a semi-autobiographical novel by the American writer Louisa May Alcott (1832–88), about four sisters – Meg, Jo, Beth and Amy – growing up in genteel poverty in Massachusetts. Alice is the little-girl heroine of *Alice's Adventures in Wonderland* (1865) and *Through the Looking Glass* (1871) by Lewis Carroll (real name Charles Dodgson, 1832–98). *The Tale of Mr Tod* (1912), one of the animal stories for children by the English writer Beatrix Potter (1866–1943), features a badger named Tommy Brock, who steals the Flopsy Bunnies, intending to eat them, but is thwarted when, while he is engaged in an altercation with Mr Tod, a fox, they are rescued by Benjamin Bunny and Peter Rabbit.

NOTES

p. 291, *named after a Mr Theodore Bear*: Teddy bears are in fact named after the US president Theodore Roosevelt (1858–1919), perhaps as a result of an incident on a hunting expedition in Mississippi in November 1902, in which the then president refused to shoot a captured bear. The episode was soon after satirized in a political cartoon in the *Washington Post*, which is said to have inspired the creation of the first "teddy bear".

p. 291, *'Pop Goes the Weasel'... 'Oranges and Lemons'*: Traditional nursery rhymes. For 'Nuts in May', see also first note to p. 276.

p. 292, *bombilating*: Buzzing, humming.

p. 293, *busbied*: That is, wearing busbies, tall military headdresses made of fur, worn as part of the dress uniform of soldiers of certain regiments of hussars and artillerymen.

p. 294, *Excelsior*: A reference to Longfellow's poem 'Excelsior' (1841), in which the word – Latin for "higher" – is used as a refrain designed to convey a sense of aspiration: "The shades of night were falling fast, / As through an Alpine village passed / A youth, who bore, 'mid snow and ice, / A banner with the strange device, / Excelsior!" (ll. 1–5). The popularity of the poem led to the word's adoption in English, in which language it is used to mean "Ever upwards!" or "Onwards and upwards!" For Longfellow, see also second note to p. 117.

p. 295, *'Christmas Comes But Once a Year'*: A phrase apparently originating in the instructional poem *Five Hundreth Pointes of Good Husbandrie to as Many of Good Huswifery* (1573), by the English poet and farmer Thomas Tusser (*c.*1524–80): "At Christmas play and make good cheer, / for Christmas comes but once a year." It also occurs in the poem 'A Christmas Carol' by the English poet, pamphleteer and hymn-writer George Wither (1588–1667), and as the title and refrain of a poem by the English poet and novelist Thomas Miller (1807–74). Thomas may have had in mind a musical setting of one of these poems.

p. 295, *gas bracket*: "A metal pipe, usually of ornamental shape, projecting from the wall of an apartment, at once to support and supply the gas lamps or burners" (*OED*).

p. 296, *Quite Early One Morning*: First broadcast on the BBC's Home Service on 31st August 1945; first published in *Wales* (Autumn 1946) and collected in *QEOM*, from where the text is taken.

p. 296, *Caruso's, sweeter than Ben Davies's*: The Italian operatic tenor Enrico Caruso (1873–1921) and the Welsh operatic tenor Ben Davies (1858–1943).

NOTES

p. 296, *bombazined*: That is, made of bombazine, a twilled dress fabric of worsted and silk or cotton, traditionally used for mourning clothes.

p. 297, *Cody-bold*: A reference to the American hunter and impresario William Frederick Cody (1846–1917), better known as "Buffalo Bill", famous for his travelling "Wild West" show.

p. 298, *laver bread*: A Welsh dish made by boiling laver (an edible seaweed), then dipping it in oatmeal and frying it.

p. 298, *sorbo*: A kind of sponge rubber.

p. 299, *Charles Morgan*: The Anglo-Welsh playwright and novelist Charles Langbridge Morgan (1894–1958), author of novels such as *My Name Is Legion* (1925), *Portrait in a Mirror* (1929) and *The Fountain* (1932), and the plays *The Flashing Stream* (1938), *The River Line* (1949) and *The Burning Glass* (1953).

p. 299, *Parchedig*: "Reverend" (Welsh).

p. 299, *Aber.*: The University College of Wales, Aberystwyth, now known as Aberystwyth University.

p. 301, *Holiday Memory*: First broadcast on the BBC's Third Programme on 25th October 1946; first published in *The Listener* (7th November 1946) and collected in QEOM, from where the text is taken.

p. 301, *monkey nuts*: Peanuts.

p. 302, *blancoed*: Blanco is a substance used primarily by soldiers for whitening belts and other equipment.

p. 303, *luke*: Lukewarm

p. 304, *from Mumbles... Ballantyne Islands*: For Mumbles, see fourth note to p. 87. "Henty-land" is a reference to the English writer G.A. Henty (1832–1902), author of many patriotic tales of adventure, many of which were set in far-flung lands, including *Out on the Pampas* (1871), *With Clive in India* (1884) and *On the Irrawaddy* (1896). "Ballantyne Islands" are South Pacific islands such as the one depicted in the adventure novel *The Coral Island: A Tale of the Pacific Ocean* (1857) by the Scottish author R.M. Ballantyne (1825–94), about three boys who survive a shipwreck.

p. 304, *Atlas-muscled Mounties... man*: The "Mounties" are the Royal Canadian Mounted Police, the national police force of Canada, founded in 1873. It is proverbially said that they "always get their man", a phrase that has been traced to a report in the *Fort Benton (Montana) Record* in April 1877, which, commenting on the arrest of three whiskey smugglers by two tenacious Mounties in the town of Fort Macleod in the Canadian province of Alberta, stated that "they fetch their men every time".

NOTES

"Atlas-muscled" is a reference to the American bodybuilder Charles Atlas (1892–1972), who developed a bodybuilding programme known as "Dynamic Tension", which became world-famous in the 1920s due to its memorable advertising campaign. "Pemmican" is a paste made from pounded dried meat with melted fat and other ingredients, and condensed into a cake. It was originally made by some North American tribes and was later adopted by explorers due to its high nutritional value and transportability. The "gold-rush wastes" are those of the Klondike region of the Yukon, in north-western Canada, where the discovery of gold in 1896 led to an influx of as many as 100,000 prospectors, who rushed to the area to try to make their fortunes.

p. 304, *larrikin*: An Australian term for an unruly or violent youth.

p. 304, *looked at Ilfracombe*: The seaside resort of Ilfracombe in Devon is visible from Swansea Bay, on the other side of the Bristol Channel.

p. 305, *Wall of Death*: A fairground attraction consisting of a large wooden cylinder, around the inner circumference of which stuntmen ride motorcycles or other vehicles, held in place by centrifugal force and friction.

p. 305, *Becher's Brooks*: Becher's Brook is a fence jumped during the Grand National, an annual horse race held at Aintree, near Liverpool.

p. 305, *Valentino-black*: A reference to the actor Rudolph Valentino – see first note to p. 51.

p. 305, *Oxford bags*: Baggy trousers.

p. 306, *The bell rang for Blaina*: A reference to a poem, numbered simply 'XV', by the Welsh collier turned poet Idris Davies (1905–53), from his 1938 collection *Gwalia Deserta*, a title meaning "Wasteland of Wales". The rhythm of the lines deliberately follows that of the nursery rhyme 'Oranges and Lemons' (see also fourth note to p. 291): "'Oh what can you give me?' / Say the sad bells of Rhymney. / 'Is there hope for the future?' / Cry the brown bells of Merthyr. / 'Who made the mine-owner?' / Say the black bells of Rhondda. / 'And who robbed the miner?' / Cry the grim bells of Blaina" (ll. 1–8). Blaina, a small town in South Wales, was then a mining community. The poem is better known today as a folk song, after it was set to music, with the title 'The Bells of Rhymney', by the American folk singer Peter Seeger (1919–2014) in 1957. The song was famously covered by the American folk-rock band the Byrds in 1965.

p. 306, *Milford Haven*: A town in Pembrokeshire, south-west Wales.

p. 306, *breathing fire and Sousa*: The fairground ride containing the gondolas is playing one of the famous military marches by the American composer John Philip Sousa (1854–1932), author of, among others, 'The Stars and Stripes Forever', 'Semper Fidelis' and 'The Liberty Bell'.

p. 307, *The Crumbs of One Man's Year*: First broadcast on the BBC's Home Service on 27th December 1946; first published in *The Listener* (2nd January 1947) and collected in *QEOM*, from where the text is taken.

p. 308, *the River Elusina… sabbath*: Both quotations are taken from a passage in *The Compleat Angler* (I, 1) – a literary exploration of the art of fishing by the English writer Izaak Walton (1593–1683), first published 1653 – in which Walton lists a number of rivers possessing magical properties that are "reported of them by authors of such credit that we need not deny them an historical faith". Walton attributes the information in the first to Aristotle, adding in a marginal gloss: "In his *Wonders of Nature.*" The reference, however, is obscure. The second is attributed by Walton to the Jewish historian Flavius Josephus (*c*.37–*c*.100 AD), who writes in his *History of the Jewish War* (VII, 5) of a river that is static for six days of the week but runs on the seventh (that is, the opposite of Walton's description). Walton's report matches, however, that of a river in Judea given in the *Natural History* (XXXI, 18) of the Roman statesman Pliny the Elder (23–79 AD).

p. 308, *jacky-jumps*: Jumping jacks, small fireworks.

p. 308, *brocks*: Shatters, falls to pieces.

p. 308, *the eighth programme*: In September 1946, three months before this piece was broadcast (on the Home Service), the BBC launched the Third Programme, a national radio station devoted to the arts, whose output was of a notably more cerebral nature than that of either of the existing networks, the Home Service and the Light Programme. (In 1967 the Third Programme became Radio 3.) The joke here is perhaps that the ladies are listening to a (non-existent) radio station of even greater intellectual refinement than the Third Programme.

p. 309, *sea pinks*: A plant, also known as thrift, that produces pink flowers and grows on sea cliffs and mountains.

p. 309, *Joseph coats*: A reference to the "coat of many colours" made for the biblical Joseph by his father, Jacob. See Genesis 37. Possibly Thomas is also punning on the other meaning of the word Joseph: a long riding cloak worn chiefly by women in the eighteenth century.

p. 310, *played old Harry*: Played the Devil; made mischief.

p. 312, *The Followers*: First published in *World Review* (October 1952) and collected in *PS*, from where the text is taken.

p. 312, *camiknicks*: Camiknickers, a one-piece undergarment for women combining camisole and French knickers.

p. 312, *Earthquake in Japan*: Perhaps a reference to the earthquake that occurred in the sea off the south coast of the Japanese island of Hokkaido on 4th March 1952, causing a tsunami. Thirty-three people were killed and hundreds more were wounded.

p. 313, *too young and too old*: There is perhaps an echo here of Byron's *Don Juan* (1819–24): "Too old for youth – too young, at thirty-five, / To herd with boys, or hoard with good threescore" (XII, 2, ll. 1–2).

p. 314, *marocain*: A dress made from ribbed crêpe of silk or wool.

p. 315, *Lon Chaney... Hoot Gibson*: Hollywood actors of the silent and early sound eras. Lon Chaney (1883–1930), known as the "Man of a Thousand Faces", was famous for his villainous roles in *The Hunchback of Notre Dame* (1923) and *The Phantom of the Opera* (1925), among others. The reference may also be to his son, Lon Chaney, Jr. (1906–73), noted for his roles in horror movies including *The Wolf Man* (1941) and *Son of Dracula* (1943). The other film actors listed are Richard Talmadge (1892–1981), a German-born stuntman turned actor; Milton Sills (1882–1930), a matinée idol in the 1920s; Noah Beery (1882–1946), a character actor who appeared in *The Mark of Zorro* (1920) opposite Douglas Fairbanks (1883–1939); Richard Dix, the archetypal rugged hero in films such as the epic Western *Cimarron* (1931) – see also first note to p. 42; Slim Summerville (1892–1946), known for his work in comedies; and Hoot Gibson (1892–1962), a rodeo champion who became one of the leading actors in the Western genre.

p. 316, *shingle*: A short, tapered haircut for women popular in the 1920s and 1930s.

p. 317, *Warner Baxter*: The American film actor Warner Baxter (1889–51), famous for his roles in Westerns including *In Old Arizona* (1928), as well as for his performances in other genres.

p. 317, *'Daisy'*: See note to p. 74.

p. 320, *A Story*: First broadcast as part of the programme *Speaking Personally* on BBC television on 10th August 1953; first published in *The Listener* (17th September 1953) and collected in *PS*, from where the text is taken.

p. 323, *swole*: Swelled.

p. 324, *Shoni-Onion Breton man*: The name "Johnny Onions" – or "Sioni Wynwns" in Welsh – was applied to onion sellers from the Roscoff area of Brittany who travelled annually to Wales and other parts of Britain to hawk their wares, and were a common sight in the early twentieth century. The tradition began in 1828, when a farmer named Henri Olivier sailed with a boatload of pink onions to Plymouth, where he quickly sold his cargo, making a significant profit in the process.

p. 325, *Quelle un grand matin, Monsieur*: "What a great morning, sir" (French).

p. 325, *bach*: Welsh for "little", used as a term of endearment, usually after a name.

p. 326, *'Asleep in the Deep'*: A song with words by the English lyricist Arthur J. Lamb (1870–1928) and music by the American composer Henry W. Petrie (1857–1925), written in 1897.

EVERGREENS SERIES
Beautifully produced classics, affordably priced

Alma Classics is committed to making available a wide range of literature from around the globe. Most of the titles are enriched by an extensive critical apparatus, notes and extra reading material, as well as a selection of photographs. The texts are based on the most authoritative editions and edited using a fresh, accessible editorial approach. With an emphasis on production, editorial and typographical values, Alma Classics aspires to revitalize the whole experience of reading classics.

 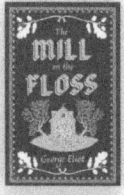    

For our complete list and latest offers

visit

almabooks.com/evergreens

101-PAGE CLASSICS
Great Rediscovered Classics

This series has been created with the aim to redefine and enrich the classics canon by promoting unjustly neglected works of enduring significance. These works, beautifully produced and mostly in translation, will intrigue and inspire the literary connoisseur and the general reader alike.

THE PERFECT COLLECTION OF LESSER-KNOWN WORKS BY MAJOR AUTHORS

almabooks.com/101-pages

ALMA CLASSICS

ALMA CLASSICS aims to publish mainstream and lesser-known European classics in an innovative and striking way, while employing the highest editorial and production standards. By way of a unique approach the range offers much more, both visually and textually, than readers have come to expect from contemporary classics publishing.

LATEST TITLES PUBLISHED BY ALMA CLASSICS

473. Sinclair Lewis, *Babbitt*
474. Edith Wharton, *The House of Mirth*
475. George Orwell, *Burmese Days*
476. Virginia Woolf, *The Voyage Out*
477. Charles Dickens, *Pictures from Italy*
478. Fyodor Dostoevsky, *Crime and Punishment*
479. Anton Chekhov, *Small Fry and Other Stories*
480. George Orwell, *Homage to Catalonia*
481. Carlo Collodi, *The Adventures of Pinocchio*
482. Virginia Woolf, *Between the Acts*
483. Alain Robbe-Grillet, *Last Year at Marienbad*
484. Charles Dickens, *The Pickwick Papers*
485. Wilkie Collins, *The Haunted Hotel*
486. Ivan Turgenev, *Parasha and Other Poems*
487. Arthur Conan Doyle, *His Last Bow*
488. Ivan Goncharov, *The Frigate Pallada*
489. Arthur Conan Doyle, *The Casebook of Sherlock Holmes*
490. Alexander Pushkin, *Lyrics Vol. 4*
491. Arthur Conan Doyle, *The Valley of Fear*
492. Gottfried Keller, *Green Henry*
493. Grimmelshausen, *Simplicius Simplicissimus*
494. Edgar Allan Poe, *The Raven and Other Poems*
495. Sinclair Lewis, *Main Street*
496. Prosper Mérimée, *Carmen*
497. D.H. Lawrence, *Women in Love*
498. Albert Maltz, *A Tale of One January*
499. George Orwell, *Coming Up for Air*
500. Anton Chekhov, *The Looking Glass and Other Stories*
501. Ivan Goncharov, *An Uncommon Story*
502. Paul Éluard, *Selected Poems*
503. Ivan Turgenev, *Memoirs of a Hunter*
504. Albert Maltz, *A Long Day in a Short Life*
505. Edith Wharton, *Ethan Frome*
506. Charles Dickens, *The Old Curiosity Shop*
507. Fyodor Dostoevsky, *The Village of Stepanchikovo*
508. George Orwell, *The Clergyman's Daughter*
509. Virginia Woolf, *The New Dress and Other Stories*
510. Ivan Goncharov, *A Serendipitous Error and Two Incidents at Sea*
511. Beatrix Potter, *Peter Rabbit*

www.almaclassics.com